A REASON

TO

Also By Michael Kerr

DI Matt Barnes Series

A REASON TO KILL
LETHAL INTENT
A NEED TO KILL
CHOSEN TO KILL
A PASSION TO KILL
RAISED TO KILL

The Joe Logan Series

AFTERMATH
ATONEMENT
ABSOLUTION
ALLEGIANCE
ABDUCTION

The Laura Scott Series

A DEADLY COMPULSION
THE SIGN OF FEAR

Other Crime Thrillers

DEADLY REPRISAL
DEADLY REQUITAL
BLACK ROCK BAY
A HUNGER WITHIN
THE SNAKE PIT
A DEADLY STATE OF MIND
TAKEN BY FORCE
DARK NEEDS AND EVIL DEEDS
DEADLY OBSESSION
COFFEE CRIME CAFE

Science Fiction / Horror

WAITING
CLOSE ENCOUNTERS OF THE STRANGE KIND
RE-EMERGENCE

Children's Fiction
Adventures in Otherworld
PART ONE – THE CHALICE OF HOPE
PART TWO – THE FAIRY CROWN

A REASON TO LIVE

BY

MICHAEL KERR

ISBN 9781-549823282

Jesus said unto her, I am the resurrection,
and the life: he that believeth in me, though
he were dead, yet shall he live.

~ John 11.

When all rational explanation has been investigated carefully and dismissed, then the extraordinary, however improbable and bizarre, is not as hard to believe and accept.

~ Michael Kerr.

BOOK ONE

LIFE AND DEATH

CHAPTER ONE

BLACK and sinister; a portent of doom, the shadow clung to the ground describing wide circles over the undulating terrain, giving stark warning of the predator that wheeled high above on a rising thermal of warm air, casting its dark, menacing shape on the sand and rocks far below.

The cottontail rabbit hopped out from the shade of a clump of mesquite, paused to sit up, nose twitching, sensing the danger a fraction of a second too late.

The redtail hawk struck like lightning, smacking into the rabbit at incredible speed. Fur flew as sharp talons clenched deeply into flesh and a razor beak darted at the fear-frozen prey's throat.

Fifty yards from where blood soaked into the siliceous particles, the sun glared hot and bright through the bedroom window, as Cal threw back the single cotton sheet and swung up to sit on the edge of the bed. He rubbed at his sleep-filled eyes and looked at the clock-radio on the nightstand. The ruby LCD read 8:02.A.M. He was running just a tad late, and that would cost him his life.

Cal Morgan was a deputy sheriff in Pershing County, Nevada, working for and alongside his father, Henry, who answered to Hank to all but strangers and felons. Hank had been re-elected County Sheriff for the past twenty-some consecutive years now, and thought that, given time, he might grow to like the job.

Cal had only been back in Benson's Creek for two years. College, and then several years' in the LAPD had kept him away far too long. He had left home a restless young man, eager to spread his wings and step on as much of that 'greener grass' that the outside world was growing as he could. He had returned home a married man, his wild oats sown, and disenchanted with the rat-race of big-city life.

The notion to return to the slower-paced small town roots of his childhood had just crept up on him, as a bulb will push up through warm, damp soil and just grow and grow. Chrissie, his wife, was not only enthusiastic over the idea, but downright pushy in wanting to quit L.A. and head for the hills post-haste. The move had been the right one, up until now, and the past two years back in Nevada had been nigh on perfect.

Benson's Creek had no logical right to still exist as a successful community. Passing trade and tourists were a rarely experienced luxury, and the mining days were long gone. To find the small backwater, travelers had to leave I-80 at Imlay, to head northwest on first blacktop and then gravel towards the Kamma Mountains, south of the ghost town of Sulfur, and then on farther, out to the edge of the Black Rock Desert. If they reached the Lava Beds – that stretched as far as the eye could see from the top of Sawtooth Knob – then they had missed the Creek.

Cal had met Chrissie in Los Angeles. Once upon a smoggy day he had pulled her over for a speeding violation, and it was love, lust, or both at first sight. They had married within six months of that fateful meeting on Santa Monica Freeway, and soon after had made the decision to tear themselves away from the growing pollution and violence of the City of Angels and hightail it to what Chrissie dubbed 'Nowhere, Nevada'.

The drive-by shooting of Cal's partner had been the final straw that broke the proverbial camel's back.

It had been a quiet Monday, midmorning, when Cal had left the black and white at the curb on Fairfax and walked into Enrico's diner to pick up two cups of coffee and ham on rye sandwiches for himself and Eddie Meyer, who had stayed in the unit, monitoring the radio and reading the sports pages.

As Cal walked back to the door with his hands full, the windows imploded and bullets strafed the diner, taking out an elderly guy who had just sat down and lifted a cheeseburger to his mouth; a slug drilling through his neck and knocking him off his stool. Cal dropped to the floor, and scalding coffee soaked his shirt front as he drew his Glock. The shooting had lasted less than five seconds; a single burst of automatic fire. Keeping low, Cal had pushed open the door, just in time to see a dark blue Chrysler's tail lights glow red as it braked hard and swung into an alleyway.

Eddie had spilled out onto the sidewalk as Cal pulled open the cruiser's door. Blood was pouring from the two bullet holes in his head, but somehow he was still conscious.

As Cal reached past Eddie to call it in on the radio, his partner gripped the cuff of his pants leg. It had been the first and last time that Cal would have to use those two terrible words; 'Officer down'. By the time paramedics got to him, Eddie was gone, and his wife and two kids were just a half hour away from having their life turned to shit.

Crackheads' with AK-47's were still a year or two away at that time, but their forerunners were blazing the trail. Senseless killing, just for kicks, was all part of the big American dream, which was quickly becoming a nightmare.

At the time she met Cal, Chrissie was working for 'Symposium'; a glossy lifestyle magazine. She was a sub editor with a background in journalism. Moving to the back of beyond had been a personal challenge to her fiercely independent nature, but by maintaining her contacts, and with the invaluable aid of her computer, she had been able to reach out from her new desert home and continue to work, freelance.

Chrissie was twenty-seven, four years younger than Cal, and stood a lithe five-seven, barefoot. She had become tanned honey-gold by the Nevada sun, and her eyes were darker than her shoulder-length mahogany hair. Chrissie was happy; a lot more contented than she had been in the city, where she had never known whether her husband would arrive home safe and sound at the end of a shift, or if someone else would knock at the door with news that would shatter all her hopes, plans and dreams. She had never made a big deal of it with Cal, but had feared for his life every single day. Oh, he was still a cop, but being a deputy in Pershing County was probably safer than selling ice-cream at Knotts Berry Farm back in Smogville, which they still returned to for the occasional weekend to visit Chrissie's parents in Brentwood, and to see the dwindling number of friends that they had remained in contact with. But it was always a relief to be back on the road again and heading for home.

Cal stretched, yawned, and shuffled his feet into the moccasins at the side of the bed, before standing and padding through to the bathroom for a quick shower.

"Coffee's poured," Chrissie called from the kitchen, hearing him up and about. He toweled himself dry, then wiped the steamed-up mirror clear enough to see himself in, always meaning to shave first then shower, and always forgetting to. Looking at his reflection, Cal was reasonably happy with the craggy, handsome face that smiled back at him. There were already a few threads of gray hair skulking among the black at his temples, but he chose to think that they added character; a distinguishing touch. His eyes were 'Newman blue', or so he had been told – always by women – that many times that the compliment had started to become irksome. He stood five-eleven, but claimed to be spot on six feet, and was lean and muscular, with broad shoulders and a trim waist. He was an above average specimen, and knew it.

He sauntered through to the kitchen, hair still dripping, wearing only a Disney bath towel around his waist. He picked up the mug of coffee from the counter and went out onto the back porch to join Chrissie, who was already taking in the fresh morning air and the warming rays of the sun.

"Good morning, sweetheart," Cal said, bending to kiss her full lips as she looked up to greet him.

"Mmmm, nice," she purred, getting up from the rocking chair that had been outside the house when they had moved in, and which she had immediately renovated and claimed as her own. "I'll pour you some fresh coffee, that'll be stone cold."

Chrissie reached for the mug, then deftly dropped her hand to his waist and relieved him of the towel with the speed and stealth of a baseball-ground pickpocket.

"Wow. No wonder Mickey's smiling," she giggled, feasting her eyes on his semi-turgid member.

Now standing as naked as a jay bird, but keeping a straight face, Cal spoke in his most official tone. "That was an act of gross indecency, Ms. If I had the time I would ask you to assume the position, put the cuffs on you and run you in...to the bedroom, for some further lewd acts." They both burst out laughing, and hugged each other.

"I love you, Morgan," she said.

"I love you too, you sneaky little towel thief," he replied. "Now give it back, before we both make me late for work."

Snatching the towel from Chrissie's hand, Cal scooted through the screen door, barely escaping a slap that was aimed at his retreating butt. Ten minutes later he reappeared, buckling his Sam Browne and adjusting his sidearm. In khaki uniform, complete with Stetson, western boots and wearing mirrored shades – which really annoyed Chrissie – he looked as Eastwood had in the old movie; *Coogan's Bluff.*

Chrissie walked down the steps with him, holding his hand as they crossed the yard to the Jeep. "See you later, poser," she said, smiling, and then kissing him through the open window, after he had climbed in, closed the door and keyed the ignition.

"Missing you already, honey," he drawled, touching the brim of his hat in a casual one-fingered salute, before gunning the engine and driving north, away from the isolated timber-frame bungalow towards the Creek, which was four miles away.

This was to be Cal's last day on earth in his present form. He would never see his beloved Chrissie again. Life was moving on, and would do so without him in it.

Thank God that the future is a closed book, and that only one page can be read at a time. The knowledge of what dire consequences may lay ahead waiting does not bear thinking about. If it could be subtly or even radically changed, then fine, but even that way could lead to madness. To see so much, affecting so many, would be intolerable. Who would want to know that a loved one would succumb the following month or year to incurable cancer? Or be privy to an impending air crash; to know that a 747 would explode in mid-air and fall from the sky to decimate a residential area, killing several hundred people. The prior knowledge of death and destruction would invite insanity. Telling people of future events would beg disbelief, then fear, and finally a shunning hatred as they came to pass. To see the following week's winning lottery numbers, race results and stock market share prices would be an attractive proposition: inside information that could be instantly employed and converted to vast wealth has its charm. But...no bad shit, thank you. Just a quick in and out of the near future with a mind full of get-rich-quick information would do nicely.

Cal was not going to reach the office that morning. He was never going to have those kids that he and Chrissie had been working on. And he would never sit out on the porch again, beer in hand, watching the sun set over the mountains with her. If he had known what was about to happen, he would not have been so relaxed, singing along with Willie Nelson, who was ironically – as it turned out – telling all who were listening how funny it was that time slipped away. As Cal sang, with the radio cranked up good and loud, he was planning a steamy night back at the old homestead, which would involve Chrissie, his Mickey Mouse towel, and maybe a liberal amount of baby oil. And as those thoughts drifted through his mind on that hot morning of July 8, 1996, he had exactly twenty minutes left to live.

CHAPTER TWO

TRUDY Henderson was three weeks shy of her sixteenth birthday. She was blue-eyed and fair-haired, and in the way she dressed and moved her chassis, nothing short of jail-bait. She was a real sex kitten. It was a natural aura. She just exuded an invisible scent that weakened most men's knees and strengthened their peckers.

Trudy lived in a double-wide with her mother, Fran, on a twenty unit site a mile south of town. The park was little more than a half acre of fenced desert, with a shower and toilet block for the use of the residents that lived in the five bricked-up RVs and ten statics' that were all owned by Warren Carlin who, with the rent from them and the income from the Sawtooth Saloon, (named after the mountain in the distance) was never going to go belly-up.

It was a strained relationship between Trudy and Fran. Most of the time they acted more like sisters than mom and daughter, but although they loved each other dearly, their bickering was on the increase as Trudy grew older. It was becoming more difficult for them to live together under the same small roof. The main bone of contention was that Trudy hated the Creek. The sand, rocks, heat and the jerk-off hicks in town felt like a worsening itch that she couldn't reach to scratch; an irritation that just got more inflamed with every passing day. Stuck in the middle of a fucking desert was not her idea of fun, and not part of a future that she allowed herself to contemplate. She had run off once, over a year back, but it hadn't worked out. She had hitched a ride out of 'Dodge' on the pillion of a Harley owned by a numb-nut biker called Chet, who was all leather and acne in what appeared to be equal amounts. After only three weeks in Sacramento, Chet had dumped her, and with no money or game-plan she had hitched back home to mom, sporting a death-head skull tattoo on her right breast, and a well-perforated hymen between her legs. So much for her first taste of civilization and sophistication. She was trailer-trash, knew it, and loathed the fix that she felt trapped in.

Trudy and Fran had got past that episode. It was not forgotten, but was forgiven; time smoothing out most of the wrinkles of bad feeling. For the past six months Trudy had been waiting-on at the Blueberry Pie diner on Main Street. The work was hot and shitty; cleaning, serving and even having to help cook when Pam, the owner, was having one of her 'bad arthritis' days. The smell of broiling burger meat and sour sweat in the confines of the sauna-hot and steaming kitchen turned Trudy's vegetarian stomach. However, the meager pay and tips gave her a certain amount of independence, and the means to take more than a passing interest in her mother's mail-order catalog, from which she ordered the most expensive Barbie-bimbo style of clothes that she could afford.

Fran worked evenings at the Sawtooth for Warren, serving drinks and generally keeping the place half clean. She dressed in low-cut blouses, and skirts that just about covered her butt, leaving little to tax the punters' imaginations. She also provided extra services after hours, either stood up against the wall in the darkness of the alleyway that ran down the side of the saloon, in a john's car, or even back at the double-wide if the price was right. And then there was Warren Carlin. The arrangement with Warren was that for a couple of blowjobs a week, the rent on Fran's trailer remained as static as the unit.

Warren was a fat, balding, lecherous pig, who showered once a month whether he thought he needed to or not. Going back to his living quarters was not a chore that Fran took on lightly, or with any degree of enthusiasm.

'You comin' through for a night-cap, Franny?' Warren would say, if in the mood, and after locking up behind the last local to stagger out into the street.

Warren always wanted the same thing. He would drop his baggy, creased pants and grimy long johns, sit in his greasy armchair and watch as Fran removed her blouse and bra, to hitch her skirt up so that he could see her thick bush of pubic hair. She rarely bothered to wear panties.

'Thanks for the night-cap, you sexy old bear,' Fran always said afterwards, somehow engineering a 'that was good for me' smile to hide her revulsion; a revulsion that was as much for herself as it was for Warren.

Fran was thirty-five, still a looker, but beginning to fray at the edges, mainly from an overindulgence of alcohol, nicotine, desert sun, and a general lifestyle that promoted ill-health and early ageing. She had been married, very briefly and just the once; Trudy being the legacy of her short foray into matrimony. The guy had turned out to be an ex-con with a chemical dependency and a penchant for wife-beating. Fran had just up and left after her first and last hospitalization, courtesy of his fists. She took her baby and what little money there was in the seedy apartment in Modesto – that she had suffered so much in – and caught the first Greyhound out of town. She had left with a single regret; that she had ever met the bastard in the first place. Trudy had not had the misfortune to know her father, and fate decreed that she never would.

Slamming the trailer door behind her, Trudy headed for the highway, pausing to wet the tip of her finger on her tongue and write: 'I'm dirty, wash me', on the side of Duke Lomax's dust-caked old Airstream, which reminded her of a silver-metal cigar tube or giant dildo.

The gravel road was just fifty yards from 'camp'. Camp being the nickname that she had christened Carlin's trailer park with when she had been five-years-old, and by which she still referred to it as.

One mile to town was not too bad, she thought. Although it was already hot and as she walked she could feel the sweat popping and running down the middle of her back. She was wearing a loose, oversize T-shirt with a grinning facsimile of her current idol, Brad Pitt on the front. The shirt was so long that it almost covered the frayed strands of cotton that sprouted from the short, ragged bottoms of her cut-down blue jeans. All that she wore apart from that was a pair of scuffed pink and white trainers. A shoulder bag swung from its strap on her shoulder; a red faux-leather number that was on permanent loan from her mother.

Back at camp, Fran was still crashed out, sleeping off the effects of a late night, too much bourbon and a 'night-cap' with Warren, which on that particular occasion had made her puke, luckily not over Warren's flabby, hairy belly, but out in the alley, after leaving the saloon by the back door. She would still be out to the world hours' later when a state trooper would hammer on the door with bad news written all over his face.

Trudy was daydreaming as she trudged along the side of the road on automatic, oblivious to her surroundings. For the umpteenth time she planned her escape from shit creek, imagining a fresh start, probably in Reno, or better still, Vegas. She knew that she had the looks to get work, even if only as a waitress to start with.

The old red Toyota pickup slowed down as the driver spotted the girl a quarter mile ahead, walking in the direction he was driving. Easing his foot off the gas pedal, the sound the hot tires made as they rolled over the loose rock chippings was like puffed wheat or eggshells being crushed. As he neared her he wound the window down and the sound increased; now a carpet of snails exploding under the soles of a thousand marching feet.

If Trudy had left the trailer just a few minutes later. Or if she had only had that glass of juice she had decided against. If only!

Trudy Henderson was in the wrong place at the wrong time. Shit was about to happen.

"Look at the ass on that," Luke growled through the cigarette that was gripped between his lips, as he brought the pickup down to walking pace alongside the girl.

"What you gonna do, Luke?" Johnny Clawson asked as he sat forward to ogle at the shapely teenager. "Offer her a lift?"

Jerry Sullivan, who had been dozing, lifted his shades to give the girl the once over. "Keep going, Luke," he said. "There's barely enough room in here for the three of us. We don't need this."

"Speak for yourself, Jer, *I* need it," Luke said as he poked his head out of the window and gave his quarry a charming, 'trust me, butter wouldn't melt in my mouth' smile. "You need a lift, baby?" he asked the girl, adopting a Good Samaritan expression which worked more often than not.

Trudy should have turned tail and ran back to the trailer park, off the road, through the sand, rocks and sagebrush. If she had, then a thousand events that followed and altered so many lives would not have taken place. But she didn't.

"Fuck off, cocksucker," Trudy said in a calm, by your leave, have you got the time please tone of voice as she looked away from him and continued walking.

Luke lost it, and the red mist rose. Instant uncontrollable anger flushed his face, consuming him. No more Mr. Nice Guy. No one, absofuckinglutely no one was allowed to speak to him that way. Especially a split-ass teenager with an attitude. He pulled the truck forward and sideways, clipping the girl with the fender as he braked, before throwing the door open and exiting the vehicle in one fast, fluid movement.

Flipped off balance, Trudy fell to the ground, startled more than hurt. And as she pushed herself up, with gravel embedded in her knees and the palms of her hands, Luke's fist crashed into her right temple, knocking her out as her head thudded onto the highway.

Johnny and Jerry scrambled out of the passenger door and ran around to where Luke stood looking down at the limp form that lay in front of him, and Johnny checked both ways to make sure that there was no other traffic in sight and said, "Now what? What're we gonna do with her, huh?"

"Let's just leave her and get the hell out of here," Jerry said, nervously shifting from one foot to the other as he scratched at the stubble on his cheek.

Luke picked the girl up – with the ease that a child might snatch up a rag doll from the ground in passing, with no conscious thought or effort – and threw her into the bed of the pickup, covering her with a piece of tarpaulin before walking back to the cab.

"Get in, boys," Luke said, grinning. "We got us pussy to play with."

He drove for approximately three hundred yards, before pulling off the two-lane onto a barely discernible dirt trail that led to an area of large boulders, many as big as semi-trucks, which fronted a backdrop of steep, red cliffs. Driving behind a large outcrop some seventy yards from the road and hidden from view, Luke stopped and climbed out onto the hot sand, his teeth dazzling white as the sun lit his broad smile.

Trudy's senses were returning. She felt as though she was slowly rising from a black abyss in an ocean that gradually grayed as she rose from its depths through ever brighter layers, with the light stretching down to reach her. Consciousness came back as she surfaced to a world of pain. Her head pounded from the blow to her temple. It felt as though a hand grenade had fragmented inside her skull; the slightest movement sending sharp bolts through her brain. Opening her eyes made it worse, so she closed them. She was lying on her back, and the rising sun had blinded her. Fire coursed through her arms and legs; a red hot flow of molten pain that seemed to emanate from her very bones. Slowly, very slowly, she turned her head to one side and eased her eyes open again, narrowed against the glare, and was so shocked by what she saw that the heat from the hot metal on her cheek went unnoticed. Icy fingers clenched in her stomach, and her heart seemed to skip several beats as she became aware of the fix she was in. She was naked, spread-eagled in the back of the red pickup with her arms and legs pinioned by barbed wire that was wrapped tightly around her wrists and ankles; the barbs biting deeply into her flesh and tearing it with the tension her limbs were under. The wire had been secured to the sides of the truck, wound around metal cleats, holding her down in an iconic pose of horizontal crucifixion. She tried to cry out, only to realize that she was gagged; her mouth covered with what she thought to be tape.

Raising her head and looking down over her pert breasts and flat tummy to the rear of the vehicle, Trudy saw three men walking towards her. She recognized one of them. He had been driving the pickup, and was the one who had spoken to her; an Indian with long black hair and a red bandanna worn around his forehead. It had been he who'd hit her, and it was him that she now focused her full attention on, instinctively knowing that he was the one to really fear.

Luke heard the wire scraping, steel on steel, and began walking across to the pickup. Johnny and Jerry followed. The girl's head was raised and she was staring at Luke with a look of mixed hatred and fear in her large blue eyes, trying to speak, grunting through the tape.

Luke took a last deep drag off the cigarette he was smoking and then threw the butt of the Winston to the ground, grinding it out with the heel of his boot as he reached the open tailgate. "Hi, baby," he said, gripping her left foot and twisting it savagely to the side, chuckling as she emitted a high-pitched whine of pain through her nostrils. "Did you sleep well?"

CHAPTER THREE

Luke Strayhorse was a Native American Chiricahua Apache, stood a stocky five-nine and was broad, muscular and powerful. His mildly arrogant expression and the way he moved gave off a self-assured and almost tangible aura of danger; a 'don't fuck with me' persona that in most cases earned him reluctant respect from those who he dealt with. It was a facet of his complex personality that he could turn on and off at will.

Luke had been born on the San Carlos Reservation in eastern Arizona, to a mother who had deserted him at birth by dying before he was delivered by section from her cooling body. His father had proved incapable of raising him efficiently, suppressing his deep sense of loss badly; the underlying resentment for his son apparent as he levied an irrational blame on the baby for the untimely death of his wife. The deadening effect of cheap, rot-gut whisky did nothing to help him cope as he slowly drank himself into oblivion. The discovery of his frozen corpse in an alley at the rear of Sitgreave's Mercantile in Show Low – following a severe ice-storm – came as no great surprise to those who had known him.

Luke had been a youngster, but had only shrugged when told of his father's death. If he had felt any emotion, he did not show it. The remainder of his childhood was supervised mainly by his paternal grandfather, who imbued his young charge with self esteem, and told him of the old ways, and of the proud heritage of the Apaches before their ruination at the hands of the whites.

Luke's traumatic birth and the subsequent years of either inattention or hostility from his father would have been a textbook case to supporters and exponents of Freud or Jung. They could have extrapolated the boy's penchant for cruelty and fundamental lack of emotional stability into a weighty tome which would, in summation, have undoubtedly led to his personality disorders being attributed to childhood imprinting, and an emotio-physical identity influenced by an uncontrollable mechanism that was patterned subconsciously from events leading back to his birth...or even before.

Truth being, Luke was just a rotten apple with a predetermined program that made him a depraved and violent human being. Perhaps he should have been left in his dead mother's womb and buried with her. But he had lived, a human stick of gelignite, sweating in the sun, ready to explode and cause mindless destruction; a homicidal psychopath. It would have made no difference if he had been born into a family like 'The Brady Bunch' in Niceville, Shangri-la. His poor start; both environmentally and culturally, only added fuel to a fire that was already smoldering within him, waiting to erupt into a conflagration.

Luke grew into a good looking young man, his features as finely chiseled as sculpted marble, with almost oil-black eyes; eyes that were hypnotic if they returned and then held an onlooker's gaze. He was a throwback to his ancestors, with a warrior spirit and an innate belief that he had a God-given right to take whatever he desired from life, and bow to no man. This ideology had, in part, been unintentionally instigated by his grandfather, who'd told him of a past that he in turn had been told of by his father and grandfather before him. Luke listened avidly to the tales of battles with the whites; of when Cochise and then Geronimo had fought valiantly to preserve a way of life on land that the Chiricahua had lived in harmony with for as long as tribal memory could regress. Luke's mind had been filled with a vision of how his people had once been, and of how they had lived in scattered groups. He imagined the days of foraging across the land, raiding the camps of other tribes, and surviving in the harsh, unforgiving desert environment, adept at living off its meager resources. Luke had been consumed by rage to hear of when the whites came, slowly at first and then in countless numbers, infesting the land like a plague of locusts; 'the teeth of the wind', to pursue a policy of genocide against all Indians, that today would be regarded as ethnic cleansing, which the present day government condemned when practiced by other foreign powers.

The whites had spread like a malignant poison ivy over land which was not theirs, driving the Apache into the mountains, or herding them onto reservations to be treated as non-persons, bent to the white mans' will. The Apaches had been subjected to pitiful treatment under the auspices of government jurisdiction, forced to endure humiliation, hunger, cruelty, and restriction of movement.

Luke listened in awe as he was told of Geronimo assuming the role of war chief, to lead a small band of his people away from the reservation and bring terror and death to the whites, wreaking havoc in the region for a decade, refusing to surrender.

Luke was in a time-warp. He wore his blue-black hair in the old way, shoulder length and held back from his face with a bandanna. He had retained his native language, only speaking English if he needed to, when dealing with whites. He had attended the Indian school; an institution conceived to eradicate the native culture, forcing pupils to renounce their language, style of dress, and even have their hair cropped in the short style of the white Americans. It had not been so long ago that boys were badly beaten – sometimes to death – for speaking in their native tongue, or subjected to having their mouths washed out with lye soap. All this had made Luke even more bitter, mean and devoid of empathy for the feelings of man or beast. He was a cold, callous individual with a bison-sized chip on his shoulder, but could appear to be amiable and well-mannered should it suit his purpose. His winning smile and softly modulated voice had parted many a girl, white and red, from their maidenheads. He was an opportunist with no particular ax to grind. Life was for pleasure, and Luke's pleasures were simple: fucking, stealing from, and hurting people, and not necessarily in that order.

For the past three years, Luke had drifted aimlessly throughout the southwest, working when necessary as a short-order cook in greasy-spoon diners, or more often than not laboring, doing odd jobs for bed and board and a few bucks. And then, while walking in the Black Mountains, just a few miles south of the Hoover Dam, a red pickup passed, and then the brake lights flared as it pulled over to the hard shoulder to stop thirty yards ahead of him. He didn't run to it, just quickened his pace to show that he was interested.

Johnny Clawson wound the cab window down as the Indian approached, watching him through the rearview mirror.

Stopping would prove to be the biggest mistake that Johnny had made in his life.

CHAPTER FOUR

JOHN Devere Clawson looked like the athlete he might have been. He was twenty-eight, six-foot one, and weighed in at a hundred-eighty-five pounds; none of it fat.

Johnny had been well on his way to becoming a pro footballer, but that was before the RTA of several years ago, and the consequences that were carved on his heart and etched in his mind, still fresh and raw; a reminder of the night that his life had been ruined.

Johnny had been out at La Jolla that evening with his girlfriend Cathy and a couple of dozen others. It had been one hell of a beach party; good music, plenty of food and drink, and even the odd joint to chill out with. By one a.m. everyone had either headed off home or vanished among the sand dunes for drunken alfresco sex.

Cathy and Johnny stepped into the surf and walked along the shoreline under a bright moon; the ebbing foam sucking the wet sand from beneath their bare feet. And as they ambled hand in hand, relaxed and happy, they discussed the wedding that they were already planning for the following spring. It was well past two a.m. when they turned and started walking back towards the rest area, where they had parked up.

"Do you want me to drive, Johnny, you're stoned?" Cathy said as they reached the car and she watched as Johnny had difficulty finding the slot in the door lock with the key.

"No, I'm fine, honest. Trust me," he replied, slurring his words slightly. He started the Chevy up and pulled across the loose gravel, out onto the coast highway to head back to San Diego.

"Lights!" Cathy snapped.

"Oops," Johnny said, smiling, turning the lights on and flipping to full beam. "All the better to see you with."

Cathy did not return his smile. He kept his speed down, concentrated, and had left the Alvarado Freeway and was heading west towards Cathy's home on Lake Murray Boulevard when he began to feel ill. The effects of the booze and marijuana took hold of him, and the air conditioning failed to hold back the sweat that was leaking from every pore. He felt sick to his stomach, and was finding it increasingly hard to concentrate; his vision blurring and making it difficult to focus on the road ahead.

The driver of the other car was doing everything right, observing the speed limit and keeping to his lane. As he saw the distant glare of approaching high beams, (which would round the curve ahead at any second), he dipped his lights. Dip don't dazzle was second nature to him, and he had never been able to understand why some morons risked causing an accident by blinding oncoming traffic.

Tony Dominquez and his wife, Vera, were both retired and in their mid sixties. Normal life patterns had been discarded, now that they were no longer slaves to an alarm clock. Tony had smashed the old clock on the day that he had retired from his clerical post at Harbor Electronics, fulfilling a promise that he had made to himself most work mornings for the twenty-eight years he had been with the company. He had never felt like that when he had been in the navy. But that was then...all of it was then, and behind him now.

It was late, but Tony and Vera had been wide awake and hungry. Tony's idea to go and eat at a twenty-four-hour downtown Denny's seemed a good one at the time, but was to prove disastrous.

Johnny rounded the curve and saw the headlights of three cars coming towards him. He knew that there was only *one* vehicle, but his eyes had lost the plot. His befuddled mind tried to concentrate and sort out the visual messages, but failed miserably.

Tony watched the weaving lights and immediately and correctly assumed that the driver was drunk. He slowed and pulled over to the side of the road, but like a ten cent nail to a magnet, the other car seemed drawn to him. He just had time to put his arm across Vera, as if to shield her from harm, when...

...Johnny actually closed his eyes a split second before the crash. And through an alcoholic, weed induced haze he heard Cathy's scream as the offside front fender of the Chevy impacted with the other car.

The dash in front of Cathy erupted towards her as the screeching metal tore and crumpled with the force of the collision. The windshield shattered into a multitude of sparkling glass cubes, which buried themselves into her face and her open mouth, to penetrate her tongue, gums and the back of her throat. She felt nothing, though. A narrow strip of metal had sheared off from the hood, whistled through the disintegrating shield and sunk into her forehead, skewering her brain as it smashed out through the back of her skull, to pin her to the seatback, killing her instantly.

Johnny felt the car rise diagonally after the initial impact, and sensed that it was cart-wheeling end over end along the highway. Everything seemed to be happening in slow motion, frame by frame. He felt no pain or fear, yet, just a childish sense of wonderment as he saw the glow of San Diego's lights, alternating with darkness as the car tumbled away through the night.

Tony thought that he and Vera were going to die. And for what? Because they had wanted a burger meal at almost three in the morning. The force of the collision to the front of his Mustang, being mainly to the passenger side, had spun the car sideways and backwards simultaneously. That, and being stationary, had almost certainly saved their lives. As a passive object, hit obliquely, the Mustang, with no forward momentum, had been shunted out of the way, not suffering the same dire fate as the other car.

Tony escaped with a broken arm and heavy bruising. Vera had fared worse, her head whip lashing back and then sideways, to smash through the side window, lacerating her face and fracturing her skull. She would however, despite being scarred, make a full recovery.

The next time that insomnia and hunger kept Tony and Vera awake late into the night, they would, without exception, settle for a sandwich at home.

Johnny woke up in Lemon Valley General Hospital two hours' after the crash. His physical injuries were multiple fractures to his legs, a ruptured spleen and concussion. With surgery and physiotherapy his injuries would heal. His damaged body could be rehabilitated, but his mental anguish would remain, a livid, festering but invisible wound that consumed him with grief, guilt and shame for what he had done. He found it almost unbearable to go on living and suffer the constant torture of reliving the events that had led up to the crash and Cathy's death. The depth of his depression deepened over the months that followed, causing savage swings in mood, sleeplessness, and a lethargy that took him spiraling down into a chasm of misery and hopelessness.

Johnny's father had used his not inconsiderable influence, and called in more than a few outstanding favors to keep his son out of prison. His business and country club connections proved invaluable. It may, on reflection, have been better if Johnny had been incarcerated for his criminal act. The guilt that he rightly felt may have been relieved to an extent, had he not only been found culpable of causing injury and death through drunk driving, but had also been punished in a manner that did not leave him feeling as though he had not made restitution fitting for his crime.

In Johnny's tortured mind, not just Cathy, but everything worth living for had died that night. His stupidity had also taken away the career in sport that he had been on the threshold of attaining. His legs were fucked. Oh, he could walk just fine; only the slightest of limps, but pro football...forget it. The support from his parents was of no help to him. Their unintentional sympathy as they treated him with kid gloves and tiptoed around him on rice-paper, simply added to his problems. His so-called friends evaporated like mist, their downcast eyes and hypocritical condolences barely masking their true feelings of contemptuous accusation. So he had spurned them, before they spurned him.

A year later and Johnny was a wreck, only coping with the aid of alcohol and drugs, which induced a level of apathy that made each day bearable. Eventually, in a lucid moment of awareness, he realized that he had to run away from the physical proximity that linked him to the past and fettered his mind with heavy chains. He had to rid himself of the people and the location which kept his pain so fresh.

Johnny skulked away in the middle of the night. The letter that he left for his parents was full of love, regrets and gratitude. He thanked them for their unswerving support and the care and devotion that they had shown him, and hoped that they could, to a degree, understand that if he were to have a future, it would have to be somewhere else; not where every sight reminded him of a past he could not bear to live with.

Taking his father's car, he headed north out of San Diego, never to return.

CHAPTER FIVE

JOHNNY met up with Jerry Sullivan in the fall of '94. He was drinking coffee in the Dogwood Diner up at Big Bear Lake, east of San Bernardino, when Jerry walked in.

"Anyone in here heading north, and could use some company?" Jerry had asked, surveying the three occupants of the diner for any response.

"It'll cost you a breakfast," Johnny said, wondering as he said it what had prompted him to speak up, surprising himself with the uncharacteristic familiarity that he had just shown to a complete stranger.

"A full breakfast for my new buddy, and make that the same for me, please," Jerry said, addressing himself to the bored looking waitress who was propping up the counter, chewing gum.

Jerry Sullivan was by nature jovial and friendly. He was a big, solid, easygoing bear of a guy, with an open, gentle, ruddy-cheeked face topped with thinning, carrot-colored hair. His hands drew most people's attention, being disproportionately large, like freckled steam shovels. It took a lot to rattle Jerry's cage, but once roused, he was a powerful and dangerous adversary, with the ability to cause serious damage to anyone who messed with him. He was thirty-one, a free spirit who lived one day at a time, ever moving on with no destination in mind and no need of one; a professional thief, he was adept at his chosen specialty of housebreaking.

Originally from Boston, Jerry was, ironically, the son of a cop. His father, Dermot, had served in the Boston police department, as had his father before him. The family roots were in County Clare, and they were proud of their Irish heritage. Jerry had been raised a good catholic boy, who had enjoyed a safe and happy childhood full of and surrounded by love and laughter. They had lived in a solid, three-storey brownstone house in Quincy, south of the city, and took their summer vacations in a rented cottage at Oak Bluffs on the island of Martha's Vineyard.

Jerry had planned on following in the family tradition and joining the department, but fate has a way of stepping in and fucking up the best laid plans and intentions. At nineteen years of age, on the twenty-fourth of December, Jerry's life took an unexpected turn for the worse, which unquestionably altered the course that he had decided to set sail on.

Dermot Sullivan was nearing the end of his shift that bleak Christmas Eve, and was looking forward to spending the holiday with his family. For the first time in several years he had two full days off, and had just used his coffee break to do some last minute shopping, picking up one or two additional gifts for his wife, Colleen, and his son, Jerry. He would, he thought, wrap them when he got home, while enjoying a large and warming measure of Irish whisky.

On his way back to the precinct, Dermot reached for the pack of cigarettes on the unit's dash, only to find it empty. Having run out, he wanted a smoke even more. He thought that the craving made him a sad man, but it highlighted what addiction to anything can do to you. All he could think of was getting another fix of nicotine. With some people it's chocolate, with others booze or heroin, and for millions like Dermot, it was tobacco. The dependency was a need that overrode all other considerations, to the point that an urgent staccato voice repeated and insisted with growing desperation that he must have a cigarette, and now. The voice of reason said, ease up, you're not a fuckin' junkie, you can do without. But he was, and he couldn't.

Dermot eased the cruiser through gray slush to the curb, and stopped outside a liquor store with his nerves already relaxing, knowing that he would be firing up a Marlboro in just a minute or two.

Stepping inside the door, he forgot all about cigarettes as he assimilated the scene that was playing out in front of him. He had walked into the middle of an ongoing armed robbery. The guy behind the cash register looked to be the owner, balding, fifties, blood from a fresh wound running from above his left eyebrow and down his cheek into a thick walrus moustache, turning it from gray to crimson. Facing him over the counter was a young black kid, no more than fourteen, and next to him, farther from Dermot, helping himself to chips, Hershey bars and other shit was another kid, even younger.

Dermot was reaching for his police special as his brain processed every detail. His main and most immediate concern was the nickel-plated Saturday night special that the older kid was waving in the air in front of the shaking owner's face. The youngster turned to face Dermot, wild-eyed and agitated.

The bullet hit him in the chest, quickly followed by two more to his stomach. *Jesus and Mary, the kid can shoot*, Dermot thought as he was driven back into the door, at the same time as he pulled the trigger of his own gun.

The slug from Dermot's .45 tore through the teenager's right eye, taking the back of his head out in a spray of blood and bone fragments and what looked like raw, minced lamb. The hot gore splashed over the second boy's face and chest, causing him to throw himself backwards away from it, which saved his life as Dermot fired again and the bullet displaced the air where a fraction of a second earlier the kid's head had been.

The boy curled up on the floor in a fetal ball, as Dermot warned him, needlessly, not to move. He then told the owner to dial 911.

The .22 caliber gun did not have the stopping power to put Dermot down. But with the situation under control, his legs gave way and he staggered, then slipped into a sitting position with his back up against the front of the counter.

"Give me a cigarette wouldya, boyo?" Dermot asked the ashen-faced owner, who had now been robbed three times in six months and had just decided to sell up and move to somewhere like Montana, or even Alaska.

Dermot managed one deep drag from the cigarette held to his lips by the store owner before drifting into the black.

Jerry and his mother were at the hospital, sitting in yellow plastic bucket chairs at Dermot's bedside when he died. The internal damage caused by the three slugs had given surgeons little chance to save his life. The massive internal hemorrhaging could not be controlled. Like a dam with cracks widening under pressure, the force of the deluge tore and pushed, filling his body cavities, extending the fissures until the whole structure collapsed, overwhelmed by the volume of liquid.

Father Bergen administered the last rites, while in numbed shock Colleen held her dying husband, whispering tearful words of love as he began to convulse. Finally, his muscles contracted and then relaxed, and his body straightened out and appeared to arrange itself neatly on the bed. With one long, last expiration of breath, that sounded for all the world like a melancholy sigh, he died. Both Jerry and his mother held their breath, waiting for Dermot to take another gulp of the antiseptic hospital air, only breathing again when blood forced open the corpse's mouth, to run from its lips down to the pillow, spreading like a wine stain on the white linen to signal his demise.

Colleen Sullivan ended her life the following year, with a cocktail of whisky and barbiturates. The official coroner's verdict was suicide, but Jerry knew that the real cause of death had been from an inconsolable and broken heart. He had watched helplessly as his mother shed fifty pounds in weight, eaten away by voracious grief.

Jerry had hit the road, and twelve years and two prison stretches later, the once would-be cop was still roaming, still thieving, with a philosophy to live footloose and fancy free; worrying about nothing. Life was short, and he had ceased to look for any rhyme or reason in what he considered a fickle and fleeting existence.

Johnny Clawson had been living in Los Angeles for the best part of a year, and only happened to be up at Big Bear because he was running— for his life. He had been dealing in coke, not the cola, but the 'real thing'; nose-candy for the rich and stupid. He had fucked up, running up a tab with his supplier that had somehow got away from him and become a serious problem. He should have known better. He knew that the Latino he was in debt to had plenty of AK-47-carrying muscle, and that he didn't take prisoners. Being sorry wasn't enough, and he couldn't meet the deadline that he'd been given. Even if he could have come up with the green – and he couldn't – he had hurt the big man's reputation, and would have probably been knee-capped as an example to other slow payers. As it stood, he was dead meat if he stayed in L.A., so took to the hills, leaving his rented studio apartment off the strip just twenty minutes before a carload of goons arrived and demolished it.

So it came to pass that the paths of Johnny and Jerry crossed, resulting in them teaming up and traveling together. Both needed a companion, though neither of them had realized it, or would have admitted to it. They just found each other's company agreeable. Hell, the bottom line was, they liked each other.

It was a hot summer's day and Johnny and Jerry were in high spirits. They had robbed two lakeside holiday cottages in Bullhead City, and were over a thousand dollars to the good. Driving south toward Hoover Dam, their intention was to hit Vegas, where they planned to increase their stake, or have fun losing it. Easy come, easy go.

It was Jerry who first spotted the solitary figure casually strolling along in the baking heat of the scorched and barren landscape.

"Hey, let's give this guy a lift," Jerry said. "Maybe even a cold beer. He looks as though he could use one. Whadya say, Johnny boy?"

"Okay, Jer, but if he turns out to be a fruit or a weirdo, you throw his ass out, right?"

"You got it."

Johnny pulled in about thirty yards in front of the guy, braking and coming to a stop on the burnt grass at the side of the highway.

"Christ, Jer, he's a fucking Indian!"

"That's okay. As long as he doesn't mention Little Big Horn, who gives a shit?"

"You looking for a ride, Tonto?" Johnny said, smiling as the Indian reached the pickup and looked in through the open window.

"Sure am, Kemosabe," Luke replied, returning the smile.

CHAPTER SIX

TRUDY ignored the pain and instinctively drew back in a futile attempt to escape from the Indian, who was now climbing into the back of the pickup. She hardly felt the further tearing of flesh as the spikes of barbed wire bit deeper into her throbbing ankles and wrists.

Luke unbuckled his belt and pushed his jeans down as far as his boots would allow. Kneeling between the girl's legs, he put his right hand under her buttocks, pulling her up and forward, so that he could enter her.

Johnny and Jerry watched in rapt silence as the Indian unselfconsciously raped the helpless teenager. Neither of them had wanted this to happen, although just by being there and not stopping him, they realized that they would be considered – in the eyes of the law – as accomplices.

"Your turn," Luke said, breathing heavily as he withdrew from the girl. "Come and get it while it's still warm."

"She can't go anywhere. Why not take the wire off?" Johnny said.

"Yeah, let's get her off the truck, it'll be easier," Jerry added, walking over to the tailgate.

Luke thought about it, but not for long. They were right. Where was the bitch going to go? Nowhere.

The wire being ripped unceremoniously from her limbs sent spasms of fresh pain searing through Trudy's entire being. Nausea swept through her in waves, like seasickness, roiling in her stomach and chest. From somewhere, a rational voice, her own, somehow detached from the proceedings, advised her not to be sick, because if she vomited while gagged she would almost certainly choke to death as her blocked mouth backed-up the surge of her stomach's contents.

Jerry picked up the girl by her ankle and swung her off the bed of the truck, face down onto the rocky ground. His cyan eyes were glazed at the sight of the naked female, and his growing lust outweighed his previous feeling of revulsion. Unzipping his pants, he then pulled the limp youngster up onto her knees, and with her head and shoulders still resting on the hot sand, he took her from behind.

Johnny watched as Jerry pounded against and into the girl. Listened in disgust to his pal's grunting as it quickened and grew louder. He was sickened. What if it had been Cathy; his poor dead Cathy? He wanted nothing to do with this; had bad feelings about all of it, and felt both sorrow and pity for the girl.

"Go on, Johnny, your turn." Luke said as Jerry shuffled to the side to make room.

"Not for me," Johnny said, his voice catching in his throat, quavering slightly. "Let's just leave her and get the hell away from here."

Luke eyed Johnny with a withering stare. "Listen up, Johnny boy," he said. "The bitch has seen us. She's buzzard bait, whether you fuck her or not. So you might as well have a piece of it."

"I'll be in the truck. I don't want any part of this, you sick bastards," Johnny said as he turned away.

"Like it or not, you *are* part of this," Luke said.

Johnny climbed into the cab, turned on the radio, loud, and then with difficulty – his hands doing a fair impression of someone suffering from advanced Parkinson's disease – lit a cigarette.

Luke strode across to the dazed girl, pulled her head up off the ground by the hair and glared down into her red-rimmed eyes.

"You're dead, bitch," he said, lowering his face to hers, almost gently taking her nose into his mouth, before biting down hard.

Forks of lightning, jagged and blinding, zigzagged through Trudy's face. The pain emanating from where the end of her nose had been was an excruciating, unbearable experience, which had to be borne. Behind the storm of pain, she could still hear the words that the Indian had said to her. They echoed around her brain... *You're dead, bitch.* And at that moment, looking into his snakelike, emotionless eyes, she knew without a doubt that he meant it. She was going to die, and there was nothing that she could do to save herself. That was when real fear hit her; a crippling, absolute dread that gripped her mind in a band of steel and immobilized her. Her brain was screaming to shut down, turn off; to not be there in that place of untenable horror. She was unable to cope with the enormity of what she knew was about to happen. Her bladder voided its contents onto the ground between her trembling legs, and she wanted to die, there and then, to avoid having to suffer whatever lay ahead at the hands of this monster.

It was not a normal fear that Trudy felt. Not one that she or anyone could contend with. The adrenaline that pumped through her, triggering the 'fight or flight' mechanism, could not be responded to.

Her mind could not adapt to a situation that prevented any form of reaction. She could neither fight nor run away, and so her subconscious was trying to fragment and crash, like a computer infiltrated by a virus. She screamed, and the scream, like Trudy, had nowhere to go. The pressure of the silent cry against the unyielding gag swelled her face, purpling it and distending hitherto unseen veins at her temples. Her eyes bulged, and blood vessels ruptured, sending red rivulets down her already blood-coated face. On the very brink of insanity, as her thoughts became an irrational, random and incoherent knot of agitation, she blacked out.

The girl's blood ran from Luke's mouth. Jerry was still knelt on the ground staring in disbelief at the lump of flesh that the Indian had spat out, and that had narrowly missed the back of his hand. It was part of her nose that the mad bastard had bitten off.

Luke grabbed hold of Trudy's wrist and dragged her across the rough, stony ground to the front of the pickup, which prompted Johnny to climb out and walk back to where Jerry was now standing, zipping up his jeans; eyes still fixed on the severed nose. Johnny took a crumpled pack of Marlboro from his shirt pocket and shook one half out, offering it to Jerry, who took it with a hand that was trembling as much as his own. Flipping the lid of his Zippo back, Johnny dragged his thumb over the wheel and a blue-yellow flame danced inside the wind-guard. With difficulty, he followed the wavering cigarette that was now between his friend's quivering lips. He then lit another for himself and took a deep drag of hot smoke, expelling it slowly.

"He...He bit her fuckin' nose off, Johnny," Jerry said, his normally ruddy face now white with an expression of repulsion wrinkling his eyes and pulling his lips back from his teeth.

"Whatever happens, Jer," Johnny said, "We've got to dump the son of a bitch. He's completely out of his fuckin' tepee."

While the other two were talking, Luke was busy.

Johnny and Jerry heard Luke's whoops of merriment, and watched spellbound as the girl bucked and writhed, emitting a loud snorting noise from the bloody stump in the middle of her face. Luke had drawn a knife from the sheath in his boot, and the ten-inch long blade glinted in the sun as with no hesitation he swept it across her smooth throat. Trudy immediately regained consciousness, and her eyes snapped wide open as her lifeblood was released from severed arteries, to spout jets into the air and down to lace the thirsty sand.

The pulses waned, became a trickle, and her blue eyes froze, dilated and fixed, staring blankly into the sun, totally bereft of emotion.

Luke knelt over the inert body and busied himself with the knife, his back to the other two as if hiding his actions. Finished, he wiped the blade on the corpse's stomach and returned the weapon to its concealed sheath as he stood up and raised his left hand to wave a raw slice of bloody flesh towards Johnny and Jerry. It bore a nipple and the blue-ink image of a deaths-head skull. With the toe of his boot, Luke flipped the body over on to its face, uncomfortable at being faced by the dead.

From the truck's Motorola, Roy Orbison balefully sang *It's Over*, and Luke sniggered, "You're damn right, Roy. It is, now."

In fact Luke could not have been more wrong. It was far from over. It was only just beginning.

"What do you think guys?" Luke said, approaching the other two, holding his macabre souvenir out for them to see more clearly. "Once this is cured it'll last forever."

"You mad bastard," Johnny said in a hushed, outraged tone of voice. "You dumb, sick Indian fuck. What did you do that for?"

"Because I think everyone should have a hobby," Luke said. "And if you ever call me dumb again, I'll cut your fuckin' ears off. Comprende, Johnny boy?"

Jerry interrupted. "Listen up, you two. There's a car coming. Now what do we do?"

Cal Morgan drove past the trailer park on his way into town. A film of sweat caused his shirt to cling to him. The Jeep's a/c unit was out, and would stay that way until he could find time to drop the vehicle off at Andy's Autos. It had juddered to a stop over a week ago, and he thought that he'd sweated off at least ten pounds in perspiration already. The windows were cranked down all the way to try and facilitate a through draft, but the desert air was hot and prickly. Never mind, he thought, another few minutes and he would be parked up and walking into the office, to immediately press a paper cone against the release on the large glass cooler, which would reward him with ice-cold water.

Cal forgot the heat and the anticipation of a cold drink in a flash; a flash of reflected sunlight that bounced off something white on the highway up ahead. He thought at first that it must be litter, blown from Carlin's park, because nothing that color crept or crawled out here. He slowed and then stopped, recognizing the object for what it was; a sneaker or some kind of sports shoe. Climbing out, he picked it up and turned it over in his hands. Judging by its size, it was a woman's shoe, pink and white, scuffed and well worn. He threw it in the Jeep, onto the passenger seat, and was about to climb back in when he heard the sound of distant music. It was unmistakably the 'Big O' singing one of his sixties ballads. Cal turned his head from right to left, zeroing in on the direction of the music's location. It emanated from up ahead to his right, probably somewhere behind the tumble of rock that ran parallel to the highway; a broken chain of sandstone cliffs that was known as Backbone Ridge, due to its outline resembling a long curved spine; the vertebrae carved out by the elements over millions of years.

Driving off road, heading for a large rent in the crumbling cliffs, Cal rounded a high shelf of rock, braking as a battered looking red pickup and the two men who were leaning against its tailgate smoking cigarettes came into view.

As he stepped from his vehicle, both of the men looked towards him, casually, and one waved a hand in greeting. Cal relaxed a little, mistakenly reading the situation as safe; something that he would never have done back in L.A. Now, as he walked towards the men, his dulled intuition led him to assume that there was no problem. He used to know better; to never take anything at face value. He had already decided that these two dudes had probably just pulled out of sight to take a leak or have a break from driving, and had no idea that they were only a hop and a skip from town and all the facilities that they could possibly need.

Several things happened in the next instant. Cal's eyes took in the whole enchilada. Looking past the two guys, he saw a leg on the ground, just visible, protruding from in front of the truck, covered with blood and only recognizable as a leg because it had a foot. At the same time he saw the furtive glance that the big, red-haired guy cast to a spot somewhere back towards the Jeep.

The smaller man said, "Is there a problem, Officer?" And in that split second Cal knew that he had blown it and seriously fucked up.

For the first time since his return to the Creek, Cal went for his gun, and as his fingers curled round the walnut stock, his wrist exploded in broken-boned agony. He spun around swiftly in reaction to the blow, just in time to see the tire-iron before it connected with his temple. He didn't feel a thing. He was out quicker than the time it takes for a wall switch to cancel the light from a bulb.

He came to on the ground in front of the pickup, lying on his side and face to face with a dead girl, who even with tape over her mouth and a bloody crater where her nose should have been, he had no doubt was Trudy Henderson, a teenager who waited-on at the diner in town, and who lived with her mother at the trailer park. Her dishwater-blonde hair, long on top but almost shaved to the skin at the sides, individualized her from any other girl in the area.

Cal's arms had been wrapped around the corpse's waist and secured at the wrists with his own handcuffs. Turning his head to look up, he saw that three men were standing just a few feet away, looking down at him. The one that must have been responsible for his present predicament and king-size headache was an Indian with black hair and wearing a bandanna; an Apache. Cal's gun hung loosely from the Indian's hand, and he knew that barring a miracle, he was going to be shot dead with his own weapon.

"You can't off a cop, Luke," Jerry said. "If you do they'll never stop looking for us. We'll end up on death row."

"He's seen us," Luke said. "And you've just told him my fuckin' name. He's got to go."

"None of this should have happened. We shouldn't have touched the girl," Johnny said. "Let's just leave him cuffed up and take off."

Luke ignored them both and held Cal's stare with lampblack eyes, which were chilling in their lack of any recognizable trace of human emotion.

"You got any tattoos, cop?" Luke asked as he slowly, purposely raised the .45 and leveled it at Cal's head.

"No. Why?" Cal said, frowning at the bizarre question.

"I collect them," Luke said, grinning as he smoothly pulled the trigger.

A deep, rolling report echoed like a thunderclap along the red cliffs, as skin, hair and bone were carved from the side of Cal's skull. The force of the shot snapped his head sideways, and a second bullet plowed through his throat, finishing him.

OH GOD, CHRISSIE! Cal's thoughts screamed in glaring orange mental neon as a brightness like an exploding star ignited in his brain, and then traveled out away from him, dimming, receding, to become a void of black infinite space. Where am I? Cal mused, as even his awareness of the darkness dissolved.

Purely for pleasure, Luke put another three bullets into the dead cop; the force of their impact making the two embracing bodies jerk together in a dance of death.

By a quarter after nine, Hank was beginning to feel just a little uptight. Cal's shift started at nine, and he was usually in the office ten minutes before that, regular as a Swiss watch, or Hank's bowel movements. If something had come up at home, he would have phoned. And if the Jeep had broken down, he would have got on the radio. Hank wasn't unduly worried, yet, just a shade rattled. He decided to give it another ten minutes or so, and then give his son a call.

"You need that freshenin'?" Mildred said, nodding in the direction of Hank's coffee mug as she watched him pace up and down the office like a caged lion.

"Thanks, Mildred, no, I'm fine." He replied.

Mildred Starkey was in love with Hank Morgan, and had been for more than six years. Nobody knew about her feelings for him. Absolutely no one. God forbid, just the thought of how she felt about the sheriff becoming common knowledge made her color up with embarrassment.

Mildred was a spinster. She had just never met the right man. Not one that she could, in all honesty, envisage being a soul mate for life. Now, at fifty-seven, it looked as though she had passed her sell-by date. But with her feelings for Hank she could still dream. She lived in a one-bed, one-bath apartment out on Boulder, which she rented from Willard Harper. Willard was a good landlord, who kept the property in decent repair and charged a fair rent. Three cats kept Mildred busy, and they were as precious to her as children were to other folk.

Mildred realized that her job at the sheriff's office, her cats, and her small apartment were her life, and gave living credence. She looked forward to every working day, just to be near Hank. He was a big, strong and honest man, with a warm and caring nature beneath the tough exterior that he wore like a bullet-proof vest. Did he suppose, she wondered, that showing too much kindness or humanity might be construed as weakness? She could vividly recall the excitement and happiness that he had allowed himself to show when his son had returned to the Creek. To have Cal back from 'tinsel-town' and working alongside him had injected Hank with a new lease of life. The friendly banter and arguments between them over everything from sport, politics, religion, working methods and even their diverse taste in music and clothes had brought the office alive, and had rejuvenated a man who could have easily gotten old before his time.

Hank had lost his wife to breast cancer, years back, and had taken it hard. Without his work he would have probably crumbled.

Pulling the handset from its retaining clip, Hank brought it to his mouth and pressed the transmit button. "Control to unit two, receivin', over?" he said, releasing the button and listening to static for a few seconds before trying again.

"Control to unit two, come back now, over."

There was more hissing and crackling, but no reply. After several attempts, Hank tossed the handset onto the desk, too irritable to take the extra second to return it to the spring-clipped recess on the side of the transmitter. He reached for the phone and dialed his son's number.

Driving north, out of town towards Cal and Chrissie's place, Hank expected to find the Jeep broken down at the side of the highway. He would give Cal a tongue-lashing for not having his radio switched on, although if it had been in working order, surely Cal would have used it to call in for assistance. Chrissie had said that Cal had left the house at eight-thirty-five. It was now nine-thirty, and Hank was pissed. This was a poor start to the day. He had told Chrissie that he would have Cal phone her, just as soon as they got back to the office, to save her worrying over what her lug of a husband was playing at.

Just two thirds of a mile out of town, Hank saw buzzards circling over Backbone Ridge. The presence of the scavengers could mean anything. An old coyote with worn down teeth and slow reactions may have lost the fight for life, starved and dehydrated, succumbing grudgingly to nature's unforgiving process. Hell, he could think of a dozen reasons to explain the raptors' interest in that spot, but none of them rested easy with him. Gut reaction stopped him from driving by, and the tire tracks leading away from the road only deepened his growing feeling of apprehension.

The Jeep sat heavily on its slashed tires, with both doors wide open. Hank braked hard, exiting his cruiser on the run as he drew his gun. He knew before he reached the bodies that his son was dead, and his world collapsed with him as he sagged to his knees, tears welling up, his head shaking slowly from side to side in stunned disbelief.

Cal had been handcuffed face to face to the body of a young girl, who appeared, from the injuries that he could see, to have been tortured and mutilated. Cal had a bone-deep gash on the side of his head, and a neat, round crimson bullet hole in his throat. The slug had taken away most of the back of his neck, and the sand was saturated with blood from both of the cadavers. Hank could see at least three more bullet holes in his dead son's khaki shirt. Whoever had done this had enjoyed it; had killed for the pure pleasure of the act, not for gain.

Through his devastating grief, and while still trying to comprehend the enormity of his loss, Hank felt something else; a cold helpless fear as he realized that as soon as he had contacted the state police, he would have to face Chrissie and tell her that his son, her husband, had been murdered and was gone from them forever.

CHAPTER SEVEN

HANK Morgan was a fit looking fifty-five year old, standing six feet two and only carrying ten pounds excess weight. He still had a thick head of hair; steel-gray now and kept short, not quite a buzz-cut.

Returning from Vietnam – still a young man – with a purple heart and a truckload of bad memories, Hank had joined the Sheriff's Department, to several years' later stand for the office of County Sheriff; a post that the sudden, natural death of old Roy Moffat had made vacant. He had got the job and was still in post, keeping law in Pershing County, based in his hometown of Benson's Creek.

The office was small. It faced the north side of Carson Square, which was in fact a public park that boasted some yellowed, tired grass, a few gnarled live oaks, several wooden benches around an all but dried-up lake, and a weathered life-size bronze statue of Josiah Benson, the town's founder, which stood forlorn under a thick white crust of bird droppings. The park was fenced off by a palisade of wrought-iron railings (in need of wire-brushing and a lick of paint), and Main Street diverged around it.

The door of the sheriff's office led into a bullpen, by way of a spring-return fitted waist-high gate that gave access to the small, turn of the century-style room. There were two desks; one that Hank and Cal shared, and the other for the exclusive use of Mildred Starkey, their secretary, who kept the paperwork moving in the right direction, and brought some order to the chaos. Out back were two holding cells that were mostly a waste of valuable space, due to hardly ever being employed to house prisoners. The occasional drunk would spend a night sleeping it off in one of them, but the other was too full of junk and cleaning gear to afford accommodation.

Like any community, the Creek had its share of crime, but most folk were honest and hardworking citizens, who made the most of what little they had, and took each day as it came, blessing the good ones and putting the bad ones down to experience; to be learned from and strengthened by.

Main Street was the hub of the Creek, offering essential goods and services to the townsfolk and outlying farmers and ranchers. Harper's General Store was a port of call for everyone, selling: tins of Copenhagen chewing tobacco, wood-burning stoves, barbed wire, generators, tools, work clothes and most things in between. If that old buzzard Willard Harper didn't stock it, then it would most likely never be asked for. And on the odd blue-moon that he was caught out, Willard would order the item, or send one of his boys down to Reno or even Carson City to pick it up; supplying it with just a small service charge tagged on, 'so as not to be out of pocket', he always said.

As well as Harper's, the main street had a small two-teller First National Bank, a bakery, diner, The Sawtooth Saloon, Scotty's Electric's, and the usual sundry enterprises that you would expect to find, including a small Savemore food market. The only other business of note was Andy's Autos up at the junction of Main and Sunset. Andy Garner's body shop took care of just about everything on wheels in the Creek, plus he also did a fair trade in new and used vehicles; mainly 4x4 off-roaders and pickups.

The town had its share of work shy, and even a handful of downright law-avoiding types, but nothing major league. There were one or two 'working girls' who kept a low profile, and minor problems with some of the teenage population, who needed the rough edges filed down once in a while. But major crime...big city stuff, well, that was a way off back then. The last crime of any real significance – apart from parking and speeding violations – had been eighteen months back, when Billy Turpin and Sammy Evans, both from the trailer park outside town, and both still a spit off seventeen, had broken into the Sawtooth Saloon at midnight, by way of the skylight, and made off with two quarts of Jack Daniel's and a few packs of cigarettes. Hank had found the boys in the bushes next to Josiah's statue in the park, both sleeping off the effects of a full bottle of the Old No. 7 Sour mash, and laid in their own vomit. When Hank had roused them, they were two very sick and sorry-assed youngsters. Warren Carlin, the owner of the saloon had been going to press charges, until Hank reminded him of the several times he could have pulled his liquor license for various misdemeanors, which had involved after hours' drinking sessions that had got a little too rowdy.

Hank had set Billy and Sammy to work for the community, carrying out small property repairs like fence painting and picking up litter. And they were just the cleaner jobs. He had them laboring until they wished that they had never heard of Mr. Jack fuckin' Daniel's. The experience seemed to do the trick. If they went wrong again, then it would more than likely be in another county or state, where they would probably end up behind bars, not 'straightened out' by Sheriff Morgan.

The Creek had also had its murders. Although the most recent had been way back in November of sixty-three, just a week before JFK had been gunned down in Dallas. Luther Gibson had shot his neighbor's dog; just leaned over the fence and emptied both barrels of his old twelve gauge in the mutt's head, blowing what little brains it had all over the backyard. Luther had warned his neighbor, Martha Robson, at least a half dozen times that it would happen. And the day before the dog's demise, he had made it a final, last time, no more talking ultimatum.

"Martha," he'd said. "If that shit-machine of yours keeps me awake with its goddamn barking just once more, I'll shoot it dead, so help me I will."

"Luther Gibson, you mean old fart," she'd replied, her face as white as the washing on her line, and her eyes narrowed to slits with anger. "If you so much as lay a hand on my Goldie, I'll cut your miserable head off, and you can take that to the bank."

Just about everyone is guilty of making idle threats. Not many can in all honesty, hand on heart, swear that they've never done it, even if it went unheard, muttered under the breath. But with Martha and Luther it was different. They meant every word that they had said. After Luther had thrown down the gauntlet, then that was it as far as he was concerned, as clear cut as the ten dollar glass vase on his bureau. If that flea-bitten excuse for a dog woke him up again, he would do the deed. Luther was a man of his word, straight as an arrow and proud of the fact that in all his eighty-one years he had never reneged on any threat or promise he'd made. With the shotgun loaded and propped up next to the kitchen door, he was just waiting for the chance to show the old bitch that no one fucked with Luther Edwin Gibson.

Martha was scared, not for herself, but for Goldie. She had been given the golden Labrador when it was just nine weeks old, almost ten years ago. At that time, her late husband, Arnold, had been hospitalized in Imlay for over a month, and everybody but Martha had accepted that he would only leave the building via the mortuary. Too many years down the mine had resulted in him developing silicosis, that became so bad that even the oxygen mask couldn't stop the hallucinations and the passing out. The doctor had reached the point where he knew that it was all over bar the grieving, and told Martha to ready herself for the worst. But she just seemed to close her ears to any talk like that, and was not prepared to acknowledge that Arnold would leave her after nearly fifty-three years together. She made ready for his return home, sure that if not cured he would at least be back with her, and much improved.

When Arnold's brittle lungs finally froze in his chest, it was Goldie that gave Martha a reason to not just take some pills and tie a plastic bag over her head. Without Arnold, Goldie was the most important thing left in her life.

It was barely light on that bleak November morning when Luther took away Martha's reason to live. Goldie had barked once...just once, about an hour before dawn, as she heard a car backfire nearby. That was all the excuse Luther had needed. He waited, keeping watch through the nicotine-stained sheers of his kitchen window, drinking coffee and impatiently, eagerly anticipating what he would do when the old crone – who he had never cottoned to – opened her back door and let her fuckin' dog out to take a dump on the lawn.

"There's a good girl, go pooh-poohs for momma," Martha cooed as she opened the screen door to let Goldie out into the yard.

Luther dropped his coffee mug in the sink and went for the shotgun, thumbing off the safety as he strode from the house and over to the dividing fence. The dog came across to him, tail thrashing the air, looking up at him with large, trusting brown eyes as he took careful aim.

The twin blasts blew the dog's head apart like an exploding pumpkin, sending a spray of crimson flesh and brains back in a swathe that painted the grass red. Luther watched, a puckered, sunken smile lifting the corners of his denture-less mouth as the mutt twitched for a couple of seconds before going limp.

Martha witnessed the execution of Goldie from her door, and instead of breaking down or becoming hysterical, she snatched a boning knife from the rack on the kitchen counter and ran outside with purpose, deadly intent, and a turn of speed not seen in her for over forty years. Luther caught the movement as a blur from the corner of his eye, and just had time to look up and see her, but no time to avoid the blade that plunged into his neck, almost to the hilt. He dropped the spent shotgun and gripped the knife's handle with both hands, wrenching it free and holding it in front of his face in disbelief and horror, as though he were holding on to a rattlesnake. The slick blade slipped from his fingers, and he staggered backwards, his lifeblood deserting him, spraying out in rhythmic spurts to soak into the dry, gray boards of the fence, and the hungry, baked ground.

"You've gone and killed me, Martha Robson," Luther gurgled, before doing a grotesque pirouette and collapsing to the hard earth.

"I said I would, and now I have, you no good sonofabitch," Martha muttered, kneeling down to gently stroke the headless corpse of her dog.

The police had taken no pleasure in arresting a frail old woman who had lost her only friend and constant companion so violently. Luther Gibson had been a vindictive and heartless man; no loss to anyone. But the law is the law, and it was impossible to overlook a crime of such magnitude. Martha was charged with murder, but her heart gave out before they even had chance to transfer her to Carson City for arraignment. The incident had made the national networks, brought the leeches from TV-land into town; which was good for trade, but a pain in the ass for the mayor and the Sheriff's Office.

The murder had been a rare high – or low – light in the Creek, not reflecting the normal slow and easy pace of life in the close-knit community. The town had been and still was usually laid-back and mellow, making it easier to understand why Hank's son, Cal, had become a little complacent. In the two years that he had been back, he had lost his street-wise edge. His instinct for real trouble was dulled as he relaxed, and the tension, which he had not even realized affected him had melted away. The ever present subconscious readiness for danger, which he had worn like a second skin back in L.A., had been eroded, and the lapse had proven fatal.

CHAPTER EIGHT

JIM Clayton was thirty-two; a handsome guy of the tall and dark variety, who was just reaching that stage in the game when you begin to be aware of your own mortality, and realize just how short life really is. It was also a time when he was starting to use the gate, instead of short-cutting by leaping over the picket fence like a teenager.

Jim, along with Brad Atherton – a buddy since seventh grade – ran a successful and respected advertising agency in Washington D.C., which was not yet frightening the really big players, but was enjoying the patronage of several high-powered accounts; accounts that attracted a welter of the smaller 'bread and butter' clients' to their door.

Jim had married Linda in the August of 'eighty-eight in a picturesque, white, clap-boarded chapel in the shadow of the Blue Ridge Mountains in Front Royal. Just family and a handful of very close friends had attended, and following a brief honeymoon on Captiva Island in Florida, they had moved into a beautiful, up market house on a select subdivision in Chevy Chase, in the 'burbs of D.C. They missed the mountains and down-home atmosphere that they had both grown up in, but commuting was out of the question.

Linda Clayton, née Clark, was still in her twenties, albeit by a hairs breadth, with the big three-O knocking at the door. She was tall, willowy, and had no need for makeup on her clear and unblemished skin. She was going through a rough patch in the fall though, to say the least. Her father, Daniel, had died in April at the ripe old age of just fifty-three. He had been mowing the lawn that day; a serious business, trying to get those stripes just so. Suddenly, and with no forewarning of impending doom, his heart had blown up and he was dead before he hit the ground, missing the ensuing spectacle of the runaway lawnmower as it slewed across the grass, disfiguring his perfectly aligned stripes and taking out an ornamental concrete deer, before finally crashing to a stop against the driver's door of his beloved powder-blue, '58 Plymouth. His habit of always stringing the Dead Man's handle up had proved a little foolhardy: not that was aware of the outcome.

Being sixty pounds overweight, predominantly inactive, and smoking three packs of cigarettes a day, Daniel Clark had certainly put in the work for his fatal cardiac infarction.

Linda's mother, Janet, had not stopped grieving, and was withdrawing from life as most people know it, drowning in a sea of misery and gin, her loss consuming her, taking away her appetite for both food and living. Linda was too far away to see as much of her mom as she would have liked to, and to be honest, when she did visit, she returned depressed and upset, having spent her time sat with a gaunt and haunted person who hardly recognized her, and who seemed to have mentally regressed to escape a reality that she could not face. Linda did her best, dividing that most precious commodity, time, between Jim, her teaching post, and the 'stranger' in Front Royal who had been her mother, but was now a preoccupied and monosyllabic stranger.

Life took a new turn for Jim and Linda. They had not used any form of contraception since their wedding night, and had gone through the full gamut of emotions as time slid by and the patter of tiny feet eluded them. They had both undergone tests, and apart from Jim having a negligibly low sperm count, everything had checked out fine. Sam Braedon, their MD and friend, sat them down in his office and rambled on about stress, trying too hard, and even tight underpants. Linda attempted to lighten up the proceedings by assuring Sam that Jim always wore loose-fitting boxer shorts. Sam's final recommendation was that they should just relax and enjoy 'it', especially at the right time in Linda's cycle, and let nature take its course. With his fingers crossed, Sam bet the farm on them needing to convert a spare room into a nursery in the not too distant future.

Linda said nothing to Jim, but her period was almost two weeks late, and for someone as regular as she had always been, it started her thinking...maybe, and what if?...and, it can't possibly be?

The next evening, Jim arrived home shortly after seven. He came through to the kitchen loosening his necktie as he casually tossed his briefcase onto the cushioned bench in the breakfast nook. He then took Linda into his arms and kissed her on the lips.

"So, how has your day been?" Jim asked, meaning it, wanting to know, and not just making small talk.

"Jim, sit down, I've got something to tell you," Linda said, feeling anxious and jittery, speaking too fast, and needing to unburden herself of her secret. Wanting to share it.

Jim poured coffee, slipped onto the bench facing her, and waited. Linda just grinned at him inanely. And he suddenly knew what she was about to tell him. It was the combination of the high color in her cheeks, and the excitement dancing in her sparkling gray eyes that conveyed what she had not yet put into words. Her normal mood of late had been tinged with the sadness of her father's death, and deep concern over her ailing mother. Tonight there was a dramatic change. It was as if her maudlin thoughts had been subdued, pushed back into a deep recess of her mind. Jim said nothing, just enjoyed the glow of elation that rippled across the table at him in almost tangible waves. This was her party, and he wanted her to tell him the good news in her own way, and in her own time.

"Shoot," he said. "What have you done, won the lottery?"

"No, better than that," Linda said. "I...I'm...I think I'm pregnant. But it's not definite, and...and..." And they were on their feet again, in each other's arms, both wet-cheeked, trading even wetter kisses. Linda pulled back, just far enough to be able to look into Jim's eyes. "I was late, Jim. And I'm never late. So I bought one of those testing kits, and the result was positive. I did it twice to be sure. I'll call Sam tomorrow and make an appointment to verify it."

Jim took a deep breath, every fiber of him hoping that it was true, and that they wouldn't be let down like a punctured tire.

Westwood Clinic: July 8, 1996

Linda was in a third floor private room at the Westwood Clinic, Bethesda, following Sam Braedon's recommendation to the facility, and subsequent arrangements that he made with a golfing bud, who also happened to be on the clinic's board. It was pricey, even with a special rate, but if you can afford it, what the hell, Jim had reasoned.

The initial ultrasound scan had been unclear, to the extent that the obstetrician had at first thought that Linda was expecting twins. The double image on the monitor seemed positive, but further scans showed a single fetus; they were expecting a boy. The choice of names took little more than a minute for them to decide on. They agreed that he would be christened Daniel, after Linda's father, and

James, after Jim and his dad. Their son would be known as Daniel James Clayton.

Daniel entered the outside world at 8.55 a.m. on the morning of July eighth, and his parents and the medical staff present at the birth would not forget the event— ever.

The birth itself was without incident; a perfectly normal textbook delivery, and the room was lit with smiles, congratulations, and above all the crying of a healthy newborn baby boy.

Daniel was placed in Linda's arms, and as she held him close, marveling at the miracle that she and Jim had created, reality melted. An electrical surge brightened the overhead fluorescent bars in a brilliance that could not be sustained, and with a series of loud cracks – that sounded like cannon fire – they exploded, sending a fusillade of hot, glittering glass particles down onto the room's occupants. All power to the third floor was out, and had it been night, the events that followed would not have been witnessed. No one moved. It was as if time stood still, freezing them, transfixing them like so many mannequins; just dummies placed around the bed in carefully arranged poses, which mimicked a store window display or a waxwork exhibit.

The air in the room shifted, visibly wavering and blurring, similar to the effect seen when driving on a desert road on a blistering day; the distant shimmering making the blacktop appear liquid in appearance. A low, pulsating throb emanated from the empty space above Linda and the infant. It was an indefinite submarine sound that seemed to burst from the depths of some alien and parallel universe.

Only baby Daniel could move. His head turned away from his mother's breast, where it had briefly rested, and his eyes opened wide and then narrowed, as though he were struggling to bring his vision into focus on each of the still figures. His mouth opened and closed rapidly, in the fashion of a gasping, beached fish. Then slowly, clearly, with a deep and resonating adult male voice, he cried out. "OH GOD, CHRISSIE...WHERE AM I?"

With a loud fizz of white noise, normality returned. Daniel lowered his head back down to Linda's bosom, and the distant sound of passing traffic and nearer voices of alarmed staff drifted back into the room. Only the debris of the shattered lighting, which covered every surface, glinting in the sunlight, remained as physical evidence that anything untoward had taken place in room 103 that morning.

Shit happens. Sometimes there are no answers. There was no answer or reasonable explanation for what had taken place after Daniel's birth, and it wasn't something that could be rationalized. It had been pure Twilight Zone; weird stuff that Rod Serling would've been happy to develop as an episode for TV. It defied belief, and the farther down the road that Jim and Linda got from it, the more unbelievable it became. It was an incident that could not be forgotten, but as the days built into weeks and then months, they found that they could almost deny it, to consign it to a corner of their minds where it could gather dust and molder like a dead rat mummifying in a neglected, cobwebbed attic.

As the years passed with no further 'events', Jim and Linda settled to a life that was richer and more fulfilling, now that Danny was a part of it. They had all but dismissed the strange happening of that faraway July day; but would soon be reminded.

CHAPTER NINE

"WHAT the fuck did we do?" Johnny said; the question leveled more to him than the other two as he knelt with his palms on the hard, burning ground in front of him, as if supporting the burden of guilt that his bowed shoulders seemed weighed down by.

"You two check the Jeep for anything worth having, and smash the radio," Luke said, dropping to one knee to frisk the body of the deputy sheriff. He took a money clip that held a paltry thirty bucks, plus ten rounds from the gun belt, and a pair of mirrored shades from the shirt pocket. Emptying the girl's shoulder bag, he came up with just eight dollars and a pack of Wrigley's gum.

Johnny and Jerry took a pump-action shotgun, a box of cartridges, and a Nevada road map from the Jeep. With tubing from the pickup they then siphoned off two gallons of the cop's gas into an empty container of their own, and found another full two-gallon can in the rear of the vehicle.

Luke held the hot barrel of the Desert Eagle to his nose and savored the smell of cordite from the muzzle, before pushing the gun under his belt as he rose and walked across to the others. Drawing his knife once more, he slashed the Jeep's tires, and then reached inside under the steering column to cut through the un-cased electrics.

Jerry drove the pickup, and they followed a dirt road west across the Lava Beds. Their newly acquired road map intimated that they would be able to avoid main highways all the way to California.

"Where are we heading?" Johnny said, still feeling numb from the carnage of the last hour.

"Once we're over the state line, we can find a place to hole up for a few days," Luke replied. "Somewhere remote like a ghost town or an old mining camp. There are hundreds of them."

"Ten bucks says we fry," Jerry said, staring fixedly ahead through the windshield to the horizon, the muscles of his cheeks twitching, his nerves almost shot.

"That's not funny, Jer. Not funny at all," Johnny said.

"You're right, it isn't. Let's make it twenty, huh?"

"Fuck you. We didn't need this shit."

"I know that, and you know that, but Tonto here is obviously still pissed over what happened at Wounded Knee."

"For fuck's sake shut up whining. It's over, and we move on. That's all there is to it. What's done is done," Luke said, folding a stick of the purloined gum into his mouth and adjusting his new shades. "It was no big deal."

Ed Cooper had a passion. It was much more than a hobby or pastime, it was his life. He was a prospector and explorer. If he wasn't out doing it, then he was planning for when he next would be. Obsession would be a fair term to use for his all-consuming pursuit, and Ed would be the first person to agree with that particular label.

Ed had retired from the Pearce Mining Corporation – where he had been a surveyor – eight years ago, on the very day that he hit sixty. He now felt fitter and was more active than he had been for many years.

His retirement was comfortable. He was financially secure, having received a substantial gratuity, and being paid a reasonable inflation-proof pension. With careful investments, plus insurance policies that had now matured, he had no worries in that area.

Ed had mining in his blood. His grandfather, Owen, had been a candle-carrying miner at Grass Valley's Empire Mine, north of Sacramento. And Ed's father, James, had followed in the old man's footsteps, literally.

Ed held the deeds to a bungalow with white stucco walls and a red tiled roof, set in a quarter acre on a quiet subdivision on the outskirts of Susanville. The house was in excellent order, the garden well-tended, with a feature of Bougainvillea that he'd pruned carefully over the years into trees to form a canopy over the porch out back. But the house was more a base of operations than a home. His real home was a Winnebago; a twenty-seven-footer that he traveled in and lived on most of the time. The motor home gave him the freedom to explore and stay at the many uninhabited towns that, although privately owned, were remote and waiting for rare visitors like Ed, who revered and respected their almost forgotten place in the nation's history.

He was a loner by choice, who had never married, and blamed his single status on his awareness of just how selfish he was with both his time and predilection for his interest. He had negotiated around two near misses over the years, and was currently fending off the unsolicited advances of Rebecca Buller, a blue-rinse widow who lived opposite him, and who was forever at his door, plying him with home-made apple pies, chocolate chip cookies, and assorted bait. He was too well-mannered to tell her just what to do with them, and so found himself having to smile and work to keep the woman at arms' length. Being an introvert and set in his ways, the man hunters' of this world put the fear of God in him.

A good time to Ed's way of thinking was wandering the desert and examining rocks, hoping to find specimens with a decent grade of ore. He had not been able to find a woman that shared his antisocial interest, and the truth was, he was content with his lot, wanting nothing more from life than what he already had.

Ed's thinning white hair was topped by an ancient felt hat: a hat that his father had worn before Ed was even born. It was as creased and weather-beaten as the man below its brim. Ed's face and arms were like tanned leather from long exposure to the elements, at odds with clear and youthful flint-gray eyes that burned with intelligence and the open capacity to still be amazed and elated at what life had to show him. His slight frame was wiry, and his grace of movement belied the advancing years.

On the afternoon of July eighth, Ed was driving the Winnebago off a dirt road, down a rutted track into a low, wide canyon; its backdrop the rising, rocky hills that stretched northeast, culminating in the seven thousand foot high peak of Eagle Mountain. He stopped momentarily to inspect the rusted, buckshot metal sign that still bore the name of the long dead township. The faded and flaking paint had left little more than an impression of lettering, which proclaimed that this was Sunrise. Below the name, scratched into the metal and standing out in rusted scrawl was carved: 'population nil'. Ed chose to believe that the epitaph was left by the last person to leave town; someone who'd still possessed a sense of humor. Driving on, he passed decaying wooden buildings, warped and leaning, but still standing in defiance of time and nature. He was on what had been Main Street, the center of town, a quarter mile from the tract of miners' houses that were located well away from the commercial district. Ed marveled at the weathered saloons and storefronts, trying, as he always did, to imagine the bustle of life that had filled this now sad husk of a town. Moving on, he headed out towards the skeleton of the ore mill that rose, still clad in bleached boards, a half mile distant. He parked up in the shadow of the mill, next to a broken-backed utility wagon that was slowly being consumed by time, and overgrown with sagebrush.

Lowering the motor home's striped awning, Ed set up a small fold-away table and sat outside in a wicker chair, taking the air and slaking his thirst with an ice-cold can of Coors. Forty yards from where he rested absorbing the atmosphere, twisted remains of rail tracks led into the entrance of the mine.

Finishing his beer, Ed went back on board, pitched the crushed can into the waste-bin, and then took a flashlight from the cupboard above the refrigerator, checking that it worked before stepping back out into the sunlight. He pulled his hat forward from its precarious position on the back of his head, and set off towards the mine's entrance. This was to be a quick look-see; just an appetizer. The entrée was to be saved for the next day, after due preparation and a good night's sleep. For the moment he would just tantalize himself with a short incursion into the main tunnel.

Luke was now at the wheel. They had crossed the state line and were heading north on 395. After traveling just a few miles, and being overtaken by a police cruiser, Luke became uneasy at being back on a main highway, and so turned off at Ravendale.

Jerry was first to see the pockmarked sign welcoming them to Sunrise.

"Let's check it out, Luke," Jerry said. "I need to stretch my legs and take a piss."

"Okay, you got it," Luke said, driving down the wide slope and into the center of the ghost town, continuing through to scout the area and make sure that they had the place to themselves. Up ahead stood the shell of an old mill, which appeared to be the last building in town. Luke decided to turn there and park up back on Main Street, already positive that this would be a perfect sanctuary to take refuge for a few days.

"Shit! Look," Johnny said, pointing at a gleaming motor home which was visible through gaps that looked like missing teeth in the ore mill's ramshackle walls.

Without hesitation, Luke drove around the side of the building and parked next to the other vehicle. Turning off the ignition, he pushed the dead cop's shades high up on his forehead, where the sweat-dampened bandanna held them in place. With an appraising eye he looked over the dusty but late model Winnebago.

"Our new home, boys," Luke said, smiling at his companions. "And ain't she just beautiful?"

Ed entered the mouth of the mine. Timber-backed, corrugated iron doors that had once forbidden entry now lay flat and entwined with weeds, their rusted hinges having lost the fight to hold them upright against the man-made opening in the rock face. He turned on the flashlight and stepped into the darkness, playing the powerful beam onto the floor, walls and roof of the tunnel. He noted that the square set timbering appeared solid, and that there was little loose debris, which would have signified movement; a shifting of wood and rock. Following the rail ties for perhaps thirty yards, Ed stopped to examine an ore cart that had been abandoned, still full, as if waiting to complete a journey that it never would. Directly behind the cart, opposite each other, were the entrances to two side tunnels. He chose not to continue any farther along the main passage, but to enter one of the smaller offshoots. He took the left one, and within ten yards was brought to a stop as the beam revealed an open vertical shaft in front of him. It was approximately eight feet square, and prevented any further advance. Ed made a mental note that should he wish to explore this tunnel during his stay, he would employ a couple of the several sturdy boards he had passed, that would no doubt bridge the chasm. Enough for now, he thought, turning to retrace his steps.

With only a few feet separating him from the entrance, Ed heard people talking; the sound coming to him suddenly as the blanketing effect of the rock lost its effect. He stepped quickly to the side of the tunnel and inched his way forward until he was able to look out furtively and seek the source of the voices.

There were three young men standing next to his camper. The tallest one, with red hair, was yawning, his arms outstretched and slightly bent at the elbows, spine arched backward as though he was working knots out of aching muscles. One of the other two boarded his vehicle, and the third, who was a Native American, stood with his head slightly cocked to a side, listening, his eyes roving, seeking movement. The urge to run from hiding and confront them was too strong to repress, and with adrenaline pumping, he left the concealing darkness. Fortunately for Ed, the Indian turned to face the camper, drawing a gun from his belted jeans. Ed froze as the sunlight bounced off the blue steel of the weapon's barrel. He backed up, not taking his eyes off the figures, or the gun, until he was once more hidden from sight. He had made a stupid move. These three men gave off a dangerous aura. If they found him, he would be hurt or killed, of that he was sure.

They quickly took stock of the motor home's contents. There was plenty of canned and dry goods, and a refrigerator packed with mainly bacon, eggs, milk, and four plastic-harnessed packs of Coors. The closets and drawers told a story, for while there was an abundance of men's clothes, there were no women's or children's. Books and magazines all seemed to be of a specialist nature, of mining and surveying. And one drawer held nothing but rock samples, another, small hammers and tools that they did not recognize. Two cherries on an already tasty cake were a bottle of bourbon, and more importantly, the keys to the camper, that were still hanging from the ignition, which Luke retrieved before walking back to the side door.

"Come on," he said. "Let's lock it up and go find him, he can't be far away."

"You're sure it's just one guy?" Jerry said. "There could be a couple of them at least."

"No, there's just one old rock-hound, believe me," Luke replied as he knelt on the sandy ground, examined it, and then moved a few feet and knelt again, before standing and looking directly towards the mine's entrance.

"He's in there," Luke said. "And my bet is that we're looking at the only way in or out. He's dead meat."

"How do you know that he's definitely in there?" Johnny said. "He could have wandered off anywhere."

Luke pointed at barely discernible indentations where the shallow sand had been displaced. "I see one set of fresh footprints heading straight towards the mine. There are no others, and they don't come back out, so he's trapped."

Neither Johnny nor Jerry could see any footprints in the apparently undisturbed sand, but they both believed that Luke could, if only for the reason that he was an Indian, and as such, in the movies, was thought to be able to track anything that moved, and hear stagecoaches, cavalry and the like approaching from twelve miles away, by putting his ear to the ground; and even be able to tell how long a camp had been quit by the coldness of the fire, or the freshness of any shit left at the scene by horse *or* man.

"There's no need to bother with him," Jerry said. "Let's just rubbish the pickup, take the camper and blow. The guy will probably never make it out of here on foot; not without water."

Luke shook his head. "We can't take the risk. With him out of the way and new plates, we're home free. I don't want to be wondering whether he made it out and reported his fuckin' wagon stolen. He's got to go."

Ed watched and waited. The trespassers went aboard his Winnebago, and then, after several minutes, stepped back out and stood talking. The Indian knelt and studied the ground, moved a few feet and repeated the act. Ed was too far back from the entrance to be seen, but his skin crawled and tightened when the Indian seemed to look straight at him, as if the darkness were nonexistent. After more talking, all three of them walked towards the mine. Ed was amazed that the man that he thought was Apache could see anything on the hard, rocky ground. He panicked, turned and ran, far too fast for safety, into the dark belly of the mountain, his heart racing as he scurried into the earth like a frightened gopher fleeing from a hawk. He forced himself to slow down, lucky not to have tripped blindly over the rusted rails and oak ties beneath his feet. Taking deep breaths and attempting to rein in his stampeding nerves, he stopped and told himself to think...think…think.

"We need a light," Luke said, stopping after walking just a few feet into the tunnel and finding it impossible to see more than a few yards ahead through the murk. "Johnny, go get a flashlight. I saw one in the cupboard next to the refrigerator."

"Keys...I need the keys," Johnny said.

Luke handed him the keys and then started walking farther into the tunnel with Jerry just a step behind him.

Johnny shouldn't be gone more than just a couple of minutes, and that wouldn't be soon enough for Jerry, who had a secret and intense problem with dark, enclosed spaces. It was not quite a real phobia, but as near to one as two books can crowd each other on a packed shelf.

Up ahead, Ed had formulated a plan of sorts; nothing long term, just a stopgap to hopefully avoid the immediate threat of being caught.

Picking up two of the long and sturdy boards he had spotted earlier, he made his way to the ore-cart and turned into the narrow, left hand branch tunnel. The boards were over ten feet in length by almost one foot wide. Ed risked a two second burst from the flashlight to ascertain exactly where the lip of the shaft was. Kneeling at the edge, he pushed the first plank out into space, his flashlight now placed safely behind him, away from any danger of being accidentally knocked into the pit. Holding the end of the plank in his left hand, with his right hand gripping the edge as far down its length as his arm would reach, he held the weight, and felt blindly for the far rim with the other end. Yes! He found solid rock and pushed the timber maybe a foot further. He then slid the second board over the first, confident that the combined thickness of the two would be strong enough to hold his weight. Retrieving the light, he turned it on, and without pausing, and with the speed of a barefoot fire-walker over hot coals, he crossed the plank bridge. From the other side, he pulled the timbers to him, to separate himself from the following men and feel a little safer as he moved off, carrying the planks with him, sporadically spraying light ahead to seek out any other hidden danger.

Johnny quickly caught up with Jerry and Luke. The small, cylindrical flashlight that he had found was not very powerful, but would have to suffice. They reached the ore-cart that sagged on its rusted axles, and stopped, confronted by a choice of tunnel entrances.

"Which way?" Johnny said, playing the weak beam over the smaller openings of the side passages.

Luke lit a cigarette and smiled that knowing, annoying smile; the one that said, pity these poor imbeciles, who are blind even in daylight.

"Just shine the light onto the ground, Johnny boy," he said. "No, more to the left...right a bit...there, stop." Once more he hunkered down to examine the ground. "That way," he stated, nodding in the direction Ed had gone. "Let's go."

Johnny entered the narrow rock arch first, the small light throwing out only a weak yellow cone in front of him. It lacked the power to cut any real distance into the gloom; as effective as car headlights on a dark, fog-bound night, reflecting back off the miasma to strain the eyes. The batteries were dying on him, and as he smacked the barrel of the flashlight into the palm of his hand in a vain attempt to beat more life and light into it, he stepped into space, and the forward momentum of his stride took him over, head first into a black hole.

CHAPTER TEN

THE scream reached Ed – who was a hundred yards farther along – as the muffled cry traveled past him to announce itself to the deepest reaches of the multifarious tunnel system.

For just a second, Luke thought that Johnny had tripped, and was reaching down to help him up when the scream told him that Johnny had fallen far lower than ground level. He stopped so fast that Jerry walked into him, nearly taking them both over to wherever Johnny had gone. A thick and almost tangible soup of silence enveloped the cavern, and the loss of the flashlight rendered them both immediately blind.

"What the fuck's happened? Where's Johnny?" Jerry said as he attempted to control a primal fear as the oppressive blackness gnawed at his brain, urging him to take flight like a trapped bird frantically beating its wings, beak opening and closing rapidly, and heart skittering as it darted in every direction, smashing into unseen barriers.

"He's fallen down a shaft," Luke said, feeling with his hand over the ground around him and finding a golf ball-sized piece of rock. "Keep quiet," he said, "while I drop a stone over. I want to see how deep it is. Okay?"

"Yeah, do it," Jerry said, standing motionless, just hanging on to his wits by a very thin, fraying thread.

Luke's fingers found the rim of the shaft, and thrusting his other hand forward, he released the stone and counted. "One...two." A muffled clump came from below.

"So, how deep is it?" Jerry asked, hearing the sound of rock striking rock.

"Deep enough," Luke answered, and then he shouted down the shaft. "Johnny, can you hear me?"

Only a dull echo bounced back at him in reply.

"How do we get him up?" Jerry whispered, as though the dark was a listening enemy.

"We don't get him up. The fall will have killed him, and we've got no light and no fuckin' ladder."

Jerry wanted to argue, but believed that Johnny must be dead. And he wanted out of the man-carved catacombs more than he had ever wanted anything else in his life.

Slowly, retracing their steps, they made their way back to the mouth of the mine, to fresh air, warmth, blue skies and space.

"Fuck it!" Luke said, stopping at the entrance. "Johnny's got the keys to the camper. We'll have to go back."

Jerry edged away from the tunnel. "You've gotta be kidding, man. I'm not going back in there, it gives me the creeps. Look what happened to Johnny. It isn't safe."

"Yeah, look what happened to Johnny," Luke said, a sly edge to his voice. "What if he *is* still alive? Maybe he was just knocked cold. He might have a broken leg or something, and not be able to climb out. He's your buddy. Can you live with that, not knowing if he could have been saved, huh?"

"Okay, okay. What do we do?" Jerry said, knowing that the Indian didn't give a fuck about Johnny, just the keys. But the bastard was right. Despite the fear that the prospect of going back into that dark warren instilled in him, he would. He had to help Johnny, or at least satisfy himself that he was beyond saving.

"We make torches, find some rope, and then go check him out," Luke said.

Johnny opened his eyes and thought that he had gone blind. There was no light, not a glimmer, just solid cloying darkness. His initial fear subsided as he realized what had happened and where he was. He had fallen, and the flashlight must have been broken. He heard Luke shout to him from somewhere above, asking him if he was still alive, and relief swept through him. He attempted to shout back, 'I'm okay' in answer, but there was no sound. He shouted again, but his voice had gone, he couldn't respond. He was lying on his back, tried to move, to sit up, but couldn't. His body would not react. There was no pain, nothing. He had no sensation of feeling at all. He could hear Luke and Jerry talking, though not what they were saying. Their voices became fainter. Oh, God, they were moving away and leaving him. Silence settled on him like a heavy blanket. This was worse than any nightmare. He was cloaked in a sightless world, totally helpless and so very alone. Johnny felt the cold paralysis spreading through his lungs, gripping them, slowly compressing them. And as his chest ceased to move, he began to see lights, like glowing dust motes dancing on a black canvass before his unblinking eyes; lights produced by his oxygen-starved brain. For a moment he was back on a dark highway, with Cathy by his side, and everything was going to be just fine. And then the bright illusory dust dimmed and died, taking Johnny tumbling away again, into the eternal night that awaits all men.

Johnny had locked the door. So Luke used a tire iron from the pickup to force the flat end into the Winnebago's door jamb, and with one sharp jerk forced the lock to gain entry. In a footlocker they found a thick coil of blue nylon rope, probably thirty or forty feet in length. It was knotted at regular intervals, obviously intended to be used for climbing.

"Go find some pieces of wood that we can use as torches. And get a can of gas from the truck," Luke instructed Jerry, who was standing near the door now, staring off vacantly, lost in heavy-hearted thought.

"Uh, right," Jerry said, wandering off towards the ore-mill and its abundance of kindling.

Luke gathered an armful of shirts and underwear from a closet shelf in the bedroom, took them outside, and sat in the wicker chair, ripping the garments into strips while he waited for Jerry to return.

With six, three-foot-long lengths of sun-dried timber, their ends bound tightly with gas-soaked cloth, and carrying the knotted rope, they made their way back to the edge of the pit that had swallowed Johnny. Wedging a plank – that from the brightness of their torches they had found in the main tunnel – into crevices at either side of the small passage, six feet back from the drop, Luke tied one end of the rope to it, pulling hard to test its effectiveness, satisfying himself that it would bear his weight. Moving back to the edge, he then threw the coils over into the darkness.

"You're a lot heavier than me, Jerry, so I'll go down. You sit on the plank and hold the rope, just in case it gives."

Leaving Jerry with one burning torch, Luke lit another from it and dropped it down the shaft. The flaming flare hit bottom, spluttered, then regained its brightness. From the flickering, yellow glow he could see Johnny on his back, twenty or more feet below him, and unmoving. Luke slipped over the rim, and hand over hand, and with his feet against the rock, walked his way down the vertical and almost smooth wall.

"How is he?" Jerry shouted, unable to see anything from where he was sitting on the plank, leaning back and holding the rope taut.

"He's dead. Looks as though he broke his neck," Luke answered, quickly retrieving the keys from one of Johnny's jeans pockets. He then settled to the task that was his real reason for returning. He pulled the cop's gun from his waistband, wiped it clean with his bandanna and then pressed it into the corpse's hand, ensuring that Johnny Clawson's prints were on the stock and trigger. He then tucked the weapon into the dead man's pants, under his shirt, against the fast-cooling skin of his belly. Lastly (and he thought this a nice touch) he removed the blood-encrusted piece of tattooed flesh, and after further wiping, pushed the gruesome souvenir into Johnny's pocket. This would be the first and last time that he would ever relinquish one of his trophies.

"I'm coming up," Luke shouted. "You ready?"

"About time," Jerry said.

Back on board the camper, cleaned up and drinking cold beer, they discussed their options. Jerry was all set to get the hell away from the place. Head for somewhere big and busy and stay under the radar. Frisco seemed ideal. He could vanish there to start afresh and put this nightmare behind him.

Luke listened to Jerry's proposed plan. "That sounds fine," he said. "But there's still a guy in that mine who could cause us plenty of grief. He's going to report his vehicle stolen, and the cops are going to be crawling all over this place like flies on dog shit. They'll find Johnny's body and have more to go on than they have now. We've already made a clean getaway, so let's not fuck it up. Christ, for all we know this guy could have seen us arrive. He could give our descriptions."

Jerry closed his eyes, feeling tired and defeated. He knew that Luke was right. He didn't want to get caught, or spend the rest of his life running and looking over his shoulder. All he wanted to do now was off-load this psycho and get back to his safer solitary existence.

"So how do we flush him out of there?" Jerry said. "He probably knows the layout of this place like the back of his hand. He could have already got out. There could be more than one entrance."

Luke shook his head. "There's only one way in and out of a mine like this," he said, almost sure that he was right. "One of us drives off in the camper and hides it. Then we stake out the entrance and wait. He's going to be wary, but he'll come out sooner or later, and when he does and finds that his fancy motor home is missing, he'll believe that we've gone. Then we can introduce him to Johnny, and dump some rocks over the bodies. They'll probably never be found."

Luke handed Jerry the keys, and he drove the Winnebago on to Main Street and parked up outside the false-fronted façade of the Flamingo Saloon, completely out of sight from the mine. He then walked back to the mill to rejoin Luke, hiding behind weathered boards, many of which now leaned from the upright, gradually reaching for the horizontal as the passage of so many years and weather cowed them into submission.

Time passed, and the dappled craze of light and shadow crept down the building as the sun sank lower in the western sky.

"Wake up," Luke said, shaking Jerry roughly by the shoulder. "It's nearly dark. We need to be nearer, in case he tries to make a break for it during the night."

It was a long vigil. Jerry huddled under a blanket from the camper, still freezing, finding it hard to believe that this was the same desert terrain that during the day baked in over a hundred degrees of arid heat. It didn't seem to bother Luke, who just squatted impassively at the other side of the mine's entrance, giving the impression that he could stay that way forever if necessary. Jerry was not only cold to the bone, but restless, praying for dawn to break. He also had a lot of time to replay the events of the last twenty-four hours' in his mind, and each time he did it just seemed to get worse.

They say that a picture is worth a thousand words, and as Jerry looked across at the still figure of Luke Strayhorse, he saw something that chilled him even more than the low temperature. In the half-light of pre-dawn, Luke was staring at Jerry, averting his eyes just a fraction of a second too late to hide the intention that his cold gaze held. Jerry knew from just that fleeting glance – as surely as he knew bears' shit in the woods – that Luke intended to kill him. The Indian was going to leave nothing to chance. Jerry was just another loose end to be dealt with; a witness to be silenced. When the time came, Luke would leave Jerry under the same pile of rocks as Johnny, and do his best to find the poor bastard who had so far avoided them, and murder him too. How Jerry had read all that from just an instant of eye contact was beyond him, but he did know that if he let nature take its course, he would die.

A blaze-red melted to cadmium-orange and seeped into the dark-blue vault of the sky; the stars appearing to wink out as the sun rose to serve up another new day.

“I’m starving, Luke,” Jerry said later, a pained expression on his face as he massaged his stomach. “I’ve got to eat something.”

“So go and get something,” Luke said. “And bring me a beer...and some cigarettes if you can find any. I’ve only got one left.”

Jerry stood up and flexed his aching legs, before walking across to the empty door-frame at the rear of the mill, which they had returned to at sunrise. “No problem,” he said.

“Oh, and Jerry,” Luke called after him. “Just one thing.”

Jerry felt weak with apprehension. “Yeah,” he answered as calmly as writhing nerve ends would allow him to.

“Keep out of fuckin’ sight.”

Jerry nodded and somehow stopped himself from breaking into a run; forced himself to stroll along the dusty track towards the gray, weathered buildings.

“Lordy...Lordy...Lordy. Yeesss!” Jerry shouted aloud as he put the Winnebago into drive and pulled away, along the street, up the hill and out of Sunrise. He had done it, escaped, and was now putting distance between himself and the psycho Indian, who had caused so much death and misfortune. He didn’t know whether to laugh or cry, and ended up doing both simultaneously.

Luke heard the engine roar into life and knew instantly that Jerry was decamping. On impulse hc ran towards the pickup, intending to give chase, but gave up on the idea, knowing that he would not be able to stop a vehicle the size of the motor home, which had a driver at the wheel who was obviously pissed off with his company, and who had more than likely guessed that Luke was planning to whack him.

“Fuck him,” Luke muttered. Jerry and whoever was hiding like a rat in the mine could go to hell. He’d had enough. It was time to move on and put this escapade behind him. It irked him that he hadn’t finished up business in the way that he had planned to, though, and determined to learn from this and cover every base in future.

Pouring a can of gasoline in and over the pickup, Luke walked backwards away from it, leaving a trail of the flammable fluid on the rocky ground. Lighting his last cigarette and adjusting the shades over his eyes, he knelt and touched the lighter flame to the quickly evaporating fuel.

Luke ran, his mood lightening as the hot blast from the exploding truck hit his back and blew him along even faster. He laughed aloud.

He was a free spirit, heading southwest, dismissing all that had transpired as trivial and incidental. His time with the two whites had been a pleasant diversion; one of many. He was already looking forward to his next exploit, whatever it may be.

Ed stayed in the mine for another night before daring to warily make his way back through the maze of tunnels. Using the boards again, he re-crossed the shaft that had claimed one of the men who had meant him harm. He paused and directed the beam of his flashlight down, putting a dozen rats to flight as he surveyed the spread-eagled corpse that was now reduced to eye-less and ravaged carrion, its stench already rising, sour and cloying from the depths. He moved on, reached the entrance and let his eyes adapt, before stumbling out into the brightness. He studied the burnt-out pickup, and his table and wicker chair, both over on their sides next to the space that had occupied his Winnebago. He walked out of Sunrise and headed east; the brim of his hat pulled down over his sad but determined eyes.

The police cruiser pulled in behind the old man. He was limping down the middle of the blacktop, swaying, hardly able to stay on his feet. The cop at the wheel hit the horn and the man stopped, turned, and shuffled towards the car.

Ed had never been so pleased to see the police in his life. He had a lot to tell them.

BOOK TWO

REBIRTH AND REUNION

CHAPTER ELEVEN

THREE days short of his twenty-first birthday, Danny Clayton felt like a million dollars; the luckiest young man on God's green earth. Four mega events were about to happen in his life. The first was that he was going to reach that somehow magical if overrated age of twenty-one. The second was that he would be joining his father's advertising agency, and thirdly, far more important than the other two, was that he was getting engaged to his high school sweetheart, Sarah Mitchell. Yes, Saturday the eighth of July 2017 was going to be a hallmark day for Danny, and he could hardly bear waiting for it to dawn.

The fourth and what would prove to be the most significant event was not known to him, but would prove to be far more momentous than the other three, in what was going to be a sudden and dire twist of fate.

Jim and Linda Clayton were riding high, and had done very well by most people's standards. Following the premature death of his business partner, Brad Atherton, whose Cessna had nose-dived into a vineyard just a mile south of Dulles Airport, Jim had been running the agency, and as both major shareholder and CEO, had steered it from strength to strength. The success of the company had resulted in a very comfortable lifestyle for Jim and his family. Linda had even taken a two-year course in business studies, and had joined the firm, though only on a part-time basis. They had relocated to Alexandria in 2009, upgrading to an eighteenth-century colonial house that they had renovated tastefully and sympathetically to suit their needs, while still retaining its old-world charm. The three-storey building was spacious and yet simple in design; reception rooms flanking a large central hall, highlighted by a dramatic oak staircase. The whiteboard exterior looked out onto a long, tree-lined approach, set well back from Seminary Road. To the rear of the property, the gardens incorporated a tennis court and large, heated swimming pool. Jim's hard work, good reputation and flair had brought him a portfolio of prestigious accounts that told him he had a lot to smile about. He was now in what he considered to be middle-age, and overjoyed that his son had decided to pursue a career in the family business.

Danny had grown into a fine young man, good-looking, with an even disposition and a warm, caring personality that seemed to engage and uplift all who met him. Jim and Linda felt blessed to have him as their son. Danny was their only child; not for the lack of wanting or spiritedly trying for more, and certainly not as a result of tight underpants, due to Jim still having worn loose boxer shorts ever since their late doctor, Sam Braedon, had brought the subject up before Danny had been conceived.

It was going to be a big day. A large marquee had been erected – for the 'do', as the impending party had been dubbed – at the rear of the tennis court. A highly-rated fifteen-piece band had been hired for the evening, and a brand new Corvette Targa, in flame red with black leather upholstery, that Danny had drooled over in the showroom was, complete with ribbon, sat in the spare garage, ready to surprise him.

Jim was as excited as anyone could be as the eighth approached. He was not only celebrating his son's coming of age, but would be officially welcoming him into the agency. Announcing the news to friends, colleagues and invited business associates would be a special moment in his life. The evening was also an engagement party, and Danny would announce that himself. His girlfriend, Sarah, was a lovely girl, and both Jim and Linda could not have been happier for the two youngsters.

On the big day, Danny and Sarah had a slow lunch at Landini's on King Street, just the two of them, savoring each other's company. They were taking some time-out before the big night and the hustle and bustle of up to three hundred guests, who they would have to share themselves with. Following the meal, they ambled down to The Torpedo Factory and browsed through the many art and craft shops, just talking, planning, scheming and dreaming.

Making their way out onto the planked dockside, they held hands and gazed north up the Potomac River to D.C., and to the sun-splashed landmarks of the Washington Monument and Capitol Building. And as the distant jets dropped over the city to land at Reagan National Airport, they became temporarily lost in their own individual thoughts, gathering themselves for the night ahead. It was, to Sarah, as though life were a cake, sectioned into separate distinct slices by the big events, be they of extreme happiness or deep sadness. Each was a milestone that denoted a new beginning. Tonight, she mused, was a stepping-stone, to be reflected on later in time as a symbolic start to their future together. This was a day of heady weight and importance.

By eight p.m., the evening was swinging. The band played music to satisfy all tastes and ages, save for lovers of the classics. Outside caterers had furnished a lavish buffet, and waiters ensured that glasses did not stand empty and idle for long.

At exactly ten-thirty, as pre-arranged, the music stopped and the lights dimmed. Everyone lit sparklers from candles that flickered in glass flutes on each table, and the lead guitarist led the gathering into song with a slightly upbeat rendition à la Eric Clapton of 'Happy Birthday to You' that resonated in the night air. Jim was then handed a microphone, and asked the guests – as the applause died down – if they would take their seats.

"Tonight is very important to Linda and myself," Jim began. "Our son, Danny, is twenty-one today, and we congratulate him and thank him for being the boy that he was, and the young man he has grown into. He has always...so far, made Linda and I very proud to be his parents. We are also over the moon with his decision to join the agency. He starts in a couple of weeks time, and I want him to know that his future boss, me, expects great things of him. Now, Danny has an announcement of his own to make."

Jim handed the microphone to Danny as he took his seat and grinned broadly at his slightly embarrassed looking son.

"Tonight has been terrific," Danny started in, moving the mike a couple of inches further from his mouth as it shrieked with feedback. "You all being here has made a special occasion extra special. There could be no better moment than this for me to share the news with you that Sarah and I have chosen tonight to become engaged." He gently urged Sarah to her feet, before continuing, "And just to make it official," he said, pausing to conjure a diamond solitaire ring from a pocket. "Sarah, will you marry me?"

Sarah held out her left hand for Danny to slip the ring on her finger, leaning forward to the microphone as he did, "Yes, I will," she whispered in a small voice that would have been inaudible without the electronic aid.

Applause, the sight of myriad glasses held aloft in toast, and the shouts and whistles fell on deaf ears as Danny and Sarah kissed; and the band played on.

A little later, Jim and Linda, accompanied by Sarah's parents, Ted and Jean, made their way across to the dimly lit garage block, with Danny and Sarah in tow and wondering why they had been led away from the festivities. Jim pressed the fob and the garage door rolled smoothly up into the ceiling recess, to reveal a brightly lit interior and its ribbon bedecked, red occupant. Danny's mouth fell open at the sight of the shining, flame-colored Corvette.

"Is this one hell of a day? Or is this one hell of a day?" Danny said, hugging his parents, and then the others, as tears misted his eyes.

It was late when the last guests bid their farewells and left. Both Danny and Sarah were exhausted from the combination of nervous tension and elation that the evening had evoked. The hundreds of individual congratulations, hugs and handshakes, plus the dancing and more than their usual intake of alcohol had left them feeling wrung out. Sarah's mom and dad were staying over, and the six of them agreed on a relaxing poolside nightcap before calling it a day.

Danny was hot, his clothes clung to him, and his feet burned and ached in the new leather shoes that encased them. The pool beckoned; a rectangle of brightly lit turquoise temptation in the humid night. He went to don his shorts; the others foregoing a dip, content to just take a load off and sit down.

For perhaps the three thousandth time, Danny executed a running dive into the clear water. But for the first time he badly misjudged the maneuver, diving at too steep an angle, smashing his head on the non-slip, textured bottom of the pool. He felt his head split open, and although still conscious, was powerless, losing control of his limbs; his brain sending dazed messages to a body that refused to respond.

Drifting upwards, Danny studied the cloud of blood that billowed out from the gash like crimson octopus ink. He had read somewhere that blood appeared green or black in water, so why did his look such a vibrant cherry red? What a stupid thing to do, he thought, before passing out.

Jim leapt into the water as he saw Danny break the surface face down in a mushrooming slick of blood. And with Ted's help he manhandled his son's limp body up onto the edge of the pool surround.

"He's breathing," Ted said.

"Linda, dial 911, we need an ambulance," Jim shouted as he placed a chair cushion under his son's head. Jean held a towel to the gaping wound to staunch the bleeding, and Sarah held Danny's hand, talking to him, urging him to wake up.

CHAPTER TWELVE

HE was in free fall, feeling weightless as he spun and tumbled through a towering mass of cumulus cloud, rushing to impact on an unseen earth below. And yet he felt calm, detached and inquisitive as to why he was plunging from the sky. As in a dream, the absurdity of the situation was lost to him. The cloud became whiter, more solid, and his body suddenly surged with weight and substance, gaining speed and careering with dizzying impetus, before stopping with a mind-jarring jolt as he became conscious.

His eyelids were gummed, sticky with sleep, resisting as he strove to force them partially open. Everything was still; a frozen landscape of Arctic white, with no horizon or depth to give perspective. This must be heaven, he thought. I'm dead, and this is what comes next.

The face appeared above him as a pink blur, floating a foot from him, taking shape as he fought to focus on it. Concerned eyes framed by a beautiful face gazed back at him. A small smile formed on sculpted rose-petal lips as they opened to speak. At first the words made no sense. They were just warm sounds, jumbling incoherently in his mind. This had to be an angel speaking to him, and he could not translate her heavenly words, only smile back at her, too tired to even attempt to understand the language of the divine messenger.

"How are you feeling?" The nurse asked, studying the patient's eyes, checking his pupils, and noting their even dilation and contraction.

No response. A niggle of concern. He should be able to answer. Again, "How are you? Can you hear me?"

His eyes met hers with a growing comprehension that gave expression to his face, which was now animate, not vacuous as before. She wiped his sleep-filled eyes and then his brow with a warm, damp cloth.

"Danny, if you can hear me, answer me. Are you okay?" she said, slowly and clearly.

In a dry, croaking voice that he didn't recognize, he answered, aware now that this was not a celestial being, but a young woman in uniform; a nurse?

"I...I'm fine, I think," he said in a weak whisper. "But why are you calling me Danny?"

Doctor Benjamin Carlisle was concerned. His patient, Daniel Clayton, had suffered a concussion. X-rays and initial tests had shown no intracranial bleeding or brain damage, and the swelling was minimal. The only significant injury had been a deep laceration high up on Danny's forehead, which had required suturing. More tests had been scheduled, due to the length of time that he had remained unconscious, although all vital signs were stable. Ben could find no apparent reason for the comatose state that the young man had been in for more than two days.

When the nurse had paged him, Ben fully expected his patient to be awake, suffering nothing more serious than a splitting headache and a bruised ego, following his half-assed dive into a swimming pool. What he found was far more disturbing.

After coming round and talking to the nurse, Danny had begun to rant hysterically, and even tried to get out of the bed with the intention of discharging himself from the hospital. It had taken two burly orderlies to restrain him and strap him down. Ben had listened to his ravings, and then injected him with five mill' of valium, monitoring his pulse as the sedative took effect.

Cal woke up confused and frightened, his mind whirling with fearful apprehension. Where was Chrissie, or his dad? How could he have survived? Where was he? And why had the nurse and then a doctor insisted on calling him Danny? The questions coalesced and overwhelmed him. He lay still, his fists clenched; nails biting into his palms; mouth as dry as sand; teeth stuck to the inside of his lips, and his tongue feeling like a thick wad of cotton batting. *Calm down, calm down. Just get a grip. There must be a simple explanation. I just don't know what it is, yet.*

He tried to move, planning to get out of bed and find someone to answer his questions, but he had been restrained. Looking down, he studied the padded, buckled straps that held his wrists in place, and knew that under the sheet that covered him, his ankles were similarly bound. Across his chest was another strap, unyielding despite the built-in quilted comfort that it afforded.

As he took a deep breath to scream for attention, a guy in a white coat entered the room and walked over to the side of the bed.

"You need answers," White Coat said. "I'm going to sit down and give you some, so try to relax and take it easy. I'm here for one reason only...to help."

The doctor poured water from a Perspex ewer into what looked like a kid's beaker fitted with a lid and a spout to drink from. "Here, you look as though you could use a drink," he said, holding the pea-green beaker to Cal's lips. "Not too much, just sip it."

Cal swilled the cold water around his parched mouth, and then slowly let the liquid trickle down his throat. He started to speak, but his voice sounded raspy and a little slurred. He needed another larger sip of water. He coughed after drinking it and then tried to talk again, and his voice was smoother.

"I'm confused, but I'm in control," he said. "So please, take the hardware off. I don't need tranquilizing or restraining. And I have no intention of going anywhere until I know what's happening. I just panicked when I first came round."

The man who studied Cal was a big guy, overweight, his gut pushing hard against the too-small coat he had somehow squeezed himself into. He had a shock of thick, graying hair – a little wild and on the long side – and a full beard that was going to white at the cheeks. His eyes were dark, a burnt umber, kindly, yet intense and perceptive behind the gold-rimmed spectacles, which with his head lowered he was peering over the top of.

"I'll buy that," he said, finally. "And in case you're interested, I'm Dr. Ross Fairburn."

As he talked, Ross unbuckled the straps with quick and practiced ease, and then sat down in a chair at the side of the bed, his eyes not leaving Cal's.

"So let's go nice and slow," Ross said. "For openers, tell me your name, age and date of birth, and the last thing that you can remember before waking up in here."

Cal replied with no hesitation. "My name is Cal Morgan, I'm thirty-one, and I was born on March twenty-eighth, nineteen sixty-five. My last memory is of being shot, out at Backbone Ridge. Right now I need to know if my wife and dad know where I am, and that I'm still in one piece."

Ross found it difficult to mask his shock and gather his wits. He inwardly readied himself for the reaction that he knew he would get when he told this young man the facts, as he knew them. The next few minutes were going to be like walking through a minefield, blindfolded, and he would need all of his experience and training if he was to prevent either of them from standing on one. The resulting explosion could put his patient over whatever edge he might already be hanging from by his fingertips.

Ross was a consultant psychoanalyst, specializing in the treatment of serious mental disorders; particularly amnesia and related phenomena. His base of operations was The Fairfax Clinic in downtown D.C. on 10th Street, just a stone's throw from Ford's Theatre, where Lincoln had been shot. He split his private and retained work down the middle, sharing his time between three hospitals around the city. He was married, with his silver wedding anniversary just six weeks away, and also his fiftieth birthday looming, ten days hence. His wife, Louise, kept humming the old Hawaii five-O theme tune, to remind him of both his age and the destination she had decided on for a celebratory anniversary vacation. Ross was beginning to feel like the middle-aged man he was, and although not a crisis, found himself indulging in more than a little self-help therapy.

This case had appealed to him. It had caught his attention and interested him from the moment that Ben Carlisle had phoned him and discussed it.

Ross and Ben had gone through medical school together, with a mutual interest in neurology, girls and beer, and the resulting friendship had lasted down thc years.

Ben was now head of neurology at The Belmont Medical Center in Arlington, and had asked Ross if he would like to get involved with the case. The patient was the son of Jim Clayton, one of Ben's golfing buddies, who Ross had met once or twice socially.

The basic facts were that Danny Clayton – a previously fit and intelligent young man – had head-butted the bottom of the family pool over forty-eight hours ago. The head injury he had sustained appeared minor, and all should have been well. Instead, he had remained unconscious; comatose for the best part of two days, and had flipped when he came round, having to be sedated to prevent him doing harm to himself or staff. Ross had decided to interview the Clayton boy and see where it led.

Ross had experience of a similar case; another head injury that had resulted in a chronic mental disorder in a thirty-six-year old man who had no prior record of mental illness. The patient had become schizophrenic, and was to hang himself four months after diagnosis. He had left a rambling six page suicide note, stating that he was an emissary of God, and realizing that no one would believe him, or follow his teachings, was going back to heaven for the time being, to where he knew that he was loved and appreciated.

The workings of the mind never ceased to amaze Ross. Its function as the seat of human intellect was as mysterious as the secrets of the universe. The brain's awesome power as it floats with such fragility; a mass of convoluted nervous tissue encased in the brittle helmet of the skull, defies understanding. It can be teased and probed, its responses recorded and measured. It can even be dissected posthumously, and some of the aberrations that occur can be recognized and treated, but the complex investigation of the conscious and unconscious; the striving to rationalize the two in patients' minds, is still to a large degree, hit and miss. The understanding of cause and effect, and even successful treatment rarely unlocks the secrets of the psyche. Dealing with mental disorder is as precarious as a one-legged funambulist trying to balance a hundred feet up in a force ten gale...without a pole.

"Here goes," Ross said to the young man, who looked both tormented and anxious. "To everyone but you, you are Daniel James Clayton, born and raised in Washington D.C., and up until recently, problem free. Then, half-loaded, you did a kamikaze dive into the family pool, cracked your head on the bottom and wound up in here in a coma with mild concussion and quite a deep cut to your forehead. Now you're up to speed, and we have to take it from here." Ross paused, but there was no immediate response, so he continued. "Your parents and your fiancée have looked in on you while you were out of it. They all recognize you, so mistaken identity isn't a possibility."

Cal had listened, hung on to every word that the doctor said, letting it repeat, running over it and replaying it. But it made no sense; wouldn't sink in. He felt light-headed with the enormity of what he had been told. He *knew* who he was for Christ's sake. What was this idiot talking about?

"What I'm going to tell you now is really going to blow your mind," Ross said with bated breath. "This is something that you will have to accept as true and take on board before we go any further. You need to get a real good grip and nod your head when you're ready for the bombshell."

Cal could see the look of genuine concern in the other man's eyes. He caught the slight tremor in the voice, and saw the perspiration forming at the doctor's hairline. He now felt fear worming into his brain, clamping his bladder in steel jaws, turning him ice-cold, raising goose bumps on his arms and tightening the skin on his neck.

"Okay," he whispered, his mouth bone-dry again. "Hit me with it."

Slowly, eyes locked on his patient's, Ross said, "Today is July eleventh, in the year two thousand and seventeen."

A grave and almost unholy silence filled the room as they stared at each other. Cal's id, or consciousness; the sense of being which made him an individual entity, rebelled. A pressure akin to a car tire being inflated to bursting point filled his mind as the astonishing news ricocheted around his brain. Two thousand and seventeen! He could not break eye contact with this harbinger of doom, who had just told him that twenty-one years of his life had evaporated. It was impossible to compute, and he didn't know how to deal with something that he could not allow himself to accept as being a fact. It was not conceivable that it could be a reality. Therefore he must be dreaming. But he knew that he wasn't.

When something is so irrational and frightening that it cannot be absorbed, then the mind has to find a way to cope and preserve its sanity. If it can find no acceptable solution, then it has to escape or shut down.

Cal escaped. He jumped. Part of his awareness snaked out at the doctor with the speed of a striking cuttlefish; invisible tentacles from his mind passing through the man's eyes, to spread throughout his brain, invading the neural pathways and absorbing the data therein.

Cal looked out from Ross Fairburn and saw the stranger who lay on the bed looking back at him. He sifted through the memories and thoughts of the person he now inhabited; a passenger and observer only. He knew that the doctor had no knowledge of what was taking place; was unaware of this ultimate invasion of privacy. It was in some way like being a stowaway on board a ship, or a parasite whose host is oblivious to the clandestine trespasser within.

Ross was listing his options of what could be causing the young man's symptoms. Had he become schizophrenic? Could a sudden disconnection between Danny's thoughts and feelings have taken place, causing a delusional state? Or was this even more complex? Only time would tell.

Cal realized that an element of his being had remained in the body on the bed. A part that was strong enough to operate on automatic;

on the same level that he had sometimes experienced while driving; when he had driven several miles completely unaware of his actions, negotiating his way through traffic without mishap, and amazing himself that he had not crashed into another vehicle or left the highway.

He felt his hold slipping. He was withdrawing from the doctor's mind, his perception rushing back through a maze of light and color. And with a snap as powerful as a fully-stretched rubber band being released, he was once again a single entity, whole again yet drained of energy. The 'jump' had exhausted him, though had at the same time somehow instilled calmness. He felt a new capacity within, which enabled him to accept that which was happening in a slightly detached and philosophical light. In the space of transferring back and forth between the two minds, he had found respite from the trauma, and strength to face the unknown.

"Did you understand what I just said?" Ross asked, wondering if Danny had comprehended the implications of what year it was, in relation to the date he had said he had been born on.

"Yes, I heard you, and it gives me one hell of a problem. One that won't improve while you continue to think that I'm Danny, or that I'm either schizophrenic or deluded."

Ross felt challenged. How could this young man have known precisely what he had been thinking? Had he read a telltale expression that Ross had let show, and just guessed along the right lines as to the thoughts behind it? That had to be the case, because the alternative was mind-reading, and that was strictly for stage shows, firmly set in the realms of entertainment. But there was something more, a gut feeling and inkling that this patient's syndrome might not conform to any textbook yet written. Ross had a foreboding that the normal methods that he used for diagnosis may not prove to be of any value. He may just have to throw usual classifications and procedures out of the window and go with the flow on this one.

Danny – if that was who he really was – had fallen asleep, as if suddenly and wholly drained of energy like a spent battery. Ross walked across to the window, absently looking out to the distant myriad rows of tombstones at Arlington Cemetery, which erupted gleaming white and tooth-like from their regimented sockets of verdant sward.

Standing in quiet rumination, Ross felt a charge, as if a low voltage was running through him. There was no foundation for it, but he had the premonition that he was on the threshold of a revelation.

CHAPTER THIRTEEN

CAL awakened to find that the nightmare was still a reality that could not be left behind in dark and twisted dreams. He was still in the hospital bed, though not restrained or alone. The nurse put down a paperback that she had been using as a foil to ward off boredom, and left her chair to approach him, glad of the diversion from the late Jackie Collins' disconcerting insight into shallow Hollywood life.

"Hi," Charlene Garner, the nurse, said with a smile. "Can I get you some juice? You must be parched."

"I need to take a pi...a leak," Cal said, sitting up and swinging his legs over the side of the bed, momentarily looking for moccasins that were not there. The sudden movement caused instant pain. It felt as though a power drill had started up behind his forehead and was biting into his skull from the inside. Clenching his teeth and screwing his eyes tightly shut, he sat and waited for the imaginary bit to withdraw.

"Not a good idea. Let me get you a bottle," Charlene said, walking across the room to open an internal door that led into an en suite bathroom.

Cal stood up, followed her and said, "Now that I've got this far, I'll try it free-standing." He smiled weakly, feeling sick to his stomach.

Urinating, the thought struck him that for the first time in his life he was holding another man's penis. The saving grace was that he was holding it with the other guy's hand. This was extremely weird shit; Looney Tune stuff. God help him, he actually grinned at the absurdity of it all. He flushed the pan, turned, and jumped back a pace, a grunt escaping him as he caught sight of his reflection in the safety mirror that was screwed to the wall. Gripping the cold stainless steel basin with both hands, he moved the stranger's face closer to the mirror's surface and studied the physiognomy that he had seen briefly through the doctor's eyes.

The young man who faced him had striking viridian eyes, and the face was strong and even-featured with a pleasant mouth, straight nose and firm, dimpled chin. The hair was thick, mid-brown, and swept back from the taped gauze pad on his forehead. It was collar length, but well cut. Some of Cal's old vanity resurfaced as he found himself thankful and relieved that he was not trapped in some bald and wrinkled octogenarian, drifting in and out of reality – whatever that might be – with Alzheimer's or something equally intolerable.

As he emerged from the john, Dr. Fairburn arrived.

"You could have passed out, trying that," Ross stated. "Here, take a load off, let me give you a hand."

Cal allowed a supporting arm, and gingerly walked back to the bed, the soles of his bare feet frigid from the cold, gray vinyl floor-covering. As he sat and faced the doctor, a sudden sensation of panic, that felt as though timorous butterflies were fluttering in his stomach and chest, took hold of him as he contemplated being trapped in another body, a generation apart from his prior life and the people that he loved. Slowly, with difficulty, he calmed the beating wings and brought the skittish insects to rest on ethereal shrubs of purple buddleia. An inner strength; a steeliness of spirit pushed the predicament onto a back burner of his mind to simmer, while he dealt with the present, not the past.

He was alone in a strange land. But why was he alone? Where was this Danny Clayton, whose body he occupied? He searched his consciousness, but could find no trace of another personality in the depths of his being. If Danny was aware of what had happened, then he must be trapped, suppressed and terrified in the bowels of a nightmarish prison; his mind and body commandeered, while he was floundering in some black-hole state of limbo.

If you are there, Cal thought, just hold on and let's both hope that this resolves itself. This is a journey that neither of us planned on taking, but we're stuck with it for the time being. If you can hear me, Danny, try to hang in there and ride this out with me.

Cal felt better for sending the message, even though he realized that it may not be reaching any cognizant destination. He imagined his thoughts speeding across a great void of deep space, like a satellite that NASA had sent up, complete with information and diagrams, to show our limited intelligence and negligible capabilities to any alien Tom, Dick or little green Harry that randomly came across it.

The nurse, who had left the room, returned with scrambled eggs, toast and fresh orange juice, which Cal eagerly devoured; his new body's hunger triggered by the smell of the food. Draining the last drops of OJ, he pushed aside the wheeled table and turned his full concentration to the doctor, who had urged him to eat, and had sat leafing through papers and making notes.

"So, how are you feeling this morning?" Ross asked. "Any change?"

"Just the same problem, Doc. I'm either completely insane, or I'm the reincarnation of who I told you I am, complete with a full memory of my past life. Where does that leave us?"

Ross smiled. "I hope that together we can make some sense of it. But first we have another problem that needs to be dealt with." The smile faded from Ross's face as he continued. "Down the hall are three people who love you...er, Danny, and are worried sick at the moment, attempting to grasp all of this. I've told them that physically you're fine, but that the accident has affected your memory. I've held back the fact that you claim to be someone else at this stage. One step at a time, eh? The bottom line is that the parents and fiancée of Danny Clayton are waiting to see him, and I don't think that it would be right to deny them. Do you?"

"I'm missing people myself," Cal said. "So I have a fair idea of what they must be going through. Let's get it over with."

Cal saw a shadow of concern flit cross the man's face.

"Don't worry, Doc. I'm not going to be too radical. But please, wheel them all in together. I'd rather not have to go through this more than once."

Jim, Linda and Sarah entered the room and stood just inside the door, crowded together and looking a little uncomfortable and nervous. They observed him as though he was a fetus preserved in a jar of formaldehyde; disturbed concern in their expressions.

Cal had never seen them before in his life. They were utter strangers to him, but he saw and felt the waves of anxiety. He had no wish to distress them more than they already were. No one spoke, and so he broke the initial awkward silence.

"Please, sit down," Cal said. And at the sound of his voice they moved, the spell broken as though he had waved a magician's wand. They approached the bed and sat on the plastic chairs that Ross had placed around it for them.

"Uh, er, Danny has something to tell you in his own words, folks," Ross said, apprehensive that the situation, which involved an added element, would if unleashed cause immeasurable stress to both his patient and the visitors.

"I'm sorry," Cal said. "But at this moment I really don't recognize any of you. The bang on the head must have caused amnesia, but I'm sure the doc here will sort it out."

Linda began crying softly and grasped Cal's hand, squeezing it tightly. He held hers firmly in return, trying to give some comfort to the distraught woman. Jim shook his head slowly, as if in disbelief that his son did not know them, or even himself. Sarah waited until Linda sat back, and then leant forward and kissed Cal lightly on his cheek.

"You'll be fine," Sarah said in a firm voice. "It will all come back, and until it does, don't forget that we all love and need you. I'm going to pester you every day. So even if you don't know me now, you sure as hell will know me very soon."

Ten minutes later they left, saddened by Danny's failure to become aware of whom they were, but heartened that he was otherwise on the mend. They were optimistic that he would soon regain his memory, and prayed that he would quickly be back with them, in mind as well as in body.

"You need a break," Ross said to Cal as he made to leave the room. "When I come back we'll go for the whole nine yards. Okay?"

Cal gathered his thoughts and tried to form a game-plan. He knew that he would have to go back to Nevada at some stage, but had no idea what he would do once he got there. He felt a rising anger, which began to twist his guts as he pictured the grinning face of the man who had shot him. Somehow in his misery, overcome with thoughts of his wife and dad, he had not got round to facing the incident that had put him in this incredible predicament. Laying back on the bed and closing his eyes, he relived the minutes that had led up to what should have been his death. He saw again the mutilated face of the Henderson girl; part of her nose missing, throat gaping wide, and eyes staring off sightless to some distant ambit. The three bastards who had done it had got to be brought to book, to pay for their horrific deeds, if they had not been apprehended. It was the sicko Indian that Cal concentrated on. As a cop, Cal had seen his type before; a monster who viciously killed for the pure pleasure of the act. The Indian had been of that breed; a sadist with no empathy for others, incapable of remorse or guilt. Something hard and cold weighed heavily in Cal's stomach. It was unbridled hate. The murderer had killed his body, but he had survived, was alive, and rightly or wrongly he wanted revenge. He would cut the Indian's heart out in reprisal for what he had done that long gone day.

Ross returned after about an hour to find his patient in an entirely different frame of mind; one that Ross had not been previously privy to. The anger was rolling off the young man in waves, and he seemed oblivious to the doctor's presence.

"Do you want to talk?" Ross said.

Cal blinked, clearing his mind of murderous thoughts – for the time being – and nodded. "Doc?" Cal said, implying a question.

"Make it Ross, would you?"

"No problem. If you humor me and call me Cal."

"Deal, for the time being. Do you want to start the ball rolling?"

"Yes, Doc, uh, Ross. I have a real problem. I know who I am. I have a full recollection of a life, complete with names, dates and events that can be verified, that I need to off-load. It's important to me that someone else believes me."

"Hold it, just a second," Ross said, placing a pocket-sized recorder on to the locker top next to the bed. "This will save time, and notes." He pressed the record button and gave Cal his full attention.

For the next hour Cal recalled his memories, weaving a rich tapestry of his former life, from infancy up until waking up in Danny's body. He furnished Ross with the names of his parents, grandparents, and all of his relatives. He listed the schools and college that he had attended, and even gave his badge number and details of his time with the LAPD, that seemed to defy invention. Tears flooded his eyes as he talked of his return to Benson's Creek with his wife. He even told Ross of the small crescent-shaped birthmark on Chrissie's left buttock and of the deep, ragged scar on his father's leg, which had been self-inflicted, accidentally, with a chain-saw, back in seventy-four. He gave the names of streets and stores, the makes and models of automobiles and the names of their owners. He supplied phone listings, and could even recall almost word for word what President Bill Clinton had been promising the nation in a TV speech he had made the week that he, Cal, had been killed.

"Well?" Cal said. "What do you make of all that? Have I somehow created this character Cal Morgan, complete with detailed day-to-day memories that I know will check out? Are you still so sure that it's really Danny Clayton in here?" And he tapped the side of his head with a finger.

Ross pressed the stop button on the recorder and sat back, dumbfounded. "I need a cup of coffee, Cal," he said. "How about you?"

"Black, please."

"Sugar?"

"No."

Ross made his way down the corridor to the vending machine adjacent to the nurses' station and fished in his pocket for quarters. The vivid details that the young man had given him appeared to be too intricate and complex to be summarily dismissed as the prefabrication of a damaged mind. But Ross was still looking for rationality. There had to be a logical explanation that excluded reincarnation.

"There you go," Ross said, handing Cal the Styrofoam cup and sipping the bitter, machine-brewed concoction from his own as he slumped back down heavily into the chair. "What you have told me is astounding," he continued. "But there must be an explanation. So to exclude any neural complication, we need to schedule another CAT scan and an EEG."

"Remind me exactly what are they in simple English, Ross?" Cal said.

"A CAT scan is a computerized Axial Tomography scan," Ross said. "Basically a series of X-rays; pictures of the brain. And an EEG is, wait for it, an Electroencephalogram, which records electrical activity in the brain. These tests will tell us if everything is still functioning within normal parameters, and will hopefully rule out anything that might be causing an aberration...anything physically untoward."

"And if the tests come back clean. Then what?"

"Well, uh—" Ross began, but Cal interrupted.

"Think of a number. A six digit number. Now."

Cal locked eyes with Ross and metaphorically jumped to propel tendrils of his consciousness that once again spread through the other mind, integrating with it.

Ross thought that Cal's request was totally unrelated to their conversation; an added symptom perhaps, to be noted. But the forcefulness with which he had been instructed to think of a number triggered an unwitting response. Ross thought of his wife's date of birth, October twelve, seventy-one: 10-12-71.

Cal let go and snapped back.

"Okay, Ross. Here's something for you to take on board as you look for logical answers for my condition," Cal said "You just thought of the numbers 10,12 and71, which is your wife Louise's date of birth. Am I right...or am I right?"

No, that can't happen! Ross thought, feeling immediate revulsion and a sense of invasion, knowing that he had been cerebrally raped. He felt violated to the core of his being. Mental privacy is the last bastion of personal defense, separating each individual from all others; a sanctuary that no one should be able to enter.

"Are you reading my thoughts now?" He said, white with controlled rage, but at the same time in awe, and fearful of the implications that the demonstration he had just been subjected to conjured up.

"No," Cal said. "I have to consciously enter your mind. I only did it to make you appreciate that this is not something that your experience or training can prepare you for. Or that you can explain away with some pat diagnosis. I need you on my side, Ross, and you won't be until you open your mind to the impossible and start looking at this with a blank sheet. I *am* Cal Morgan, and that's a fact."

Ross had the sudden urge to start smoking again; a habit that he had weaned himself off over twenty years ago. "From where I'm sat, what do you think you would make of all this?" He asked, not knowing at that moment what to believe any more.

Cal shrugged. "I don't know what I would think if I were you, Ross. I'm just a dead cop, not a shrink. Do your tests again, but check out all that I've told you. I think when you find out that everything on the tape that you made is bona fide you'll be able to call me Cal not just to humor me, but with conviction."

"I'm on your side," Ross said. "Remember that. I'll check out your story and arrange for the tests. Just promise me that you'll keep out of my head from now on, will you?"

Cal hesitated. "I can't promise that, Ross. I'm fighting for my sanity and identity here. My survival is at stake in the middle of all this science-fiction shit that has happened to me. I'll do whatever I think necessary to protect myself and know what is happening around me. If I believe that you or anyone else is lying to me, or not looking out for my best interests, then I'll check it out. All I can promise you is that if I'm going to do it, I'll tell you first. That's the best I can give you."

"I'm not going to lie to you, or keep anything from you, Cal. That's not what I do. I expect a certain amount of trust, though. In fact complete trust if I'm going to try to help you. Please don't abuse this...this power or whatever the hell it is that you possess. It's trespass and amounts to…to spiritual theft. Having the ability to do something doesn't automatically give you the right to do it."

They nodded solemnly at each other, having reached a level of mutual understanding. They were now both clear on the other's viewpoint.

"I'll arrange for the tests to be done. Why don't you take a little time out from the problem and watch some TV? You'll probably find plenty of re-runs of stuff that you were watching back in the day," Ross said, the smile returning to his face.

After Ross left, Cal studied the unfamiliar remote control that the doctor had handed him. He managed to switch on the wall-mounted TV, and spent a few minutes watching CNN. The talking head was spouting the same kind of gloom and doom that newscasters always had done. Only the names of the current players' on the world's stage had changed. He channel-hopped and ended up watching an old episode of Star Trek, more at ease with Kirk and Spock; their familiarity reassuring. He fell asleep with the image of Leonard Nimoy, hand raised in split-fingered greeting, telling him to 'live long and prosper'.

Ross conferred with Ben Carlisle, bringing him up to speed with a summary of his session with 'Danny'. He ran off a copy of the tape for Ben to listen to, and mentioned the mind-reading incident. Ben listened, but was disbelieving.

"The tests should shed more light on the problem," Ben said. "Don't be surprised if we find a mass that we must have missed. It would explain a lot."

"I'm as confused as the patient at the moment, Ben," Ross said. "Does that mean I might have a tumor?"

CHAPTER FOURTEEN

BACK at the clinic, Ross replayed the tape of his conversation with Danny and made notes on a legal pad, listing key names and dates. He then jabbed the intercom button and asked Kelly, his secretary, to come through to the office.

"Kelly, I've got some work for Mike if he wants it. Would you get him to give me a call ASAP? And run a copy of this off for me, please?" he said, passing her the sheet that he had all but filled with details that might prove to be the ravings of a madman.

Kelly Stadler had worked for Ross for almost four years now. And on several occasions the doctor had employed the services of her brother, Mike, to check out certain facts, and the status and credentials of some prospective private patients.

Mike Cassidy was a PI. He had spent twenty years with the D.C. police department before putting his papers in and swapping his detective's badge for a gumshoe's license; a line of work that he had now been in for coming up to five years. Divorced, and forever being hounded for overdue alimony payments, Mike needed all the work that he could lay his hands on, just to keep his head above water. Ironically, divorce cases and associated marital problems brought him the lion's share of his income. Process serving, skip traces and the suspected infidelity of both men and women accounted for almost seventy percent of his seedy workload.

Mike was a throwback to the Mike Hammer image of a private eye. His office also doubled as living accommodation; an old leather-covered sofa, his bed. The cracked, frosted glass panel of the door advertised his agency to anyone who could manage the four flights of stairs. And the legend: MIKE CASSIDY INVESTIGATIONS in flaking gold paint, not leaf, welcomed all potential clients.

The office was a mess. Cash flow, which was always at ebb tide, prevented Mike from moving to a more up market location, or from employing a secretary who would have brought some semblance of order to the apparent chaos that reigned. The furniture, apart from the sofa, consisted of a second-hand battleship-gray desk, three matching and scratched five-drawer file cabinets, a shabbily upholstered swivel chair on squeaky castors, and an almost presentable re-covered armchair for visitors. The single internal door from the office led into a cubby-hole of a room that was barely large enough to accommodate the toilet, cracked sink, water heater and small refrigerator that it held. The ancient Kelvinator and the dented coffeemaker that clung to its top were both plugged into an extension cable, which Mike had jury-rigged under the door from the main office. In sharp contrast to the gloomy and impoverished surroundings to the left hand side of the office desk stood a unit that held a PC with 56k modem and a seventeen inch monitor. On the shelf under the PC was a compact fax and telephone unit with answer phone interface. Mike could accomplish much fact-finding from the relative comfort of his office. He was an experienced user, and hacking into various agencies saved a lot of shoe leather and dead-end inquiries. The only other item in the office that was of any real worth – and kept in immaculate condition – rested in a holster in the top right drawer of the desk. Oiled and gleaming, his loaded .38 Chief's Special was an old and faithful friend which was hopefully now redundant, but remained both reliable and accurate in his hand, should he ever need to use it.

Mike was a powerful man, a shade over six-feet tall, still muscular and supple, and possessing a natural strength that belied his fifty-three years. His face was craggy and dependable looking, with sharp flint-gray eyes that stared out uncompromisingly below a furrowed brow and short sandy hair that was threaded through with silver.

Time in the Marine Corps followed by his police career had molded a complex man; a man who had known extreme hardship and violence, but who savored peace and avoided conflict by choice, if possible, but was not afraid of it.

An incoming call pulled his attention away from the paperwork that was the bane of his life.

"Pick up, Mike," Kelly said, knowing that he usually preferred messages to be left, which he would get back to if and when it suited him.

Mike picked up on hearing the voice of his kid sister. "Hi, Kel. Everything okay?"

"Yeah, we're all fine," she said, meaning by all, her husband, Steve, and Mike's nephew, Gary. "When are you going to drop by for dinner? Gary doesn't see enough of you. And you know that you're his hero; The Great Detective."

"Soon, sis, soon. So what can I do for you, huh?"

"You could call in at the clinic. Dr. Fairburn needs something checking out, and it sounds urgent."

"I'll be there in a half hour. See you then," he said, racking the phone.

Mike drank the last mouthful of lukewarm, gritty coffee from his 'Lord of the Rings' mug – that Gary had bought him a couple of Christmases back – and replaced it on the ring-marked desktop. He then removed the .38 from the drawer and took it through to the cubby-hole, stashing it in his wall safe, which was concealed behind the hinged and rust-spotted mirror above the sink. He then headed for the door. Doc Fairburn always paid up front in folding green, which made him a priority in Mike's book.

"Please, take a seat, Mike," Ross said, motioning to the plush chair in front of his solid oak behemoth of a desk.

The light, spacious and richly furnished office of the doctor always sent unashamed pangs of envy through Mike, who could imagine his old sofa up against the far wall, in the shade of the massive yucca plant that stood there, and which would itself have taken up half of his paltry office's space.

"I've got a few names and dates that need checking out, Mike," Ross said. "Top of the list are those of a cop and a girl who may or may not have been murdered, back in ninety-six. All I need is some verification for now." He pushed a piece of A4 copy paper across the desktop to Mike, which appeared to be solid with names, dates and places.

"I'm on it." Mike said as he folded the list and slipped it into the inside pocket of his navy windbreaker.

Ross withdrew an envelope from his pocket. "This should be enough to start the ball rolling," he said, passing it to Mike. "I need something fast. So anything that you come up with, however small, I would appreciate a call."

"I'll be in touch." Mike said, standing and reaching over to take the envelope and then shake hands, cementing the contract.

"Thanks Mike. I'll most likely be at the Belmont Medical Center if you can't reach me here. Kelly will know where to contact me."

CHAPTER FIFTEEN

CAL was wired up. Nurses had wheeled in a contraption that looked like a polygraph, and had spent several minutes attaching leads to various points on his head with round adhesive pads holding them in place, linking him to the cumbersome machine. As if on cue, as they finished up, Ross entered the room accompanied by the other doctor, Carlisle.

"This is the EEG, Danny," Ben Carlisle said. "The procedure is pretty straight forward. We're going to ask you to imagine a series of mental pictures, and all you have to do is formulate them in your mind as clearly as you can. This machine will give us a printout of brainwave activity, and then we should be able to see if there are any anomalies. If you're ready, I've just got two more contacts here that need to go on your eyelids, and then we can begin."

Cal was sat in a chair next to the gizmo, which he still thought of as a glorified lie detector. The apparatus stuttered into life; a low humming sound announcing its preparedness to begin its machinations.

"Okay, Danny. I want you to visualize the President standing outside the White House to the left hand side of the front door, holding a folded newspaper in his right hand and looking across the lawn to a large square table with people sat around it."

Cal imagined Bill Clinton sporting a manufactured smile of sincerity that was probably the envy of many a second-hand car dealer.

"Any problem with that?" Ben said.

"No. I just pictured Clinton as you asked. I find him dangerously amusing," Cal replied.

"Next," Ben said, taking into account that the patient appeared to believe that the current president was one that had not been in office for many years. "Imagine that you are on board a space shuttle. The right cargo door is open, and below you, the Earth is revolving."

Cal concentrated. He could see the Earth spinning on its axis in space. He could even picture the outline of North America, its 'penis' – the state of Florida – hanging flaccid in the southeast. The planet was predominantly blue, with cotton-candy clouds loosely wrapping it in sparse, broken swathes.

For over an hour, Ben Carlisle asked him to construct scenarios in his brain, that Cal realized mainly involved spatial abstract content. It was as if he was being tested on whether he could properly visualize left and right, and 'see' objects in the right context in relation to where they should be. He felt that he had succeeded in mentally translating the required information correctly. He hadn't been aware of any black spots.

A nurse began detaching the contacts from his head. He removed the two from his eyelids himself.

"Can you give me a clue?" Cal asked the doctor. "Anything heavy show up?"

"Briefly," Ben said. "There seems to be only one area of concern. Anything that I asked you to envision that appertained to the last couple of decades drew a blank, or presented you with difficulties. Your mind is refusing to acknowledge a specific period of time. You perceive that you have no recollection of events that have taken place during the last twenty years."

Cal's face hardened. "Twenty-one years to be precise, Doc. You find it impossible to believe that this is not brain damage," he said, beginning to feel angry at the doctor, whose mind was closed to anything outside his expertise.

"Calm down, Danny. We're trying to eliminate any possibility of injury or morbid reason for your problem. That's what the tests are for. We need to pinpoint the reason for your confusion," Ben replied.

"One," Cal said in a cold, firm voice. "I am *not* Danny Clayton. And secondly, all your tests are going to prove is that there is no apparent damage to my brain. Once you appreciate that you'll want to brush the problem aside by deeming me mentally ill. Christ, with your mind as tightly shut as a duck's ass, I could wind up being committed to some funny farm for the rest of my life."

Ben looked first to Ross and then back to Cal, trying to formulate words that would pacify the patient before he became hysterical. And as he did, Cal jumped.

Invading the mind of Ben Carlisle proved an invaluable revelation. The good doctor was convinced that his patient had suffered an as yet undetermined injury to his brain, and that his delusional fugue state was a symptom of the damage. The EEG had not disclosed expected abnormalities, but he was confident that the CAT scan would uncover some trauma caused by the accident, or even the presence of a tumor.

If it did prove to be a physical mass, then he could hopefully excise it successfully and return the young man to his family, cured. There was no room in Carlisle's mind for any of his colleague's mumbo-jumbo. The possibility of another personality inhabiting the patient was a non-starter. If the scan was negative, then Danny was suffering from a mental disorder. Ben's mind was firmly closed to any supernatural explanation.

Probing deeper, Cal studied the man's life, past and present. At that moment, Carlisle's strongest subconscious thoughts were concerning his mistress, Anne Howard, a girl over twenty-five years his junior, who would be joining him this weekend at his beach cottage on Chesapeake Bay, near Fair Port. Ben planned to buy her the gold and jade bracelet that he had seen her admiring in a Georgetown jeweler's, and give it to her during a lobster and champagne meal at the Mobjack Inn on Saturday evening.

Cal withdrew from the less than respectable mind of Ben Carlisle, letting him finish his doctor to patient patter of condescending bullshit, before speaking.

"I can appreciate that your professional expertise and basic beliefs make it impossible for you to have an open mind, Doc," Cal started. "But I'm not asking anyone to believe that I'm Napoleon or Jesus Christ. I've given Ross evidence of my real identity, complete with precise details that if found to be true, could only be known to the person I claim to be. When the facts tie up with what I've said, then what tests will you carry out?"

Ben shook his head resignedly. "When you find that this person did not exist, then I'm sure that you will want to know the real reason for your problem, young man. Until then, I can understand your frustration and reluctance to accept that the nasty accident that you sustained has, temporarily I hope, caused this confused state."

As the Doctor turned to leave the room, Cal spoke again, stopping the man in his tracks. "By the way, Ben," he said. "I hope that your mistress, Anne, likes the gold and jade bracelet that you intend to give her over bubbly and lobster at the Mobjack. I'm sure that she'll just love it."

Ben stopped, rooted to the spot as unmoving as an oak tree for the best part of ten seconds. Then, gathering his frayed wits, he broke free and rushed from the room without turning and with no further comment.

"Was that really necessary, Cal?" Ross said, looking concerned and feeling a little fearful, but also amazed at the young man's demonstration.

"If you could read his mind, then you'd know it was," Cal said. "And after I've had the scan and the results come back clear, then I'm checking out of this place."

Later, back in his room and alone, Cal stretched out on top of the bed with his eyes closed; running through memories of a past that he knew was gone forever. There could be no way back through time. Twenty-one years and a stranger's body separated him from all that should have been. If this was reincarnation, then it sucked. It was a curse to be able to remember a previous existence. Doubly so because he was occupying another hapless person's body and mind. Not only was his life ruined, but a second life had been presumably wiped out; erased in the process.

The light tap at the door broke his brooding reverie.

Sarah entered the room and came over to him and kissed him, her soft lips brushing his cheek, giving him no time to pull away. He caught her scent, fresh and provocative, the feminine fragrance taking him back for just a second to a sun-filled clearing in a lush forest of pine and spruce; a blue check tablecloth spread out on the grass, and Chrissie handing him a plate of finger food. It was the memory of a picnic up near Tahoe, which to Cal had been enjoyed less than three months ago. Linear time; the rational passing of one minute to the next throughout life, had in some incredible way been disrupted. In his mind it was as if a section of celluloid had been cut from a film and dumped onto some mystical cutting-room floor. Twenty-one years of frames discarded; the film then re-spliced with scant regard to continuity. He felt as though he had passed through a portal, into a parallel world that was out of sync from where he should be.

Sarah sat on the edge of the bed and took his hand gently in her own. The warm touch re-focused his attention to the here and now.

"Danny," she said. "I've been feeling lost, confused and even angry at what's happened. And I know that if I feel like that, then you must feel much worse. It's so damn frustrating. I'm not sure how to deal with it. I love you and need you, but you don't even recognize me."

"Sarah," Cal said, sitting up, placing the pillow behind him for support, and at the same time using the maneuver to disengage his hand from hers. "You deserve to know the truth. I'm not suffering from amnesia. This isn't simply a case of not remembering. I have a full memory, but not of anyone by the name of Danny Clayton. My memories belong to another person; a guy by the name of Cal Morgan."

Sarah stared at him open-mouthed, as though he had just confessed to being a serial killer or being gay and in love with a butch and HIV positive Mafia hitman.

"That's just...well it doesn't make sense," she said. "The bang on the head has done this. But how can you suddenly think that you're somebody else? What do the doctors say about it?"

Cal shrugged his shoulders. "We expect life to follow an orderly, logical path. Strange events and impossible sounding occurrences are only supposed to happen in fiction, or to other people. But this is happening to me...us, and it isn't going to go away, it's for real. The injury to Danny's head somehow brought me back into existence. I was murdered in nineteen-ninety-six, and now I'm back. Call it reincarnation or anything you like, but Danny is not in here. I'm sorry. Christ, I can even read minds, and God knows what else I might be capable of."

Sarah had drawn back from Cal and her face was ashen. "This is crazy," she said. "Who do you think you are, Sam Beckett out of that ancient TV series *Quantum Leap*?"

"That only came on the tube in eighty-nine," Cal said. "Just seven years ago to me."

Sarah studied him thoughtfully, seeing that he truly believed what he was saying, and needing to show him that what he had just told her was a figment of his imagination.

"So do it," Sarah said. "Read my mind. Give me some proof that there is more to this than just abnormal after effects from the accident. Please help me to understand."

Cal did not want to enter Sarah's mind. He knew that it would be full of Danny, and feared seeing the young man as a real person while inhabiting his body. For the moment he could keep him at arm, or mind's length, as an abstract. It was bad enough using him, without having to face him, even if only in Sarah's mind.

He looked at the need in the young woman's eyes and knew that if he didn't perform what felt like a magic trick, then she would never be convinced, and so he relented.

"Okay," Cal said. "I'll do it, once only. Think of something unique. Something that no one, especially Danny, could know. Invent an image so complicated that there can be no ambiguity, no chance of you doubting that I would have to be able to see into your mind to know what it is."

Sarah concentrated with her eyes closed, and thought of a cat. Playing with the mental image, she turned it into a dark blue china ornament with sparkling green emerald eyes. She added a large red-on-white polka-dot scarf, and as a final touch, had it smoking a menthol cigarette, set in a long ivory holder. She even gave her creation a name; Cleopatra.

"Ready," she said, smiling thinly at Cal. "Make me a believer."

He flew into her eyes, his mind blinkered, ignoring the lifetime of memories and experiences that rushed to enter his brain, crowding in, up against barriers that he erected like a solid brick wall.

Sarah's strongest current thoughts stood out. He could see the three-dimensional image floating in her psyche for him to view. His projected self moved around it, studying the details of her make-believe conception. Within seconds he was back, wholly within himself again, relieved that he had been able to mask all but that which she had constructed for him to see.

"Well, are you going to do it?" Sarah said.

"Do what?" Cal said. "Tell you how weird your dark blue, green-eyed China cat with the red and white spotted scarf and smoking a menthol cigarette in an ivory holder looks? Or whether I think that Cleopatra sounds a suitable name for her?"

Sarah's hands flew to her face, cupping her mouth and chin. It was impossible. He *had* read her thoughts and described exactly that which she had only just imagined. There was no thread of skepticism, just astonished awe at what had taken place. She opened her mind, looked at him with new perspective, and found hardness; an experience of life in his eyes that Danny had not possessed. And his voice, though so familiar, had an accent, a slight drawl that she had failed to notice until now. Could it really be true? Could some other...person have taken up residence in Danny?

They talked for over an hour. Cal's personality shone through, overshadowing the physical presence that had denied his existence. He told Sarah of his past life, infusing it with such vivid detail and depth that she knew that she was in the company of a lost soul; a man back from the dead.

Cal got up and paced the room, and Sarah acknowledged that this man even moved differently. His mannerisms individualized him, and even though his DNA, fingerprints and dental records would confirm him to be Danny Clayton, they would be false witnesses to his true identity.

Leaving, but promising to return, Sarah did not kiss the man that she now believed to be a stranger by the name of Cal Morgan. They had agreed that she should discuss what had transpired between them with Jim and Linda, although the thought of doing it was daunting to Sarah. How could Danny's parents possibly accept such a seemingly bizarre situation?

CHAPTER SIXTEEN

AT nine a.m. on July thirteenth, Kelly buzzed Ross from the outer office.

"Dr. Fairburn, I've got Mike on the line for you."

"Put him through, please."

"Hi, Doc," Mike said. "I've got a few answers for you. But it might be better if I drop by...if you still want them soonest. A written report will be a day or two."

"Can you make it now?" Ross said.

"I'm on my way," Mike said, and rang off.

Kelly ushered her brother into Ross's office as soon as he arrived, with no formalities, as instructed.

"Good to see you, Mike," Ross said. "Take a seat." And once the PI was settled. "What have you got for me?"

Flipping open a slim, leather-bound notebook, Mike smiled. "All the answers to the details you needed checking Doc," he said, scanning his jottings. "Names, dates and places, all on the money and a lot more besides. First, (he paused to pull some folded paper from his inside jacket pocket), here are some copies of newspaper coverage of a double homicide that took place in ninety-six. There are photos of the deputy sheriff and the girl who were offed, uh, I mean murdered."

Ross took the papers, to unfold them and look at the monochrome image of Cal Morgan. The headline above it read: PERSHING COUNTY DEPUTY SHERIFF BRUTALLY MURDERED IN DOUBLE DESERT SLAYING.

"It's believed that three guys were responsible," Mike continued. "One of them was found at the bottom of a mine shaft, dead, with the cop's gun on him. The other two vanished into thin air. There was an old prospector at the mine who saw all three of them and gave descriptions of the two that got away. He even overheard one of their names. You'll find all that stuff on the second sheet, and I'll put everything in my report."

"What about the cop's wife and his father, anything on them?" Ross said.

Mike nodded. "The wife, Chrissie, remarried a few years' later. She has two teenage daughters and lives in Sacramento. Morgan's father is in his seventies, still living in Benson's Creek. The old guy was a widower, but he married again, the year that he retired from the sheriff's department."

"I don't know how you do it, Mike. Thanks. What do I owe you?"

"You paid enough up front to cover it, Doc. I'll get the full report to you in forty-eight hours if that's okay?"

Ross nodded, rising and walking round the desk to see Mike to the door. "I'm not sure," he said. "But there could be some follow up work on this one. I'll let you know."

"Anytime," Mike said. "Music to my ears. I'm only a phone call away."

CHAPTER SEVENTEEN

MANDY Kepple was full-bodied and sexy in a cuddly kind of way. Her face was pleasant, but if studied closely had a hard edge; a cynical expression of barely concealed contempt, that added a decade to her nineteen years.

Mandy was a working girl, hustling for trade in the close proximity of Sky Harbor International Airport in Phoenix.

It was late on a hot, sticky midsummer night, and she had not had a very profitable evening. Two blowjobs at thirty bucks each was not enough to be able to call it quits. There was cab fare and a baby-sitter – who didn't come cheap – to be paid for out of whatever she made.

Three other girls were still working the street, moving out of murky doorways to negotiate services and prices with any of the curb-crawlers who actually had the balls to stop, and were not just eyeballing the merchandise.

Mandy decided to give it another thirty minutes before heading for home. She was pissed at the world tonight and in particular with her patent leather high-heeled shoes, that were killing her.

Home to Mandy was a seedy, three-roomed, roach-infested apartment in a tenement building that should have been condemned and torn down decades ago. A neighbor looked after her son, Jason, and charged ten bucks an hour to sit in front of Mandy's TV instead of her own. Mandy shook her head. Christ, she thought, I should start a child minding service and give up hooking. It's an easier way to earn a living...well, maybe not.

Jason had been the result of a quick fuck with a high-roller who'd refused to wear a rubber. That was back at the time when she had just started on the game, and he had paid well to ride bareback, so she took the risk, only to fall pregnant. She had fully intended to have an abortion, but kept putting it off until flushing it was no longer an option. Jason was now eighteen months old, and she loved the kid, who had given her life a little purpose; a reason to keep off hard drugs, and the ability to act a lot more responsibly than she had been doing before he came along.

At sixteen, Mandy had plucked up enough courage to flee from an abusive father, and a mother who had known what was happening but was too afraid and cowed to interfere. For as long as Mandy could remember her father had visited her bedroom at night. She could recall as a five or six-year old being touched between her legs, and being made to hold and fondle him. By the time she was eight, she was an expert, having completely mastered all aspects of sex. The first time that her father had entered her, it had hurt beyond belief. He had felt so big and hard inside her that she had thought she might split in two. She was left sore, bloody and crying, and he had scolded her for acting like a baby. Thereafter he took her most nights. She had become used to his heavy, sweating body, his wheezing and grunting, and most of all his dick inside her. She believed that it was normal. He had told her that all little girls who loved their daddies did these things, but that it was their big secret, not to be shared with anyone.

God, how she had grown to hate the dirty old bastard. She had prayed that he would get cancer and die. And on her sixteenth birthday she had left home, never to return. She had not gone to the police, or ever told anyone of the abuse she had suffered. She just lived with the psychological scarring, and a deep sense of shame that rightfully belonged to her perverted father, who felt none.

Since her escape, and armed with a practical and comprehensive carnal education, Mandy had decided that it was payback time. As far as she was concerned, men only wanted one thing, so she provided it, at a price. They could all pay in hard cash for what her sick father had taken freely for so many years.

The Chevrolet had stopped, and the driver called out, startling her back to the present and the job at hand, or wherever the agreed price deigned that he put his member. With a slight swing of her wide, mini-skirted hips, Mandy sashayed over to the car, her heels clipping on the sidewalk, and her leather skirt hugging her ample buttocks.

"Can I do somethin' for you, handsome?" Mandy said, resting her fleshy forearm on the sill of the open car window, surveying the face of the prospective john.

"You sure can, sweet thing. Fifty bucks worth," he replied, holding a crisp bill to the light for her to see.

Mandy walked around the front of the Chevy and climbed into the passenger seat, instructing the punter to head west on Washington Street. A minute later she pointed to the entrance of a parking lot, which was still open and manned. Mandy had an arrangement with Paulie, the attendant. She paid him in kind every Monday night in the back of his station wagon, with no money changing hands.

The punter turned into the alleyway at the side of the lot and drove fifty yards down it into darkness before stopping. Only derelict buildings witnessed the car's arrival.

"What the fuck are you playin' at, buddy?" Mandy said. "I use the car lot that you just passed."

"S…Sorry, love, I'm a bit nervous," he said with a worried look and a slight stammer.

He was maybe in his early forties, and even in the poor light Mandy could see that he was an Indian. His features were chiseled, good looking in a harsh but interesting way, and framed by collar length ebony hair that had just a tinge of gray at the temples. But it was his eyes that mesmerized her. They were intense black pools that held her gaze and somehow weakened her resolve.

What the hell! She reached across and unzipped his pants, releasing his stiff penis with professional dexterity. *Fifty bucks is fifty bucks.*

Mandy bobbed her head down to take him into her mouth, wanting to get it over with quickly and call it a night.

The blow to the side of her head paralyzed her. She didn't black out, but lost all control of her limbs as her muscles became instantly rubbery, sapped of strength and unable to respond to her commands to move. She felt nauseous as her vision blurred and became a mottled canvass of swarming red and black pixels. As if detached from the events, Mandy felt her skirt being pushed up to her waist. Her panties were in the plastic shoulder bag on the seat next to her, not worn while she was working. Also in the bag was a mace spray that she carried for just this sort of unprovoked attack, but which on this occasion would remain unused.

He stopped and reached down as if to retrieve something from the floor, and Mandy heard a tearing sound, familiar to her, yet unrecognizable in her panic.

He wound the tape tightly around her head, sealing off her mouth but ensuring that her nostrils were not obstructed, before pushing her forward, to once more – though purely coincidentally – have her face next to his still turgid penis as he taped her wrists together behind her. Pulling her head back he waited until she had regained her senses, taking a perverse delight in her wide-eyed bewilderment as she fully appreciated her predicament. Sliding the strap of her top from her right shoulder, he fingered the delicate rose tattoo that had initially singled her out for his attention.

"That's a neat little posy you have there," he remarked, bending forward, his tongue darting out to lick the ink bloom. "Now, listen up, sweet thing. I want you to spread those fat little legs of yours just as wide as you can, and earn your money. If you try to mess with me I'll bite your fuckin' nose off. Do you understand?"

Mandy nodded vigorously, grunting frantically as a mind-numbing sense of foreboding immobilized her with a fear far stronger than the bonds that held her.

Luke ran his fingers through her thick wedge of pubic hair, before placing both of his hands under her buttocks and tilting her pelvis up so that he could enter her with ease. And as he fucked her, he reached down and pulled up the cuff of his jeans, to withdraw the long, wide-bladed knife from the sheath in his boot. Pausing, still inside her, he sliced the tattoo from her shoulder with one swift stroke.

Mandy bucked and writhed, eyes bulging and a muffled, mewling sound escaping her nostrils as her nerve ends transmitted the pain to her terrified brain.

Now experiencing what he considered to being a mind-blowing high, Luke put his face to hers and bit down hard on her nose, his clenched teeth sawing back and forth to tear it free.

Appetite for sex and blood now almost totally sated, Luke put the tattoo souvenir of his conquest into his jacket pocket, then moved aside and folded her, pushing the top half of her body down so that her head was between her legs, nearly touching the floor of the car. Gripping a handful of her long, lacquered hair, he pulled her head back, and with expert precision, cut deeply. The blade entered Mandy's neck below her ear, traversing across her throat to sever her major arteries and windpipe. He felt the satisfying give as the head came up and back toward him; the yawning wound affording it an unnatural freedom of movement.

Mandy felt no pain now, just an icy coldness that seemed to flow back from her hands and feet into her stomach and chest, and finally her brain. As she bled out in the dark well of the Chevy, a single last thought crossed her befuddled mind; *Why daddy, why*?

Luke pulled the trunk release handle, got out of the car and quickly hefted the limp body from the front and tipped it into the open waiting compartment, where it flopped face down, large buttocks jouncing in the weak light from a small courtesy bulb. She brought to his mind the image of a beached whale, sagging under its own unsupported weight. He covered the cadaver with an opaque, blue plastic sheet and then pushed the lid down, to lock away the hundred fifty plus pound slab of dead meat that was now just evidence to get rid of as soon as possible. Back in the driver's seat, he checked the hooker's gaudy shoulder bag, removed the cash and smiled at the sight of a mace spray, which had undoubtedly given the stupid bitch a very false sense of security. He held the crumpled red cotton panties he found to his nose, inhaling the faint yet unmistakable scent of her sex, and then pushed them back into the bag and deposited it under the seat along with her shoes, which had fallen off inside the car and were slick with blood. Once more he climbed out of the car, taking a liter bottle of water from the back seat and rinsing his hands and face, drying off with a red bandanna he pulled from the back pocket of his jeans.

Starting the Chevy, he headed east through Mesa and out past Tortilla Flat, not stopping until he reached the isolated edge of the Horse Mesa Dam.

Laboriously wiping the steering wheel and all surfaces that he may have touched, including the shoes and bag, Luke opened the car's windows, put the transmission into neutral and with his ass against the trunk, pushed the Chevy over the high rocky cliff, to send it into one of the deepest stretches of the dam.

Standing at the edge, he lit a cigarette and waited for the car to fill with water, tip forward and sink ship-like, vanishing in a surge of foaming, bubbling blackness.

Finishing the cigarette, Luke flicked the glowing butt after the stolen automobile, for it to be extinguished on the now glassy surface that separated it from Mandy's final resting place a hundred feet below.

Taking the fresh trophy from his pocket, he admired the artwork under the pale moonlight, before wrapping it in the damp bandanna – within which he had enfolded so many similar mementoes of past kills – to place it in the inside pocket of his scuffed leather jacket, which he fastened up to the collar against the cold night air, and to cover his blood-smeared shirt.

Heading for the highway at a slow jog, Luke mentally tallied up the slivers of preserved, tattooed skin that he had harvested from disinclined donors throughout the years. They were all safely stashed at the cabin, where he cohabited with his aunt. This fresh specimen would make a fine addition to his collection, and bring the total to thirty.

CHAPTER EIGHTEEN

CAL woke up in a cold sweat. The Indian's face had appeared vividly in his dark dream, looking down at him with evil intent. Cal's gun had materialized in the killer's hand, pointing at his face. And as the phantom muzzle flashed, Cal shot upright with a film of perspiration coating his skin; the bed and pillow soaked from every pore of his body, caused not by the temperature of the room, but from an undiluted state of pure fear.

Cal felt him, and knew beyond any doubt that he was still out there. Be it providence or whatever, Cal was back and would somehow find his executioner and take care of what was now unfinished business.

After the CAT scan, Ross dropped by. Cal had showered, shaved, and then got dressed in freshly laundered jeans and a short-sleeved sports shirt, left by Sarah. The clothes had belonged to Danny. He also wore a pair of Danny's socks and Nike training shoes, which were comfortable but seemed very thick-soled and heavily padded, making his feet – to him – look enormous.

Ross placed a slim hard-shell briefcase on the bed, flicked the catches open and lifted up the lid.

"I've got some news for you," Ross said. "But before we get to it, do me a favor. Describe Cal Morgan in detail."

"Testing me again, huh?" Cal asked with a wry grin on his face as he sat back in a chair next to the bed and muted the TV with the remote before, interlocking his fingers behind his head and crossing his legs. "In my opinion I was one handsome son of a gun: a lean, mean machine, five-eleven...six-one with my boots on. Black hair, combed back, a little gray at the sides. I had Paul Newman-blue eyes, is he still alive?"

"'Fraid not." Ross said. "He died eight or nine years back. And the description you gave me of Cal Morgan is pretty good. Although the handsome bit is a little narcissistic on your part. Here look." He removed a photocopy from his briefcase and handed it to Cal, who stared at the image of his former face. It was from a photo that Chrissie had taken of him back in ninety-five. He had been sitting out on the stoop, and she had shouted, 'Hey, handsome', and as he'd looked up, she'd taken the pic.

It was another painful flashback. He was transported back to that bright morning. The tears welled, threatening to wet his cheeks, causing him to swallow hard in an effort to hold them back. "Yes, Ross, that's me. Does everything else check out?"

"Word for word, name for name and date for date, so far," Ross said. "I have no idea how this can be happening, but for what it's worth, I believe you. I accept without reservation that you are Cal Morgan, God help you. In some way you've survived death. Hell, if there *is* such a thing as reincarnation, then it's something that no one has any memory of, and if they do, they remember a past life as another person. This is a new twist, and it turns everything that I've believed in all my life upside down and inside out."

Ross handed Cal the copies of news reports that covered the incident. "These will fill you in on what happened following your...uh, murder," he said. "I have a PI, a reliable guy, digging around for me. He even found out that you're…widow remarried. I'll let you have a copy of his full report when I get it."

"Thanks for this, Ross," Cal said as the headlines of his death and the shock of knowing that Chrissie had married again branded themselves into his brain. "I was secretly wondering if I might be insane; that I may have somehow created all this and was believing a complicated delusion. Now I don't have to try and question my memory or doubt the truth. I'm back, I can read minds, and all I have to do now is work out how to deal with what has happened to me."

Ross put his hands up, as if pushing his palms against a wall. "Hold it. Slow down, Cal," he said. "A lot of the time, if not all of the time, life doesn't provide answers or reasons. You may have to accept the here and now; take it one step at a time and go forward and build a new life. Like it or not, you're in a new time and a new body. There is no going back."

Jim, Linda and Sarah arrived while Cal was watching CNN again. He was trying to familiarize himself with some of the current issues, and work out what was happening in the new millennium; bring himself up to date. Most of it went over his head. It was going to take a long time to assimilate his new surroundings and acclimatize to this strange new world, that had moved on without him.

Everything was familiar, but out of true. He felt more a time-traveler than a dead man reborn. The only saving grace of his return was the time factor. He could, he supposed, have popped back into existence a century or a thousand years in the future. That only a little more than two decades had passed was in some way a bonus. The bridge that spanned the gap in his life had not cut him off entirely from his past.

He turned off the TV, and rather than stay in the small hospital room, led his visitors down the corridor to the spacious day room, to drink coffee and talk. They sat in comfortable easy chairs, Sarah next to Cal, Jim and Linda opposite, with a low glass-topped table between the two couples.

“This is difficult,” Jim began, looking ill at ease, and visibly trembling with nervous tension. “Sarah told us everything, and...well, there is a strange coincidence that Linda and I have tried to forget. Something unexplainable happened the day that you...Danny was born. It was an event that we put behind us, and hoped was of no consequence; that it would never have to be mentioned again.”

Jim related what had taken place all those years ago. He recalled the moments following Danny’s birth; the shattering lights; the power cut, noises, and the apparent warping of reality.

“The reason I’ve told you all this,” Jim continued, gripping Linda’s hand as he forced himself to speak, “is because our son was born at the exact time and on the same day that Sarah says you claim to have been murdered. Our baby, just a few seconds old, spoke as clearly as I’m speaking to you now. He said, ‘Oh God, Chrissie’, and then, ‘Where am I?’ That was it. Everything returned to normal, and if it hadn’t been for the debris in the room, and the fact that other people were present, we may have tried to kid ourselves that it didn’t happen, and that we had just imagined it. Sarah told us that Chrissie is the name of Cal Morgan’s wife. Is that right?”

“No,” Cal replied. “She *was* my wife, then my widow, and now I’ve been informed that she remarried.”

“I’m sorry,” Jim said. “There’s one other thing. When Linda had an ultrasound to check the baby out, it showed what looked like two babies, twins. But one was indistinct, a blurred image. And when they tried again it had gone. They thought it had just been a glitch of the equipment.”

Jim and Linda both seemed to sag in their chairs, unburdened yet still unable to understand any of it. Cal nodded and looked from one to the other with heartfelt sympathy. He was as confused as they were, and could truly empathize with their fear and sense of loss.

"I had no control over what happened to me," Cal said, feeling a little defensive, as though they thought that he had stolen their son; body snatched him. "If I could return Danny to you now, then I would. But I have no awareness of him. One second I was shot, and the next I woke up to find that twenty-one years had passed, and that everybody thought I was Danny."

"We're not blaming you for what has happened," Linda said. "We just thought you should know that whatever is happening now started at the precise moment in time that you were, uh...you died and our son was born. There was some link between you. You must have been part of Danny from the very beginning."

Jim cleared his throat with a nervous cough. "Ross told us that you will be checking out of the hospital as soon as the test results come through, if they're clear."

"That's right," Cal said. "I know that whatever the problem is, it isn't one that doctors will be able to solve."

"So stay with us," Linda blurted out, almost as a plea. "Whatever you decide to do, start from our home. You'll need clothes and money. You have a dilemma, and even if we don't know you, you're as close to Danny as we can get. And he is probably in there with you on some level. We want to help. No pressure, just stay with us for as long as you need somewhere as a base."

Sarah took Cal's hand and squeezed it hard. That single act said a lot more to him than any words. It said, please do it, let us be a part of your life. We know that you are not the young man who has been taken away from us, but we need to know you. We couldn't bear to lose our only link with Danny.

Cal's decision was in part, but not totally, mercenary. He cared about these people's feelings. But the hard facts were that he *did* need money, clothes and a place to gather himself and make plans; a base of operations.

"I'll give it a try, if you're sure that you think it's for the best," he said. "But I'll be going back to Nevada soon. I have to lay the ghosts of the past to rest before I can even start to try and build a new future."

At ten a.m. on July fifteenth, Ross gave Cal the news that they had both expected. "Ben Carlisle asked me to tell you that there is no pathological explanation for your condition. For reasons we both know, he seems reluctant to tell you himself. The scan and other tests show no anomalies, and I know that you are not mentally ill, so the best I can do is arrange therapy to help you come to terms with what has happened."

"Thanks, Ross, but no thanks. Lying on a couch and talking about it won't make it go away or change a damn thing. I'm all packed and ready to ship out. Sarah is waiting to pick me up when I give her a call."

"Okay, Cal, but stay in touch. I'll get the rest of that information to you shortly. Also, be aware that you may suffer unexpected emotional trauma, and God knows what else that we have no precedent to study. I don't believe for one minute that Danny Clayton has just ceased to exist. He's in there with you, even if you can't sense him. Don't bank on him staying suppressed forever. His personality could reassert itself at any moment, and that could be catastrophic. If it should happen, neither of you may be able to deal with trying to coexist in the same brain. I'm now beginning to think that reincarnation could be the answer to many problems associated with what you would probably call split personality. It could be a hitherto unacknowledged cause of all sorts of disorders, primarily schizophrenia." Ross handed Cal a business card. "I've put my home and cell numbers on there, Cal. If you need me, pick up the phone, day or night. One of those will reach me."

They shook hands. Ross left feeling out of control of a situation that he wanted to be involved with. Probably the most significant case that he was ever likely to come across was about to drive away. He hoped that he could continue to function with the mundane, now that a real enigma had tantalizingly crossed his path.

Cal phoned Sarah, and forty minutes later they were driving from the hospital to Alexandria. The journey gave Cal the fresh air and space that he had been missing. Marshmallow clouds skittered across a sapphire sky, and the greenery and buildings that flashed by brought back color after the blandness of the Belmont's decor.

Sarah drove fast and talked nervously. The sensation of being alone with someone who appeared so familiar, but was in fact almost a stranger, was daunting. It had been different in the hospital. Other people had been nearby; nurses hurrying about their duties; doctors on their rounds; the building alive with distraction. Now it was just one-on-one, with a man who only looked like Danny; whom she loved so dearly and missed so desperately.

They reached Jim and Linda's and found a barbecue in progress next to the now infamous swimming pool, that such a short time ago Danny had entered, and Cal had exited from.

"We thought that you had been cooped up indoors for long enough," Linda said to Cal. "It's far too nice a day to be in the house."

"Perfect," Cal said, looking around at the house and extensive grounds. "You and Jim have a lovely place here, away from the maddening crowd."

"Beer?" Jim said, proffering a chilled bottle of Bud Ice.

CHAPTER NINETEEN

MIKE Cassidy was burning the midnight oil over a hot computer. The cop killing of so long ago intrigued him, and he wanted more details, for himself as well as for Ross. It transpired that a guy who'd been found down a mine shaft with his neck broken had been in possession of the dead cop's gun, and a piece of the dead girl's breast. The portion of flesh had a tattoo on it and incorporated the nipple. The mother of the dead girl had identified the illustration. Jesus! Mike couldn't properly imagine the horror of having to inspect a small separate piece of your murdered daughter's body. He shivered. As for the other two perps, they had never been apprehended. Mike had called in a favor from an old friend, Richard Cole, a field agent with the FBI, who he had known for over fifteen years. Rich was going to check the MO and look for comparisons. Mike thought that it was a long shot, but if the same wet work had been carried out on other women, or men, then the bureau would have been involved, assuming a serial killer was responsible.

Used properly, the computer was the criminal fraternities biggest enemy; one that could gather and collate information nation or world-wide.

Mike had a gut feeling that these wackos had struck more than once. Biting off the victim's nose and removing a tattoo before cutting her throat seemed ritualistic. The mutilations performed on the girl had been kept from the media, for obvious reasons, but Mike had hacked into the main Nevada police terminal and picked it clean of all information he deemed pertinent to the case. Working quickly and re-routing his inquiries through five locations on two continents – that terminated at a user code belonging to a London-based insurance company – gave him a pretty good chance of avoiding detection, should they even realize that their system had been illegally infiltrated.

The descriptions of the two fugitives, given by a prospector, Ed Cooper, who was now deceased, were on file. One had been described as being a Native American with long black hair and wearing a red bandanna. He had appeared to be in his twenties, of medium height, and was presumed to be an Apache. The other guy had been Caucasian, big, built like a Kenworth semi truck and well over six-feet tall, with thinning red hair, and in his thirties. The pickup that they had driven had been torched, and the plates had been taken from another vehicle. They had stolen the witness's RV, which had also been found burnt out a few days later and over three hundred miles northeast of the mine. No usable latent prints had been lifted, and the case remained unsolved and still open, though very cold.

At nine-thirty a.m. a special delivery put Mike back in front of his monitor. Rich had come through for him. The package gave up a memory stick, and the data on it exceeded Mike's expectations by a country mile. There were no case file numbers or anything to show where the information had originated from, just a small typed note that had been wrapped around the stick. It read: 'Now you owe me!'

Mike inserted the stick in the USB port and was confronted with one file: R-SKIN. He brought it up on screen and began to read Rich's anonymous communication:

> LIST OF DECEASED CONFORMING TO MO AS DISCUSSED:
>
> It is believed that this list is partial; incomplete due to the placement of corpses in locations that made discovery highly unlikely.
>
> All victims were raped.
>
> All victims had suffered partial removal of nose by human bite.
>
> All victims had tattoos excised from body.
>
> All victims had throat cut – cause of death – from left to right. Large partially serrated blade used in all cases, believed to be the same weapon.
>
> Six of the victims were known prostitutes (P).

Name	Age	Date found	Location	Known tattoo details
Patricia Miller (P)	18	Mar '90	Tucson, Ariz	Rose – rt buttock
Claire Masters	21	Jul '91	Provo, Utah	Chain – rt ankle
Emily Hope	23	May '93	Gallup, N. Mex	B/fly – lft shldr
Kim Gray (P)	19	Dec '94	El Paso, TX	Heart – u-lft arm
Ruth Marlowe (P)	27	Apr '95	Denver, Col	L/birds – rt breast
Trish Henderson	16	Jul '96	Benson's Creek,	Nev Skull – lft breast
Tina Lopez (P)	17	Aug '98	Barstow, Calif	Celtic cross – lwr back
Martha Crowther	15	Feb '98	Indio, Calif	Eagle – rt shldr
Barbara Fox (P)	20	Jun '03	Flagstaff, Ariz	Heart – lft buttock
Connie Patterson	18	Sep '04	Santa Fe, N. Mex	Lizard – rt forearm
Sue Jacobs (P)	19	May '08	Prescott, Ariz	Rose – lft neck

Extracts from lab reports and forensic evidence. Condensed:

The samples of blood, semen and hair collected from all deceased – apart from Trudy Henderson – are from only one and same individual.

His blood type is AB Positive. He has predominantly black hair.

Only partial latent prints have ever been found.

From DNA it is conclusive that suspect is Native American Indian.

Footprints found at three locations identical: Size 8 western style boot with heel. Depth of impression in relation to ground density gives guesstimate of suspect's weight to be approximately 175 pounds.

The psychological profile on this guy is now as thick as three D.C. phone listings. So cutting out the repetition and mumbo jumbo, I've picked out the main points of interest. The behavioral science boys are still having a field day with this one. They always give these creeps a handle (unofficially), and this one has had a couple over the last twenty-odd years. He started off as the Tattoo Killer, and then with the DNA profiling they tagged him as Cochise. I'm sure that these profilers spend most of their time dreaming up nicknames and drinking coffee. The overall consensus is that he started killing when he was young, and is now in his forties. Background is thought to be the standard broken home scenario: probably desertion by the mother when he was pre-puberty age. Women are thought to have become objects of hate and usage to him; a commodity to get off on and discard after humiliating and mutilating them. The real buzz for this SOB is to dominate and cause suffering. He has no apparent wish to interact with his victims, apart from screwing and killing them. All were found with their arms bound and mouths gagged.

He wants them subservient and unable to communicate with him. It seems that he has a prefixed game plan and sticks to it. He stalks his intended prey like a hunter, with a proclivity to usually select prostitutes. The homeless and hitchhikers are also fair game to him, as are any isolated females who happen to be in the wrong place, for them. The tattoo collecting is thought to be a conscious need to have a souvenir; a trophy of his kill. *This* redskin takes tattoos instead of scalps.

He is more than likely a charmer, who can display a likeable personality. He may spend interludes dormant, living within

> normal parameters, and is possibly involved in a long-standing relationship, probably with an older, maternal woman. It is apparent that he can function in a way that does not cause alarm or suspicion. He is cunning, clever and extremely organized and dangerous. He has nothing to prove, has never contacted any law enforcement agencies, and has no subconscious need to be apprehended. This isn't some weirdo who craves attention or wants to play games with us. His 'mission' is purely personal.
>
> It's fair to assume that he is in a line of work that affords him the chance to travel without attracting attention. His home base is almost certainly in the Southwest. The geographical locations of the recovered bodies tell us that.
>
> I don't know why you would want this stuff, Mike, but if for some reason you're looking for this psycho, and get a lead...call me. DO NOT try to take him down by yourself. He's an expert at what he does, and hasn't made a mistake yet.
>
> When you have digested this stuff, make it vanish.

That was it. Mike scrolled through the report twice, then made a backup copy of the memory stick and locked the original away in his safe. He was bemused. How could Ross Fairburn be tied into this? What possible connection could the doctor have with an unknown serial killer who prowled the Southwest? Mike had questions that wouldn't wait.

"Come in, Mike. What have you got for me?" Ross said as Mike took a seat and removed more folded paperwork from his pocket.

"I've got some answers, and a whole bunch of questions, Doc," Mike said. "To start with, did you know that the cop killer that you're interested in is still on the loose, has never been identified, and is probably cutting someone's throat as we speak?"

Ross frowned, picked up a paperclip and started straightening it out as he fought with his conscience, but said nothing.

"Come on, Doc'. What's your connection to a sicko that the FBI have been after for well over two decades? He isn't a patient of yours, is he?"

"Christ, no, Mike, I don't know anything about him. Only what you are telling me. This does concern a patient, but he isn't the killer. You know that I can't get into this with you. It would be a breach of doctor/patient confidentiality."

"I realize that, Doc. If you or your patient want any more information...and I have plenty, then you'd better talk to him and arrange a meet. Don't forget that my work involves protecting clients' interests as well. If you know anybody who is trying to find this psycho, then they are going to need to know just what they're going up against. And they will definitely need all the help they can get."

"Why would you want to be involved, Mike?"

"Because this smells of unfinished business, and the more I find out, the more intriguing it gets. It also scares the shit out of me, and it's been a long time since I've experienced this combination of emotions simultaneously."

Ross scratched his beard, and then gave the PI a wan smile. "Give me a few hours', Mike. I'll get back to you later today. I think it would be a good idea for you to be in on this. But believe me; you have no idea just how strange this case is. If my patient agrees to see you, then you may just decide to back off when you know the full facts."

CHAPTER TWENTY

ROSS parked on the herringbone patterned brick forecourt outside the house and was met by Linda Clayton as he climbed out of his ageing but beloved Porsche.

After asking Linda how she and Jim were bearing up, Ross followed Linda through the house and out back to the pool, where Cal was swimming.

"Surprise visit," Linda called, purposely avoiding the use of either Danny or Cal when addressing the stranger in her son's body. "Ross needs to speak to you. I'll go and rustle up something cool to drink, and a snack."

"Hi, Ross," Cal said, pulling himself out of the pool and joining the doctor, who had already taken a seat under the sun shade that sheltered a large, round wrought iron table with a mosaic-tiled top. "So, what's with the house-call? It must be important to bring you out here without even phoning first."

"Well, for starters, Cal, the guy that shot you and murdered the girl is in all probability still out there, alive and well in body, if sick in mind. He's a serial killer who the FBI has been attempting to run down for decades."

Cal brought his fist down hard on the tabletop, causing Ross to jump at the sudden act. "I knew it!" Cal exclaimed loudly. And then barely audibly to himself. "I could feel him; sense that he was still alive and free."

Ross told him about Mike Cassidy, his interest, and his request to be involved.

"I hope you aren't, but if you are planning to look for this deranged killer, then I would strongly recommend that you have Mike on board, Cal. He wants to be in on it, and he's a professional; an Ex-Marine and ex-cop. He could help."

"What have you told him about me?" Cal asked, wary of strangers.

"Nothing. He has no idea why I wanted the details about a deputy sheriff's death. It's up to you. He has more information, but he wants to be included. If you okay it, I'll get back to him."

Cal was excited. He wanted to know everything that the PI had dug up. "Do it, Ross, please. Set up a meeting, but tell him the background first. See how he reacts to the idea of dealing with a cop that he thinks is dead. He may just decide that we're both as crazy as shit-house rats and lose interest."

Cal drove Danny's brand new Corvette to the Fairfax Clinic the following morning. Mike had arrived almost an hour earlier and listened in amazement to the story that Ross told him. It made no sense. It was not a scenario that he could accept; even though the doctor seemed convinced that it was the truth.

Kelly showed Cal into the office for the scheduled meeting, and Ross told her to hold all calls until it was over.

"Cal Morgan, meet Mike Cassidy," Ross said, introducing the two men to each other. They shook hands, both appreciating the other's firm grip, neither liking to shake a limp, dead fish hand that did not respond and lay in the palm in passive acceptance of the greeting ceremony.

"Let's have some coffee and get to it," Ross said, pressing the intercom and asking Kelly to arrange refreshment.

"First hurdle to get over, Cal," Ross said. "Is that Mike finds reincarnation and assorted sundry supernatural powers just a little hard to swallow at the present time."

Cal stared into Mike's eyes and saw the stony look of cynicism. Without hesitation, he jumped into the gumshoe's mind. The process was becoming easier with practice, more fluid and smooth; almost a natural act, as normal as talking or swallowing. He engulfed Mike's brain, saw his life, absorbed his thoughts, and picked out the highlights and useful tidbits; the choice morsels, collecting them as though he was plucking products from a supermarket shelf and placing them in a cart. His power was growing. And the part of his consciousness still in Danny's body was as strong as the part of him that was in Mike. He was fully aware, totally cognizant in both locations. He left Mike. There was no sudden snapping recoil now, just a flowing return to oneness.

"So, you're the deputy that got capped in Nevada back in ninety-six, right?" Mike asked with no hint of mockery, but also no trace of belief in his voice.

"Yeah," replied Cal. "And you're the ex-marine who watched his buddy, Roy Benedict, get offed during operation Urgent Fury in Grenada. You watched as he ran for the chopper you were on. Even managed to get a hand to him, but had to let go as he was nearly cut in half by bullets. You saw him writhing on the ground as the pilot quit the scene."

Mike could not have moved faster if someone had thrown a rattler in his lap. He shot to his feet and involuntarily backed up three paces, before stopping to stare wide-eyed at Cal in both anger and bewilderment. He knew without any misgiving that his thoughts and memories had been hacked into with far greater speed and efficiency than he could steal from a database.

"Also," Cal added, now on a roll. "I know everything that your FBI pal, Rich Cole, gave you. So if you want to call it a day right here and now, do it."

Mike was lost for words. He sat back down and the pregnant silence was only broken by Kelly knocking at the door.

"Come in, Kelly," Ross said.

Kelly opened the door and vanished again for a few seconds before entering the office carrying a silver-plated tray that held fine bone-china cups and saucers, a pot of coffee, jug of cream, and a bowl of brown cane sugar. She placed the tray on a low, elliptical-shaped, marble-topped table that seemed to grow from the burnt orange pile of the expensive Axminster. "Thanks," Ross said as his secretary glided from the room.

"If you were...*are* who you say, then I take it that you're going to try and nail this guy, correct?" Mike said, the interruption having given him time to recover from the initial shock of the mind-reading exhibition, to adapt, as most people can to an event that until it takes place would be viewed as outlandish and inconceivable.

"Does that mean you're now a convert? Because any doubts will impede what needs to be done." Cal said.

"I know what you just did. But I admit that without the demonstration it would have been easier to believe that Elvis was alive and well, and living in Howard Hughes style reclusion in a loft at Graceland," Mike replied, a forced smile on his face.

"How do you think I feel?" Cal said. "Waking up after a gap of twenty-one years in someone else's body is heavy shit, believe me. Oh, and just as a bonus, Mike, at no extra charge, the combination to the safe behind your bathroom mirror is, 20 left, 6 right, 12 right and 14 left. Inside, along with your Chief's Special, are eight hundred dollars in an envelope, your divorce papers, and the memory stick that Rich sent you and asked you to get rid of. How's that for just a little more proof that I'm the real McCoy?"

"Whoa," Mike said. "Enough, I'm sold. No more, please, I'm a believer. Are you doing it now?"

"No, and I only did it because there's no way you would have ever believed this stuff without solid proof to back it up. Ask Ross, he's been there."

Ross nodded at Mike. "That's right, Mike. I got the shock treatment as well."

"I suppose it could be termed illegal entry, if there was a law to govern this sort of thing," Cal said. "But giving a practical demo saved a lot of time. You've got to admit it's an attention-getter."

"So now what?" Mike said. "How do you plan to catch up with a perp that the police in several states and the FBI can't run down?"

Ross poured the coffee as they talked, the strong aroma of quality Colombian filling the room.

"I've got an edge, Mike," Cal said, putting his index finger to his right temple. "I know two things that no one else does; his name, and what he looks like close up."

"You know the Indian's name? What is it?" Mike said.

Cal smiled. "Sorry, Mike. I'm not about to say anything that you might take straight to your fed friend."

"Give it up, Cal," Ross said. "Let the authorities deal with it."

Cal's head jerked in Ross's direction. "The authorities have had over twenty years to deal with it, and they haven't come up with jack shit," he snapped. "As a cop, I never did approve of Bronson-style vigilantism, but now that it's personal, I can see the attraction. I believe that this is probably why I'm back; to deal with it myself."

"You need backup," Mike said. "Let me help you track this scumbag down."

"Thanks for the offer, but it isn't your problem and—"

"The hell it isn't my problem!" Mike exploded. "This motherfucker is everyone's problem. As far as we know he's still out there, mutilating and killing young women. You're not the only one who has suffered at his hands, so get real and accept my help."

Ross stood up and raised his arm to shake the other men's hands. "I'm not happy with what you two may end up trying to do," he said. "So I'll take my leave before I hear anymore. Just remember, Cal, contact me if you have any psychological problems. And be careful. This guy obviously doesn't take prisoners."

Ross left them to use his office, already running late for an appointment over at the George Washington Hospital.

Cal sipped his coffee as he thought over his options. He had seen Mike's mind and knew that the PI was a tough and tenacious professional, both capable and intelligent. He could not wish for a better ally.

"Okay, if you want, you're a sworn-in member of this two-man posse, Mike. I plan to head out to Nevada this weekend. I doubt that he's there, but I need to go back to where this all began."

"So when do we fly out, Saturday?"

"We don't. We drive out. If we flew, we'd have to pick up transport when we got there, so we might as well rent an RV here."

"Why an RV?"

"Because I'd rather we didn't leave a trail of motels or a paper trail in our slipstream."

"Okay, partner. So tell me who we're after, and exactly what happened the day you bought it?" Mike said, framing the question more as a stipulation to show trust, than a request.

"OK. But no FBI, this is a private party."

Mike nodded. "You got it."

Cal put his empty cup down and fisted his right hand into his left palm as he took a deep breath. "The Indian who shot me is called Luke. Just before he pulled the trigger, one of the other guys said; 'You can't off a cop, Luke. If you do, they'll never stop looking for us'. And he was right, because I'm back, and I'm looking."

Mike looked a little disappointed. "You mean to say that all we have is the first name of an Indian who may be living somewhere in the Southwest? That's a needle in a field of haystacks' job, Cal."

"O ye of little faith," Cal smiled. "He's an Apache. Don't forget I've seen him. So he is most likely from Arizona. There will be people who know him, or knew him. And we don't have to rely on a vague description. One of my hidden talents is art. I spent my life sketching, just as a hobby. So I can draw a pretty good likeness of him; one that anyone who has seen him would be able to recognize him from."

"Have you done one yet?" Mike said.

"I've been sketching him since I left the hospital. The last one I did is as good as having a photograph of the guy, if I do say so myself."

Cal reached into the inside pocket of the blue linen sports coat – that he had chosen that morning from an extensive range of clothes in Danny's wall-length fitted closet – and passed a folded piece of white cartridge paper to Mike.

"The sketch at the top is how the sonofabitch looked back in ninety-six. And below is how he might look now," Cal said as Mike studied the two pencil drawings.

"So this is the one man war party that we're after?" Mike said, absorbing the images that unbeknown to him bore a striking resemblance to Luke Strayhorse.

"Believe me, Mike. He might have a few more lines, have grown a moustache, or have gray hair now, but overall, that's him. You are looking at...what do the profilers call him, Cochise?"

"I really think we have a chance, Cal," Mike said, suddenly enthusiastic; the name and sketches giving him the belief that they could run him down. "With these and what I got from Rich, we can trace and nail the sonofabitch." Mike fleshed out the drawings in his mind, added color, imagining a three-dimensional face before him. He found it hard to put the sheet of paper down. Cal had somehow captured a look in the eyes that was intense and almost hypnotic; twin pools of liquid pitch that projected a self-assurance that only thinly veiled the pure evil that lurked beneath their surface. He could almost taste the pleasure that capturing or, if absolutely necessary, killing this piece of shit would give him, when the time came.

"Will you organize a decent motor home, Mike? And don't go for cheap and shabby," Cal said. "The cash is no problem, it's covered. I'll break the news to Jim, Linda and Sarah that I'm heading out west, and we'll leave Saturday, early. Phone me when you need credit card details for the transport."

Jim had given Cal Danny's MasterCard, telling him to use it as though it were his own. Now he would have to spend some time practicing the forging of Danny's signature.

Standing, Mike took one more look at the sketches of the Indian, then refolded the sheet of paper and handed it back to Cal, now eager to make arrangements for the trip.

After Cal left the clinic, Mike chewed the fat awhile with Kelly, arranging to go to her place for a meal that evening, and telling her that he would be going on a business trip of indeterminate length, come the weekend. He held back the details, just saying that it was a skip trace.

Out on the street, Mike found himself walking on air, adrenaline already percolating in his veins at the thought of the imminent adventure, which would take him away from his seedy surroundings for what he hoped would be a couple of weeks at least.

Cal told Jim and Linda that he was going to Nevada. They accepted – with no choice in the matter – that he needed to go back and take a nostalgic look at Benson's Creek, and the people who had been a part of his life, even though he knew it would be impossible to make his true identity known, especially to his father. What he did not tell them, was that after leaving the Creek, he intended to track down the man who had taken his, and God knew how many other people's lives.

"Whatever happens, keep in touch, please," Jim said. "Let us know that you are okay. Remember that Linda and I are here for you, and take this." He handed Cal an envelope containing a large amount of cash and more plastic. "Just put it in your pocket, son, and use what you need. Money is the least of our problems at the moment."

Cal noted that Jim had called him, *son*, but also that he had said it in the way that an older man would address a much younger guy, not in a paternal way; it had just been a figure of speech.

"Thanks, Jim," Cal said, accepting the envelope. "I *will* need cash, so I won't refuse it. When this trip is over, I'll be back. After all that I've lost, I think I'm part way qualified to know just how much you are both hurting. Maybe this is just a temporary thing. Ross believes that Danny is still in here with me, and that he could pop back at any time. Like it or not, I may just vanish as quickly as I arrived."

Sarah had become a good friend, and more, a companion. She was someone that Cal could confide in. He enjoyed being around her. She made him smile, and picked him up when he mentally began to sink into a mire of self pity. He sensed that she was more relaxed with him now; that she had begun to know him as a real person, separate from Danny.

On the Friday, Sarah drove Cal over to Manassas, where they stopped off at Ruby Tuesday's for brunch. From concealed speakers, Travis Tritt – who Cal had never heard of, but thought sounded wicked – was bemoaning the plight of the working man, as though he drove a semi truck for a living, or put cars together in a Motown plant.

"I'll be going to Nevada tomorrow with Mike Cassidy," Cal said as casually as possible, as an aside to the main business of devouring a cheeseburger and fries.

"You could have given me more warning," Sarah said. "I'll go home and pack, after I drop you off."

"Hell, no, Sarah," Cal said, taken aback. "You can't come with us."

"Why not? You need to go off and deal with your past. So I'll be there as part of your present. I want to be with you, Cal."

"No, Sarah. You want to be with Danny. You hardly know me, Cal Morgan, and that is who I am. Don't you see that you're trying to reach out to someone who doesn't exist in me? They say that looks are only skin deep, and in my case that's spot on."

"You bastard!" Sarah spat through gritted teeth, causing a passing waitress to turn her head toward their table in brief alarm. "Of course I see Danny every time I look at you. But I also see *you*, looking out through his eyes. I see you as a separate person from Danny, an individual. You think differently, move differently. Christ, I know who you are, and I want to go with you, so please do not patronize me or try to push me away. I'm going to Benson's Creek with or without you."

"Nice speech," Cal said, having listened to the tirade with such concentration that his burger had been held poised, halfway between plate and mouth throughout. "But it could be dangerous, and Mike and I will have enough to worry about without having to look after you as well. I promise I'll come back. Will that do?"

"No, Cal. And if you knew me just a little better, then you would know that once I've made up my mind, I don't change it. What time do we leave tomorrow?"

CHAPTER TWENTY-ONE

MIKE called by to see Brad McCoy, another ex-cop, who had been his partner for four years in the department, and who he had known for much longer than that. Brad now owned The Real McCoy, an RV center just off the Beltway on I-66, where he sold or rented any size or make of motor home that could be named. If the model wanted was not on his extensive lot, or in the showrooms, then he would order it in. Mike decided on a fully loaded Chevrolet Cobra Phoenix 6.5 T.D. six berth model, and Brad cut him a good deal, giving him ten percent discount on the month's rental that Mike paid up front, and even waiving the security deposit.

Brad kept plying Mike with gritty re-heated coffee that was beginning to take on the consistency of liquid tar, as they mulled over a score of old cases they had investigated. Brad was now raking in more money than he had ever made as a cop, but missed the rush that being on the street had given him. Selling campers and playing golf was no substitute for stakeouts and taking down felons. As Mike made to leave, Brad even offered him some work; checking the credit status of prospective buyers who wanted installment plans.

"Thanks for the offer, Brad," Mike said, shaking hands. "Let's discuss it when I'm back in town."

Saturday morning at nine o'clock, Mike pulled up the driveway to the Clayton's house and hit the horn on the Cobra's steering wheel. He had been up most of the night preparing for the trip, feeling too wired to even contemplate sleep. His .38 was cleaned, oiled and packed, as was a 9 millimeter Glock that he was taking along for Cal. The pistols, with a box of shells for each, would remain hidden away until they hopefully closed in on their quarry. Mike had also stopped off at a Safeway in Alexandria and stocked up the vehicle's refrigerator and cupboards with basic necessities. In a way he felt as though he was about to set off on a vacation, not a manhunt. At best, this trip should be no more difficult than many of the skip traces he had chased down. At worst, it could end up with people being killed. On a subconscious level that he was hardly aware of, Mike enjoyed his line of work. The unpredictability and diversity of each case made every day dissimilar and therefore more interesting. He could never have been a desk-jockey, or pursued what might be considered a 'normal' nine-till-five job. It was horses for courses, he supposed.

"All set?" Mike asked as Cal appeared at the front door carrying a large duffel bag and a large expandable rolling suitcase. "Looks as though you're toting enough luggage for two, buddy."

"He is," Sarah said, following Cal out.

"You must be kidding," Mike said, turning the ignition key, killing the engine and then exiting the vehicle. "This was never part of the deal, Cal. There's no way that Sarah can go on this picnic. You should know better."

It took a while for Mike to accept that Sarah was joining the team. He reluctantly acknowledged that it would appear more innocuous; a young couple on vacation, with dad along. Although he was not happy with the dad-tag, and made it quite clear – for the record – that Sarah was about as welcome as a leper in a shopping mall. Cal had even resorted to telling Sarah the truth, hoping that it would deter her. He'd laid it on the line that the trip to Nevada was just a prelude to what was to be a search for a psycho who collected tattoos the way some folk collected Franklin Mint plates.

Sarah had paled at that, and pulled the right side of her shorts down, just far enough for Cal and Mike to see the delicate heart-shaped garland of roses tattooed on her hip.

The two men admired both the shapely hip and the intricate design. Cal diverted his gaze with difficulty, surprised that his face felt the same color as the artistic blooms. He blushed with uncharacteristic embarrassment.

"I hope to God that your pretty picture isn't some kind of omen," Mike said gruffly as he stepped back into the RV, to start it up and swing the Cobra round in the circle driveway and roll out onto the main road, to leave Alexandria on a journey of ultimate confrontation: one that they may not have so eagerly set off on had they known what horrors lay ahead.

"Well, campers," Mike said, back in holiday mood. "Just another two and a half thousand miles, give or take, to our first port of call."

Hank Morgan was now seventy-six. The ravages of time; the desert sun, and the constant gnawing grief over his long dead son had carved deep lines in his worn face. Rain, frost, heat and the passing of countless seasons can fracture and erode the hardest rock, and

Hank was not as granite-hard as he had spent most of his life purporting to be. He still stood tall, although the years had marginally stooped his six-two frame. His eyes were also more lackluster, not sparkling with a love for life that he had once embraced. His hair was still thick, though gone to snow-white. Age had also conferred on him a blossoming gift of arthritis, which had sunk its sharp, hot fangs into his hands and knees; the crippling venom slowing him up some, but not stopping him.

After Cal had been laid to rest, Hank had struggled to make sense of a life that had first taken his wife to an early grave, and then his son from him. If it were all part of some vast eternal plan, then it sucked, and he could neither understand nor forgive it. God's sense of humor never ceased to amaze and dishearten him, to the point that he chose to turn his back on the concept of an almighty creator being a feasible possibility. The chaos theory, based on unpredictability became a far more appealing and rational doctrine to adopt. His work as sheriff probably kept him on the right side of a fine line that he could so easily have crossed. Without his obligation and professional pride in serving the community, he may well have slipped into irrevocable melancholia. Filling his days with the problems of others helped keep his own at arms' length. And of course there was Mildred. For the first few months after Cal's death, Mildred had nearly force-fed Hank, forever fussing round him like a mother hen. And then as time distanced him from the tragedy, dulling the pain as he moved inchmeal through the stages of grief, Mildred became more than a concerned and caring friend, she became a staff for him to lean on; an essential part of his life.

It had been twelve months before his retirement that Hank finally succumbed and asked Mildred to marry him. They tied the knot within twenty-four hours' of Hank handing in his badge and took a trip to Yosemite to mark an end to one chapter of life and the beginning of another. On their return to the Creek, home for Mildred became Hank's two bed bungalow out on Sulfur Spring Road, just a few minutes walk from the amenities of Main Street. They were happy together, enjoying life at a slow and easy pace; their pensions and savings adequate for their modest needs.

Cal had made a good decision by choosing not to fly out to Nevada. Several days living together in the close confines of the RV gave the three of them the time that they needed to really get to know each other and fine-tune relationships.

The night before they left Virginia, Mike – not being a fan of satnav – had flipped through the pages of his dog-eared road atlas to work out what to him seemed the most practical route to Benson's Creek. He'd decided to first head northwest to Chicago, then pick up I-80, which would take them all the way west to Nevada.

Mike and Cal took turns at the wheel, and, by choice Sarah took charge of the galley, as she called the small dinette. She did her best to serve up proper cooked meals rather than TV dinners and instant food, which if left to their own devices the other two would have subsisted on.

The motor home had two bedrooms; one at the rear with an en suite bathroom – which Sarah immediately commandeered without argument, to give her maximum privacy – and another, much smaller. The main cabin area was well furnished and roomy, carpeted in deep Wilton of a nondescript color that Sarah insisted was oyster, Cal thought mushroom, and Mike decreed gray. A shower opposite the galley was a luxury that each of them used every day. And the second toilet meant that the one adjacent to Sarah's bedroom was used by her exclusively.

After living for so long in his shabby office, Mike was already contemplating buying the RV off Brad on their return, reckoning that it would vastly improve his quality of life and go a long way to easing the back pain that he blamed on the lumpy sofa in his squalid workplace.

Cal's initial euphoria waned, and he became more morose and withdrawn as they neared and then eventually crossed the state line into Nevada. He was lost in another time to Mike and Sarah, his mind now reliving a life that he knew could not be recaptured by physically returning to a geographical point of reference. After passing through Imlay, on the last few miles of gravel road that led to the Creek, he sat at the dinette table staring out at the barren landscape, clenching and relaxing his fists, suffering mental turmoil.

Sarah was tense with concern, but left Cal to his thoughts, staying up front with Mike.

"Maybe coming back here was a bad idea," Sarah said in a low voice.

"It was Cal's call. He needs to do it." Mike replied.

They rolled into Main Street, and Mike brought the Cobra to a stop next to a small park that was fenced around with railings. Cal looked out at the now dark green painted palisade, through the scorched bushes and twisted tree trunks, his eyes drawn to the sun-dappled head and shoulders of Josiah Benson; the visible part of the statue still splashed white by ill-mannered birds.

"That was one hell of a trip, guys," Mike said, massaging the back of his neck to loosen taut muscles that ached after driving for a lengthy spell.

"So this is the place that you've told us so much about," Sarah said to Cal, attempting to prize him out of his hardening shell.

"Uh, yeah. This is it. Must seem like the boonies to you two city folk. And stop worrying, Sarah, I'm fine, honest."

Sarah knew that Cal was far from fine, and neither was she. When she looked at him she still saw Danny, the twenty-one-year-old who she loved. But her feelings were becoming confused. Guilt snapped at her mind with spasmodic, vicious bites, eating at the edges of her consciousness as she admitted to herself that she was becoming attracted to the man behind the façade of Danny. Christ, Cal Morgan was old enough to be her father. He had been born way back in nineteen-sixty-five, which made him fifty-two. That *was* older than her dad. But he had no knowledge of the last twenty-one years, so was he still only thirty-one? Or would he be classed as the same age as the body that he inhabited? It was all too befuddling to work out.

Cal surveyed the street. It was as if parts of it had undergone drastic changes overnight, with some businesses altered beyond recognition. The Blueberry Pie diner had been renamed The Lite Bite, but still served the same function. The Sawtooth Saloon had been modernized, and now professed, in large blue and red neon-tube lettering, to be The Eldorado Lounge. Harper's General Store had retained a measure of its former rustic charm, although it now displayed its wares through a lot more plate-glass frontage than it had boasted previously. It was just called Harper's now, the general store tag having been dropped.

Cal's forlorn gaze lingered on the sheriff's office, and his throat tightened as sadness and nostalgia welled up and swept through him; a tide of emotional pain. To him only a very short time had passed since he had worked there with his dad.

"Come on, Sarah," Mike said. "Let's go explore, and leave Cal to acclimatize." He could see that his friend needed space to try and put things into some kind of perspective; to absorb the fact that he had been away from his hometown for over two decades, not just a few weeks.

CHAPTER TWENTY-TWO

IT was pure coincidence. As Cal sat reviewing his last memories of that terrible, fateful day, he brought to mind the image of the big, red-haired guy, who had been standing behind the Indian, and wondered what had become of him. And at exactly the same time, Jerry Sullivan was thinking of him, from a hospital bed in Boston.

Jerry was now down to eighty pounds, a sunken-eyed skeletal figure, virtually unrecognizable as the former burly individual he had been. The cancer had started in his right lung, and following radical surgery and chemotherapy, he had gone into remission. That had been two years ago. He had begun to think that he had beaten it, but then it resurfaced with a vengeance. Now, the insidious, creeping invader had lodged in his colon, and was feeding, growing, spreading, reaching out its mutated cells to consume him from within. Jerry knew that he was dying, and reviled the mindfuck system that insisted on keeping him alive. The miracle of modern medicine – on his unsolicited behalf – had decreed in its wisdom that it served some edifying purpose to prolong his fear and pain, supposedly in the mistaken belief that total loss of dignity and no measurable quality of life was for some reason a state worthy of preserving for as long as possible. The increasing amount of morphine that they were administering would finally release him from his suffering, though, and he would slip into a welcome coma; a precursor to death, which would end his torment; a torment that could not be reversed at this late stage, even should they find a miracle cure that day.

What a crazy world! No other animal would be allowed to suffer in such a way. It would be considered criminal, cruel and inhumane to prolong its agony and misery in the manner that they were protracting his. He sorely wished that he had taken himself out, before being unable to have any say in the matter. Between the Hippocratic Oath that took the life-preserving obligation too far, and the religious factions that decried euthanasia and actively fought any form of mercy killing becoming legalized, countless thousands of terminally ill patients needlessly died wretchedly at the archaic legal system's whim.

Jerry had settled down at the turn of the century, finding love and stability with a girl who he had lived next door to as a child. Keeley had been a non-Catholic divorcee, raising a ten-year-old son alone, when Jerry had returned to Boston. It was love at first sight. He was smitten the second that he set eyes on her. A mutual friend had introduced them at Carson's Irish bar, and Jerry was hooked, on the line, and in the keep-net before the evening was over. He went straight, finding a driving job with a local dumpster-hire company, and soon after that he married Keeley, taking on the role of husband and stepfather with a gusto and commitment that amazed him. He had never felt so contented or happy. Although once in a while he opened the trapdoor to the dark attic of his mind, in which were stored the closeted memories of his murky past. His regrets were many, but all paled into insignificance when he relived the episode in Nevada. The memory could still bring him out in a cold sweat in the hours' of darkness, to knot his stomach with the sensation of live worms twisting and writhing in his gut. The replay of the terrible events swirled through his mind unbidden, vivid and nightmarish. He had always wished that he could go back and somehow change what had taken place. If only he and Johnny had not stopped to give that fucking Indian a lift. If they had just kept going...If...If. That young girl had suffered so much, and he couldn't lay off all the blame on Luke. The bastard had not forced *him* to take his turn with her; but she shouldn't have died. The Indian had gone fucking berserk and mutilated and murdered her. Jerry's mind refused to edit the carnage and gory details. For what seemed the millionth time he saw the Apache bite her nose off, and was sickened to recall that he stood back and watched as her throat was cut.

And then the hick cop had turned up, and yet again he had stood by as the cop was shot dead, like a dog in the street. It had been *so* wrong, all of it. The memory loop kept playing. Now he was in the ghost town again, with Johnny dead at the bottom of a mine shaft. All that had stopped him winding up next to Johnny, covered in rocks, had been a sixth sense that the Indian meant to kill him. He had escaped in the camper, leaving the dumbfuck Apache out there. He hoped that a fucking rattlesnake had bitten him in the ass. Although it would probably have been the snake that died from the bite, killed by the poison that Luke was full of.

Jerry had been convinced that he would be caught, even though he had wiped the motor home clean and torched it. But with time, and each mile farther east he traveled, the safer he began to feel. The only person who could sing was Luke, and he wasn't likely to tell anyone...unless he was ever arrested. A small part of Jerry had always waited for a knock at the door, or a hand on his shoulder; ever expectant that the past would catch up with him.

Now, lying tubed-up, so weak and in constant, if dulled pain, he felt light-headed and nauseous. Everything seemed to look distant, and through paper thin, half-closed eyelids, Keeley appeared to be moving away from him, spinning as she receded. He raised his bony left hand from the sheet and revolved his index finger to signify that he was dizzy. His right hand was being held firmly by his wife, but he could no longer feel her grip. Keeley looked down at her dying husband, unable to hold back the tears as she waited for the inevitable.

Jerry hated the dark. And now he was engulfed by it, being sucked down into a vortex of pitch black Delphic blindness. His mind screamed in silent terror as death entered him, to make its presence known; to overwhelm his frail existence and drag him horror-stricken into the unknown.

The scrawny hand lost its feeble grip, and Keeley realized that Jerry was no longer looking at her, or anything. His eyes slowly rolled back in their sockets, and his shallow breathing stopped.

Jerry had left the building.

CHAPTER TWENTY-THREE

A cobalt sky slashed through with rapier-thin clouds met Cal as he stepped down from the RV and made his way over to the Lite Bite to join Sarah and Mike. He had decided that he wanted company, needing relief from his scrambled thoughts. He joined them in a window booth, and all three ordered the works; bacon, eggs over easy, hash browns, and pancakes with maple syrup; enough to well and truly contradict the establishment's name. Later, as the waitress paused to freshen their coffee, Cal noted the name printed on the plastic tag that was pinned to her blouse.

"Cindy," he said, attracting her attention. "I wonder if you could help me."

"Shoot. What can I do for you, handsome?" Cindy said, smiling and running her tongue over her top lip in coquettish fashion, briefly giving the wad of gum in her mouth some respite. The way in which she had addressed Cal and the intimacy of her smile was not lost on Sarah, who acknowledged that it caused her to feel a slight but unmistakable twinge of jealousy.

"Does Hank Morgan live hereabouts?" Cal asked the girl.

Cindy looked out through the window. "He sure does, hon. And if I ain't mistaken, and I ain't, he just walked into Harper's store."

"Thanks," Cal said, abruptly rising from his seat and heading for the door.

Mike's hand gripped his shoulder before he had time to make the street.

"Don't do it, Cal, let it go," Mike urged. "You'll only open an old wound and start it bleeding again. Whatever you say to him, there is no way that you can expect him to believe you. It's too off-the-wall, and you know it."

Gently, but firmly, Cal gripped Mike's hand, pulled it free and said, "I have no idea what I'm going to do. But I have to see him, up close. He's my dad for Chrissake!"

Cal entered Harper's and was taken aback by the extensively altered interior. The long oak counter had gone, and the clutter of barbed wire coils, steel pails, tools and other sundry goods had also vanished from the front of the store. It had always been a jumbled mishmash that only old man Harper and his sons seemed to have a mental map of, enabling them to lay their hands on whatever was required within seconds. Now, sterile aisles under the harsh glare of overhead fluorescent bars met the eye. The rear of the store had been extended back, and the packaged products on metal shelving stretched away in an overall blandness that reminded Cal of countless supermarkets, devoid of character and instantly forgettable.

Hank was at the far end of the first aisle, checking out a pair of rugged Timberland boots. Cal made his way – as if browsing – to within ten feet of him, before his dad looked up, and being stared at, nodded, the way one does when in close proximity to someone making eye contact. Cal was hardly aware that he had jumped. He was suddenly in his father's mind, soaking up his life, seeing his mom again, and himself as a baby; a boy; a teenager, and finally as an adult. His dad was still grieving; the sadness simmering like a pan of stew on a low light. Hank missed Cal every day that dawned, and would go to his grave mourning his son. Cal slipped back, away from the poignant pain.

"Are you okay, son?" Hank said with a quizzical expression in his concerned eyes. "You look as though you just saw a ghost. I'm not that frightenin', am I?"

Against his better judgment, every nerve end jangling with a mixture of trepidation and excitement, Cal made a decision.

"Do you believe in life after death?" Cal blurted out. "By that I mean in a continuation of an individual's spirit? Is your mind open to the possibility of it being a fact?"

Hank's eyes narrowed. "You a Mormon or somethin', boy?" He said. "You tryin' to sell eternal life to me, just because I'm gettin' to an age that makes me a lot nearer to heaven or hell than most folk?"

"No, sir," Cal said. "I'm asking you if you can be told something personal, which is so incredible that it might just give your old heart a seizure, or cause you to clip me one on the chin."

Hank looked long and hard into the young man's eyes, and saw sincerity, desperation and sadness; not the look of someone deranged, or a salesman. In fact it was a strangely familiar look, disturbing but benign. He had not lost his cop curiosity, and found himself intrigued.

"Spit it out then, son. I'll risk it," Hank said, almost regretting opening the door to whatever might follow. "Just call Doc Johnson if I keel over from the shock of what you plan on tellin' me and don't get back up."

Cal smiled. His dad had not lost his sense of humor, or his inquisitiveness. "I've got an RV parked up over there," he said, pointing through the front window to the Cobra. "Opposite the Blu...The Lite Bite. Come on board, have a beer, and give me a few minutes of your time. I promise that it's important to both of us."

Again, Hank studied the young man, checked his body language, his overall demeanor; ran a sanity check. He could sense no sign of threat.

"Lead the way, son," he said. "It's not often these days that my nose gets to itch over much. But I'm tellin' you now, if you start in on tryin' to sell me the good book, or any other goddamn thing, I'm outta there. Understood?"

Mike watched Cal and the old man board the RV, and saw Cal raise the palm of his hand and push it towards the diner. The gesture was obvious...stay away. He swapped worried looks with Sarah. It appeared that they were going to be drinking Cindy's coffee awhile longer.

"Shoot," Hank said, sitting at the dinette table and looking around, admiring the luxury of the motor home's interior.

Cal gathered his thoughts, formulating a way to begin as he handed a chilled can of Bud light to his, as yet, unknowing dad.

"Okay, here goes," he said, taking a deep breath. "If I told you that I had died, and then after a long period of time had woken up and found myself in someone else...in their body, could you...*can* you look past how bizarre that sounds and imagine that it could be true?"

Hank shook his head and said, "No, son. I can see that you mean what you're sayin', but why pick on me to tell this stuff to? Or do you tell it to every stranger you run into that'll listen?"

"No, just you. And if you can handle it, I can turn your life upside down, hopefully for the better. But the shock will be the biggest that you've had in twenty-one years."

Hank froze; an icicle fast-freezing to form up the length of his spine. What could this young man possibly know about events that happened at that specific time?

"Are you from a newspaper or TV station?" He inquired brusquely. "Because all of that was a long time ago, and I don't think that there's any new ground to cover."

Cal shook his head. "I've got some new ground that needs covering, concerning what happened. And you'll want to know what it is, I promise you."

"Nice 'n' easy," Hank whispered. "Lay it on me."

"First," Cal said. "Forget how I look. Just open your mind and listen with your heart, because every word that I am about to say is the absolute truth. I had no intention of speaking to you about this, but when I saw you, well, commonsense went out the window. I had to let you know."

Hank was gripping his beer can so tightly that it was being crushed, forcing the contents out of the top, to foam and pool around his hand on the table.

Cal continued. "When Cal was six-years-old, he took your service revolver out the back of the house onto the stoop and fired it. The recoil knocked him on his butt, and you came running. He'd dropped the gun, and you picked it up, and then helped him to his feet. You took him back into the kitchen, and he thought he was going to get the biggest whupping of his life. You didn't hit him, though. You sat him down and talked about how dangerous guns were, and the harm that they could do in the wrong hands. You asked him to promise not to touch one again, until he was older and could be taught how to handle one properly, by you. Oh, and the bullet that he'd fired had gone through his mom's best damask tablecloth, which had been out on the line drying."

"Stop!" Hank said, choked, with tears running freely down his furrowed cheeks. "You can't know that. Nobody does."

"Nobody but you and Cal," Cal said.

Hank pushed himself up from the table. "I'm too old to start believin' in X-File crap, and you have no right to—"

"Listen," Cal said, firmly. "There are two people across the street that didn't believe at first. But they know who I am now, and so do the doctors at a hospital in Washington D.C. So whether you believe it or not, you're going to have to accept that however impossible it seems to be, it's true. I'm Cal, and I'm back."

Hank slumped back onto the bench seat, ashen, shaking his head in denial.

"Dad," Cal said. "How do you think I feel? One second I was being shot dead, and the next I was waking up in a hospital to find I was in a stranger's body, thousands of miles and twenty-one years later."

A calculated expression formed on Hank's face. "After Cal's mom died, I took him on a trip to Disneyland," he said. "Then we drove down to Tijuana; even haggled for and ended up payin' too much for a couple of real Mexican sombreros. Question is, can you tell me the name of the motel that we stayed at for three nights in San Diego? It's a name that Cal never forgot."

Cal smiled. "Nice try, Dad, and sneaky. No wonder you were the sheriff for so long. Truth is, a couple of weeks after mom died, you were getting worried about me; the way I started withdrawing into myself and hardly eating. So you took some leave and we did go on a trip. But it wasn't to Walt's place. We went up to Fort Pack Lake in Montana and stayed at the Hell Creek Lodge for ten days, fishing, canoeing and rock climbing. It was the best time of my life, and followed the worst. It helped me accept that mom was gone, and went a long way to straightening my head out. Do you remember the guy who owned the lodge? He had one eye and the biggest, bushiest, blackest beard that either of us had ever seen, and he scared the shit out of me."

As Cal finished reminiscing, tears filled both men's eyes.

"Cal, can that really be you in there? I want to believe it, but it's so damn impossible."

"You'd better believe it. I can tell you every detail of my life up to being murdered. I don't understand why, or how, but I'm back. I love you, Dad, and I'm sorry that I messed up that morning at Backbone Ridge. I was careless."

"I love you too, Cal. You just took over twenty years of lead weight off these old shoulders."

Father and son, now reunited, embraced, and both found more meaning and purpose again; a reason to live.

"I'm going to introduce you to two special people," Cal said. "They're keeping out of the way, over at The Blueberry Pie."

"You mean The Lite Bite," Hank said, smiling. "It hasn't been called the Blueberry Pie since Pat Evans sold up and high-tailed it to Florida, back in oh-two."

Hank phoned Mildred and told her that he was going to be awhile, and that he was having a beer with an old colleague. It wasn't a lie.

Cal waved across to where Sarah and Mike were watching the RV, and they hurried across the street.

Mike and Sarah sat opposite Cal and Hank at the table and talked. Sarah told Hank the story of how Danny had suffered the head injury, and that Cal had somehow taken his place when he regained consciousness. Mike filled in on how he had become involved, and of the inquiries he'd made for Ross Fairburn on Cal's behalf, and that he had found all the details that Cal gave about the murders in ninety-six to be true. Everything had checked out.

Hank listened, still astonished at what he now believed was some sort of miracle. He was overjoyed that his son was back, but also felt a deep sympathy for Sarah, and for Danny's parents, because his and Cal's gain had been their loss.

"I can sense your empathy and feeling of awkwardness, Mr. Morgan," Sarah said, reaching out and placing her hand over Hank's. "Please don't talk or act as though you were walking on glass. I'm so happy for you and Cal. Everything will work out. Life has a way of sorting things."

"Make it, Hank, would you, Sarah? Mr. Morgan sounds a mite stiff and formal."

Mike and Cal brought Hank up to speed with the information that they had on Cal's and Trudy Henderson's murderer.

"You mean to say that the crazy sonofabitch is still out there, still killin'?" Hank said.

"We've no way of knowing whether he's alive or dead, Hank. We're going with the belief that he's still above ground," Mike said. "He's a serial killer and on the FBI's most wanted list. The rewards on this scumbag would keep us all out of gainful employment for at least ten years, if we nailed him."

"What're you plannin' on doing next?" Hank said, addressing Cal.

"Run him down, Dad. With his name and knowing what he looks like, (he showed Hank the sketch), it'll just be a matter of time before we catch up with him. He's got to be stopped, and I want to be the one to do it. By that, I mean us." Cal said, looking at Mike.

"Where do you plan to start?"

"Arizona. Apache reservations. We only need to meet up with one person who knows him, and he's history."

"What makes you think that if you do find someone who knows this low-life that they'll talk?" Hank said, frowning.

"They don't have to talk or tell Cal anything," Sarah said. "He has a hell of a new party trick. He can read minds."

The next morning, Hank left home early and walked into town. He had arranged to meet the others and go out to Backbone Ridge with them, to the spot where he had found Cal's body. It was the first time he had ever physically been back to the crime scene, although he had returned there daily in his thoughts, never able to eradicate the location from his mind. Even returning with Cal in his new guise did not allay the numbing abhorrence that the site had instilled in him.

Pensively, Cal studied his surroundings, reliving what should have been his final minutes on earth. This was the spot that he felt was the real beginning; the starting point of his quest to settle what had gone down here so long ago. He had thought that returning to the ridge would in some way be an enlightening experience, but there was nothing. Rocks, sand and mesquite possessed no minds that he could tap into for information. There was no lasting imprint of that day's outrage lingering like a ghostly episode, eternally replaying the appalling moments. No spiritual residue remained, unable to rest until fitting retribution was exacted. It was just a harsh, barren and god-awful place that brought vivid scenes of brutality back to torment him.

On the drive back to town they were all silent. It was Hank who finally broke the funereal mood that had settled over them like a damp blanket. "I told Mildred about this, Cal," he said. "I couldn't keep it to myself. We don't have any secrets. I sat her down and laid it all out, just the way it happened, from when you came up to me in Harper's."

"And what did she say, Dad? Could she even begin to believe any of it?"

"Well, she credits me with more horse sense than I deserve, and tends to think that there's more to heaven and earth than meets the eye. Said if a cynical old fart like me believed it, then it must be true. She wants to meet you. So if the three of you would do us the honor...dinner's at eight, sharp."

Mildred watched the two men and the girl as they stepped down from the RV and made their way up the path to the door. Hank had described the young man who claimed to be Cal, and she studied him intensely as he approached the house; part of her frightened to the core for Hank, in case this was some kind of hoax, or something even more cruel and maleficent.

Opening the door, Mildred bid them enter and led them through to the living kitchen, where Hank was sitting at a large pine table.

"Pleased to meet you all," Mildred said reticently, hoping that she *would* in retrospect be pleased to have met them, at the close of the evening. "Sit yourselves down."

With introductions over and freshly-brewed coffee in mugs before them, Mildred turned her attention to Cal. "Hank tells me that you're Cal, back among us somehow," she stated, her voice neutral, as was her expression and direct, unreadable hazel eyes.

"Yup, Mildred. Straight out of 'Ripley's'. So, believe it or not, I'm really here. I look different, but underneath I'm still the same loveable hunk who pecked you on the cheek every morning when I came into the office."

Mildred was taken aback, and had she been holding her coffee mug, would have probably dropped it. "I...I want to believe this so much," she said. "So will you humor an old woman and let me ask you something that only Cal and I know?"

"No problem, Mildred," Cal said. "But make it good, because I don't want you to have any misgivings. Half-believing isn't enough. I want you to be totally convinced, so give it your best shot."

Mildred paused, looking somewhere into the middle distance as she reached back in time to pluck an incident from her memory: one that if recalled by this claimant to Cal's identity would substantiate the truth of it beyond any possible doubt.

"I had an old cat," Mildred began. "And one morning I brought him into the office. He was under the weather, and I was worried about him. Do you remember that morning?"

Cal smiled and nodded. "Yes, Mildred. It was in the fall, late October, and you carried him into the office in a big cardboard box. It had an old cardigan that he favored on the bottom of it, and you'd thrown a couple of his favorite toys in for good measure. He was as black as night, long-haired, and with a crooked tail that was the legacy of an altercation with a car. You called him August, after Dan August; a TV cop played by Burt Reynolds, way back in the dark ages; an actor I know you had a crush on. Well, I tried stroking August that morning, not au fait with his savage disposition, and he ended up hanging off my chest, claws in so deep I thought I was doing a sun dance. My shirt was shredded and bloody, and all you could say was, 'There, there, August, be nice. Cal won't hurt you'. It must have taken five minutes to separate us. You had always joked that he hunted coyotes in preference to mice, and after that episode I didn't doubt it."

"Oh, dear God, Cal!" Mildred said, reaching across the tabletop to grip his hand with hers. "I don't understand how this can be, but I know that it's you in there." She blinked rapidly, her eyes glistening with tears.

Sarah helped Mildred with dinner; chicken fried steak, mashed potatoes, corn on the cob and gravy. And while they cooked, the three men – all ex-cops – swapped career details and told heavily embellished stories as they drank beer out back on the decking.

It was a good down-home meal, and a perfect evening that filled the air of the bungalow with laughter and more than a little love. With the RV being parked up outside the house, they allowed themselves an over-indulgence of alcohol. No one was going to be driving that night.

It was late when Hank and Mildred's guests finally said goodnight and wove their slightly inebriated way across to the motor home. They were giggling like teenagers as they stumbled to the vehicle's door, where Mike, on his fourth attempt, managed to locate the lock with the key and gain entry.

The sun was up, and after an early breakfast they were ready to leave. Hank and Cal walked a little way from the house; father and son, taking a few minutes out to make their hopefully only temporary farewell to each other. Hank had his arm draped over Cal's shoulder, unashamedly enjoying his son's nearness and wishing that it could be for longer.

"Son, I know that you have to do this," he said. "But do me a favor. If you get close to the bastard, call in the cavalry. Don't risk gettin' killed by this prick again. You might just wind up stayin' dead next time."

"I'll play it safe, Dad. And when it's over we can spend some quality time together. How does that sound?"

"That sounds just fine, Cal. We have a lot of time to catch up on."

Cal did not remind his dad that hardly any time at all had passed for *him*. It was Hank's life that had rolled by in real time, and even that was no secret to Cal. He had absorbed all of his dad's life to date when he forged the mind-link in Harper's store.

They hugged each other, and then walked back to the others.

Mike took the wheel, and as they pulled away from the brick bungalow with the white picket fence, Cal and Sarah waved from the rear bedroom window of the Cobra, until the elderly couple who stood at the gate was out of sight.

Heading back to I-80, Cal was a different person from the wrung-out and maudlin man who had arrived at the Creek. He was checking the road map and humming along to the stereo, that was playing that old outlaw, Willie Nelson; who was warbling *On The Road Again*, in that clear, reedy and unmistakable voice of his.

BOOK THREE

THE HUNT

CHAPTER TWENTY-FOUR

HOME to Luke was a large, solid, one-storey structure. Saddle notch joints anchored the corners, and the logs were packed with lime for insulation. A deep porch extended the length of the frontage; an addition built on in the thirties. The dwelling had stood for eighty winters, and there was no reason why it shouldn't stand for eighty more.

The cabin stood in a large clearing, surrounded by alder, aspen and pine in profusion, north of Bonita in the Coronado National Forest. Its location rendered it hidden, a half mile from a highway that in winter was closed more often than it was open.

Luke's aunt, Belle Morita, had lived in the cabin for over thirty years, and Luke had used it, and his aunt, for a great many of them. This was his base of operations, just south of the San Carlos reservation. He still had many acquaintances and associates on the res'; men whom he would meet with on occasion at a roadhouse called The Buckeye, which was situated on the outskirts of Bylas. It was a seedy bar-come-diner; a rundown joint patronized exclusively by Indians. Its large graveled parking lot was a trading post for hot automobiles, the fencing of stolen goods, and all manner of illegal transactions.

Belle had turned sixty, but was still a trim and striking woman, not beautiful but handsome, and not yet gone to fat. Her raven hair was streaked silver, and usually worn in beaded braids, which framed a face of strong character, with high prominent cheekbones below oil-black eyes.

Belle's uncle, Charlie, had died in the winter of eighty-six, and lain frozen to the cabin floor until the following spring. He had been ravaged by a variety of critters, and was reduced to gleaming bones by the time they found him, which had slowed up official identification. The coroner had eventually ruled, from scrappy dental records, that the remains were those of Charlie, and released the skeleton to Belle, having no idea of the cause of death, but finding no evidence to suggest foul play. Belle had been the sole beneficiary, and had inherited the cabin, its contents, and a few hundred dollars. She had moved into her new home the week after laying what was left of Charlie to rest.

Belle had no children, and had not remarried after her husband, John, had been drowned in a flash flood back in seventy-eight.

Luke had started visiting Belle soon after she had moved in to 'Charlie's place'. He began to call regularly and stay over, enjoying the remoteness of the cabin's location, and eventually the warmth of his aunt's body, which she was only too eager to pleasure him with. It was not until the fall of ninety-six that he had moved in on a semi-permanent basis, staying through till the spring of the following year; holed up and lying low.

Belle knew that Luke was a thief, and that his main source of income came by way of dealing in stolen cars. He avoided regular work, and would have no truck with authority or officialdom in any guise. He led a clandestine life, appearing and vanishing like a lone wolf in a blizzard, giving Belle no indication of when he would materialize, or for how long he might stay. He looked after her, though. He always gave her money, and sometimes a lot of it. And his lovemaking was much appreciated. She enjoyed sex, and he more than satisfied her needs. The relationship between them had become a bond, developing to an extent that neither of them had anticipated, or would have admitted to. For disparate reasons, each had become a little dependent on the other.

Winter was Belle's favorite season. Luke would settle in for a couple of months, keeping the cold-room stocked with dressed game that he trapped or shot. And she kept the shelves of the earthen cellar packed with mason jars full of pickles and preserves. To Belle, winter was clean, white; a peaceful and tranquil time of year that she always wished would last forever. The log fire gave them warmth, and oil lamps allowed her to weave, sew and read by.

Luke had his own bedroom, not that he slept in it often. But it was his private domain; a place to be alone and have space when he craved solitude. The room was Spartan, with few furnishings: a bed, chest of oak drawers and a closet. Bright rugs featuring bold tribal designs – that Belle had woven – were scattered across the sturdy floorboards. The solid timber closet, that Luke had built, stretched across one side of the room, wall to wall, serving a dual purpose. Behind the clothes and the false back was a spacious hidden compartment that housed his prized possessions; items that were for his eyes only; a black museum of macabre specimens.

The secret cache held a gleaming, stainless steel Colt Python, several boxes of shells, an ornately-worked, pearl-handled derringer, and twelve thousand dollars in bills no larger than fifties. On a separate shelf stood a padlocked metal ammo box, which was the citadel in which he stored his trophies. Individually wrapped in waxed cloth were thirty slivers of human flesh, each cured and preserved for posterity. Luke would, when the need arose, take them from their dark crypt and lay them out on the bed's patch quilt, in the order in which they had been collected. Each one triggered – with perfect recall – the vivid memory of the hunt, and the pleasure that had preceded their harvesting. All bore a unique illustration. This was an assortment of tattoos that served as a scrapbook of good times had; a mummified record of past conquests, sexual pleasure, mutilation, and ultimately, death. Luke would fondle each one in turn, as foreplay to the main event.

He sat naked and cross-legged on the bed holding one of the thin, ovoid-shaped piece of human leather. It was perhaps five inches in length by three at its widest, impregnated with the inked image of a rose; the red petals now a faded orange, due to the tanning process. At the broadest edge, the fragment bore a now dark brown circle of aureole topped with a wrinkled, gathered nipple. He placed the supple remnant onto his left thigh, smoothing it with the palm of his hand to feel the cool, moisturized flesh cling to him. He stroked the nipple with his thumb, his eyes closed, head back slightly, right hand encircling his erection, slowly masturbating.

As usual, it all flooded back to him as clearly as though it were just taking place. He had picked the bitch up near Salt Lake City in the late summer of nineteen-ninety-two. She had told him that her name was Dawn, and that she was hitching west to Frisco.

Luke could even rekindle the smell of the black vinyl covering of the diner's bench seats, and the powerful combined aroma redolent of fried food, sweat, stale cigarette smoke and coffee, that clung to every surface and pervaded the air, as much a part of the establishment as the fixtures and fittings. He had eaten with her, talked and joked, and then paid the check and offered to take her as far as Reno, where, he told her, he lived with his wife and two daughters.

The girl accepted the lift, even hinted that she would be happy to show her gratitude, if he knew what she meant. Oh, yes, he knew what she fuckin' meant all right. What she didn't know was that she would get far more than she intended to give. He remained friendly and talkative as the boring little slut started to tell him the story of her pathetic and worthless life.

Taking a left onto a back road from Riverton, Luke told her that it was a short cut and linked up with I-80 west, which was the truth. After fifteen minutes, he pulled off the country road and drove the stolen station wagon down a tree-lined track, stopping well into the side under cover of thick foliage, a hundred yards from the little-used gravel top.

It was almost too easy. The dumbfuck whore thought that he wanted a quickie or a blowjob before continuing on.

Luke let her unzip him and take him into her mouth. Her hot lips and flicking tongue withdrew after a few seconds, and she sat back, pulling her calico skirt up to her waist and quickly slipping off her panties. She fumbled under the seat, found the lever that released it on its track, and pushed it back to its limit, to give her room to spread her thighs and display her shaven pubes for Luke to admire by the ambient light.

That was when he hit her. His fist connected with such force that he felt and heard her cheekbone fracture. Her head bounced off the side window, and she slumped forward, rendered unconscious by the double impact.

Dawn drifted back, confused and not knowing what had happened. She was outside the vehicle now, cold and naked, with the moonlight shafting through the trees, painting the scene in stark blue-black and white. Her mouth was covered, and her arms were bound behind her back, causing her hands to dig into her spine. The man, who she had wrongly believed to be harmless, was squatting next to her, silent and also naked, watching her. She cringed, pulled back, her face alive with red-hot pain. He reached out and ran his finger over her breast, tracing the outline of the bright red rose tattoo. Bringing his thumb into play he pinched her large and rigid nipple with enough force to bring even more tears to her streaming eyes, before pushing her passive, shaking legs apart and moving between them, entering her quickly, deeply.

Luke had lowered his face to hers, took her nose into his mouth, sucking it, exploring the nostrils with the tip of his tongue, before lodging his bottom teeth against the septum and pressing his top incisors against the bridge. As he reached a shuddering climax, he bit down, slowly at first, twisting, wrenching with his strong teeth, tasting the warm, salty blood as it flowed into his mouth, to then ejaculate inside her, moaning and biting harder, taking the nose away from her face to spit the bloody lump between her heaving breasts.

As Luke reached across for his booted knife, Dawn went into seizure, jerking spasmodically, the irises of her eyes upturned, with only the whites of the bulging orbs shining in the moonlight. She felt nothing as her tattoo and nipple were removed, and was unaware of being turned over onto her stomach. He was tempted to wait, to see if she would regain her senses to meet death aware of the event. But time was of the essence, and he thought her too far gone. He was sated, and impatient to finish up and be rid of her.

Clasping her forehead with his left hand, he pulled the head back hard, stretching the upturned neck, before inserting the tip of the heavy blade under her right ear and drawing it deeply across her throat to sever arteries and cut through the larynx. The deed done, he dropped the head back to rest face down on the damp grass, and wiped the blade on her buttocks as he savored the hot, coppery smell of the spurting blood, and the sound of the liquid, gurgling fight for breath that accompanied it. With one powerful spasm, Dawn kicked out her legs stiffly, and then went limp and was gone, beyond further harm.

The bitch had been carrying. He found a small, expensive-looking derringer in her purse, along with three hundred dollars.

After cleaning up, he smoked a cigarette while the body partially bled out. He then threw the slack carcass into the rear of the wagon and covered it with a blanket.

Driving back southeast, he stopped at Strawberry Reservoir, twenty miles east of Provo, and fed the station wagon and its cargo to a watery resting place.

Reliving the night in Utah, with his emotions fired by the trophy that lay on his thigh, Luke came, his eyes and mind closed to the present, and with a luster of perspiration coating his body. As his heart rate slowed and his member wilted, he gathered himself and drifted back from vivid reverie. He wiped himself dry of sweat and semen before carefully, reverently returning the memento to the rest of the collection, and replacing the box back into the secret compartment of the closet.

Later, joining Belle for dinner, Luke was in a relaxed and buoyant mood.

CHAPTER TWENTY-FIVE

JUST before dawn with the skies still ink-washed and clinging to the night, the outline of the Cobra was barely visible against the towering backdrop of rock monoliths that stood dark sentinels in wait of the new day.

They had parked-up south of Tonopah, just a half mile off highway 95, and spent the night in splendid isolation. They had agreed that there was no pressure to rush pell-mell in their search, and were happy to take time out, to 'smell the flowers', so to speak.

As they traveled south and east to the area that they suspected the killer might be, they were open to distraction. After all the years that had passed, whatever challenges that lay ahead would not be helped by their charging at them overtired and edgy. Better that they should remain fresh and as relaxed as possible, though not complacent. They now appreciated that they had started on what might prove to be a long and dangerous manhunt.

Sarah wanted to spend the following night in Vegas. She had never been out west, and Las Vegas was a place she had always intended to visit. Cal and Mike acceded to her wishes without argument, and the three of them were now looking forward to a quick sojourn into the bejeweled capital of gambling and entertainment.

The sun rose, turning the darkness blood red, then flame orange, and finally salmon pink before it crept over the eastern horizon and painted the sky a cloudless powder-blue. Another scorching day was assured as they finished up scrambled eggs and coffee and set off to follow the highway down past the cauldron that was Death Valley, to head south to Sin City, also known as the City of Lights.

Mike found a large open-air parking lot just off the Strip and only a couple of minutes walk from the casinos. They showered, and then sat at the table enjoying iced tea, now dressed casually in fresh, clean clothes that marked a change from the shorts and T-shirts that had become their usual garb.

Cal had visited Vegas several times. The singer, Dean Martin, had been a particular favorite of his dad's, who had made numerous trips to see Dean in cabaret. In the heyday of the late fifties and early sixties 'The Ratpack', as they were tagged, appeared at the Sands Hotel regularly. Dean, Frank Sinatra, Sammy Davis Jr, Peter Lawford and Joey Bishop performed a blend of comedy and song for their audiences, which was a loosely scripted and usually irreverent feast of fun. They were now all dead, as so many of the actors, singers and sportsmen and women that had not survived the twenty-one years that Cal had been on what he thought of as the Dark Side.

Cal somehow repressed a mood that threatened to assault him like a tropical depression. His respite from life had shown him, graphically, how brief and fragile the allotted span of mortality is, and how all hopes, fears and fickle perception of self importance are but a fleeting and petty insubstantial moment of little consequence. Carpe Diem, he thought. Seize the day by the throat and face tomorrow if and when it rears its ugly head. It amazed him just how adaptable the human mind is. However traumatic and whatever life threw the average person's way, the id, or core of the spirit – whatever we are or have become – seems to be able to assimilate, digest and accept change, be it for the better or unimaginably worse. The mystical organic computer that we call the brain sifts and sorts all incoming data, and feeds it to the appropriate pending or to-be-dealt-with trays. If he could be killed and then somehow be regurgitated back from the unknown at a later date and in another physical form...and be able to accept it, well, he should be able to deal with anything now. The uniqueness of sentient life had taken on more weight and spiritual meaning. He knew that whatever he was, he existed separately from any form that he might inhabit. He was an abstract force to himself, with no comprehension of why such a transitory existence is ordained by imprisonment in such a feeble host.

They stood in the enormous main lounge of Caesar's Palace. Sarah was open-mouthed as she marveled at the sheer acreage of the flamboyant gambling hall, which she thought of as a Sodom-like saloon of cathedral proportions. She had imagined that these colossal desert cash depositories were big, but being there in-situ was still a shock. She could almost taste the fever; a near tangible atmosphere of greed and frenzied expectation that ran through the building like static electricity. With few exceptions, most players would leave materially and spiritually poorer for the experience. Some would leave desperate, inconsolable, and astounded at their reckless stupidity, but as unable to control their vice as most addicts, who cannot restrain the personal demons that habituate and encourage them to overindulgence.

Stopping in front of a bank of slots, hesitating, trying to decide which one to play, Sarah stepped forward to feed the bar-coded ticket that she had purchased into the one nearest to her.

Cal suddenly felt light-headed, experiencing a fleeting dizzy spell that passed as quickly as it had come. He then felt isolated; alone. The cacophony of voices and music receded, and his vision blurred. This was followed by a pull; a mental tug that focused his attention with razor-sharp clarity on a particular machine, which was four along from where they stood. He was subject to the same presentiment that he likened to anticipating a phone call just before the appliance rang, knowing who would be on the line when he picked up. It was on a par with that of whistling a tune, only to then turn on the radio and hear it being played. It was sixth sense; a fleeting perception of an event about to happen. Who knows what causes premonition? But ignore it at your peril. Last minute changes of plan, due to an unreasonable yet insistent sense of doom have saved many people from becoming statistics of fatal air crashes and other disasters.

Cal just 'felt' the draw, and his feelings were wired to that one particular machine.

"No, Sarah!" Cal said, grasping her hand as she was about to feed the ticket into the slot. "That one." And he pointed to the source of his mental magnetism.

Sarah saw the rapt expression in Cal's eyes, and with no hesitation, just unconditional trust, walked over to the nominated slot and fed it. Unlike both Mike and Sarah, Cal was not surprised at the subsequent big win.

"Yeesss!" Sarah shouted, punching the air in triumph. Mike just stared quizzically at Cal.

"Don't ask, Mike," Cal answered the unasked question. "I just felt that it was set to pay out. It was a hunch...well, more than that. I knew that it would."

Small wins, jackpots, and twelve casinos later, they returned to the RV, fifty grand ahead of the game. Cal's 'hunches' had not failed them. Every designated slot paid out. Problem for Cal was that virtually all the coin-operated slots had gone, consigned to history.

Feeding paper to the machines was not as exciting as using quarters or dollars.

Sarah brewed fresh coffee, and they sat reflecting on the rewarding evening that they had enjoyed and profited by. With curtains drawn against prying eyes, they counted the crisp bills a second time, laughing, exhilarated, all three of them momentarily forgetting their mission and attendant problems, excited by their wanton plunder against the fixed odds of Vegas.

"Mike, do me a favor, will you?" Cal said. "Call your buddy in D.C. and cut a deal for the Cobra. Buy it. Let's call it part of your fee."

"I'd already thought of keeping it," Mike said. "I kinda like the idea of living on it. This trip has picked me up, turned me around and knocked some sense into me. I've been in a sad rut for too long now. I think it's about time I found a new direction and some purpose."

"Settled then. And tomorrow night we hit a few more casinos. Pick up, say, another fifty grand before we move on." Cal said, grinning, pleased with his new-found ability.

Sarah looked doubtful. "It seems like stealing, Cal. I don't know that I feel comfortable with it."

"Stealing!" Cal exclaimed, almost choking on his coffee. "Sarah, Vegas was born with mob money. It still exists to part punters from their bucks as quickly as it can. That is its sole mercenary function and purpose. The glitz and big name entertainment are just the lure and the dressing; bait to reel in the fish. The place thrives on greed, and has no consideration for losers. Taking a few thousand off them isn't going to cause a ripple, but it gives me a perverse pleasure to stick it to them."

"Right on," Mike said, by way of agreement.

Sarah put her hand to her mouth, to cover a mischievous grin. "It *was* fun," she said. "And when you put it like that, I agree. Why should they have it all their own way?"

They felt like down at heel project kids who had found a five dollar bill in a storm drain among the leaves and detritus; dirty, muddied, but still legal tender. Someone else's bank note, that they thought would burn their fingers, or suddenly erupt with a piercing klaxon warning that would bring the rightful owner or the cops down on them in a fury of condemnation. But having taken it and fled the scene, they felt the thrill of unexpected good fortune, and gloated over the windfall.

"If you ever need a manager, Cal, look no farther. I'm here, ready, willing and able," Mike said with a smirk lighting up his face.

Cal felt grubby and tired. It had been a long day and the appeal of another quick shower and then bed was irresistible.

"A shower and bed for me, guys," he said through a yawn.

"Yes, I think I'll hit the sack, I'm pooped," Sarah added.

Mike was still buzzing, on a high. "Well I'm wide awake," he said. "You two youngsters just can't go the distance. I'm going out for a couple of drinks, and maybe I'll catch a late show. I'll see you kids in the morning."

"Be careful, Mike," Sarah called as he closed the door behind him.

Sarah settled on the seat in the dinette, with just the radio on. The perimeter lights of the parking lot glowed dimly through the thin drapes, casting soft shadows on the opposite wall of the RV. The peace was almost an antithesis to the frantic atmosphere of the nearby Strip. She relaxed, finishing her coffee while Cal showered. She heard the swish of the cubicle's curtain, followed by the steady thrumming of water on plastic. A sudden thud was presumably Cal dropping the soap, and her cheeks flamed as she imagined him bending down naked to retrieve it. She was confused, her emotions shot. Why was she here out west, hunting for someone who had killed a complete stranger so long ago? She had originally wanted to be with Cal in case Danny suddenly resurfaced, to be there when or if it happened. Now, she had feelings for Cal, and they were deepening, developing with every day that passed. Was this being unfaithful to Danny, who apparently no longer existed? Her loyalty to the past was being slowly eroded by her attraction to Cal. She was fighting it and felt extremely guilty. It was an unfathomable and absurd situation to be in.

Cal stepped out of the shower cubicle with a towel wrapped around his waist, his hair combed back from his forehead, and droplets of water running down his chest.

"Sorry, Sarah, I thought you'd gone to bed," he said, quickly retreating to the bedroom, to return within seconds tying the belt of a thick, white terry robe. "How about a nightcap before we hit the road to dreamland?"

Approaching her in the diffused light, he noticed the tears on her cheeks; went to her and placed his hands on her shoulders, not needing to read her mind to know the reason for her distress, which was an open book in the glistening mirrors to her soul.

"I know that this is a crazy situation, Sarah," he said. "It doesn't make any sense, but we're both stuck with it. I've got past the initial shock. Christ knows why anything happens, or what life is all about, I don't. All I do know is that crying over spilt milk doesn't help. Part of me is still sick at heart over what might have been, but another part that is gaining in strength is telling me that it's only now and here that really counts and that I can be certain of. You've just got to take the ball, run with it and see how far you can get. I know that catching this guy isn't going to put everything back to how it was for either of us, but it gives me purpose at the moment to get up every morning. I also like being with you," he paused, before adding, "and with Mike. Don't forget, Sarah, like the song says: yesterday is dead and gone, and tomorrow's out of sight."

Sarah looked up into Cal's eyes and saw a fusion of disparate emotions vying for supremacy; concern, loneliness, even simmering rage, and most of all a disconsolate and overwhelming sadness. What happened next was as natural as blinking...they kissed. It was a long, deep, gentle kiss, which melted their melancholy and felt so right. Their tongues flicked, probed, met, and it seemed an eternity before Cal pulled away and sat down, stunned at what had just transpired between them.

"Wow!" Cal gasped. "What happened?"

Sarah smiled, but said nothing. There was nothing to say. Realization of how they both felt had been released through the warmth and tenderness of the kiss. Sarah reached out for his hands, as they both gazed poignantly into each other's eyes.

"Where do we go from here?" Sarah whispered, her words cleaving through the charged atmosphere.

"Anywhere we want to," Cal said. "I'm through needing reasons for anything."

"Let's go to bed, Cal, now," Sarah said. "Before I can think of a reason why I shouldn't, and before Mike gets back."

They embraced and then headed for Sarah's bedroom.

CHAPTER TWENTY-SIX

MIKE had a couple of drinks in the Mirage and then left, preferring to find a small bar off the Strip that offered less grand surroundings and a more intimate atmosphere to relax in. As he walked, he marveled at his uplifted frame of mind. He felt ten years younger than he had done before leaving D.C. How easy it had been to just plod along in the mire, getting nowhere fast. The last decade had slipped by almost furtively, with no discernible meaning, leaving nothing to show for its passing. He had been lost in a morass of habit and self-inflicted solitude, just functioning on auto pilot like a robot, and barely scratching a decent living. It hit him hard to admit what a mess he had dug himself into. This trip was definitely the kick in the ass he'd needed to jump-start his life and reassess his priorities. He was enjoying himself for the first time in years, and it felt good. Being with Cal and Sarah had turned him around, and although they didn't know it, they had given him the chance of a fresh start, that he would not fuck up.

He found a suitably rustic drinking hole, The Harlequin, which was squeezed between a burger joint and a pawnbroker's shop. He propped up the bar for over an hour with sour mash whiskey and the wall-mounted TV for company. He left feeling mellow and slightly under the influence, and headed back in the direction of the Cobra, lost in thought, mainly over Cal, and the knowledge that he was miraculously returned from the grave with unearthly powers. Shit, he was the embodiment of a fictional Stephen King character; a Johnny Smith from *The Dead Zone*, but without the brain tumor.

Benny Filmore had seen Mike earlier in the evening in the company of another younger guy and a broad. They had dropped a jackpot in Circus-Circus, and Benny had followed them into Bally's and watched as they did it again. He had then been distracted by a friend for all of ten seconds and lost sight of them. But now he found himself sitting less than ten feet from the older guy at the bar of The Harlequin. It was odds on that this half-bombed bozo was carrying a stack of green that was burning a hole in his pocket, and Benny would be only too happy to relieve the schmuck of it.

Benny was an opportunist thief who by day worked for 'Sunset Inc' driving a waste disposal tanker, emptying septic tanks in the Greater

District of Las Vegas; a far cry from the neon lit glamour associated with this shithole in the desert.

Benny was twenty-seven, and had spent half of those years in one kind of institution or another: his last stretch of two years duration having been up in the state pen' in Carson City for handling stolen jewelry. He had tried to sell it to an undercover cop who was wired and being videoed from what had appeared to be a U-haul van; which just about summed up Benny's luck and level of intelligence. Nowadays he stuck to mugging. Cruising the casinos like a hungry shark, he watched for winners, and then followed them, hopefully to some quiet, ill-lit location, where he could smack them over the head and rob them while they were too dazed to defend themselves.

Benny was a weasel of a man, slender-bodied, with thin, sharp facial features. His close-set beady eyes were separated by a long, pointy nose above a small, pinched mouth and weak receding chin. His hair was mousy and lank, eaten into by a bald spot that was expanding on his crown. His movements were quick and furtive. He was a predator on the unwary, or as in Mike's case, courtesy of whiskey, the unable.

Keeping his distance, Benny followed Mike as he made his way farther from the glare of the Strip, down another side street that led to the Oasis parking lot. Benny almost shimmied from shadow to shadow, gaining on his mark, not wanting him to reach the well lit area further down. He gripped the end of a twelve-inch long lead pipe that was secreted up his coat sleeve; an essential aid to his nefarious work. Rolling this drunk, he imagined, would be a piece of cake. Quickening his pace, narrowing the gap between them, he smiled, pleased to see the guy weaving as the fresh air increased his level of inebriation.

Cal sat bolt upright, startling Sarah who had been lying with her arm across his chest, almost asleep, mentally replaying every blissful moment of their prior lovemaking.

"What is it, Cal?" She said. "What's the matter?"

"There's something wrong. Mike's in trouble," he said, leaping from the bed, pulling on his shorts and running from the room. Throwing back the side door, he stepped down from the RV and spotted Mike approaching the entrance to the lot. He also saw the figure behind him, who was raising his arm as if to strike.

"Behind you, Mike, look out!" Cal shouted, breaking into a run, ignoring the rough concrete that tore at his bare feet.

As Benny started to swing the pipe in an over arm arc, a voice of alarm pierced the night. The guy in front of him went down on one knee as the weapon descended, and although it made contact, it was only a glancing blow.

Mike dropped as he heard Cal's shout of warning, a fraction of a second before he felt a sudden impact to the side of his head. He spun, ignoring the pain, and thrust his arm out in reaction to the attack, driving his closed fist into his assailant's diaphragm.

Benny crumpled to the sidewalk, curling into a fetal ball, moaning and clutching at the nerve center in his solar plexus that Mike had struck with a devastating punch.

Cal reached Mike and helped him to his feet, simultaneously kicking the length of pipe away from the fallen man's hand, wincing as his bare toes struck the lead. He then knelt next to the writhing figure, frisking him, searching for any concealed weapon. Satisfied that the mugger was clean, he turned to Mike, who rested his hands on Cal's shoulders for balance, dazed from the blow that had creased his temple to cause a thin ribbon of blood to run down the side of his face and neck, where it soaked into his shirt collar.

"Are you okay, Mike?" Cal said, concerned at the sight of the blood, not knowing the extent of the wound.

"Yeah, thanks to you, pal. He would have probably put me in intensive care if you hadn't shouted. Lucky for me that you were looking out at just that second, huh?"

"I wasn't," Cal answered absently, glancing down at the groaning mugger. "So what do we do with this piece of garbage, take him to the cops?"

Mike looked thoughtful, and then shook his head.

The faces of the two cops glowed green, illuminated by the radiance from the dash lights and on-board computer screen. Dawn was only just beginning to prod at the darkness; although even in the side streets it was never fully dark in Vegas.

Phyllis and Brian Brent stepped off the sidewalk and waved the LVPD cruiser down. They had been taking Felix, their poodle, for a walk; sleep now being an elusive and snatched feature of their ageing lives, taken in small amounts at any time that suited them, now that they were both into their second decade of retirement.

"What can we do for you folks?" Officer Lee Manville asked as he pulled to a stop next to the old couple, with the unit's window cranked down.

"You can drive another fifty yards on and deal with the guy that you'll come across," Brian said.

"It's disgusting," Phyllis added, grunting as she bent down to stroke the old, fat poodle that sat wheezing by her side. "Indecent, is what it is. I swear I don't know what the world's coming to," and to Brian. "Come on, dear, I want to go home, and so does Felix."

The couple walked off into the gloom behind the cruiser, the sound of Phyllis complaining, and Brian saying, "Yes, dear, no dear," fading under the engine's purr.

Lee drove on, at a crawl, almost immediately seeing the figure ahead of them, pinned by the headlights.

"Fuck me!" Officer Tommy Dacascos said as Lee pulled to the curb and stopped.

Benny was securely bound to the lamp post, completely naked, with his legs and feet glistening wet from being peed on by Felix just minutes before. Written across Benny the weasel's stomach in black felt-tip was the message: I am a thief. This time I fucked up. Please arrest me!

The cops knew Benny of old, and were tempted to just leave him there to face the ridicule and taunts that daylight would surely bring him. They knew that whatever lies he told them, he had without any doubt asked for what he'd got, and should be thankful that whoever had tied him up bare-assed had a sense of humor. He could easily have been left seriously injured or dead. Lee and Tommy both burst out laughing as they noticed the two large cartoon eyes that had been drawn with ink marker above Benny's diminutive pecker. The cruiser's video was rolling, and this footage would remain in the top ten unofficial clips for a long time, only topped by that of a loaded couple making out on the shoulder of US 95 against the trunk of their Pinto, so far gone that they ignored the cruiser and finished up their al fresco coupling to the delight of the two cops who – for the sake of art – just kept filming, and then bust them when the act was completed.

Benny was untied, then cuffed and taken in. Indecent behavior in a public place was the initial charge. Benny wasn't emptying shit now, he was in it.

Sarah bathed Mike's head, and then dabbed the wound liberally with peroxide, which foamed and made Mike suck in his breath and pull away.

"Baby," Sarah said, applying more just out of devilment.

Mike poured himself a stiff drink and again thanked Cal for the warning that had saved him from being rolled, and more importantly from being seriously injured. Sarah told Mike how Cal had shot out of bed when he had suddenly sensed that he was in some kind of trouble. Her statement disclosed more than Cal's added ability, and Mike was pleased that the two of them had 'got it together', though said nothing.

"I just had a powerful premonition that you were in danger," Cal said. "I didn't know what from, just that you were at risk."

"Whatever powers you have, buddy, they're getting stronger. What next, I wonder?" Mike said as he reached for a pack of Winston and fired one up.

"It frightens me, Mike. I think I would settle for just being normal, whatever normal might be."

"Shit. If you were a mere mortal I would probably have had my skull caved in. Instead I got away with a graze and a headache. You know what they say, if you've got it, flaunt it. You're using this stuff for the good, so think of it as a gift, not a curse."

Cal smiled and patted the PI's shoulder. "Thanks, Mike, I'll try to look at it that way from now on."

They spent the next night as planned, relieving the casinos' cash-filled coffers of just over another sixty thousand dollars, finally quitting at the MGM Grand and walking back to the RV with the sound of tumbling, rushing waterfalls of tokens still ringing in their ears, which was a generated sound effect, not real.

The following morning after a breakfast at Denny's, they left Vegas and headed east through Boulder City and across into Arizona. Hours later, Mike pulled the Cobra into a large shopping precinct on I-40 at Ash Fork, west of Flagstaff, and dropped Sarah and Cal off outside a large supermarket to stock up with provisions.

"I'll get some gas and check her over," Mike said, nodding to the Amoco station farther along. "I'll meet you back here and we can load up, then go get some lunch, okay?"

Cal and Sarah waved in acknowledgement as he drove off.

Mike noticed the dark blue Dodge as it cruised by. It was probably only happenstance, but a Dodge the same color had been parked up between two campers in the shade of a row of lofty palms at the Oasis' lot in Vegas. Thinking back, he was almost sure that he had also seen it – or one like it – in Benson's Creek, outside The Eldorado Lounge. He couldn't be absolutely certain that it was the same car, but he was wary of coincidences. It was against his nature to believe in them. He decided to watch and see if it parked up. If it did, he would make a note of the plate number and have a look at the driver. He kept his eye on the suspect vehicle as he stopped next to the pumps, and watched as it left the precinct and headed off east. He must be getting paranoid. Nobody knew their location, or what business they were embarked on.

But someone did. And it was the driver of the dark blue Dodge.

An hour later, the cupboards and refrigerator of the RV were packed with provisions. Even a couple of bottles of Johnny Walker Black Label – Mike's favorite tipple and becoming as popular with both Cal and Sarah – were in the designated booze cupboard. They walked across to a Ho-Jo restaurant and settled at a window booth, all three of them famished. Thanks to their exploits in Vegas, they could now eat out as and when the fancy took them, and even purchase more expensive and varied groceries. Money was no longer of any concern. Cal had not felt at ease spending Jim's cash. Now they had their own, and plenty of it.

By mid-afternoon they had left Flagstaff behind and were driving through Oak Creek Canyon, entering the area that was known as Red Rock Country. They stopped at Pine Flat Camp Site, having covered more ground than they'd intended to in one day.

The canyon area and nearby town of Sedona were amongst the most popular and scenic locations in the state. Movie makers had long since recognized the natural splendor, and had used the unrivalled backdrops for countless flicks; mainly westerns.

They sat outside the Cobra at a picnic bench, enjoying the early evening air and the proximity of other people around them, who all seemed to be families on vacation. The aroma of chicken and steak slowly frying on a dozen or more grills wafted through the campsite on the light breeze, causing them to salivate, not from hunger, just the redolence of char-broiled meat, heavy in the air.

Children laughed and played. And a collie dog mesmerized Cal with its acrobatics as it leapt and twisted to take a Frisbee from mid-air, snatching the plastic disc time and time again with unerring ease until the teenager throwing it was called for supper.

The normality of the trio's surroundings seemed apart from them. It was as if they were onlookers, separate from other people. They were not on vacation, or even innocent travelers passing through, and the knowledge that their planned assault on the area just a few hours' drive to the east – where they would attempt to find the trail of a killer – somehow alienated them from their fellow man.

They had decided to spend the following night near Show Low, and then crisscross the Fort Apache Indian Reservation, starting at the tribal headquarters and then canvassing gas stations, diners, roadhouses, bars, and anywhere else that their quarry may frequent.

Mike and Cal devised a working plan for when they began their inquiries. "Cal and I go in, and you stay on board, Sarah," Mike said. "I'll ask if they know this guy and show them the sketches. Cal can verify whether they do or not by checking out their thoughts. Sound okay?"

Sarah frowned. "It sounds fine. But won't that just give him an edge, if someone warns him that we're on his case?"

"It's the only way to go, Sarah," Cal said. "If somebody warns him, then so be it. There isn't a lot we can do about it. But if anybody does know him, then I'll know, and with any luck I might even find out where he is. Even if he is tipped off, he won't know who we are or why we want to find him. Plus, I can always scare the shit out of whoever might tell him that we're sniffing around. A little mind-reading exhibition followed by an explicit warning to keep quiet should do the trick."

CHAPTER TWENTY-SEVEN

IT was late August. They had visited reservations trying, as yet unsuccessfully, to get a fix on the Indian, who unbeknown to them was at that time in Las Cruces, New Mexico, delivering a Cadillac to a regular buyer whom he often stole vehicles to order for.

"I gotta Pontiac for delivery in El Paso," Fat Al barked in a voice that had the gravely sound of a man who had smoked too many cheap cigars for too many years. "You wanna take it down for me, Luke, and bring a Mustang back tomorrow?"

Luke nodded and took the keys, paperwork and bills that the chubby little man held out to him with stubby, hairy-backed fingers.

Fat Al Parker had dealt with the Indian for going on ten years, but didn't like him. Luke was, and always had been, too arrogant. He also oozed menace, with a stare that Al thought would most likely cause a mountain lion to back off and slink away from him. But he was reliable, and would steal, deliver or pick up anything on wheels in the Southwest, if the money was right.

Al supplied stolen vehicles that he already had buyers lined up for, and most of his hired help were ex-cons, crack heads or just plain dumb, and as undependable and untrustworthy as lawyers and politicians. The Apache was the only one worth spit.

Out front on the lot were Al's legit cars. They were all Junkers, but as squeaky clean as freshly washed dishes, capable of standing up to any checks. It was the other side of the business that made the tax-free big bucks. His Mex mechanics ran the chop shop alongside the regular work, and had usually wiped out a car's history before it was even reported stolen. Al was a rich man, thanks to his 'fuck the law, and double fuck the IRS' attitude.

There was no mystery as to why Al was called Fat Al. He weighed in at just over three hundred pounds, and none of it was muscle. He stood five-eight, but his ideal height for the weight he carried would probably have been eight-three, had there been a chart in existence outside of a zoo that dealt in that sort of math. The folds in Al's face almost buried the small porcine eyes that darted restlessly, never seeming to settle or focus on one particular object for more than a fraction of a second. It was his toupee that stole the show, though. It lay limply across his pate, a disheveled black mass that could have been any nondescript pelt of dried out road kill. His white sideburns protruded from it in stark contrast. Not surprisingly, Al was a bachelor, and paid to get his rocks off with any of the local hookers that could survive a few pulverizing minutes under his elephantine bulk.

"See you tomorrow, midday," Luke said, leaving the office to Al and the rafts of blue-gray cigar smoke that hung in the humid, stale-sweat air below the tar-coated and cracked ceiling.

Luke drove in silence with the radio off, not in the mood for shit-kicking ditties or inane commercials. When he was driving, he thought and planned. He had a need, that when upon him was intense and undeniable. The fix he needed was sex, and not freely given. Belle supplied that. He needed a piece of *unwilling* ass that was fresh and fearful of him, to calm his raging blood. He had an overpowering urge to give it to some bitch in El Paso that night. Just thinking of the hunt, capture, and the control that he would exert over some helpless whore caused an uncomfortable erection that ached against the tight denim of his jeans.

Luke had never tried to justify his actions to himself or anyone else. He had known since being a young boy that his anger, hatred and propensity for cruelty were a result of many conflicting emotional hang-ups. His mother had checked out during his birth, and he had not forgiven the bitch for depriving him of a normal childhood. And his father had been a weak-livered piece of shit who, instead of raising him right, had abandoned him for the bottle, unable to cope with what cards life had dealt him. Then there was the whole fuckin' white race. He had grown up being treated like a second rate citizen in his own country, where being an Indian was an affront to a society that had tried to do the same to a whole race of people as it had done to the buffalo. He was a pragmatist, who knew that he would never –as a poorly educated Apache – be a member of a country club, playing golf with business buddies. Or ever drive to a detached, up market house in a custom-built Lincoln. Well, fuck them all! He would vent his feelings in whatever way he wished. On his bucket list was the plan to break into some rich dude's home, truss him and his family up, and then do his thing to the cocksucker's wife and daughters, before cutting the guy's eyes out and letting him live, to remember the last thing that he ever saw for the rest of his life. Shit, he was going to do it. It wasn't an if, it was a when.

He dropped the Pontiac off and then booked into The Palomino, a hot-bed motel next to the Mexican border, with the lights of Ciudad Juarez mirrored on the surface of the muddy Rio Grande at its rear. It was a flea-pit, used mainly by hookers to entertain their johns. Luke registered as John Aquino, not that the sour-breathed slob in the office gave a shit who he was, as he took the cash and then threw Luke a room key, seemingly without missing a frame of the old *Ironside* repeat that was showing on his portable TV.

Luke took a tepid shower, having to run the sand-colored water for a long time until it eventually cleared. The bathtub he stood in was ringed with a crust of scum, and hairs of every shade and type imaginable clogged the plughole.

He dozed on the bed until it was dark, then left the room and walked four blocks before even looking for a suitable vehicle to steal. It was from an ill-lit lot at the rear of a bar that he took a suitably dirty, nondescript Chevy Blazer, hot wiring it within thirty seconds, before driving away unseen.

Stopping several blocks away, he checked the 4x4 for anything of value. A folded canvas ground sheet stowed in the back was the only significant find. It was an item that could hopefully be put to good use later. With luck he would have finished with and dumped the Blazer before it was even missed. He drove to a red light district and began to cruise the streets, hunting for the right prey, extremely selective in his choice of victim.

Conchita Alvarez was eighteen; an olive-skinned beauty with shoulder length, blue-black hair. She was just five-feet-tall, but slim and well-stacked, showing off her ample cleavage with a low-cut, tit-popping, crushed velvet purple top. It was a hot and humid Texas night, and she could feel the damp and sticky sweat in her unshaven armpits and also trickling down the middle of her back. She needed the chill of a car's air-con to give her some respite from the muggy street, even if only for a few minutes as she conducted business in the front seat in the darkness of Seminole Street, which backed on to deserted freight yards. If a punter wanted more than a quick fuck or blowjob in his vehicle, then the Braden Hotel on the same street charged for rooms by the hour.

Conchita worked days at the Odessa Laundry, slaving for long hours on a steam press for minimum wages in an atmosphere that was both damp and hot, with the clime of a sauna; a sweat shop in every sense of the word. Every passing day strengthened her resolve to improve her quality of life. She had a dream. She led a double life, projecting an image of wholesome decency and propriety to her parents and younger sister. Her mom and dad chided her for going out and returning home late several evenings a week. They believed that she was in the company of friends her own age, clubbing and partying, and they reluctantly acquiesced to her remonstrations that she needed to have fun with her peers after spending her days in the laundry. They hoped that she would soon find a nice young man and settle down.

Every cent that she made on the street, Conchita saved, and now had an unbelievable total of twenty thousand dollars stashed away. Another year of avoiding the attention of both police and pimps, and she was going to get the hell out of El Paso and move north to Albuquerque or Santa Fe. She planned to open a small business in a respectable area. Maybe a florists; she loved flowers. Or perhaps a gift shop, selling greeting cards and knick-knacks. She wanted premises with living accommodation at the rear or above it. In her daydreams she could see it; bright pastel colors on the walls, and her very own furniture, mostly built of pine. She would have freedom, independence and space, away from her squalid roots and her short yet hectic past.

The dusty 4x4 pulled into the curb. She walked across to it, assessing the driver through the open window as she approached. He was a good looking Indian, in his forties maybe, of clean appearance and with a pleasant almost embarrassed smile on his face. She pegged him as married, just looking for a little excitement on the side.

"You wanna go someplace for a little fun, honey?" she said, smiling at the guy and jiggling her tits a little as she leaned forward to give him an appetizer.

"Please," he replied, nodding. "How much?"

"Thirty bucks for the best blow job in town."

"Sounds good. Where?"

"Cash first, okay?"

Luke took a fifty from his shirt pocket and handed it to her. "I'm sure it'll be worth fifty," he said, winking at her.

After checking the bill, Conchita tucked it into her purse as she walked around to the passenger side of the Blazer and climbed in, to settle back and enjoy the steady rush of chilled air that surged from the vents on the dash and from unseen blowers nearer the floor.

"Just make a right at Seminole and park up near the freight yards. It's nice and private there," Conchita said.

This would be a quick fifty, she thought. Another couple like this and she would have had a very profitable evening.

Luke parked next to a rusted chain-link fence, and the moonlight cast a mesh shadow from it, to net the windshield and hood in an intangible pattern of ethereal diamonds. The area was rundown and deserted, and only the ambient light illuminated the Chevy's interior.

Conchita lifted her top up to release her large breasts, and began to rub her nipples with her index fingers, teasing them to lengthy firmness. Experience had taught her that this sort of display resulted in the john's coming with only the minimum encouragement from her mouth. The days of playing with flaccid dicks and having to suck them until her jaw ached were behind her.

Luke stared at her tits, his eyes widening with pleasure as she manipulated the hard knurls that projected from the firm mounds.

"That sure is a pretty picture," he said, reaching forward to touch the tattoo that was high up on her left breast. "What is it, an angel?"

"A cherub," she said, looking down at herself to also admire the winged child that adorned her smooth mammary.

Luke was in high spirits. He felt relaxed and decided not to rush with this one. She could earn her money, even though he would be reclaiming it later.

Conchita rubbed him through the denim of his jeans as he took over the pleasant task of stimulating her nipples. She unzipped him, released his hard penis and encircled it with her hand and slowly began to masturbate him, bringing him to the edge before bobbing her head down to take the glistening head of it into her mouth. She ran her tongue around the bulbous tip, and then slipped the full length slowly back and forth between her lips. As he came, thrusting his hips up, she drew back slightly, not wanting his dick at the back of her throat, choking her. She swallowed quickly, not tasting his issue, and sat up to wipe her mouth with a Kleenex.

"That was world class, sweet-lips," Luke said, stroking her cheek gently with his hand, before drawing it back, to clench into a fist and punch her hard in the temple.

The bitch screamed and reached for the door handle, apparently not even dazed by the blow. He jerked her back, ripping the flimsy polyester top, and then hit her another four times in the head and face before she finally slumped in the seat and lapsed into unconsciousness.

He looked at his stinging knuckles. The whore had cut them with her teeth; she would suffer for that.

Conchita's two front teeth had broken under the onslaught, and the jagged stumps had lacerated her already swelling top lip. Blood ran from her nose, which had fractured with an audible crack as the Indian had driven his fist into it. Her cheekbone was also shattered, lending a lopsided look to her now misshapen face.

Retrieving a reel of silver duct tape from where he had secreted it under the seat, Luke quickly wrapped it around her head, over the bleeding maw of her mouth, biting through it before pulling her sideways and toward him to gather her wrists behind her back and bind them together. He then reached down to secure her ankles, before lifting her with ease to maneuver the limp body over the back of the seats, where it fell into the rear foot well in a crumpled heap. Once covered by the canvas sheet, she was invisible to all exterior scrutiny. Luke restarted the engine, did a tight U-turn and drove away from the area.

CHAPTER TWENTY-EIGHT

CONCHITA recovered her senses, and although terrified and racked with pain, she tried to assess the situation that she found herself in. The bastard had hit her repeatedly, and from the vibration and engine noise, it was obvious that she was on the floor of the Blazer; he had compounded his assault with abduction. She was unable to move, tied securely, gagged, and under some kind of covering. She knew that he had taken her for a more sinister purpose than sex. He could have fucked her every which way he had wanted, without resorting to violence and kidnap. Panic fluttered with dark feathered wings through her mind as she faced the stark reality of her plight. This was a head case; a maniac who was going to kill her after committing whatever sick acts turned him on. She had to escape. Scared as she was of dying, it was the greater fear of what might come first and make her pray for death as blessed relief that frightened her the most, sending waves of near hysteria pulsing through her.

The blood from her torn mouth was running down her throat, and her tongue was also bleeding, cut from her catching it on the razor sharp remains of her broken teeth. Her nose and the side of her face pounded with searing bolts of white-hot agony, that every movement of the vehicle amplified and inflamed. She was trussed up like a Thanksgiving turkey, unable to move her limbs an inch. There was no give in whatever he had used to bind her: no leeway to give her a flicker of hope; a spark of light at the end of a long black tunnel of approaching doom.

The tape that covered her mouth moved. The blood that coated her face in a crimson slick had acted as a barrier between her skin and the adhesive. Slowly, painfully, opening and closing her throbbing jaws, she worked the tape up until it was over her top lip, no longer restricting her breathing, and allowing the blood to flow out onto the carpet, not down her throat.

Sucking in air, Conchita was astounded at the pleasure that just being able to breathe freely gave her. Ridding herself of the gag was significant. Now she was in a position to scream and bite, given the chance. But even though that might delay the inevitable for a moment or two, it could not help her escape while tied up and helpless.

A voice in her mind was chanting...*You're going to die! You're going to die!* She suppressed the negative thoughts with willpower and a stronger more determined mantra: *The fuck I am! The fuck I am!*

Luke was pissed. The bitch had taken a lot of subduing, and it had resulted in him having to damage her face, which disturbed him. He preferred that they remain good looking while he played with them. He had suddenly lost interest in this one. She could keep her fucking tattoo. This was an episode that he did not want a reminder of. All he wanted now was an isolated spot to get rid of her. He would not follow his usual pattern; would just strangle her slowly and dump the body, before torching the Blazer and heading back to the motel.

Still well short of the city limits, the warning light blinked on to alert him to the fact that he was almost out of gas. This, he thought, was turning into a real fuck-up of a night. He would be glad to see the back of El Paso come the morning. He smashed his fist against the dash with enough force to shatter the Perspex that covered the glowing fuel warning light.

Pulling onto the next service station forecourt, he stopped at the pump farthest from the office and checked that the bitch was still hidden from view under the sheet. He then emptied her purse of folding money and opened the door.

As he stepped out, everything happened at once. A guy in a sedan pulled in behind him, cut his engine and got out, just as the screaming started.

She had one shot and knew it. The psycho had stopped, and as he opened the door she heard another vehicle pull up.

"Help! Murder! Call the police! Rape!" Conchita screamed at the top of her voice, throwing her weight against the back of the seat repeatedly as she relentlessly kept up a tirade of loud pleas for assistance.

The screams from the 4x4 echoed around the roofed forecourt, and Luke froze momentarily as the other motorist stopped and stared, first at him, then the Blazer, and finally towards the office, where the young attendant inside was now taking a lot more than a passing interest.

Within less than three seconds, Luke ran through his options and made a decision. If it hadn't been for the guy in the locked office, he would have gutted the other driver on the spot and taken off. But with another witness sat next to a phone that course of action was pointless. He ran across the brightly lit forecourt and into the relative darkness of a side street. He knew that he had only minutes to find alternative transport and get clear of the area. As he ran, he imagined the driver of the sedan cautiously approaching the Blazer, to find the source of the screaming as he uncovered the lucky wetback bitch.

Pausing to test door handles of cars that were parked up at the curbside, Luke's mind whirled: the other driver was probably running to the office, shouting for the attendant to hit 911 and get the cops and an ambulance.

Relief. The driver's door of a dark Oldsmobile was unlocked. He climbed in and surpassed his own record for hot-wiring a car.

The incident would already be being reported to the emergency switchboard. Details being asked for, giving him more precious seconds to abet his escape.

He snapped the shift into drive and pulled away, slowly, twenty, thirty yards before he flicked on the lights.

The nearest units would now be heading for the gas station, looking for a guy on foot, maybe running.

He took a ramp onto I-10, which ran through the city, and within less than two minutes took an off ramp onto Texas Avenue. He parked up in the first dimly lit and deserted side street that he came to and then quickly wiped the wheel and all other surfaces that he may have touched, before strolling casually away, hands in pockets, now a long way from the scene. He headed back to the motel, reaching it without further incident.

Conchita was taken to ER at Memorial Park Hospital, badly injured about the face, in a great deal of pain, and although in mild shock, fully aware of just how lucky she was to be alive and able to feel anything. Fearful that her covert self-employment would be unveiled, she lied to the intern who treated her, and then to the police who questioned her the next day.

"So, did you know the creep?" Detective Don Kenney asked her, after she had undergone surgery to her face and had slept for twelve hours.

"I accepted a lift home," Conchita said slowly through swollen and sutured lips. "He started to get fresh, and I lost my temper and slapped his face. He just went berserk and started beating on me."

"But he tied you up and put you in the back of his vehicle. What did he say to you?"

"He knocked me out. I came to just before he stopped at the gas station, and then I screamed for help. That's all I know."

"So what did he look like?" Don said.

"He was a Mexican, in his late twenties or early thirties I think. He seemed nice…trustworthy, Conchita lied.

Had she given a full and accurate description of her attacker, and mentioned his interest in her tattoo, or admitted to being a hooker, then the assault might have been taken far more seriously than it was. But she was not about to give any information that might disclose her clandestine profession.

The only other witness was the guy who had fortuitously pulled up behind the Chevy Blazer, and his description was vague. He had removed his glasses before stepping out of the car, and could only confirm that the attacker had probably been Mexican and of average height. The attendant had caught a brief glimpse of Luke as he ran off, but could add nothing. They had a description that fitted thousands of males in the city.

Luke was home-free. The Blazer was a mass of prints, including his, but, as no one had been raped or murdered, the assault was just another run of the mill crime; low priority stuff. That same evening had produced one fatal shooting, several knifings, two rapes and various other crimes in the city, all before midnight. Conchita's mishap hardly rippled the pond. The case was assigned and immediately filed at the bottom of a very large pile of ongoing investigations; consigned to a dusty wait of considerable duration before it would see the light of day.

Luke picked up the Mustang from Arroyo Auto's and headed back north to Las Cruces. His mood was black, and he had hardly slept the previous night. The anger and frustration of the fuck-up still knotted his stomach and boiled in his brain. The bitch had escaped him, and would have given the pigs a detailed description. He felt vulnerable and in danger, not his usual confident self. She had succeeded in doing what no other whore had ever done before. She had made him run, afraid, like a fuckin' mangy dog with its tail tucked between shaking legs. The next piece of ass would suffer unmercifully to appease this affront. He would not just take a tattoo, he would flay the bitch like an elk; skin her alive, and completely.

After dropping the car off at Fat Al's and collecting his payment, Luke hitched a lift west in a Peterbilt to Willcox on I-10, then headed north on foot, off-road to the cabin and Belle. He planned to spend a week or two laying low until things cooled down. He was unaware that he was in the clear, thanks to Conchita and her false statement.

CHAPTER TWENTY-NINE

RICH Cole knew that Mike was good. He had a gut feeling that his old friend had made the dark blue Dodge. It was time to change wheels.

After tailing them at a safe distance, keeping several other vehicles between himself and the RV, Rich decided that they had stopped for the night at Pine Flat, and so drove back into Flagstaff and off-loaded the Dodge. At five-thirty the next morning, after a meal and a few hours' sleep, he was back in wait, a few hundred yards north of the campsite, now behind the wheel of a tan Trans Am.

Rich was on special assignment, playing a long but strong hunch. Being a friend of the PI did not compromise his duty as a federal agent as he continued his search for the serial killer.

After Mike had contacted him, asking for information, Rich had met with his supervisor, Paul Nicholl, at HQ in D.C. and discussed Mike's interest in the slaying of the girl and the deputy sheriff that had taken place back in ninety-six.

"What do you read into it, Rich?" Paul had asked, taking a sip of coffee from his ever present National Zoo mug.

"It's a lead, boss, and we need one. We're at a dead end with this and going nowhere fast. Mike is a no-nonsense pro'. He operates as a gumshoe now, but he's as sharp as glass and never misses a trick. If he needed to ask me for information, then he must be onto something."

Paul had jabbed his gold-rimmed spectacles further up the bridge of his nose; a habit that was exacerbated when problem solving or decision making, which was most of the time.

"Why not just lean on him for what he's got," Paul said, running a finger through his mustache to the corner of his thin-lipped mouth. "Point out that this is a live federal case that he has stepped into, and that we wouldn't want to think that he was withholding evidence or obstructing justice. Because if he is, Rich, his ass and his license are ours."

"That isn't the way to go with him, Paul. Believe me, I know him. If we push him, he'll just seize up tight as a clam with whatever he has. If he is after the son of a bitch, we can let him lead us in. He's hot shit at finding people who don't want to be found."

Paul had thought it through. He knew that Rich could have been running his own field office by now, if he had wanted to, which he didn't. He had an aversion to being sat fattening his ass behind a desk and playing politics.

"How do you want to play it?" Paul said, standing, as if to ward off the extra pounds that had already begun to widen his desk-bound butt. "Give him some off-the-record help and see which way he runs once he has the ball?"

Rich nodded, and Paul walked across to the coffeemaker that was wheezing like an asthmatic; zoo mug in hand, ready for refilling.

"Okay, Rich. Feed him and stick with him." Paul said.

Rich had sent Mike all the information that they had, bar autopsy reports and photographs. All the relevant facts were on the stick, and from the second Mike received it he was under the twenty-four hour surveillance of four operatives on six hour shifts. It had paid off, and when Mike rented the RV and picked up the young couple, Rich followed. A check on Danny Clayton and Sarah Mitchell drew a blank, with no feasible link between them and the serial murders. But Rich knew that his friend was on to something. Patience and time would make things a lot clearer, and Mike's motives would surface. All he had to do was keep with them.

Rich had passed out overall top of his section at Quantico back in two-thousand. He was now over forty, but was a Peter Pan type, hardly seeming to age, looking to be in his early thirties. In appearance, he was the consummate agent; average. He blended into a crowd and became faceless. Standing five-ten, he was lean and fit, with mid-brown hair and a physiognomy that would not be remembered or easily described, unless studied very closely. They say that the eyes are the mirrors of the soul, and if that is true, then it was evident in Richard Cole. His clear gray eyes could be ice cold or ember hot, reflecting his inner feelings to a trained observer. He loved the natural world, had an eye for pre-Raphaelite art, particularly the English painter, Millais, and by contrast had the propensity to be ruthless and efficient in dispatching his duties, with extreme prejudice if necessary.

Rich did not conform to the stereotype dark suit, tie and raincoat image of a fed. That was for the movies, TV, and Special Agents on high profile duties. Rich wore what worked. In this case, a baggy Red Sox T-shirt, creased chinos, Nikes, a baseball cap and shades.

Rich experienced the odd flurry of gooseflesh on his arms as he tailed Mike across the west, which was a good sign. Something was going down, if only for the reason that Mike Cassidy never took vacations.

CHAPTER THIRTY

IT was midday when Cal pulled into a rest area just north of Whiteriver. There were no facilities. It was just a deserted and scenic off-road clearing with a scattering of timber picnic tables and benches, which were splitting, warping out of true and bleached gray by the sun.

Sarah made sandwiches, and they watched the local newscast on the small portable as they ate and sipped chilled beer. Once finished the make-do meal, Mike took advantage of the stop to check the tire pressures, oil and water level. Leaving the regulated cold air of Ol' Betsy – as Sarah had christened the Cobra – was like walking into a blast furnace; a dry, skin-cracking heat, relentless and unforgiving, even driving rattlers and scorpions under rocks in search of shade.

Sarah began washing up the plates as Cal braved the merciless heat and went for a walk. He had a lot on his mind and was in need of a short spell in his own company, feeling emotionally wrung out; a fragile package of mixed feelings, the wrapping paper split and creased, with the string holding it together now loose and frayed. He was confused, at odds with the thoughts that eddied and whirled like so many autumn leaves in a windy corner of his mind's backyard. The reunion with his dad had been his salvation, giving him the bridge that he had needed, which was a solid link spanning the chasm of past and present. The irrevocable loss of Chrissie and the life that they should have had together was a constant source of pain, but one that had been dulled by the unexpected fresh tide of emotion that Sarah had evoked in him. He had begun to be overwhelmed and excited by his growing attraction to her. He was experiencing all the symptoms of that indefinable state that is labeled, love. They had both lost an invaluable, irreplaceable person from their lives, and he hoped that their blossoming feelings for each other were not just a reaction to compensate in the wake of that loss.

Daydreaming, lost in thoughts of what might have been, and speculating on what may lay ahead, he wandered over a hundred yards into the hostile desert that bordered the blacktop and rest area.

The coyote loped from saguaro to mesquite, its pale enigmatic eyes locked onto the slowly approaching figure. Inquisitive yet wary, it kept a predetermined distance between itself and the smell of possible danger.

Cal stopped as his peripheral vision caught the movement of the lean prairie wolf. He turned to face it, and their eyes met in silent communion. Not knowing why, and with no conscious intention, Cal jumped, mentally sliding into the canine brain, also watching from where he stood, as part of his self explored the animal's being.

Christ! He was in an alien environment. A world bereft of real thought or constructive memories. There was an acute awareness of shape and perspective, and a sharpness of eye and sense of smell that made human sight and the ability to detect odors almost pitiful. But he could find no form of language, just basic feelings; a positive acuity of well-honed instincts. He sensed curiosity, as the animal studied the large upright creature before it. It noted every fractional movement, and the smell of the intruder to its territory triggered extreme caution.

Cal found a purity of spirit in the coyote's mind. It possessed a clear, clean, crisp and uncluttered view of life, unburdened by greed, desire, or a need to prove anything, or to have power over others. Its only apparent purpose seemed to be one of survival, with food being a central motivating factor. Through the hot air, Cal caught the scent of himself; a musky, sour-sweat odor that filled his host's nasal cavities and by some chemical coding system dismissed him as potential prey. He could also recognize the bitter scent of the cacti, and the pungent tarry odor of the mesquite bushes. His superior intellect – though inferior senses – gave him a sense of power over the beast that he had not experienced with human beings.

On sudden impulse, Cal attempted to control the coyote's actions and imagined it sitting like a pet dog, and urged it to comply; willed it to obey him.

Not knowing why, the coyote promptly sat on its haunches, confused and frightened by its wayward actions. Cal pushed harder, and the animal lay down and rolled over, as if to have its belly scratched like a pet dog, exactly as he had visualized it doing. Bidding it to rise and join the *him* that was separate from it, they both walked back to the RV. The wild animal appeared to be at ease, walking to heel as commanded by silent and undeniable order.

Mike grasped Sarah's arm and pointed, watching in dumbstruck wonder as Cal and his four-legged companion ambled casually towards them.

"Pass me some steak, please," Cal said when he reached the open door, and Sarah went to the refrigerator, returning with a large cut of raw beef, to hand it to Cal with a smile of entranced bewilderment on her face.

Cal passed the meat to the animal, tasting the cold juices and blood and feeling the mouth begin to salivate as sharp teeth sank into the flesh.

Thankful for the incomparable experience, he patted the creature's head and then withdrew wholly, back into himself, leaving the animal to its own devices.

The coyote stopped eating, blinked, and stared in surprise at each of them in turn; the slab of meat forgotten for a moment, jutting from its dripping jaws like a massive, bloody, malformed tongue. The spell broke, and it turned and loped away, head flicking back repeatedly to ensure that it was not being followed or attacked from behind. It stopped at what it considered a safe distance and lay under a thorny bush, facing them as it devoured its first and most likely last cut of choice beefsteak.

Cal felt that he had become more by sharing that brief time as part of another species. He understood, to some small degree, that other life forms were in no way inferior to man, just fundamentally different, and in a way more noble and honest with no hidden agenda. What you saw was what you got.

"You were inside it!" Sarah said with a mixture of awe and excitement in her voice. "You actually went inside an animal's brain...that's just incredible."

"It sure was," Cal said, his eyes shining with the enormity of what he had done. "And I found that I can do more than just visit and read thoughts. I can take control and manipulate. At least I could with that old boy."

Cal related his experience and the sensations of sharing the coyote's mind. Mike and Sarah were astounded by his abilities.

"That must have been wonderful," Sarah said. "You must be the first human being to ever have had that kind of encounter."

"Maybe so," Cal said. "And I feel privileged to have been able to do it. If I could do it with people as well, just think how it would help when we find the killer."

"So try it with me," Sarah said. "You need to know if you *can* do it, and I'm a willing volunteer."

"Sarah's right, Cal," Mike said. "We do need to know just what you can do. It could save our lives. But try it on me. If you can make me do something against my will, well, I think you could control anybody."

Cal shrugged. "Okay, Mike, I'll try it with you, just to check it out and see if it's possible."

Entering Mike's mind, Cal continued to talk to him from the other side of the table. He was surprised to find that Mike was ready for him, and had tried to put up a mental barrier like a firewall against any invasive trespass, convinced that there was no way that the motor functions of his brain could be taken over and manipulated.

Mike blinked rapidly as a repeating order was directed into his frontal lobe; the part of the brain that is associated with movement. He swallowed several times and squeezed his eyelids shut in determined but futile concentration to fight Cal off.

Sarah watched in silence. She was amazed to see that Cal was still talking, apparently relaxed and showing no outward sign of trying to occupy Mike. But it was obvious by Mike's reactions that something *was* happening. Sweat was now running down the PI's reddening face, and his hands were clenched, white-knuckled on the tabletop.

Rising slowly, Mike walked to the front of the Cobra. He had become apparently calm, although he was moving jerkily, stiff-legged, reminiscent of Mary Shelley's famous monster. He unlocked the glove compartment and withdrew his .38, checked that it was loaded, and then climbed out of the driver's door into the lung-searing heat. Cal stood up, walked to the side door and stepped outside, with Sarah close behind him.

Mike made his way to the edge of the parking area and stopped facing out towards the desert, standing directly in front of a large saguaro cactus that pointed heavenward; a thirty foot high, ridged and spiny green finger, which had stood resolutely at attention for perhaps fifty years.

Assuming a firing stance with his right shooting hand cupped in his left, and the left side of his body slightly forward, braced and balanced, Mike emptied the gun into the leathery giant, almost amputating the top ten feet of the spiked trunk. He continued pulling the trigger of the empty pistol until Cal withdrew his control and left his friend's mind.

Mike stood motionless, smoke curling from the hot muzzle of his weapon, staring at his handiwork in disbelief. He then turned and walked slowly back to Cal and Sarah, the gun now hung loosely in his hand, by his side. He stopped six feet from them, squinting against the sun's glare and shielding his eyes with his free hand to stare at Cal.

"Holy shit! You did it," he said. "I didn't believe you could, but you did. You made me discharge my gun at a fucking cactus. I couldn't feel you making me do it. I just had a compulsive urge to blast away at that overgrown pot-plant."

"It's mind-blowing," Sarah said. "You have the power to control people. It's...it's awesome."

Mike gripped Cal's shoulder, firmly. "Never let the government, military or anyone else know what abilities you have, Cal," he said in an almost threatening tone of voice. "They would sell their souls to have a weapon as potentially powerful as you are under their control. They would treat you like a lab rat. Believe me, I've seen some of the cogs at work in the machine, and it's not a pretty sight."

CHAPTER THIRTY-ONE

LOUISE Gorman was a prim and matronly sixty-nine-year-old spinster, who had taught at the Indian school for over forty years and had been appointed to the position of principal in nineteen-seventy-six; a position that despite her advanced age, she still held. An unattractive – by most standards – and asexual entity, Louise wore loose, shapeless clothing, nondescript and neutral gray, from her wattled neck down to her old-fashioned laced, black leather shoes. Her hair was as gray as her garb, scraped back from her sallow face and worn in a bun. Horn-rimmed, bottle-glass thick spectacles magnified her stone-washed, rheumy eyes, and the whole package effectively promoted the image she had subconsciously nurtured since her gawky and unhappy teenage days.

As a young girl, Louise had been emotionally crippled by rejection, not just by her peers but at all levels, and had sought solace in academia. Now an ageing woman, she was trapped in the deep and lonely furrow of a sterile life that she had plowed with her own hand.

Sarah emptied the stale, wet grounds, put a new filter in the basket and added fresh coffee before switching on the coffeemaker, while Cal and Mike went into the agency school.

After being kept waiting – sitting on a wooden form like a pair of recalcitrant pupils summoned for admonishment – for almost fifteen minutes, they were ushered into the austere office of the school's ageing principal.

"Well?" The terse, one word question greeted them in a tone that demanded that they state their business and leave with all due haste.

"We're trying to locate a man that we believe may have attended this school back in the late seventies or early eighties," Mike began with no preamble, showing his credentials to the suspicious, frosty woman who sat before them, an oversize antique desk conspicuously setting her apart from the rest of the drab room and her unwelcome visitors. "To be honest," he continued. "It's more than likely that he has been involved in a number of very serious crimes. All we have is his first name, Luke, and an artist's impression of how he looked in nineteen-ninety six, and what he may look like now."

Mike unfolded a photocopy of Cal's drawings and pushed it across the polished desktop to the forbidding and remote principal.

Louise had no intention of divulging any information to the two men. Confidentiality regarding all pupils past or present was not a negotiable commodity. If they had a valid reason for making inquiries, then they should go to the police. With a bony, chalk-white index finger, she pulled the piece of paper towards her and gave it a cursory disinterested glance, before freezing, the skin of her scalp and the nape of her neck tightening as her eyes locked on the striking and unmistakable likeness of Luke Strayhorse, who stared back at her from the two black and white images on the sheet of paper that she now gripped tightly in both hands.

Shuddering and closing her eyes, Louise was back in her early days at the school, at the time that she had first had the misfortune to meet the then thirteen-year old Indian boy. His attendance had been poor, which pleased all the staff and most of the other pupils. She remembered that from the outset she had found his attitude to be one of arrogant defiance of authority, and that his favorite weapon had been dumb insolence. At times he had refused to communicate with more than a scornful smirk on his face, and a cold, malevolent stare of undisguised hatred in his fathomless ebony eyes.

Louise, as all the teaching staff, had reprimanded the boy on countless occasions, berating him in front of his peers in an attempt to embarrass him to no avail, finding it impossible to breach his armor of impenetrable disdain.

A sleepless night was the reason, not an excuse for causing Louise to lose her temper on that long gone August day. Her air-conditioning had developed a labored rattling over a period of several weeks, finally deciding to expire on one of the hottest nights of the year. The resulting heat had left Louise tossing and turning, sweltering in her own sweat, without even the sigh of a breeze through the open window to give respite.

The following morning, Luke had been sat looking out of the classroom window, hands clasped behind his head, and an obnoxious smile playing at the corners of his cruel mouth.

"Luke Strayhorse!" Louise shouted. "Will you stop daydreaming and pay attention?"

Luke looked at the teacher as though she were a cockroach that had ventured out from under a baseboard in broad daylight, and then turned away with exaggerated contempt, yawning to register his boredom with the lesson, and a complete disregard of her request.

Louise lost her temper, which was a highly unusual occurrence, and marched down the aisle between the scratched and ancient desks, to stop in front of the Indian's now grinning face. She lashed out, slapping him hard; the sound of her hand against his cheek a whiplash crack that echoed around the now hushed room. The force of the blow, charged with unchecked anger, stung her palm and knocked Luke's head sideways. He had been taken off guard, not expecting an assault from the frail looking and usually timid woman. Quickly regaining his composure, he smiled broadly at the now ashen-faced teacher, then stood, ran his fingers through his thick black hair and casually walked to the door.

"Thank you, ma'am, that sure got my attention," Luke had said, winking at Louise, smiling, but not with his eyes, before vanishing through the door, a tuneless whistle accompanying him as with hands stuffed in his jeans pockets he left the building.

It was at a little past six that evening when Louise arrived home. She had attended a staff meeting that had included a lengthy evaluation of the Strayhorse boy. No positive recommendation as to how to deal with him had been forthcoming, but it was decided that his flouting of the system and unacceptable behavior would be the sole order of business at a special meeting the following week, when a decision as to his future at the school would be made. Staking him out in the desert with wet rawhide tied around his neck had been a suggestion from Albie McCammon, the science teacher. They had all laughed, but without exception thought the idea admirable.

Entering the kitchen of her modest, county-owned, timber-framed house, Louise went directly to the refrigerator for fresh, cold milk. Her pet and companion of the last five years had been a black and white cat, which she had named Barnum, having found him abandoned and starving as she made her way home from a circus in her home town of Sioux Falls.

Barnum would have normally been at her feet already, rubbing against her legs, attentive and purring loudly. She wondered what was keeping him otherwise engaged as she pulled open the door of the old Frigidaire. And then she knew. Her eyes fastened in horror and disbelief on the severed head that stared out, not at her, not at anything anymore. Barnum's head rested on a plate; the pooling blood already congealing like a thick, gourmet sauce around the ragged neck. The cat's lips were drawn back in a frozen grimace, teeth flecked red, tongue lolling out to one side. The green eyes, their pupils dilated, held an accusing expression; a look that Louise would see in nightmares for the rest of her life. A small piece of paper was taped to the fur of the cat's forehead, between its ears. Written on it in large block capital letters were the words: TEACHER'S PET.

Standing transfixed, her eyes riveted to the sickening sight of the decapitated cat's head, and her hand still clamped to the door handle as if glued there, Louise's misery at the loss of her pet was equaled only by her loathing and unbound fury at what 'that fucking Indian kid' had done. She knew with the same certainty that she knew the sun would rise in the east that Luke was responsible. The cold-hearted, callous little bastard was showing her that she had hit him where it hurt. His enormous pride had been wounded when she had struck him, and that had triggered this warped act of revenge.

Her stomach cramped, and she pulled her hand free from the refrigerator and ran to the sink, almost making it before vomiting. The sour, noxious stream hit the edge of the counter, splashing back at her, some finding the sink but most covering her dress and the quarry-tiled floor. Louise cried out, and screamed aloud as more hot liquid was ejected. She lowered her head over the sink, holding on to it with both hands as her body began to slump, her legs almost devoid of strength, shaking and threatening to give way.

After several minutes, with her throat aching and strands of bile-ridden saliva hanging from her chin, she reached for a towel and wiped at her mouth, crying and trembling at the outrage that had been visited upon her. With clothes covered in her stinking juices, she staggered back to the open refrigerator and gently lifted the head from the glutinous platter, to wrap it in the old cardigan that Barnum had always slept on. She searched the house, yard, and the garbage bin for the body, but it was nowhere to be found. She did find the window that had been forced open to gain entry, though, and phoned the police to report the break-in and the vile act that had been committed, naming Luke as the person who she believed...*knew* had done the vile deed.

Over two months had passed, and although Luke had been questioned, the matter had remained officially unresolved. It was the boy himself who had confirmed his guilt. He approached her after class one afternoon, hanging back to be alone with her. He had chuckled and said. "I just love pussy and givin' head, Ms," and then he mewled like a cat and was gone, striding away along the corridor, laughing as he went.

Mike said nothing as he watched the woman stare with revulsion at the drawings. An uncomfortable silence lasting for over a minute passed, before she looked up and studied them both, pushing back the piece of paper as though it were soiled toilet tissue, her owlish eyes steeling as she came to a decision.

"He was a pupil here," Louise said, clearing her throat and reaching for a pitcher that stood on a large green blotter, to half fill a tumbler with water and take a few birdlike sips before continuing. "He was the most wicked person that I have ever met. The only person that, God forgive me, I have ever wished harm to. His name is Luke...Luke Strayhorse. He is a Chiricahua Apache and used to live out on Bear Flats Road with his grandfather, but that was back in about nineteen-eighty.

"When the old man passed on, he just vanished and never came back. I think he had an aunt that he was close to, but I never knew her name or where she lived."

Cal had been reading Louise Gorman's mind from the second that Mike passed the drawings to her, and knew that she was holding nothing back. He had experienced the pure unadulterated hatred that still simmered within her for the Indian, not diminished, even with the passing of so many years. She still suffered bad dreams, her tormented visions of Barnum's head, usually spinning on a plate of gore, screaming as it sprayed blood around the interior of the refrigerator and out onto Louise, who in her appalling nightmares was for some symbolic reason always stood naked before it, her body cold, bathed in yellow light from the small bulb that lit the Frigidaire's ghastly and animated contents.

Cal pulled back from the oppressive hidden misery of the loveless woman's emotions, relieved to escape from her bitter thoughts and memories.

Back on board Ol' Betsy, Sarah poured them coffee, and Cal confirmed that what he and Mike had been told was the truth. He also told them the full story of the 'teacher's pet'.

"She wouldn't have told us a damn thing if Luke hadn't been such an evil bastard," Cal said. "I would've seen it all anyway, but it's nice to know that he is probably so despicable that anyone who knows him will most likely be only too happy to drop him up to his neck in whatever pile of shit is to hand."

Mike scribbled notes on a yellow legal tablet. "So we know his full name now: Luke Strayhorse. And we also know the tribe he is a member of, and that your sketches of him are right on the money, Cal," Mike said. "That old crone looked as if he'd walked into the room when she saw them."

Later, as they drove away from the school, Mike was feeling exhilarated with the jumpy edginess that he always felt when he was closing in. He believed – wrongly – that they were nearing the end zone, and that they would soon track the Indian down. With confirmation of his appearance, and more importantly his surname, Mike thought that within a couple of days the hunt would be over.

Cal parked up off the main highway in a sheltered stand of trees next to Cedar Creek, which appeared to be a peaceful, private location to spend the night. As he helped Sarah cook up a chili, Mike unpacked his laptop and hacked into agency after agency, in what was proving to be a vain attempt to get a lead on the Indian. The guy was a phantom. No credit cards, bank accounts, or even a driver's license. There was nothing to be found under the name of Luke Strayhorse. It was a dead end.

"This is one careful dude," Mike said, giving up on the computer. "He seems to be a non person. Looks like more legwork. What we need now is to meet up with someone who knows him, or we could be going round like headless chickens forever."

Cal smiled. "Don't worry, Mike. We're close. It's just a matter of time before we lift up the right rock and uncover him."

Sarah shivered, her appetite gone. She had none of Cal's paranormal abilities, but was suddenly overwhelmed by an acute sense of foreboding; a fleeting touch of doom that caressed her and then moved on. She found her hand on her thigh; as if to protect the tattoo that lay beneath her shorts.

CHAPTER THIRTY-TWO

He stayed at the cabin until the last week in September. After returning from his last trip, Belle had found Luke to be more uptight and agitated than she had ever seen him before, but knew better than to question him over his visibly jittery demeanor. Over a week passed before he started to settle and become more sociable, relaxing and not staying in his bedroom for lengthy periods.

They went for walks together, spending hours on the deer trails that crisscrossed the area in the vicinity of the cabin. Belle relished the light breeze that filled the forest with the scent of pine, causing the sunlight to dance in a silvery kaleidoscope of dappled freckles through the canopies of the trees. Most days they would make their way down to Turkey Lake, a deep turquoise stretch of mountain run-off, clear and pure, its quality unadulterated by human infestation around its lush banks. They would swim naked in the chill water and then enjoy vigorous sex before dressing under the late summer sun. Luke sometimes fished with a line, catching fat bass that Belle would gut and then bake slowly over a small fire. As they sat picking the fresh and succulent flakes of white meat from the bones, Luke seemed at his most relaxed and happiest, showing a side of his nature that at times could be loving and caring; the eye of the storm. But Belle knew that not far beneath the surface dwelt a cold and callous spirit that was predominant in his make-up. He was an enigma, even to himself.

On the last Monday of September, Luke asked Belle to drive him north to Bylas. And as she put distance between the Jeep and the cabin, she sensed him becoming detached, drawing inward, already separate and mentally apart from her.

Stepping from the vehicle, Luke handed her five, hundred dollar bills, and then nodded and walked away with no word of when he might return, just a slight wave of his hand as he turned his back and departed. Belle knew his habits, though. He was governed by the seasons, and winter was not far off. He always spent winter at the cabin, and would no doubt be back before the first flurries of snow fell on the high ground. He would probably reappear before the end of October.

As Luke crossed highway 70, a truck the size of a barn roared by. When it had passed and the slipstream of dust that clouded the blacktop cleared, he was gone from Belle's sight; vanished as though he had never been.

Luke entered the Buckeye, leaving the dust-laden brightness behind as he walked into the murk of the sleazy roadhouse. Two Indians that he knew looked in his direction, nodded, and then continued with their game of pool. Another four slapped dominoes loudly on the red Formica top of a table, enjoying their noisy and verbal enterprise. The juke was playing Kristofferson singing *Me and Bobby McGee*. He was a singer that Luke half-liked, even if he was white and sounded like a bullfrog with a sore throat. Luke had caught one of his concerts almost thirty years ago in Phoenix, and had enjoyed the guy's laid back, stoned approach. Kris appeared to be a poet and free spirit, who didn't give a fuck about being politically correct, and let you know where he was coming from, even at the risk of being unpopular. Luke had identified with him on some level that he couldn't quite put his finger on.

"Tequila," Luke stated, glancing at Nina, who was the live-in barkeep. She stopped wiping the counter down and filled a shot-glass with the clear spirit, pushing it across to him, her somber and disinterested gaze showing undisguised boredom.

Nina had been living with Larry Loloma, the owner of the dump, for nigh on twelve years, and had been meaning to leave him for the last six of them, but supposed that she never would.

Larry Loloma had the dubious honor of being the tallest Apache in the Southwest. He stood a hair's breadth under seven feet tall, and could have doubled for Will Sampson, the actor who'd played the Chief in the old Nicholson movie, 'One Flew Over the Cuckoo's Nest'. Larry also had a beer-gut that was bought, paid for, and was now a permanent feature of his enormous anatomy.

"Fat Al's been tryin' to get hold of you," Nina said, nodding towards the pay phone.

Luke returned her nod and took his drink down to the end of the bar, to where the phone was fixed to the wall.

Al's rasping voice answered on the second ring, mumbling through the cheap cigar that he gripped between his stained and ill-fitting dentures.

"Yeah, Al, what you got for me?" Luke said.

Al coughed up tarry phlegm and spat it out of the side of his mouth into a metal waste bin; a practiced habit that he accomplished without disturbing the stump of his dollar smoke. "If you can get your sorry ass over to Tucson tomorrow mornin', early, there's a Buick needs pickin' up at Coronado Cars, and then droppin' off at Laguna Motors in Yuma. There'll be a Thunderbird ready to bring back to me. Okay?"

"Let them know I'm coming. I'll see you Thursday," Luke said, and then hung up.

Lenny Jackson was a big man with a big mouth. One of his pet hates happened to be Indians, although he also despised blacks, Hispanics and anyone else who wasn't white with English as their first and only language. He made Donald Trump seem positively liberal. Lenny was a bigot and a racist at heart; just your average, common garden Nazi-type moron. He was lazy and dirty, happy to wear the same underwear and socks until even the dog slunk away when it found itself too close or downwind of him. The man looked unpleasant, acted sour, and smelled worse.

As a mechanic at Coronado Cars, Lenny was at best adequate, only working efficiently if pressed, supervised and chided. His father, George, would have let him go, son or not, but Lenny's mother insisted that he kept the no good son of a bitch on. Why she doted on the idle wretch, George had never been able to figure out.

George was in the can when Luke arrived to pick up the Buick. Had he not been, he could have saved his son – who had never met the Indian – a shitload of grief.

"Whatever you want, we ain't got it, so take a hike," Lenny growled as Luke strolled into the office.

Luke's eyes narrowed. He tensed up, but ignored the stranger's demeaning attitude and remarks. "I don't want trouble, hoss," he said. "I'm here to pick up a Buick to deliver over in Yuma. If you just give me the keys and paperwork I'll be on my way."

Lenny strode out from behind the counter and lowered his unshaven face to within three inches of Luke's.

"When I say take a hike, boy, you take it," he spat, his face purpling with rage. "So vamoose Geronimo, pronto."

Luke was all for not causing a scene, preferring to keep his low profile intact. But the slob stepped over the magic line by prodding him in the chest with an oil-grimed, nail-bitten finger to emphasize his point.

Luke was fast. He took the offending digit in his hand, clenching his fist around it and snapping it backwards in the blink of an eye. There was a loud crack as the finger broke like a dry twig, followed by an even louder bellow of surprise and pain, that was cut short as Luke drove the heel of his other hand into the ape's throat. Standing back, Luke watched in mild amusement as Lenny crumpled to the floor, gasping for air and seemingly uncertain as to whether his broken finger or throbbing throat was the priority, but finally, and quite rightly in Luke's estimation, deciding that his bruised windpipe was the main attraction to concentrate his attention on, which he proceeded to massage with his uninjured hand as he dragged small amounts of air in shallow and obviously painful gulps.

George came through from the back in a hurry, not wiped off, still fastening his pants, alarmed into vacating the toilet by the scream he had heard and recognized as being made by his son. Seeing Luke stood there, he stopped and assessed the situation, noting that Lenny was hurt, fighting for breath, but not beyond repair.

"He ask for it, Luke?" George said as he finished buttoning up his flies.

"Begged for it, George."

"Might just teach him a lesson, eh?"

"Doubt it."

"Well, as maybe," George mused, reaching under the counter and withdrawing an envelope and a set of keys. "That's for the dark green Buick out back. Best if you get gone now, before the boy feels fit enough to suffer some more."

Luke took the proffered paperwork and keys and made for the door. "See you later," he called back. "And George, the boy could do with hosing down, he's stinking the place up something awful."

Lenny croaked an unintelligible profanity from where he now sat with his back up against the wall, but showed no inclination to stand up and instigate a rematch.

"That was Luke Strayhorse you just met," George said, helping Lenny to his feet. "You might want to keep it in mind that he's one dangerous and able motherfucker, son. If we didn't go back aways, he might have just left you for dead."

CHAPTER THIRTY-THREE

LUKE was picking up the T-bird at Laguna Motors in Yuma as Mike brought the Cobra to a stop in the parking lot of a strip mall on the outskirts of Globe.

Antelope Hills was a large complex that as well as being a hypermarket boasted a First National Bank, pharmacy, deli-bakery, restaurant and various other retail outlets all under the same roof. Fast-food diners and gas stations proliferated in its shadow, littering a half mile drag next to highway 70.

"We need to do a full shop," Sarah said as she finished stocktaking the dwindling supplies. "We're low on just about everything."

"I better go pilfer the kitty," Cal said, walking past her, going to the bedroom and removing a wedge of their Vegas money from its hiding place, which was the bottom of the laundry basket in a pillow case, under a pile of not too dirty T-shirts, underwear and towels. "Okay, campers, let's go and spend," he said, reappearing to hand Sarah six hundred bucks in crisp fifty dollar bills, and dividing a further four hundred between himself and Mike. "Let's shop till we drop."

Locking the vehicle, which Mike had parked prominently in the front row of the lot, facing the main entrance of the market, they collected three shopping carts and entered the cool air of the food hall. Following Sarah up and down the aisles as she worked through a lengthy list, the two men talked.

"Where next?" Cal asked. "Any ideas?"

Mike nodded. "We're only about twenty miles from the tribal capital of the San Carlos reservation. We can start there and see if they have any record of Strayhorse. Apart from that, all we can do is keep targeting the usual type of places that he might use, and keep our fingers crossed."

An hour later, with the carts piled high, they returned to the RV and stowed everything away.

"Now that's over with, let's grab a bite to eat," Cal said, scanning the several restaurants that bordered the lot. "How about that?" He pointed to a building in the shape of a giant sombrero, aptly named, El Sombrero, and obviously home to a varied selection of Mexican fare.

Sarah ordered chicken fajitas and took a plate to the salad bar, while both Cal and Mike decided to pig out with a full Mexican platter. All three of them had chilled beer in tankards; the condensation misting the glass and running down it to soak the cardboard coasters.

Rich Cole was at the other side of the lot, sat in a window booth of an Arby's, watching and waiting for them to return to the RV as he hurriedly ate a cheeseburger and washed it down with muddy, gritty coffee from a paper cup.

Tailing the motor home had been a laborious, zigzagging trek south since they had reached eastern Arizona. Mike and the young couple had meandered down through the Fort Apache reservation, stopping at every honky-tonk, gas station, bar and roadhouse. It had been a tiresome and time-consuming journey. And now it looked as if they would follow the same pattern on the San Carlos reservation. Rich had spoken to some of the people that Mike and the Clayton boy had questioned, and now knew that they sought an Indian guy in his forties whose Christian name was Luke. They had been showing drawings of him to everyone, but had – as far as Rich could assess, and due to the fact that they were still searching – not been able to get a fix on him as yet. No one had given Luke's surname; most could smell a cop or fed at fifty yards, and did not feel obliged to give him the time of day. Also, Rich could not take the time to check out every place that they stopped, at risk of losing them. Had he met Louise Gorman, he would have struck gold. But she was one of many he had skipped in his endeavor to keep the RV in sight.

Rich was relying on Mike's tenacity. He had faith that his friend would inadvertently lead him in. Mike was a dog with a bone, and would keep worrying it for the marrow. Come the right time, Rich would step in and officially take over, and that, he knew, would stretch his friendship with the PI to the limit. Mike would be seriously pissed and offended at being used and followed, but would, as a fellow pro, accept that in Rich's shoes he would have done exactly the same.

The official that Cal and Mike spoke to at the tribal headquarters was surly and tight-lipped; not just unhelpful, but downright ornery. He refused to confirm or deny whether he had ever even heard the name, Luke Strayhorse. But his body language spoke volumes at the mention of the Indian, and his eyes widened in recognition as he glanced at the drawings that Mike held up in front of his face.

Cal entered the old Indian's mind, examined his life, and garnered his memories with less effort than it would take to turn on a faucet and fill a glass with water.

Samuel Joseph was seventy, and the mention of Luke's name immediately brought back memories of Bill Strayhorse, Luke's father. He had worked alongside the man for over four years, mainly patching blacktop for the highways department back in the sixties. He recalled that Bill's wife had died during childbirth, and that Bill had taken it badly. The grief had eaten him away, consumed him, and he had not recovered from the loss, drinking heavily to dull a pain that would not abate. It had been Samuel and a friend, Lou Moreno, who'd found his body. It had been frozen, solid as a side of beef in a meatpacker's cold room, lying in a doorway at the back of Sitgreave's Mercantile in Show Low. Samuel remembered that even the vomit that pooled under Bill's face had been rock hard, with glittering crystals formed on its surface, sealing in the smell. He could vividly recall the police having to chip the corpse free from the ground with their snow shovels, and that when they had lifted the stiffened body, the frozen spew had come up with it, protruding from the mouth and stuck to the side of the head like a massive growth that had filled the body and was overflowing from gaping rictus jaws.

The boy, Luke, had been maybe nine or ten years old at the time, but had shown little if any emotion at the loss of his father. Samuel believed that the kid was without normal human feelings, and had been born plain evil; not molded that way by neglect or environment, which were the excuses that do-gooders always threw up to absolve the behavior of the heartless, worthless and dishonest. No, Samuel had been raised in the old ways, and fervently believed that bad spirits could return, taking over new-born souls to perpetuate evil throughout a hundred generations. As far as he was concerned, Luke had a dark demon in his heart, and would never be any good, just a dangerous blot on the land.

The boy had been taken in by his grandfather, now long passed, and Samuel shuddered as he remembered the old man recounting a story of a time he had seen the boy's rotten streak. He'd told Luke to take six puppies from a litter of eight out into the backyard and drown them, leaving two to suckle on the bitch. Later, checking to see if the boy had been capable of performing the task he'd been given, the grandfather had stepped out onto the porch and watched from the shadows. He had seen Luke bite the head off the last struggling pup, to then remove it from his mouth and place it next to the bloody heads of the others that he had lined up in the dirt. The boy had been sitting cross-legged, rocking backwards and forwards, humming to himself with contentment. Blood had been dripping from his mouth, and a glazed, dreamy look of near ecstasy was on his face. His grandfather had said nothing, just retreated from view and gone back inside the house, disgusted and slightly afraid of what inhabited the youngster.

As Luke grew, so did his capacity for violence. His desire or need to inflict pain and suffering becoming the hallmark of his personality; flowing through his being like a raging torrent, stifling and drowning any commendable qualities that attempted to surface.

The last that Samuel had heard of Luke, he had been traveling a lot, but was supposedly still in the area, and in contact with his aunt Belle who lived somewhere near Safford. Damned if he could remember the woman's surname. He had probably never known it.

Cal left the old man with his ghosts and walked out of the building with Mike, saying nothing until they had rejoined Sarah on board the RV.

"Anything?" Mike said, his expression showing that he expected nothing.

Cal grinned. "We're getting warmer. This is his patch. He has an aunt by the name of Belle who lives somewhere near Safford, or did."

Cal told them Samuel's recollections of the young Luke, and of his father's fate. The more they found out, the worse the man that they were looking for appeared to be. A picture was beginning to take shape of this modern day renegade's life, and they felt that the noose was gradually tightening around his neck as they gathered each small morsel of information. He was no longer an elusive specter, but flesh and blood; a human being who could be found and stopped.

"We'll stay on highway 70," Mike said, running his finger over the road map that was open on the table in front of them. "It'll take us through Bylas, Geronimo, Pima, Thatcher and into Safford. If we try every likely spot on that route, we may just hit pay-dirt."

CHAPTER THIRTY-FOUR

STAYING over in Yuma, Luke parked the Thunderbird outside the door of the room at the cheap motel he had booked in to. The Territorial Motor Inn sat back from the interstate, next to an exit ramp which was quite close to the city center. The motel was an ugly and uninviting hovel; a bleached wood and L-shaped complex of eighteen western style cabins, fronted by a flickering red and blue, bug-spattered neon sign that was fixed to two tall wooden poles in the graveled parking lot, buzzing and flickering intermittently as it flashed V C NCY. The missing A's were an unintentional eye-catcher that repelled rather than attracted passing trade. A hospice for the terminally ill had more charm and appeal than the Territorial, and a greater number of residents.

As darkness fell, Luke set off walking toward the downtown glow. He could feel the reassuring pressure of the booted knife pressing against his calf, and the weight of the fat roll of duct tape in his jacket pocket.

Entering a smoky, nicotine-stained bar six or seven blocks from the motel, Luke ordered tequila, and then sat for a while contemplating and anticipating the forthcoming hunt. A half hour and two more shots later, with warmth in his gut and adrenaline beginning to circulate through his muscles, heightening his senses, he left the bar. He was as excited as a kid in the gray half-light of Christmas morning, just prior to tearing the ribbon and wrapping from that first parcel; hands shaking, teeth chattering, ripping the paper frantically to uncover the, as yet, unknown gift hidden within.

Lisa McNary lived alone in an apartment in Gila Bend, but had been over to Yuma to visit her widowed mother. At twenty-seven, Lisa was now divorced and feeling as free as a bird. A shitty phase of her life was now thankfully behind her, and she was rejuvenated and able to function again as an individual, out from an oppressive relationship that had blighted her life.

Lisa's mother, Katherine, was a pain in the ass, continually moaning about everything and anything. She had become a woman with no joy left in her heart, and had the ability to demoralize the most happy-go-lucky folk within a few minutes of being in their company.

A couple of days with her mom had seemed like a small eternity and had almost driven Lisa to distraction. Blood was supposedly thicker than water, but it was sometimes extremely hard to hold on to that thought. She decided that subsequent visits would be far and few between. And she also omitted telling her mom that she was moving from Gila Bend soon. She had been offered the position of manager of an up market furniture store in Scottsdale, and had also been asked to share an apartment with a friend from her college days who lived in Paradise Valley; a beautiful suburb of Phoenix. Her life was turning round for the better.

Tossing her duffel bag into the back of the Dodge station wagon, Lisa waved good-bye to her mother, who stood hatchet-faced at the front door of the tract house for only a few seconds before going inside and closing the door without waving back. Since the death of Lisa's father three years ago, what had been a happy home had become a place of misery. Her mom had not forgiven her husband, Stephen, for going up on the roof to tighten the loose bracket of the satellite dish. He had slipped and fallen, to roll down the shingles and off into midair, to land head first on the roof of their Caddy and die almost instantly as his neck was broken.

Lisa missed her father. He had always been jovial, outgoing and loving, and was well thought of by everyone that knew him. Pulling off the highway, Lisa parked in the lot of a small convenience store, got out of the car and lit a cigarette. She smoked half of it, and then walked over to the entrance, pausing to crush the butt out in a pedestal ashtray. She was thirsty and needed a fix of caffeine before carrying on.

Back at the car, Lisa took a sip of the strong brew, and then put the cup in a holder and slipped a John Denver CD into the player before keying the engine to life.

The parking lot was ill-lit, lined with palm trees that cast long shadows across its width under the moonlight. The night air was scented with jasmine and honeysuckle, and the road appeared to be deserted.

Luke was standing less than twelve feet behind the station wagon. He had been passing as it pulled in and stopped, and had watched the young woman climb out and stand next to it and light a cigarette. She had taken a few deep drags from it and then strolled over to the main door of the store. She was slim, wearing a loose sweater with the sleeves pushed up to her elbows, and tight jeans that strained the denim taut against firm buttocks.

Angling across the lot, hands in pockets and searching the shadow-streaked night for anyone that might witness what he was about to do, Luke had just waited.

A few minutes later, as Lisa was about to put the car in drive, the door came open and she was startled at the sudden appearance of a middle-aged guy, well, over forty anyway. She thought he looked relaxed, with a casual attitude that was not intimidating. He had a pleasant, open friendly face, and he was smiling at her.

"What do you want?" Lisa said.

"Everything," Luke said as he punched her hard on the left side of her face, high up on the temple.

Another glance around satisfied him that no one had witnessed what had taken place. The woman was dazed but still conscious. He hit her again, harder, and she slumped sideways across the passenger seat and became still.

Lifting her legs up and pushing her over the center console into the passenger foot well, he climbed in and drove out on to the highway, to head south from Yuma to a rocky area bordering the Kofa Wildlife Refuge, just a forty minute drive from the store. Stopping at an isolated scenic overlook – that did not even have vending machines or restrooms – Luke parked in a corner of the dark, dirt-topped area to wind duct tape around his new acquisition's head to cover her mouth, and to also secure her ankles and wrists with it.

Finding a narrow gravel top turnoff several miles farther south, Luke killed the lights and followed the road until it became little more than a dirt track. He kept going, up to higher ground, to finally branch off by the side of a canyon with the trickle of a stream running along one side of it, and a dense stretch of trees growing on the far bank. It was a desolate location, and he felt safe and in complete control of the situation as he drove through the shallow water and parked the vehicle out of sight in a gap among the fir trees.

The moon was almost full, casting enough illumination for him to see clearly. He switched off the ignition and stepped out of the station wagon to light a cigarette and listen to the night as he looked up at the star-filled heavens. This was the good life, from which he took and enjoyed all that he desired.

Lisa's head was pounding. She was folded almost double and could hardly breathe, and although now fully conscious she kept quiet and still. It was hard to believe what had happened to her. One second she had been safe inside the car, and the next she had been attacked. Why hadn't she locked the door? Why had she stayed there and put a CD on instead of driving off first? She had not been thinking straight. She should have parked at the door of the store, where it was brightly lit.

Her mind was racing, and what she should or shouldn't have done didn't matter anymore. She had been assaulted and abducted, and was now bound up and gagged. He was without any doubt going to rape and murder her, and there was nothing that she could do to prevent it happening. Although he would have to free her ankles to open her legs and take her. And when he did, and if she pretended that she was still be unconscious, then she could lash out with her feet, kick him, and make a run for it.

Finishing the cigarette, Luke opened the rear door of the Dodge and took off all of his clothes and placed them on the rear seat, before drawing the knife from the sheath in his boot.

Terror threatened to overcome Lisa. Her thought processes were in danger of meltdown, which would render her incapable of doing anything. She wanted to survive, so concentrated on somehow remaining still and waiting for what might only be a split-second chance to turn the situation around. As the front passenger door was opened she fought for some measure of composure. She had to keep her muscles loose and her eyes closed, so that he would not be prepared for what she planned on doing.

Grasping the woman by the collar of her sweater, Luke dragged her out of the vehicle and across to a spot between two tall trees, where pine needles and twigs made for a softer surface to deal with her. Dumping her down on the ground face up, he used the keen, broad blade to cut through the tape binding her wrists, and then pulled her woolen sweater taut and slashed through the turtle neck and slit the garment down to part it at the hem. Next was the lacy bra. He sliced it open at the center, to relish the sight of her breasts as the cups fell apart to disclose them.

Lisa could not stifle a groan as the point of the blade nicked her skin.

He smiled. She was coming round. He wanted her to feel every single sensation of what he was about to do.

Jeans next. He cut through the duct tape pinioning her ankles together, and then placed the knife down while he pulled off her Reebok sneakers.

Now! Lisa thought, knowing that this was the only chance that she would get to escape. She drew her legs back, bending them at the knee to then shoot them up and forward like pistons with all the strength that she could muster.

Both of the bitch's heels struck him in the solar plexus. The explosion of pain was instant and paralyzing. He fell back and pressed both hands to his stomach and fought for breath.

Lisa did not hesitate, just leapt to her feet and took off like a scalded cat. She needed to get as far away from him as possible. There may have been time for her to climb in the station wagon, but she couldn't take the chance that he had left the key in the ignition, so just ran through the trees swerving around their trunks, tripping once over a rock, but too frantic to even feel any pain as she rolled, sprang back up and careered along what could have been a deer trail. After less than twenty seconds she left the trail and headed towards a sandstone cliff that she hoped she would be able to climb.

He took several deep, whooping breaths, and then got to his feet, to stoop and pick up the knife and lurch off in the direction that she had gone. He would find her, of that there was no doubt whatsoever, and when he did she would die slow and hard for the trouble that she was putting him to.

After only jogging for thirty or forty yards he had to stop and lean against a tree. The cramping pain in his upper abdomen was easing slightly, but he needed to rest for a minute until it became more bearable. He smiled despite the discomfort. Having to hunt her down was stimulating. It added a dimension to what would be the ultimate kill.

Lisa came out next to the meandering stream. It was little more than twelve feet wide, and only shin-deep. She stepped into the slow-moving chill water and made it half way across before slipping on slimy pebbles and falling on her ass. She was hurting, cold and petrified, but had to keep going, so got up and carried on, to step out at the other side and be faced by an almost sheer wall of rock that she knew would be impossible to climb. There was a path of sorts at the bottom of the cliffs. She jogged along it for over a hundred yards and came to a fissure that she supposed was a narrow canyon. Her only choice was to continue in the open or enter it.

He chuckled as he heard a loud splash, and headed in the direction it had come from, to reach the stream and cross it and walk along the left bank for several yards, then retrace his steps and inspect the rocky ground to the right. The wet footprints looked like just so many small dark shadows in the moonlight. He followed them, and they led him in front of a crag that ran for as far as he could see. But he was closing in. Reaching a break in the cliff that was only eight or ten feet wide, telltale drops of water where evidence that she had entered it.

After following the winding canyon for less than a minute it began to narrow, and then dead-ended. Lisa just stood and looked up at the night sky high above. She would have to somehow climb to safety. Going back was not an option. There was every chance that she would come face to face with the psycho who intended to murder her.

Luke stayed close up to one side and moved cautiously along what he thought was a gulch. The bitch had shown that she had the wherewithal to keep her head and defend herself. Perhaps she had found a length of dead branch and was up ahead waiting to use it on him like a baseball bat. Or picked up a large rock and planned to smash it into his face. He walked in a crouch, and moved silently. There was no rush. This was terrain that he was at ease in, and that gave him the advantage.

Reaching the end of what was a blind alley, leading nowhere, Luke looked up and saw her clinging to the rock like a spider only twenty feet above his head.

"Now what?" he called up to her. "Unless you can fly, you'rc dead meat."

Lisa clung on with aching fingers, looked down at him and said, "If you climb up after me I'll kick you in the face."

He laughed, and the sound of it echoed dully from wall to wall. He had no intention of climbing. There were plenty of loose pieces of rock of various sizes resting in the red sand. He selected one the size of a large orange and hurled it up at her. It missed by a couple of inches, bouncing back down to almost strike him on the head. Picking it up he threw again, and this time it connected with her thigh, but although she screamed out she managed to hold on. It was the third shot that did the trick. The rock struck her in the lower back, hard, and she fell.

Twisting in mid-air, Lisa hit the hard ground on her right side, to scream again as her shoulder broke and some of her ribs broke. She tasted blood and believed that the jagged end of one had punctured a lung.

Luke took his time. Stripped off her jeans and panties and fucked her before starting in on the wet work. And there was a bonus; a small tattoo of a dolphin on her hip, which he removed with one stroke of the broad knife blade. The coup de grâce was a single thrust of the knife into her windpipe. He then sat cross-legged in front of her and watched as she writhed and jerked, gasping breath that she could no longer inhale. Blood misted the air and spotted her lips as she frantically, vainly attempted to cling on to life.

Lisa almost welcomed death when it came. In the last few seconds of consciousness the pain seemed to dissolve, and she became accepting of the eternal peace of nonexistence that she was so close to being a part of.

Luke fucked the now cooling body again, and then dragged it behind an outcrop of rock and left it for the plentiful and varied wildlife to sniff out and devour. He then went back to the stream and washed the blood from his body before returning to the Dodge, dressing and driving back to the outskirts of Yuma, where he abandoned the vehicle unlocked with the key in the slot, in an area that guaranteed it would be stolen within minutes.

He walked the mile back to the Territorial Motel feeling jubilant. The tattooed piece of Lisa McNary was nestled in his right hand, a souvenir of a much enjoyed evening's work. He had foregone skinning the bitch; although he had promised himself earlier that he would perform the task, after his last catastrophic experience. But it would have been a pointless and uninspiring exercise. Once they were dead and beyond pain, then there was no pleasure left to be had. The episode had been fulfilling, though, and he felt well compensated for the bad experience of the last lucky piece of ass who had escaped his clutches in El Paso.

CHAPTER THIRTY-FIVE

OL' Betsy was looking in need of some TLC. Sand and morning dew had combined – over a period of time – to form a coating; a thick patina that made the vehicle look like a time-aged relic. Only two sparkling wedges of glass reflected the sun, where the wipers had kept the crust at bay on the windshield.

"There," Cal said, pointing ahead at the roadhouse that crouched squat and low in the middle of a large gravel parking lot; a grimy plastic sign atop a faded hand-painted totem pole announcing that the structure was The Buckeye. The joint, for lack of a more suitable description, was a rickety, warped, wooden building, fragile-looking and leaning off-true in several directions, making it appear as though it was about to collapse; just waiting for a strong gust of desert wind to reduce it to match-wood. The few visible windows were small, covered with rusted mesh screens that obscured any view of the interior. This was not the sort of place that attracted tourists or passing trade. It was for locals of a certain standing, who did not reckon too highly in the community's scheme of things.

An elderly Indian was sitting on the step of a sagging porch that ran the length of the frontage, his shoulder-length yellow-white hair worn in loose matted plaits protruding from a battered black Stetson that had lost all shape over many years. He sucked on a corncob pipe, and was stroking a half-starved looking, three-legged mongrel dog, with one of his gnarled and palsied hands. Looking up and squinting out through milky cataracts, he could hear clearer than see the large motor home that swept by him, its tires throwing up sand before parking up thirty yards away.

Mike stepped out into the heat, lit a Marlboro and looked about him, noticing the U-Wash machine and deciding to treat the RV to a wash 'n' wax as soon as they had been inside to question the shit-hole's owner. Cal joined him, and they walked across the lot and stepped up past the old man and his dog to the screen door. The squeaking hinges heralded their presence. Inside, the dive was rundown, sleazy and dimly lit; the noise of the air conditioner as loud as the music emitted from the dented fifties Wurlitzer that was playing a scratchy 45; Patsy Cline singing *Crazy*.

They approached a woman who was sitting idly behind the bar, and who barely gave them a glance; a picture of pure, undiluted disinterest on her hard, lined face. She was just functioning on automatic, long past even affecting a pretense of civility.

"'Scuse me, ma'am," Mike said, resting one cheek of his butt on the knife-slashed vinyl top of a stool as he spoke. "We're looking for a guy by the name of Luke Strayhorse. Do you know where we might find him?"

"Larry, git out here," she shouted, turning her head towards the closed door behind her, that had a Keep Out sign tacked to it, and presumably led through to the owner's living quarters.

After a few seconds she shouted again. "Hey, Lar—"

The door opened and a giant Indian lowered his head at least six inches to allow him egress without cracking his skull.

"Yeah, Nina, what?" He growled in a deep, gruff voice, obviously not pleased at being disturbed.

"These guys are lookin' for someone," she said, walking away to the other end of the bar.

"Cops?" Larry said, resting his shovel-sized hands on the less than clean bar top.

"No," Mike said, producing his ID to hold out for inspection. "Private. Just trying to locate a guy for someone. Does the name Strayhorse ring any bells?"

"No," Larry replied, too quickly, already turning as he spoke, dismissing Mike.

"Hey, Chief, this is important," Mike snapped at the giant's back.

Larry stopped and spun round with surprising speed for a man of such Goliath proportions, his jet eyes fixed on Mike with all the humor of a great white shark.

"Listen, cop," he hissed through clenched teeth, his jaw muscles working, bunching his cheeks. "I ain't no chief, and what might be important to you could be bowel cancer for all I care. So fuck off, now, before you find yourself in a shitload of sorrow that you won't believe."

Mike wanted to take the big man on, to hurt him and bring him down to size. He tensed, preparing to move forward, but Cal jabbed him hard in the ribs with his elbow, breaking his line of thought.

"Let's go, buddy. I'm on the case, remember," Cal said, taking hold of Mike's arm and making for the door.

Outside in the fresh air, Mike took deep breaths, trying to disperse the adrenaline overload that had hit him as he had readied himself for combat with the colossal Apache.

Cal grinned at him. "You could have got yourself squished like a bug for nothing, Mike. Have you forgotten that we don't need answers with me around, eh?"

Mike rolled his shoulders to unravel the tension that was tightening his muscles, and managed to smile. "I hadn't forgotten, Cal. I just didn't like his piss-poor attitude. He needs educating. I take it you did the grand tour of his head?"

"Yes, and it's a place I'd rather not have been."

Larry was unsettled, ignoring an Oprah rerun on the TV and pacing restlessly, he wondered what the two strangers wanted Luke for, and wished that he had let the PI run off at the mouth more, before telling him and his sidekick to fuck off. The code that he lived by prevented him from singing, especially to whites. Had it not, then he would have dropped Strayhorse into the deepest pile of shit on offer. He traced the hairline scar on his throat with his thumb, recalling vividly the night, long ago now, when Luke had cut him with the outsize Bowie knife he kept in his boot.

It had been back in ninety-nine, when Larry had owned the Bear's Claw in Bisbee; which was a misnomer. The place should have been called the Bear's Asshole, or the Bear's Armpit; something that reflected the cankerous rough house's true character, and readied patrons for the sour odor of sweat, vomit, backed up toilets and cheap liquor that permeated throughout the squalid building. The spit and sawdust saloon was a second home to every drunken Indian and ill-tempered copper miner in the district. Brawls appeared to be almost mandatory, and Larry was renowned for his skill in ejecting – with all due pain and lack of consideration – any patron who got too far out of line. He never instigated a situation, but put an end to hundreds, removing troublemakers, sometimes two at a time to deposit on the sidewalk, taking no little pleasure in cracking heads and generally inflicting sufficient pain and injury to go a long way towards reforming their behavior, at least inside his premises. Larry should have been on a retainer, or on commission for the amount of business that he put the ambulance services way.

It had been a hot Friday evening in June when Luke had entered the Claw early, his mood as dark and mean as a timber wolf with raging toothache. He had taken a bottle of tequila and a shot glass over to a corner table, to drink alone. Larry had known Luke for several years' at that time, and had known of him by reputation for a lot longer. They were on good terms, and dealt in hot cars regularly. Luke stole them, and Larry ringed and sold them on. The two men had spent countless nights drinking together and talking of the old days and old ways, both sharing a common hatred for the whites, who in the main still regarded Indians as having less worth than campfire dogs.

The Claw had been heaving on that June evening. The miners had been paid, and were converting as much of their hard-earned cash as possible into booze, before driving or staggering home, loaded.

Four of the copper-diggers took it into their heads to not only sit at the small table that Luke was monopolizing, but to move him off, not wanting the Apache in their midst.

Patrick Ross was a big, 'take no prisoners, and fight the world' kind of guy, who'd never heard the word diplomacy, and lacked the ability to use any measure of adroitness in dealing with others.

"Hey, 'buffalo who shits in grass', or whatever the fuck some squaw christened you with horse piss," Patrick said with undisguised menace in his voice. "Haul ass and let us God-fearin', hard workin' white folk rest our bones."

Luke totally ignored the miner and raised the glass to his lips, emptying the contents before reaching for the bottle to pour another shot. Had he been left alone for another hour, then the fiery liquid may have mellowed his mood. He may have just moved and disregarded the miner's comments. But he was still stone-cold sober and in no frame of mind to be hassled by the vilifying troglodyte who stood in front of him with fists clenched on his hips, glaring with undisguised animosity.

"You've got five seconds to disappear, redskin," Patrick growled, now livid at being so blatantly ignored; disregarded as though he did not exist. "If you're still in my face when I finish countin' I'm gonna rip your fuckin' head off and piss in your neck."

The big man was almost purple in the face, eyes bulging like organ stops, and with a large vein throbbing at his temple in time to the beat of the jukebox. His hands were now fisted so tightly that his scarred and callused knuckles were ivory-white.

Luke looked up and stared into the other man's eyes, unblinking and with a calm expression on his face which disguised the seething anger that roiled beneath his bland expression.

"Do it or fuck off, Custer," Luke drawled slow and easy, a smile now playing at the corners of his mouth, but not touching his eyes.

Larry watched from the bar. The miner knocked a chair out of the way with a sweep of his muscular arm and reached across the table. Larry admired Luke's turn of speed, as he grabbed a handful of the miner's thick, greasy hair and brought his face down with shattering force onto the solid timber tabletop. The Irishman's nose exploded like a cartridge in a fire; the sound audible above the cacophony of noise in the crowded bar.

Patrick Ross was already unconscious as Luke pushed him back from the table to watch him slide down in a heap, out of his sight. But the other three dummies felt lucky. They rushed in as one, but Luke had already drawn the knife from his boot, and as they saw the light flash off the ten inch blade, they hesitated, and he struck. He hit the nearest to him in the forehead with the turquoise-tipped hilt, pole-axing him like a dumb ox. The second received a straight thumb in his left eye and screamed out, cupping his hands to the eyeball, which had been popped from the socket to hang on his cheek, looking down at the floor. Staggering away, half blind, he tripped over a chair and his forehead split open like an overripe tomato on the rough floorboards, for the gusher of blood to be greedily absorbed by the parched wood.

The last of the foursome stopped in his tracks. Realizing that he had no support left he was suddenly chastened and wanted no truck with the lethal Indian who stood before him. He started to back off, his hands lowered and open, signaling with a full range of body language that he was no longer a threat.

Luke moved in a blur, grasping the retreating deserter by the throat with his left hand, to push him backwards, up against the wall with breath-stopping pressure on his windpipe, which between the viselike jaws of fingers and thumb was being slowly crushed.

As the curved blade of the Bowie rose in front of him, the choking miner felt his bladder release its hot contents, to darken the front of his jeans and run down his leg. He thought that he was going to die, and Larry thought so too. He vaulted the bar and reached them in three giant strides. Grasping Luke's wrist, he twisted it backwards, only to immediately find his hand empty, as Luke brought his arm down, snatching his wrist free and flicking the blade of the knife upwards for the tip to cut into Larry's throat, drawing a crimson line from ear to ear. It was a measured cut, not deep enough to sever arteries or cause serious damage, but sufficient to scar him for life.

"Back off, Larry, this is a private party," Luke hissed. "These ol' boys wanted to have some fun, and I don't want to disappoint them."

Larry knew that the wound he had sustained was just a warning, judged to the millimeter, and so he stood his ground, conscious of the blood that fell like a curtain to soak the front of his T-shirt.

"Let it go now, Luke. It's over," Larry said as they locked eyes. And Luke did let go, releasing the petrified miner to slide down the wall and join his fellow attackers in the sawdust. The man's face was plum-colored, his throat a constricted ball of pain; each tortured breath a thorny, razor-blade rasp that brought tears to his eyes.

Turning back to the table, Luke bent to slip the knife into the boot sheath and then retook his seat, ready for another shot of tequila.

"Come on, big guy," he said, smiling affably at Larry as though nothing untoward had taken place. "Fetch another glass. Have a drink with me."

Larry's already healthy respect for Luke had increased immeasurably from that day forth. He saw the man for what he was; a deadly wild animal who could turn in a second, even on a supposed friend. Luke had a wall around his heart; a barrier that no one could penetrate or even loosen the mortar that held the bricks of it in place. It kept him insular, safe beyond the weakness of emotions that might undermine his deep and rock hard foundations.

Larry was sure that even his superior size and strength would not guarantee supremacy over the machine that was Luke Strayhorse. He had never seen the man show fear of anything, only, as in the case of the miners, a degree of restraint, not wanting to publicly commit an act that would risk his being subject to incarceration in a white man's prison. That characteristic of self preservation had undoubtedly saved the miners' lives.

Back in the now, Larry ran his fingers over the white line of the scar on his throat and wondered what to do about the two guys that had visited The Buckeye asking questions. He knew that Luke spent time at the cabin of his aunt, Belle Morita, which was situated somewhere up off US 666 in high country. Belle was not on the phone, so he couldn't warn Luke about the private dicks. He probably wasn't even at the cabin, so he would tell him about the two guys the next time that he called in at The Buckeye. If they found him in the meantime, then God help them. They would shoot first and worry about questions afterwards if they had any idea of just what he was capable of.

CHAPTER THIRTY-SIX

CAL shook his head as he flipped out of Larry Loloma's mind. He was wholly himself again as he and Mike stepped back onto the RV. He surveyed the expectant expressions on both Sarah's and Mike's faces, and gave them a smug, knowing smile. "The eagle has landed," he said, going over to the fridge for a can of beer before sitting at the bench in the dinette section to share the 'Chief's' thoughts and recollections with them.

They listened to the full account, with no questions asked or comments made until Cal was through and sat back to finish his Coors.

"If Loloma sees Luke, he'll give him our descriptions and put him on guard," Mike said. "From now on we'd better carry guns and watch our backs. We don't want to end up being on the receiving end. Strayhorse sounds a handful, and let's not forget that we're in his backyard. If he gets wind of us he'll have the advantage."

Mike went forward and returned with the handguns and two shoulder rigs. He handed the Glock to Cal. It was black, weighed a pound and a half, and Cal was familiar with the model from his previous life. It felt comfortable in his grip.

"It's a nine millimeter Glock 17, fully loaded, and there's no external safety to worry about," Mike said.

Cal removed the magazine and also ejected the bullet that was already in the chamber. He then snapped the mag back into the stock with the heel of his hand and smiled at Mike.

"Just for a moment I forgot that you're not who you appear to be, and that you know your way around firearms," Mike said.

"What about me?" Sarah said. "I'd feel safer with some personal protection."

Mike looked thoughtful and then nodded. "Better safe than sorry," he said, reaching down, pulling up his right trouser cuff and withdrawing a small, stainless steel revolver from a soft leather ankle holster. "Backup piece," he said as way of explanation for the concealed weapon that Sarah had not known about, but of which Cal had been aware of since being in Mike's head, although he had said nothing.

Emptying the cylinder, Mike passed the pistol to Sarah and said, "Do you know how to use one of these?"

"No, not yet."

"Okay," Mike said. "This is a Smith & Wesson snub-nose .38. Get used to the feel of it, and keep it in your purse. When we find a quiet spot, I'll give you some intensive training."

Sarah held it. The pistol felt cold, strange, but reassuring in her hand. It was the first time that she had ever touched a handgun, and even though Mike had removed the shells, it felt exactly what it was, a deadly weapon.

Cal got up suddenly and walked to the door, turning to the other two as he opened it. "I must be stupid!" he said. "Here we are worrying about Loloma telling Strayhorse that we're on his case, and I've got the ability to convince him that talking about us is the last thing on earth he wants to do. You two give Ol' Betsy a wash and brush up. I won't be long."

"Larrrry!" Nina shouted for the second time in less than thirty minutes. "One of those guys is back...Wants a word."

The door behind the counter burst open and Larry came through the opening like a big old grizzly whose hibernation has been rudely interrupted, and has woken up with a bad case of hemorrhoids. He looked more than ready to slap some sense into anyone that didn't listen up real good.

"Whoa...Just hold it right there, Chief, and calm down," Cal said as Larry rounded the end of the bar like a runaway freight train. "Or the police are going to be all over the hot cars on this lot, and the truckload of computers that you've got stashed in the lockup out back. You know the one's I mean. Donny Rivers and Billy Bob Baker delivered them three nights back."

Larry stopped, head cocked to one side like a puzzled dog, worried now, trying to figure out just what the young guy's play was. If he had been a cop, then Larry knew that he would already be in custody. The big man went cold, feeling claustrophobic at just the thought of confined spaces; especially the likes of a cell.

"So just what the fuck do you want?" Larry said with a cautious but resigned tone to his deep voice.

"That's more like it," Cal said. "Just a couple of minutes of your time, in private, and then I'll be out of your face for good."

"Come on through," Larry said, jerking his head towards the back, not waiting for Cal as he moved quickly behind the bar, to duck and vanish through the doorway.

Cal had entered the Indian's mind again, not trusting him, wanting to be sure that Larry would not suddenly pick him up and break him like a twig. But the volatile giant was not planning to inflict any damage. He was just worried, bewildered, and more than a little curious as to how Cal knew so much about his business. He had decided that he must have been the subject of a stakeout. They obviously wanted to cut some kind of deal, or his ass would already be on a cot in the slammer.

"Sit down, Larry, and listen up. I'm no cop and this isn't a set up. All I want is Luke Strayhorse, nothing else. What I don't want is you running off at the mouth and warning him that he has an unofficial posse trying to nail his ass. I know your thoughts and memories, all of them. I'm in your head right now, and can even see that night when Luke cut you with that mother of a knife he keeps in his boot. You know that he's dangerous, but you have no idea just how dangerous. Strayhorse is a serial killer; a fully fledged psycho who rapes, mutilates and kills his victims. He murdered me over twenty years ago, when I came across him at the scene of one of his sick crimes. And now I'm back to stop him, for good.

"You're planning to tell him about us the next time that you see him, and that is not something I can allow to happen, so I'm going to have to convince you that talking to him is the last thing you would want to do. I am the most powerful medicine man that it has ever been your misfortune to meet. And you need to believe that, if you still want to be alive when I leave this room."

What Larry wanted to believe was that the young man was paddling his canoe with just one oar in the creek. But that didn't explain how he seemed to be reading his thoughts. Built in superstition and native belief in forces outside human ken stopped him from laughing at the guy, or rearranging his face and throwing him out. He was nervous of talk about reincarnation and all that had been implied, but still thought that this was some kind of set up; a scam that he just hadn't worked out yet.

"I think you're full of shit," Larry said, logic telling him not to entertain what the guy was trying to sell. "You get one shot at proving what you say, and if I don't buy it, I'm going to break every bone in your body."

"You got it, Chief," Cal said. "That Desert Eagle in the top drawer of your bureau should do the trick. I'm going to make you go over there and get it. Then you're going to thumb the safety off, put the muzzle nice and snug up against your temple and pull the trigger. That way I don't have to take the chance of you flapping that big dumb mouth the second you see your old buddy."

Larry attempted to cross the space between himself and Cal, with the full intention of ripping the other man's face off, now convinced that he was a candidate for a rubber room.

The big Indian froze in mid-stride, unable to move, feeling as though not just his legs, but his whole body was set in concrete. He was slowly turned around against his will, and found himself walking stiff-legged across to the bureau. He could only watch in fearful fascination as his right hand – with traitorous independence – took the pistol from the drawer, and his other equally perfidious hand flipped off the safety. He was then jerked back round to face his puppeteer, and made to walk to the center of the room. Fighting, yet powerless to resist an undeniable impulse, Larry's gun-hand slowly raised the weapon and pressed the cold steel of the muzzle against the side of his head. Beads of sweat pebbled his forehead as he exerted all of his considerable strength to no effect, trying to pull the weapon away, but feeling as though it were glued in place. His finger tightened on the trigger, and for the first time in his life he experienced the prospect of certain death, with all the emotions that accompany the irrefutable knowledge that you are about to buy the farm.

Cal used his mind with the sureness and precision of a virologist handling a phial full of some lethal toxic virus without the benefit of protective clothing or a self-contained supply of oxygen. He took the pressure off Larry's finger at a point so near discharging a bullet into the Indian's brain that his life was truly within less than a hair's breadth of being extinguished.

"Well, Chief...Do you believe?" Cal said, lowering Larry's arm to his side and allowing his hand to let the gun fall to the threadbare carpet. "I didn't need the gun," he continued in a more friendly tone of voice. "I could have just willed your heart to stop beating. I don't wish you any harm, Larry, but you had to know that I was for real, for your own good. I see that you've decided not to talk to Strayhorse. Please don't change your mind, because if you do, I'll know, and you'll see me again. And that would be a meeting you *wouldn't* survive. Oh, and Larry, make sure that Nina minds her own business as well. Your continued good health depends on it."

Larry sank into a chair, his limbs liquid, unable to hold him up. He knew that the demonstration could have been one involving pain or death, and not just an exhibition of power to instill fear. He fully appreciated that the strange young white man had a capability beyond his comprehension; awesome facilities to be respected and very afraid of.

Cal left Larry sitting there with his mouth agape in shock and with a lot to ponder. He knew that the big Indian would not discuss what had taken place in that room with anyone, especially Luke.

"If you make one mistake, he'll kill you." Larry said as Cal reached the door. Cal turned to face him and managed a pained smile. "I know that, Larry. I told you, he already has done once."

BOOK FOUR

CLOSING IN

CHAPTER THIRTY-SEVEN

THE teenage girl was obese, and perspiring profusely due to the air-con being on a low setting. Her short mousy hair was damp and stuck to her forehead, around her ears and at the nape of her neck. She leaned forward toad-like towards the laminated glass that protected and separated her from the public, physically if not verbally.

"Hi there, Demi," Mike said, having scanned the plastic ID tag on the stretched nylon fabric that fought to hold back the post office girl's breasts. "I wonder if you can help us out. We need the address of a lady by the name of Belle Morita."

Demi wasn't a hot-looking supermodel or actress kind of girl, Mike thought, but her open smile and warm brown eyes were captivating, and when she spoke, her voice was liquid silk.

Demi told Mike that it was not policy to give out addresses, but Cal picked the address of Belle Morita's cabin and its location from her mind. He had also gathered all other information that Demi knew about the woman they sought. He saw that Demi knew Belle visited Safford every second Friday to shop, driving down from her mountain home in a battered green Jeep; always parking up opposite the post office outside The Cotton Bob; a needlepoint store that was owned by her best friend, Suzanne Caitlin.

It was Monday. They had four days to familiarize themselves with the area and wait for Belle to hit town. Cal needed to get inside her head and surreptitiously learn all that he could from her about Strayhorse before they attempted to capture or, if necessary, kill him. Knowing him as Belle did could give them the edge they needed. It could ultimately make the difference between life and death, because from what Cal knew from personal experience and had seen in Loloma's mind, Strayhorse was a ruthless and sadistic piece of work; a repeat murderer who would not hesitate in killing anyone who posed a threat to him.

Back on board Ol' Betsy, they discussed the current situation.

"We're so close," Sarah said. "Wouldn't it be better to call in the police now and let them take it from here?"

"No way," Cal said with an unintentional hard edge to his voice. "You and Mike can, and probably should, back off now. But for me this is personal. This callous bastard takes life for pleasure. He enjoys causing maximum suffering to helpless victims, with no thought or feeling for them or the people that love them. He drifts through his repulsive life leaving a trail of death and misery behind him, and I want to stop him, and let him know who I am and why I've hunted him down. Rightly or wrongly I need to finish this if I'm ever going to be able to put it behind me and start over. He isn't going to get his day in court."

Neither Sarah nor Mike said anything, but both understood. Mike nodded, appreciating how Cal must feel, even though it was impossible to put himself in the other man's shoes. He could never know the trauma that his friend had suffered. But he did know that he wanted to be part of the solution, be it a crusade or just a journey of revengeful intent. He was in too deep now to even contemplate walking away. His mind was made up to stay by Cal and see it through, to whatever conclusion.

"For better or worse, you're stuck with us, Cal. We're a team," Sarah said firmly. Her face was pale but bore a fixed, resolute expression that defied argument.

The road that led up from Safford into the eastern fringe of the Coronado Forest was US 666; a number that held dark, satanic significance, and could almost be looked upon as a portent of evil, which was appropriate, given that this was where they hoped to end the reign of a devil in human guise.

As a base, they parked up at an RV campground just south of town and were soon connected up to the power and water lines. Mike had rented a Range Rover, to give them more maneuverability on the mountain roads, and because the Cobra was too high profile for surveillance work.

Once settled in, Mike decided to leave Cal and Sarah in the RV while he reconnoitered the approach to the cabin. He also wanted to give the couple some space and time to be together without his continual presence. He hadn't forgotten what it was like to be in your twenties and in love. Arming himself with a road map and binoculars, as well as his handgun, he made ready to acquaint himself with the territory, for when the time came they would be visiting in earnest and need to know the lay of the land.

"I'll be back in a couple of hours," Mike said before leaving to head south on 666.

Rich Cole was now behind the wheel of a sturdy Explorer, following Mike, but not needing to keep him in sight, knowing his approximate destination. He had parked between other vehicles on the street and watched Mike, accompanied by Danny Clayton, go into the post office, then followed the RV to a used car dealership, where Mike rented an SUV and tagged on behind the motor home to the campground. When they had settled, he returned to the post office, flashed his FBI ID, which had impressed Demi, and was told of their interest in Belle Morita, and the whereabouts of her cabin. Swearing the wide-eyed girl to secrecy, he left, to park up within sight of the campground and wait, to then tail Mike when he left alone in the Range Rover.

Rich had the old familiar tingle running through his arms; a cold sensation that tightened the skin and raised the hairs, as though they were charged with static electricity. He always knew that he was up close to impending action when the goose-flesh made an appearance. It never seemed to fail him, having always proved as sure-fire as twitching rods in a diviner's hands.

Rich had been less than twelve months out of the academy when it had first happened. He had been assigned to work in the field with a seasoned agent, who was not amused at having to wet-nurse a rookie so recently hatched from the classrooms of Quantico.

Hal Macklin was a dinosaur; a legend in the bureau. Stories of his service exploits – both true and false – had been handed down by word of mouth, probably contorted and embellished at each telling until fact and fiction blurred into folklore.

It *was* true that Hal had been a junior member of the protection squad that had been guarding Richard Milhous Nixon in nineteen-seventy-three. And it was also true that he had used extreme prejudice by taking out a would-be assassin who had infiltrated Camp David with the intention of turning a security meeting between Nixon, Haigh and several other high-profile policy makers into a blood bath. Hal's almost imperceptible limp was the legacy of two bullets from the terrorist's Uzi, which had discharged as the guy's trigger finger went into spasm, due to the shock of his skull being blown apart as Hal shot him dead. But for that act, Watergate might have remained just another anonymous if architecturally interestingly shaped complex.

At nearly sixty, Hal had still done roadwork, played tennis, and visited the gym as often as his workload would allow, and by doing so retained an acceptable level of fitness. He was a little battle-worn to look at, with steel-gray crew-cut hair, a deeply-lined face, and carrying maybe ten pounds over his best fighting weight. But he was still one of the most effective special agents in the business, and had forgotten more than most of the new generation of feds had yet to learn. His impassive demeanor was the result of being a shade jaded by so many years in the midst of the capital's political subterfuge.

Rich remembered an incident that followed a kidnapping that had gone woefully wrong and ended up with the son of a republican senator being found floating face down in the Potomac with a bullet in the back of his head. Hal and Rich had been staking out the prime suspect's girlfriend when the guy that they were after nearly broke up their brief partnership permanently.

It was two a.m. when Hal had left the car to take a leak in the bushes twenty feet away. There was no telltale illumination as he opened the door; the dome-light was switched off. And as Hal moved away into the darkness, Rich's arms had started to ripple with goose-flesh. Call it an outwardly physical manifestation of sixth sense, premonition or whatever. Rich just knew that something was about to happen. He slid his nine millimeter from the holster under his left armpit and silently exited the passenger door, crouching low as he moved to the rear of the car in search of his partner.

The silhouetted shape of a figure pointing a gun at Hal's back gave Rich no time to shout a warning. With no doubt as to the intention of the armed man, and with no hesitation, he put three bullets into the would-be assailant.

Hal Macklin threw himself sideways as the sound of gunshots split the air, to hit the ground rolling, drawing his gun as he came up onto his knees.

"He's down," Rich shouted, "at eleven o'clock, five yards from your position."

"I see him," Hal responded.

They moved in slow and low with their weapons trained on the fallen, moaning and seriously injured figure, whose blood was a spreading stain, black and effulgent under the moonlight on the grassy verge of the suburban sidewalk.

Only a few house lights came on. The residents prudently watched from behind the twitching drapes of their private bolt holes, afraid of drawing attention to themselves in these violent times; as timid and cautious as church mice.

Rich snapped a pair of cuffs on the prone man, kicking away the silencer-equipped Ruger pistol that lay on the ground next to him. The guy drew his knees up to his gunshot abdomen and gasped-moaned-cried in agony, taking no notice of the two feds; too involved with personal pain. Hal knelt and tried to determine the extent of the injuries as Rich used his cell phone to summon an ambulance and notify the DCPD.

"You made me piss my pants, shooting this turd," Hal said, his face grave as Rich hunkered down next to him.

"So sue me," Rich replied, grinning. "Next time I'll make sure that you've finished, shaken off and tucked it away before I open fire."

Rocking on their haunches at the side of the gravely injured gunman, tears coursed down their cheeks as they succumbed to a bout of uncontrollable laughter.

The guy that Rich had shot, one Julio Ramirez, lived against all odds, to serve a life sentence for the kidnap and murder of the senator's son. The colostomy bag that he wore strapped to his thigh was a constant reminder of the night when a young FBI agent had literally blown the shit out of him, leaving him in need of a permanent artificial ass-hole.

Rich and Hal had been a tight-knit double act from that night on. And on each subsequent occasion that Rich's arms tingled, Hal sat up and took notice.

Now as Rich drove with the road steadily rising higher into the cooler mountain air, and still probably two S-bends behind Mike, he felt his throat constrict and his eyes begin to sting with a misting of salty tears. He blinked them away, the highway ahead of him a watery blur for a couple of seconds. Once again he was reliving the day when his late partner had given up a long fight against the Big C that won a lot more bouts than it lost. The malignancy had grown fat as Hal had shrunk; his life sapped from him as the tumors feasted from within, with no perception of the fact that their voracity would destroy them along with their host.

Rich had been there at the end, holding Hal's hand, which was little more than a bony, birdlike and weightless claw. A shudder had run through the dying man, his sunken wafer-thin eyelids closing, and his teeth clenching against pain that was severe enough to tear through the chemical barrier that fought unsuccessfully to nullify it. The skeletal fingers tightened, and somehow Hal managed to smile and speak to Rich a final time.

"Remember that night when I pissed down my pants, Rich?" He said in a thin, rasping whisper, blood now bubbling out from the left corner of his mouth, crimson, bright and vital against the gray parchment skin.

"Yeah, Hal, it was a hoot," Rich sobbed as the legend of the bureau exhaled a long shallow breath, as if purposefully pushing the last vestige of life from his ruined body before slipping into history, no longer a person, just another statistic.

With great difficulty, Rich cleared his mind of things past, again concentrating on the job at hand. Too late, he saw that Mike had pulled into a gap at the side of the road, leaving him no choice but to drive past and keep going. He was pissed. He had allowed maudlin reverie to interfere with and cloud his thoughts. The only upside was that a week's growth of beard, plus the shades and long-billed baseball cap provided adequate disguise, even if Mike had noticed the Explorer go by.

Mike studied the track opposite him that led into the dense forest of predominantly red ponderosa pine. Belle Morita's cabin was almost a mile from the highway. He drove a further two hundred yards and pulled off the road again, this time into thick juniper, checking as he walked back on to the highway to be sure that the vehicle was completely hidden from sight. He crossed the blacktop, slipped into the undergrowth and made his way back diagonally to the trail, keeping to the edge, ready to dive for cover should anyone approach.

Ten minutes later, off to his right, a thin wisp of blue smoke gave away the cabin's location. It stood in a small clearing, hard to spot at first with the backdrop of the forest behind it; wood on wood. He circled to his left, keeping under cover, not taking his eyes off the cabin door and the two front windows.

Settling in deep ferns, Mike lifted his binoculars and closely inspected the homestead, which he knew was also a killer's stronghold and retreat.

From the other side of the trail, also hidden from view, Rich Cole watched the watcher.

CHAPTER THIRTY-EIGHT

MIKE'S absence gave Sarah and Cal the opportunity to be together for a while. And like two young lovers – which they were – left alone, they wasted no time and were soon feverishly embracing. Although they now shared the rear bedroom at night, this was a time, in daylight, when they had not had the chance to vent their feelings in a physical way. They kissed, urgently. Clumsily and over eagerly they fumbled and pulled at each other's clothing, needing to be free of it and feel the warmth and smoothness of each other's naked skin. They went into the small shower cubicle, soaped and caressed every inch of each other's bodies, licking, teasing and kissing; a sculpted knot of wet flesh, both in love and also fired by unbridled lust.

Sarah raised her right leg, wrapped it around Cal's hip, and then reached down and guided him into her, holding his testicles gently cupped in her palm as she moved against him. They tongued each other's mouths, and moved fluidly under the hot jets of water. Steam encompassed them, as joined and with sensations building in ever-strengthening waves, paroxysms of intense pleasure flooded and surged, to finally burst in a shuddering simultaneous climax. Holding, crushing each other in an almost brutal embrace, their fluids combined in warm union within Sarah.

"I love you, Cal Morgan," she whispered breathlessly, resting her head on his shoulder, her hands gripping his firm buttocks to prevent him from withdrawing.

"I love you too, Sarah," he replied, holding her close, not wanting the moment to pass.

The water had run cold before they stepped out of the shower, toweled each other dry and walked through to the bedroom naked, Cal behind Sarah admiring her slim waist, her exquisite bottom, and her long, shapely legs. His penis rose in a Hitleresque salute to the rear of the girl he loved, and Sarah, turning and seeing the evidence of his renewed ardor, pulled him through the door, pushed him onto the bed and straddled him. She impaled herself deeply, her head back, eyes closed, hands on his chest as she rocked slowly back and forth against his hardness, feeling his fingers on her aroused nipples, then slipping down to clasp her buttocks, urging them to move ever faster on him. They both came again, and she sank down into his arms, time suspended in a cocoon of love; no past, no future, just the moment. They didn't speak, both reluctant to break the spell as they drifted into a light, blissful doze in the warmth and safety of each other's embrace.

The sun was sinking low in a bruised and darkening sky as Mike drove back down the winding mountain road. The forest seemed on fire, glowing with burnished copper, gold, yellow ochre and vermilion red; a cornucopia of autumnal splendor. Rounding a curve he braked gently at the sight of three deer standing in the center of the highway. He approached them slowly, almost upon them before, as one, they leapt into the safe haven of the trees. The tranquility of the area put Mike in reflective mood. His life back in the city had degenerated into a mess that he had been too wrapped up in to be able to stand back from and properly appreciate for what it was. He now knew without any shadow of doubt that he would not return to the soul-destroying, corrupting metropolis. The last few weeks on the open road, amid the rugged, timeless beauty of the deserts and mountains, had invigorated him, cleansing and washing away the stale and self-effacing layer of apathy that had steadily and stealthily robbed him of expectation and zeal. This, now, was the happiest and most contented period he had known for many years, and he would not readily return to the humdrum, sleazy life that he had left behind him. He felt at ease here, and planned to stay out west and make it his home. Money and material possessions had never figured high on Mike's list of priorities, and were losing more ground with every day that passed. His spirit felt free for the first time since he had been a teenager. He had come full circle, and meant to live each day to the full and not let life slip by as though it were bubbling from an inexhaustible subterranean well, but savor each second, in the knowledge that time was the most precious and yet transitory gift bestowed on all living things.

Cal was still sleeping, but Sarah was dressed and outside the Cobra, enjoying the evening air, drinking coffee, her thoughts recapturing the pleasure of their lovemaking, first in the shower and then on top of the coverlet in the bedroom. She had never felt so alive or contented. Love was a potent spell, which she was well and truly bewitched by.

Mike pulled the Range Rover to within ten feet of the RV, cut the engine and stepped out, raising his hand in greeting.

"Hi, Mike, could you use a mug of coffee?" Sarah said as he ambled across the grass toward her.

"That's the best offer I've had all day," he replied, smiling, his mood buoyant, to the extent that he even tipped her a wink.

It was past dusk, and darkness had stolen the day. The lengthening autumn nights now held the promise of winter in the chill air. It was a time of dormancy, when nature regrouped and made ready to be reborn again the following spring with renewed vigor, in celebration of life.

By the time Sarah and Mike had finished their coffee, Cal was up. The three of them sat at the table, warm sweaters denoting the drop in temperature; their T-shirts and shorts packed away, now that the desert heat was behind them. Cal poured each of them a large shot of Johnny Walker Black Label as they studied the map, and Mike pointed out the location of the cabin as he described the local terrain.

"You're sure you found the right cabin?" Sarah said.

"Yes," Mike said "It's the only one in the area. There are no other properties in the vicinity, and I saw an Indian woman up there as well, who just had to be Belle Morita."

Cal checked Mike's recent images of his trip up the mountain, seeing the setting of the cabin and the woman who Mike had seen briefly outside gathering logs, obviously for the fire.

"It was her," Cal said. "I just checked, and the woman you saw was definitely Belle. I recognize her from both the 'Chief's' and then Demi at the post office's memories."

Mike slammed his glass down on the tabletop and the Scotch shot up to splatter down on the Formica tabletop. He glared at Cal with sudden, open hostility. It was a look that didn't need a mind reader to interpret. They were friends, and unauthorized entry to Mike's thoughts and experiences was a breach of trust. It offended him deeply that Cal would do it without prior discussion or permission.

"Christ, I'm sorry, Mike," Cal said in a grave and apologetic tone of voice. "I had no right to do that without asking. It's becoming second nature to me now, just like talking. I did it automatically without thinking, but that's no excuse, I know. I'll make sure it doesn't happen again, ever, unless it's a life or death situation."

Mike's expression softened. He knew sincerity when he came across it, and he could see that the younger man was genuinely upset and embarrassed at what he had done.

"Okay, Cal. No damage done," Mike said, unscrewing the lid on the bottle of the Scotch and refilling his glass.

CHAPTER THIRTY-NINE

THE sudden rap at the door made all three of them jump. They exchanged surprised glances, and Mike reached for his gun, which was in the shoulder rig on the bench seat next to him.

"Who's there?" Mike called as he moved to the side of the door, his arm flexed, finger curled round the trigger of the gun.

"Richard Cole, FBI," was the instant reply.

Recognizing the voice, and astonished and confused, Mike lowered the pistol and opened the door.

"What the fuck are you doing here, Rich? Why are you following us?" Mike said in an ill-disposed tone of voice as the realization that his earlier suspicion of being tailed had been more than an irrational foreboding.

"Let me in and I'll explain," Rich said, not moving, hands deep in the pockets of his newly purchased fleece-lined lumber-jacket.

Mike stood aside, and with a jerk of his head bid the agent step on board.

"Sarah, Cal," he said. "This is Richard Cole, a feeb that I have the misfortune to know. I think he'll confirm that he's been following us since we left D.C. I'm hoping he has one hell of a good reason for doing it." Mike's voice was cold and reserved. He wanted to know why Rich had been tailing them, and to also make it clear that the agent was less welcome than the last President, Obama, would have been at a Klan meeting.

"Please, sit down and have a drink with us, Mr. Cole," Sarah said, attempting to melt some of the ice that had entered Ol' Betsy with the FBI agent.

"Rich. Please call me Rich. And thanks, I could use a shot," he said, looking at the half full – or half empty, depending on individual perspective – bottle of Black Label.

Rich took a seat, then a large swig of the mellow Scotch that Sarah had poured him, before setting the glass down and clearing his throat.

"This is official, folks. You and I know that this is serious shit," Rich said before pausing to look Mike in the eye. "When you asked me to dig up that information, Mike, you stepped into a live case; an ongoing hunt for a serial killer, so don't act outraged or be naive with me, because this is too far-reaching to keep private or personal. I've been on your case since you contacted me, just on the off-chance that you were holding a high card that we were missing, and it looks like you were."

"So why let the cat out of the bag now? Why break cover before we've found him?" Mike said.

"Because, my friend, you're closing in. It's time to give me all you have and bow out gracefully. The bureau will take it from here on in. You're obviously certain that you know who the serial killer is. But tell me, why are you so interested in him? Why have you been scouring the Southwest for a complete stranger to you?"

Cal had been sat back, apparently just listening to the two-way conversation. In fact he had inhabited Rich the moment Mike had introduced them. He now knew the fed as well as he knew himself.

"It's like this," Cal said, enjoining the discussion. "You haven't reported in since Friday, Rich. And you won't now until this is settled. If you want to join us musketeers, you're welcome. You can be d'Artagnan, and we can take the bastard down together. But you will not take this over and—"

"Now hold it right there, son," Rich snapped, fixing Cal with a frosty, official stare, his teeth gritted and cheeks flushed with a touch of good old-fashioned pique. "You need to wise-up, and quick. I could already bust your asses for withholding, obstructing, and God knows what else. So stop thinking that you have any rights as private citizens to conduct a manhunt. You're outside the law, and you know it."

Mike and Sarah looked to Cal, as an awkward pregnant silence filled the now deathly quiet RV. It seemed to last forever, but was in reality of only a few seconds duration. And then Cal responded.

"Pour Special Agent Cole another drink, please, Sarah," Cal said. "I think he's going to need it." And to Rich. "Now, listen up and be suitably amazed, Richard Dwight Cole, originally from Muncie, Indiana. This is going to blow your conservative mind."

Rich said nothing, and by taking another sip of Scotch, registered that he was prepared to listen to whatever Cal needed to get off his chest. The fact that the young man knew his full name and where he had been born, which even Mike didn't, was enough to grab his undivided attention.

"You know," Cal continued, "that Mike is looking for this killer, whose full name by the way is Luke Strayhorse. What you don't know is that he is doing it for me. You won't believe this, yet, but I am the walking, talking and large-as-life reincarnation of the deputy sheriff who was murdered along with a young girl by the name of Trudy Henderson, back in July of ninety-six. My name is Cal Morgan, and before you interrupt I want you to know that I'm inside your head, looking at your thoughts and through your memories as I speak. I can see you and Hal Macklin laughing about him pissing his pants on the night that you shot that perp. And I know that the first time that you got laid was in the back of your dad's Buick in ninety-two by a pretty little redhead...Susan Margolis. She was wearing braces on her teeth and had a slight lisp. It still embarrasses you to recall that you slipped out at the crucial moment and soiled her gingham dress. You turned cherry-red every time you saw her after that, if you couldn't avoid her. Anything else you want reminding of, or that you've forgotten, just ask. I know everything that you know, Rich."

Rich knew that his mouth was hanging open, and that he probably looked like a retard. But he was finding it hard to assimilate what was happening. He felt completely out of his depth for the first time since maybe that night with the Margolis girl; certainly for the first time in his adult life. He was out of control of a situation that he could not understand.

Rich was an X-File fan, and enjoyed the reruns of the asinine story lines that had an almost permanently poker-faced Fox Mulder chasing aliens and supernatural entities. Rich had always felt more of an affinity with Scully, though, who believed that everything must have a logical explanation.

"Forget Mulder and Scully, Rich," Cal said, breaking into his current line of thought. "How are the arms, huh? Any goose-flesh yet? As if I needed to ask."

"Jesus H Christ!" Rich exclaimed, draining his glass in one gulp.

"In for a penny," Cal continued. "Here's another magical moment to amuse and confuse you. Take your cell phone out of your pocket and try to contact Paul Nicholl. Go on, patronize me and do it."

Rich hesitated, looking to Mike and Sarah for some insight as to what might happen next, only to be met by the attentive, intrigued expressions of an expectant audience. He withdrew the cell phone from his pocket, and at that point lost total control of his actions. A compulsion forced him to rise and walk to the door, open it and step out into the darkness. Knowingly, but now lacking the ability to resist, he tossed the phone on to the ground in front of him, then watched his own insurgent hands, as between them they unzipped and withdrew his dick to face the cold night air. At that point his bladder rebelled, voiding itself and causing him to urinate on the state-of-the-art bureau issue unit. Rich knew exactly what he was doing, but for the life of him could not find the will to fight his mutinous body.

Benevolently, Cal, within Rich, replaced the agent's pecker to the warmth and privacy of its nest in his boxer shorts and allowed him to zip up his pants, before returning him inside and re-seating the bewildered man at the table.

Two hours passed, and a second bottle of Scotch stood severely depleted by the time Cal had told his story, starting with his murder at Backbone Ridge, and then of his awakening in Danny exactly twenty-one years later. Sarah told Rich of Danny's accident, which had somehow triggered Cal's emergence. And Mike explained his subsequent involvement at the request of Dr. Ross Fairburn.

"So what do you plan on doing?" Rich said, addressing Cal, unable to deny a truth that he thought should be a figment of someone like Stephen King's strange imagination; a storyline for a weird book, not reality. "What if I still want to call in the cavalry?"

"No deal," Cal said. "We *are* the cavalry, the four of us. We don't need any more cooks in the kitchen. You can have all the kudos when it goes down, Rich. But if you try to contact Nicholl, then I'll freeze you out. I could easily instruct you to check into a motel and just eat Twinkies and watch soaps on TV for a week or two. Or have you catch a plane to Europe and play tourist in London or Paris, if that's the way you want to go with this."

Rich knew that it wasn't a bluff. "Okay, Cal, you win. All for one...and all that crap. It's just the four of us. But I want you to accept one proviso. Promise me that if possible, we take him alive. No killing for killing's sake, or for personal revenge. I don't want to be party to a lynch-mob mentality. I aim to take his ass alive, not vaporize it."

"You got it, Rich," Cal said. "If we can take him alive, we will."

Friday came, and the four of them were sitting at a table in the Load O' Bull diner over the street and with a clear view of the Cotton Bob needlepoint shop. They ate breakfast and hoped that Belle would stick to her usual routine and come to town. If she did, Cal would 'visit' with her on a cerebral level and hopefully be able to pinpoint

Luke Strayhorse's whereabouts. He would also find out much more than they presently knew about the man, his habits, and general lifestyle.

Without warning, Cal turned to Rich, who was staring into his coffee cup, deep in thought; thought that Cal was monitoring.

"You're thinking just how useful I would be to the bureau, Rich. How all this weird shit that I can do could be utilized to solve crime and Christ knows what else. Well, forget it. I'm not for sale or hire. And I'm not about to become a research project or a secret weapon to be aimed at anyone that politicians or the pentagon consider to be this week's enemies. I've got my own life to live, and service for the supposed greater good of the nation doesn't figure in it. If you try to use me after this business is wrapped, then at best you'll end up looking stupid with no proof of what I can do. Or at worst, if I thought there was a chance that you *could* cause me problems, having a fatal accident. Believe me, Rich, if you try to interfere with my life, I'll make you drive into a concrete overpass at ninety miles an hour, or just have you eat your gun. Do you copy?"

Rich listened; really listened, and knew that this extraordinary man was not issuing idle threats. He knew that this seasoned cop, who only appeared to be a twenty-one-year-old, meant every word he said. Rich was suddenly very afraid, not for himself, but because without exaggeration he realized that this man could change the world if he chose to. He was a walking time-bomb, with a potential that was incalculable.

"You're probably right," Cal said, answering the agent's thoughts. "But I don't want to change the world. After this is a done deal I just want to put these...abilities in a locked box in some corner of my mind and let it gather dust and lie there unopened."

"You may find that impossible to do," Rich said, frowning. "It's easy to let a wild animal out of its cage, but a bitch to get it back in."

Cal nodded. "I know, Rich. I know."

CHAPTER FORTY

IT was noon when the green Jeep – its badly rusted muffler growling like a cougar – pulled into a parking slot outside Suzanne Caitlin's shop. Belle climbed out and went inside to chit-chat and drink coffee for the best part of an hour with Sue, as was her custom before going off to fill her shopping list.

Sue was Belle's only true friend; the one person whom she really confided in. She knew that she could broach any subject with her, including Luke, with total confidence. Whatever was discussed would go no further, and Sue knew that she could unburden herself in the same way. The implicit trust was mutual.

Belle expected Luke back soon, now that the icy fingers of November were knocking at the door, and winter was flexing its muscles. A sharp drop in the temperature was already bringing a dusting of snow to the mountain peaks. Just the thought of Luke's homecoming caused a flutter in her stomach. She was ready for his nearness, his company, and the physical pleasures that she missed and would indulge in wholeheartedly when he returned from his travels. He would be like a husband to her, checking the cabin and making good any damage; carrying out small repairs, such as replacing the odd missing cedar shingle, and he would also cut enough cords of wood to see them through till early spring. He would only leave her to go hunting for fresh meat, bringing deer, wild turkey and other game to supplement their larder during the snow-clad months.

Suzanne had known Belle for many years and valued her friendship. Being part Chiricahua and part white had left her in a half-breed wilderness, treated as a white by many Indians, and as an Indian by *all* whites. Racism was flourishing just as healthily in this part of the States as anywhere else, but seemed to be an overlooked issue that eyes were blind, ears deaf, and backs turned to.

Luke scared Suzanne. She had never felt at ease or safe in his presence. And although she kept it from Belle, whom she knew loved the man; she could not abide him, sensing the rage and the potential for cruelty and violence that swirled just beneath the outward mask of calmness he exhibited. Belle seemed blind to his lack of normal human emotions, or only saw what she chose to. Suzanne could not help but feel terribly afraid for her friend, even though Luke apparently treated her well and made her happy. She would not be surprised if Belle died at his hands one day. And although she tried to tell herself that she was being too melodramatic, the sickly, flesh-crawling trepidation that she felt when he was at the cabin could not be diluted. Fear for Belle was in her waking thoughts, and crowded her dark dreams.

"I was in the post office, Belle," Suzanne said as she poured steaming coffee into delicate china cups, not mugs. "And Demi told me that two white men from the east were asking for your address. She said that they had a large motor home, and that one of them had subsequently rented a 4x4 from her brother, Jim, who runs the dealership out on Mission Road. Jim said that they mentioned parking up at the campground near Roper Lake."

Belle was worried. Why would strangers be interested in her? And even though Demi had said that she withheld her address, they would have no doubt found out where she lived, but had not called at the cabin. Perhaps it was Luke that they were attempting to trace. That made more sense to her. She had no idea who he knew or what trouble he may be in. She could admit to herself that in many ways he was a stranger to her, like an iceberg, with much of his life invisible beneath deep water; a well kept secret.

"What are you going to do about it, Belle?" Suzanne said, concerned for her friend.

"Nothing. I'll tell Luke about them when he gets home. He'll deal with it."

The conversation moved on to other topics; local gossip, the weather, and the sad passing of twelve-year-old Tommy Buck, who had – after a brave two year long battle – lost the fight against leukemia. Yet another victim of whites, in this instance an excess of white corpuscles in his blood. Tommy's grandfather, Nathan, had been a minor celebrity in the area. He had appeared as an extra in countless westerns that had been shot over at the Old Tucson Studios, and even had a photograph of himself stood next to John Wayne, signed: To Nathan, Happy Trails, Duke.

"See you in two weeks, if the weather holds up," Belle said an hour later as she walked out on to Main Street. But Suzanne would never see her friend alive again.

CHAPTER FORTY-ONE

LUKE was in Alamogordo, New Mexico that last week of October. He had delivered a Plymouth Voyager to a car auction house for Fat Al, and was due to pick up a Ford F150 the next day from Camino Cars and take it back to Las Cruces. He called in at Camino to check with the owner Ben Shelby that the Ford would be ready to roll bright and early the following morning, and was offered a fill-in job. Ben needed to have a top of the range Chevy Suburban delivered to the Flat Top Ranch, which was less than an hour's drive north, of Tularosa. That suited Luke just fine. He would be able to call in at Ruidoso Downs Reservation on the way and visit with an old medicine man whom he had been closer to in his youth than he had been to his grandfather, and who he'd kept in touch with down the years.

Swift Elk was not so fleet of foot these days. The aged Apache was ninety, and failing by the hour. He was now blind, and had lost his left leg to gangrene. He knew that this would be his last winter, and spent an increasing amount of time living in the distant past, which was as clear in his mind as mountain spring water, not the muddy silt that just the day before could be, as his short term memory swam under the murky onslaught of senile dementia.

Swift Elk's own grandfather had fought the whites to try to protect and preserve a way of life that had now all but shriveled up and blown away, as though ripped from the earth and dispersed by the wind like so much lifeless tumbleweed. He had never been able to come to terms with the new ways that had been forced upon his people, sapping their spirit and robbing them of their culture. The white Americans had swarmed over the land with the voracity of grasshoppers, stripping it, abusing it, and treating the Indian nations as uncivilized and less than human; believing that the Apache was in need of instruction in the white men's ways and beliefs. Swift Elk was glad that he would soon be joining his ancestors, where he would be young again in the beyond; full of life and sharp of eye.

Luke parked in the dust outside the prefabricated dwelling that was little more than a glorified hut. He was met by Swift Elk's son – an old man himself now – and ushered through to the small bedroom that was the medicine man's living accommodation.

A broad slash of sunlight filtered through the grimed and rotting sheers which hung like sand-colored cobwebs at the single small window. The brightness was diffused and crowded with drifting dust motes. And behind the haze on a wooden rail-backed chair, the old man was asleep or in a fugue; a faded black, white and red patterned blanket draped across his lap, hanging down to his remaining moccasin-clad foot.

Luke went over and knelt next to the ancient figure, at ease in front of a kindred spirit, and now carrying the flaming torch of blazing hatred that in Swift Elk was finally flickering and dying.

Sensing his presence, the medicine man raised his head a few inches, facing his visitor with opaque eyes that were lightly coated by milky cauls. Luke handed him a carton of tar-rich Pall Mall, which were grasped greedily by swollen, gnarled hands and secreted furtively into loose robes, away from the caring but prying eyes of his family, who, if they found the cigarettes would confiscate them and lecture him over the danger of losing his other leg; as if it mattered at this late stage.

Touching Luke's forehead, concentrating, now lucid and back in the present, Swift Elk gave the younger man a slow smile, revealing the one remaining yellow tooth, which stood alone and resolute in his shrunken gums.

"Yatasay, Luke Strayhorse, it is good that you have come," he lisped in greeting. "I am losing my life force and will not be here for another time of planting. This is my last winter."

"And are you ready for the journey, Swift Elk?" Luke said.

"Yes, I am happy to be near the end of the trail. It has been long and stony. I am excited to know that I will soon be reunited with all those who have gone before. I am a burden here, and have outlived all purpose."

Swift Elk had held Luke's hand as he spoke, and now his almost sightless eyes closed, the wrinkled skin around them gathering, puckering as he tilted his head back in sudden concentration.

"I see dark clouds gathering above you. A storm approaches that may take your life in its fury," the old man said, placing his trembling hands to Luke's temples, the firmness of his grip a denial of his frailty. "You are being hunted, my son," he continued, feeling the invisible emanations that radiated out from the other man; an aura that he received and was somehow able to absorb and translate into images of what might come to pass. "As we sit here, you are being sought. And among those who seek you is a man who is not what he appears to be, but much more. He is a victim of a past sin, and has returned to do battle with you, and is in your shadow. You are 'Death Walking', and if you return to your lodge, there will be much blood spilt."

Abruptly, as if drained like a run down flashlight battery, Swift Elk's hands fell to his lap, and his chin slumped forward onto his chest. His clarity had deserted him, and his thoughts were now back in a time when he was a laughing child in the Dragoon Mountains, when each day was a warm and welcome friend, not a cold and dreaded enemy.

Luke said a final good-bye to the old sage, kissing him on his gelid brow, knowing that his farewell went unheeded. He would not set foot on the reservation again. He stood at the doorway and took one last look at the ancient warrior, who appeared as a golden specter through the beam of clouded light from the window.

Driving off, Luke closed another door behind him, his apartness protecting him from grief or sadness; just feeling glad that he had been there to hear the cryptic warning. He did not understand it, but neither did he doubt Swift Elk's powers of 'sight'. He would now be watchful for signs of an unknown enemy.

CHAPTER FORTY-TWO

THE Flat Top Ranch was an isolated spread, two miles east of the highway. A large sign hanging over a rail-gate advertised its existence, and a dirt track that disappeared over rolling hills led to the ranch house, which lay out of sight behind them.

Luke pulled to a stop at the bottom of wide wooden steps that were overhung by a porch roof that ran the full length of the frontage of the house. He got out of the vehicle to be met by Jed Grodin, who stepped down to greet him.

"Thanks for bringing this beauty out here for us," Jed said, his eyes darting sparrow-quick over the Chevy, checking for damage and giving Luke a cursory inspection at the same time. "It sure looks fine and dandy. My boy Scott will be all over it like a fly on a steer turd when he gets home. It's his birthday, and this is his present from his mom and me."

"Glad I could help out," Luke said, producing one of his warmest open smiles.

Jed slapped him all buddy-buddy, ain't we pally-like on the shoulder.

"Git yourself round back to the kitchen, boy, and have some coffee and maybe a bite to eat. And while you do that I'll organize you a lift into Tularosa, and thanks again," Jed said before turning and going back up the steps with the Indian already dismissed from his mind.

The kitchen was a huge room, with other storage rooms and a large cold room leading off a passage from it. Two Mexican girls were fussing about, preparing food. One was chopping peppers, the other stirring a steaming pan that gave off a mouth-watering aroma of meat cooking in fragrant spices.

Luke accepted the mug of coffee that he was offered, but politely declined anything to eat.

"This is a beautiful ranch," he said to one of the girls. "And I can see that Mr. Grodin likes to employ beautiful staff to help run it for him."

He spread the charm on thick, like honey on a biscuit, starting a conversation with the girl who had made him the coffee, and who had looked at him with more than a little interest in her fiery, umber eyes. Within minutes she had unwittingly given him all the information he needed. He had – on the spur of the moment – decided to rob the place...and much more. The patronizing attitude of the fat-bellied rancher had provoked him, and he had determined to return and introduce himself properly to the Grodins', on his own terms.

The kitchen maid had spouted with all the restraint of an open faucet, happy to discuss her employer, his family, and their business.

Jed and Marcia Grodin had two grown sons, neither married yet, and both still living at home. Maria, the maid, lived in, with quarters adjoining the house at the rear. But all the ranch hands and the other maid lived off property. Bunkhouse days were a thing of the past at the Flat Top.

Later, after being driven into Tularosa, Luke hitched a ride back to Alamogordo, planning to return to the ranch in a couple of days, excited at the prospect of stepping into new territory, and anticipating a venture involving more risk than his usual escapades, but which held the promise of rich pickings in more ways than one.

It was almost midnight two days later when Luke approached the maid's quarters at the back of the ranch house. The pickup he had stolen in Las Cruces was hidden in a thicket of shrubs and tall jacarandas a half mile away, out of sight from both the highway and the house.

The tempered blade of his knife released the catch without a sound, and he was through the window and crossing to the sleeping figure in the bed with the speed and stealth of a hunting owl.

The girl awoke with a scream stifled, locked in her mouth, which was now clamped firmly by an unseen hand.

"Listen up, bitch," Luke said, holding the blade of the knife in front of her wide-eyed gaze, rotating it slowly so that the soft glow of moonlight penetrating the window could play on the cold steel for her to fully appreciate the predicament that she was in. "If you make a sound, I'll cut your fuckin' throat. I need to talk to you, and then I'll leave. But if you cause me any trouble, you'll be one dead wetback. Do you understand?"

She nodded, mesmerized by the gleaming ten-inch blade; its movement having the same paralyzing effect on her as a rattlesnake ready to strike would have induced in a kangaroo mouse.

Luke slowly took his hand away, ready to replace it and plunge the knife into her heart if she so much as belched. She was silent, quivering with fear, and so he moved round to sit on the bed in front of her, his hand firmly gripping her throat. He could see in the half light that she was too terrified to cause him any grief, but he was ready for any untoward action, should she suddenly panic and lose control. Sometimes you just couldn't outguess how people would react when their minds were fucked up.

"What's your name again?" Luke said, smiling at her, seeing the recognition flash across her tear-filmed eyes as she recalled his earlier more innocuous visit to the ranch.

"Ma...Maria," she stammered, now shaking uncontrollably, justifiably fearful for her life.

"Well relax, Maria. You'll be fine, if you behave," he lied. "Are there any dogs?"

"Ye...Yes. Just one."

"Where is it, in the house?"

"No. It's outside. It...It's chained up at night. It's in a kennel."

"Good girl. How many people are inside?"

Maria told Luke, and answered all his questions, describing the layout of the ranch in detail, and who was in which bedroom. She also confirmed that the house was not alarmed, and that the last upstairs light had been switched off over an hour before Luke had arrived.

He pulled the sheet back from where it rested on her lap. The flimsy nightie that she wore had ridden up and was above her crotch, showing a dark triangle between her tightly closed legs.

"Open them," he said, the flat of the blade pressing against her thigh, persuading her to part her trembling limbs and display her sex to him. He unzipped, in a hurry to be about his business, but now aroused and needing relief. He pulled himself free of the denim and saw her look down at his tumescence. Then, placing the tip of the razor-sharp blade against the outside of her vagina, he pushed her head down to his groin with his other hand, leaving her in no doubt as to what he wanted done.

Maria could feel the knife, now actually inside her. She found that her mouth was bone dry as she took him inside it, and had to run her tongue around his member to give enough lubrication to allow her to slide her lips up and down its length. She swallowed repeatedly to save gagging, as his viscous semen shot from him, and continued to suck until he pulled her up by the hair.

"There, that wasn't so bad, was it?" Luke said, withdrawing the knife, putting it to one side and holding her face gently between his hands, grinning at her. "Tell me you enjoyed it."

"I...I enjoyed it," she sobbed.

"I knew you would," Luke said before savagely wrenching her head sideways, only stopping after hearing the crack of her vertebrae, and feeling the sudden limp weight of her body as she slumped down. Her breasts still jutted towards him, but her head was twisted and her now sightless eyes stared almost backwards, as if inspecting the pine headboard behind her. Just one violent tremor ripped through her, and the only sound in the room was the familiar liquid outpouring of waste, that Luke had become accustomed to and expected from his victims, as they met traumatic, brutal death at his hands.

He entered the main house through the kitchen, where Maria had served him with coffee on his first visit. She had been entrusted with a key, so that she could start cooking breakfast before the Grodins' rose. It was a bonus to not have to force entry, and Luke appreciated the help that the now dead girl had given him.

Passing through the kitchen, he came to a large open plan hallway, turned right and climbed the wide stairway that led to the landing. The first door, if the maid had been truthful, and he just knew that she had been, was to the eldest son's bedroom.

Turning the brass knob and easing the door back, holding his breath, relieved that no squeaking hinge or creaking of wood on wood broke the silence, Luke crossed to the bed, where he could see the shadowy shape of a young man lying on his back and gently snoring with his mouth slightly open.

Luke quickly undressed, to save his clothes from being sodden by the blood that he knew would soon be flowing.

Scott Grodin awoke with something across his mouth and nose, unable to breathe, not realizing that his throat had been cut, and unaware of the blood jetting into the pillow from his left carotid artery and jugular vein. He lost consciousness and died quickly without ever knowing that he had been murdered in his bed.

Luke found seventy-three dollars in the kid's billfold and put it on top of his jeans, which he had folded neatly and placed on the coverlet at the bottom of the bed with the rest of his clothes. He then moved on.

The second son was a light sleeper, only dozing, drifting on the edge of a dream in which he was necking with Kelly Debroux in the back row of the Cineport 10 multiplex theatre at the Mesilla Valley Mall in Las Cruces. He was slowly moving his hand towards her T-shirted breasts, expecting to be stopped with his hand clamped by her forearm as it neared its intended target. Her hand dropped to his thigh, though, and he could feel his leg begin to shake as the light touch of her fingers traced the shape of his swollen dick through the thin cotton cargo pants he wore. And then something was clamping his mouth and nose, and Greg Grodin lashed out with his arm in instant reaction, taking Luke by surprise and knocking him back into the middle of the room. Greg sat up and faced his attacker, seeing only the silhouette of a figure outlined against the ambient light.

Shocked, but regrouping with lightning speed, Luke lunged forward, his knife arm arcing down towards the boy's chest. But once again he was outmaneuvered. He felt his arm deflected to the side, and as the blade scythed into the mattress, a blow to his face sent him reeling backwards away from the bed again, taking him to his knees.

Greg had driven his fist into his assailant's face and then leapt from the bed and rushed towards the door. If he had shouted for help, or not slipped in his haste to get away – falling headlong as the rug slipped on the varnished floorboards – then events may have taken a very different course. But Greg *did* slip, falling on his face, knocking the wind from his lungs.

Luke hurled himself across the room, bringing his knife down as the boy attempted to push himself up. The blade sank into the back of Greg's neck with so much force that it split his larynx and exited to imbed itself in the wood beneath him, pinning him to the floor like an insect on an entomologist's setting-board.

Scrabbling at the polished floor, breaking his nails as he scored the varnish and drove splinters up under them, Greg still fought to escape his fate. Pulling with every ounce of his dwindling strength, he tried to dislodge the knife, but Luke was knelt on his back, using both hands and all of his weight to keep the head skewered in place.

As if gargling as he drowned in his own blood, Greg struggled and then quivered and lapsed into profound stillness. With aching arms, Luke relaxed and remained motionless as he listened for any sounds that would signal that his tussle with the boy had been overheard. The house remained a silent witness against him.

He retrieved just forty dollars – which he considered hard-earned – from a pair of the youth's jeans that had been thrown over the back of a cane chair. He left the money on the bed for collection later.

Closing the door on the body and the spreading pool of warm and metallic-scented blood, Luke wiped his bare feet on the landing carpet, leaving dark smears on the pea-green pile, before heading for the master bedroom to deal with the principal target of his visit to the ranch.

CHAPTER FORTY-THREE

MARCIA Grodin came to her senses choking for breath in the dark. Unbeknown to her, Luke had slipped his left arm between her neck and the pillow, to heave her up into a sitting position with his forearm locked across her windpipe, and his knife held under her right ear; the tip piercing the skin to cause a trickle of blood to run down and soak her lemon colored cotton nightdress.

"Turn the fuckin' light on," Luke ordered in a low voice, swinging her across to the nightstand, not taking his eyes from her snoring husband as she fumbled for the switch.

Jed awoke slowly from an alcohol-induced haze, to find the light on and his wife covered in blood, being held at knife-point. It was irrational, and his sleep-befuddled brain was trying to deny the reality of a scenario that could not possibly be taking place.

"Come on, lard-guts, wakey-wakey, it's time to rock 'n' roll," said a familiar voice that cut through Jed's stupor like a thunderbolt splitting a rotten tree trunk. He was suddenly wide awake and knew that this was not a bad dream, it was a waking nightmare. The Indian who had delivered the Chevy was in his bedroom, naked, streaked with blood and holding the mother of all knives to Marcia's neck.

"What the—" he began.

"Shut the fuck up and listen," Luke said firmly and menacingly. And Jed did. "Now, here's the plan, cowboy. Your maid and both of your sons are tied up and gagged, and the phone line is cut. All I want from you is cash, and if you give it up, all of it, then I leave you trussed up and vanish. If you have a gun in here, tell me where it is, now. If you don't and I find one, I'll use it to kneecap the little lady here."

"In the drawer. There's a revolver in the nightstand drawer," Jed said, pointing to the cabinet next to his side of the bed.

"Take it out, slowly," Luke instructed. "Barrel first, finger and thumb, and toss it over here on to the bed next to me."

Jed did as he was told, throwing the gun to within six inches of the Indian, not even tempted to try and use it, knowing that he would be signing his wife's death warrant should he attempt to play hero.

"Nice choice," Luke said, admiring the handgun. "A .44 Magnum. You must think you're Dirty Harry with a fuckin' cannon like this."

Taking the knife away from the woman's throat, Luke lifted the weighty weapon, checked that it was loaded, and then stood away from the bed, aiming the revolver at Marcia.

"Now," he said, grinning at Jed. "We all go down to the kitchen, and you find some duct tape and tie wifey here up in a chair, nice and tight. Then you and me go and empty your safe and collect any other cash that you've got stashed. Let's go."

Luke followed the couple down the stairs and into the kitchen, and when Jed had found a reel of tape, Luke, keeping the gun leveled on the woman's stomach, watched closely as her husband bound her securely to a chair and then, under instruction, wound more of the tape around her head to cover her mouth.

"Back off," Luke said as Jed finished, and moved forward to check the rancher's work. "So far, so good. Now pay attention you fat cocksucker. I don't want to play games or waste time. Just lead the way to your safe, nice 'n' easy. Keep it in mind that if you try anything stupid I'll kill everyone in the house. Move your ass."

Jed walked out of the kitchen and across the hall, to open the door to his study and come to a stop at the center of the room.

"You're doing just fine, cowboy," Luke said, keeping six feet behind him, not wanting to give the man any reason to think that he might just be able to turn the situation around to his advantage. "Turn on that desk light and then open the safe."

Jed stepped over to his desk and switched on the banker's lamp; the hand-blown, green glass shade giving a soft and eerie glow to the corner of the study. He then went to the bookcase and raised his hand, feeling for the hidden catch on the underside of the third shelf.

"Careful," Luke said. "No sudden moves."

Fear and anger in almost equal measure surged through Jed. The piece of shit Indian sonofabitch was dead meat, he thought. He would see the bastard behind bars, and use a lot of influence to ensure that he did hard time, or even died inside the state pen. No dumbfuck Apache like him was going to terrorize and rob him and his family and get away with it.

Jed thumbed the catch, releasing a section of the shelf that had appeared to be just several of many books. The false spines were attached to a hinged door, which sprung back to reveal a small wall safe.

"Open it and stand back," Luke said, keeping the gun trained on Jed, steady as a rock.

Jed spun the dial, first right, then left and right again and once more to the left, his hand sweating as he pulled down the handle and swung the steel door open.

"That's fine. Now lie on the floor, face down, and don't even twitch," Luke said, moving to the safe, admiring the craftsmanship of the fake book panel that had hidden the secret cache with such realism. He reached inside and removed four banded bundles of bills and placed them on the mahogany surface of the desk.

"How much?" Luke said to the prone rancher.

"Twenty grand," Jed said, stifling a sneeze as he spoke. The carpet fibers and dust were aggravating his mild asthma.

"Any more cash in the house?" Luke said, walking over to Jed.

"Just a couple of hundred in my billfold. It's on the bureau in the bedroom."

"Well, that seems to take care of business," Luke said, stepping over Jed. "I think it's time you joined your boys."

He brought the butt of the gun down on the back of the rancher's head three times in quick succession, and the heavy blows crushed Jed's skull and pulped his brain, killing him almost instantly.

Luke knelt, and using the material of the dead man's pajama jacket, cleaned off the bloody gun to remove any prints, and left the weapon resting on the corpse's back.

It was going well. Apart from a few tense moments dealing with the second boy, it had gone to plan. He had decided to kill everyone in the house, so would deal with the woman and then take a shower, dress, collect up the cash, and remove any prints that he might have left. He had touched very few surfaces, and had made a mental note of each one.

Leaving the study, he made his way back to the kitchen, humming one of that old redneck, George Jones's songs; *It don't get any better than this*, as he stopped in front of the buxom mistress of the house, who was as yet unaware of the fact that she was now the sole owner of the Flat Top Ranch; albeit not for long enough to matter a tinker's cuss. Luke now wanted to be away from the area. Once out on the open road he would be home free, with nothing to connect him to the murders. He had come to rob and kill the overblown, full of shit rancher, and had completed his mission. The other killings had just been incidental; an added side salad to the main course. He had even, briefly, contemplated leaving the woman alive to remember this night, but she had seen him, effectively sealing her fate.

"Hi honey, I'm home," he said, grinning like a fox in a chicken shed as he grasped the front of Marcia's nightdress and ripped it away from her body. Her breasts were unattractive, sagging under both their own weight and less than youthful muscle tone. The nipples were like chapel hat pegs; large, dark, fleshy knobs that pointed down to her stretch-marked belly. Luke savored the sight of the thick mass of coarse hair that spread from around her protuberant fleshy pussy, out onto her alabaster thighs and up to the slash of her navel; golden wheat in a now less than fertile field. No time, he thought, although he was semi-hard again, aroused from the excitement of the killing, and now by the sight of the naked and tethered woman. It had already been a night to remember fondly, though neither the Mex girl or this prissy bitch had a single tattoo between them. But he had to have something by way of a trophy. Reaching down between her legs, he gripped her sex and sliced a gleaming salmon-pink portion free with a single stroke, taking a large patch of her pubic hair with it.

Marcia had tensed as the naked Indian re-entered the kitchen and walked across to her. He held the large knife loosely in his right hand, but his left hand was empty, the gun now gone. There had been no shots. Had he just knocked Jed out, or used the knife on him? Were Scott, Greg and Maria still alive? Or had this savage killed them all? She chose to imagine that the Indian would not risk killing them, and that his motive was purely robbery. To consider anything worse was unbearable. What would he do now? She could see that his penis was rising as he stood in front of her with a crooked smile on his face. He was going to rape her. She determined not to struggle, just passively let him have his way. As long as they all came out of this alive, then being raped was a small price to pay.

Marcia had not been shocked when he suddenly reached out and ripped her nightie off. She had almost expected it. Through her fear she still found herself embarrassed, though; self conscious of her slightly flabby and overweight body, which was now being inspected in detail by a complete stranger.

She closed her eyes as he reached down between her legs and gripped her vagina. She prayed that he would take her quickly and go; just get the fuck out of the house and leave them alone.

Jesus! Marcia sprung backward like a spring as sudden stinging pain lanced through her groin. The chair flew over, dumping her on to the floor where she landed heavily, cracking her skull on the tiles. She shook her head from side to side and struggled to be free, now consumed by almost heart-stopping fear as she attempted to comprehend what he had just done to her, and what he might yet do.

Luke put his blood-coated foot on her throat and steadily increased the pressure until she stopped thrashing. He saw the dire terror, hatred, and above all the silent questions in the woman's eyes as she stared up at him. They were questions that the least he could do in all conscience was answer for her.

"Yes, sweetheart," he said quietly and calmly with the gravitas that he felt his revelations merited. "They're all dead. Your husband, the boys, even the maid. I killed them all, and the good news is you get to die too."

He straddled the shaking woman's belly, not hesitating, driving the blade of his knife up under her ribcage into her heart, as at the same time he leant forward and tore her pert, slightly upturned nose from her face with his strong, even, white teeth.

The life ebbed out of Marcia as her heart was punctured. After forty-eight safe and happy years, her hitherto contented existence had been torn to shreds in just a few horrifying minutes. And in the last few seconds she had been mutilated, made aware of the loss of her husband and sons by the psychotic, naked Indian, and was now racked with agony that emanated from her vagina, nose and chest. Unaware that she was dying from the mortal knife wound, she whispered, "Kill me, finish it you bastard," as the kitchen darkened and the grinning face of the Indian, his mouth seeping with her blood, receded. She felt death enter her, fill her, and welcomed it as a friend who was saving her from a future that she could not have faced or lived with.

As the woman's eyes lost all emotion and became unseeing marbles in their sockets, Luke rose and wiped both his mouth and the knife's blade on the torn night-dress. Chewing on the gristly meat of his victim's nose, he made his way up the stairs to the bathroom and turned on the shower.

Feeling clean and contented, Luke dressed and collected up the money. The billfold in the master bedroom contained twenty bucks less than the two hundred that Grodin had said was in it. The fat fuck had short-changed him.

Standing in the kitchen, Luke reviewed the situation. He had revisited each corpse to properly appreciate his work, and had then used his bandanna to wipe off the door knobs and all surfaces he had touched. That he had left semen in the maid's body, by way of her mouth, and an unknown quantity of hair from both his head and pubic area in the shower was of no concern to him. Leaving DNA traces was a problem that he was au fait with, but chose to dismiss as being too complicated to be eradicated. They would need to apprehend him before any forensic evidence found could be of any use to them. And he was never going to be caught, of that he was certain.

With the cash in a large brown paper bag, he jogged away from the house under the cover of darkness. Back in the pickup, he drove out to the highway, keeping the lights off until he left the property and was heading south, putting mileage between himself and the scene of his handiwork. The shit was going to fly big-time at the Flat Top Ranch when the Grodin family massacre was discovered.

"Fuck it!" Luke said under his breath, slowing the pickup. The dog. He had forgotten to slaughter the dog. It had deserved to die, having proved that its worth as a guard to the ranch was seriously lacking. It was just a shit-machine, enjoying free board and lodging under false pretenses; letting the side down badly when most needed. Commonsense prevailed though, and he accelerated away, but only after giving serious thought to going back to slit its throat.

CHAPTER FORTY-FOUR

BELLE did not notice the young man who was apparently just browsing through the aisles of the busy general store. She had no idea that as he feigned interest in winter clothing, he was actually probing her mind, in particular all memories of her long-standing relationship with Luke Strayhorse. He was picking the flesh from the bones of her life, leaving nothing unseen.

In this ultimate world of virtual reality, Cal plundered her thoughts and experienced her memories in graphic detail. This was much more than Dickens' Scrooge visiting Christmas past as just an observer of specific events that had taken place. This was a high-speed dubbing of all Belle's past from birth to present day, complete with sight, sound, smell, taste and touch. Cal saw Luke as she saw him, and could even plumb the depths of her subconscious and know of emotions that she herself was unaware of. He felt the true extent of her reliance on the man, and the strength of her love and need for him. He had become the focal point in her life, with everything else revolving around his visits like the Earth around the Sun. Belle had not admitted to herself that he was the center of her small and simplistic universe. She knew that he was a dangerous individual, capable of violence. But with her he could at times be loving and warm, and had never hurt her. As with a pet dog, she thrived on the odd handout of affection and the company of her master.

The major surprise to Cal was that she had no knowledge of Luke having ever killed another human being. That was an aspect of his life that he obviously kept closed to her. She knew that the cash he was always so liberal with had not been earned by honest labor, and that it was the profit of theft, mostly from his trade in stolen cars. That and his lack of moral integrity did not bother her. Money had no memory, and she was content to accept it, as all his favors, without question.

Cal saw that Luke was an expert hunter and tracker, patient and determined, possessing an iron will and trusting in no one but himself.

Sifting through Belle's stored knowledge, he studied the layout of the cabin, noting the gun rack near the door, which held two high-powered hunting rifles and a Mossberg pump-action 12 gauge shotgun. The bedroom that Luke used was a sterile vision of furniture. At times Belle entered it to clean and change the linen, but the contents of the drawers and closet was a blank. She did not pry, even when he was away. This was the Indian's private domain; a bolt hole that was safe and sacrosanct from even her violation.

What Cal *did* know as a hard fact was that Belle would be of no help to them in bringing Luke to justice. Her loyalty to him was unbounded, and she would never betray him. On the contrary, she would kill if necessary to protect her way of life and the man she loved.

Cal would ensure that the others were fully aware of how serious a threat this woman would be when they moved against her nephew and lover. Hopefully, Cal's power to manipulate would prove invaluable and avert any possible danger when they made their play. Luke would be at his most relaxed, off guard to an extent, feeling at his safest in this sanctuary that he made his home between the killing sprees that governed his life.

Back on Ol' Betsy, Cal drew a sketch of the cabin, even drawing the furniture and including approximate dimensions. The others observed as with his pencil employed as a pointer, Cal guided them around the rooms of the building.

"As you enter the front door, there's a gun-rack to the left with two rifles and a pump-action in it," he began. "And there are three doors leading off from the main living room. The one on the immediate right is the kitchen. The next door up on the same side is the bathroom. And at the end, to the right of the fireplace is the third, which leads into a narrow hallway with a door on either side. The one on the left is Belle's bedroom, and the one facing it is Luke's. Oh, and under the rug on the living room floor is a trapdoor that opens onto a stairway down to a large earthen cellar."

Cal then went into detail, even telling them that the cellar had been dug out when the cabin was built, as a potential refuge should forest fire make escape from the building impossible. He relayed all the relevant details concerning Luke, and of Belle's feelings for him, and her total ignorance of his penchant for rape and murder. The one thing he didn't know was when the Indian would return, only that Belle expected him back soon, within the next few days. It all depended on where he was and the weather. They would just have to watch the cabin and kick their heels until he showed up.

Rich devised a schedule that gave round-the-clock cover, comprising of four hour shifts shared between Mike, Cal and himself.

They would not allow Sarah to take part in the surveillance. Not one of them could have relaxed with her out there alone. She called them all male chauvinist pigs, and they were quite happy to accede to that, but did not relent. The plan was simple. They would keep watch on the trail that led from the highway to the cabin. That way they would see Luke return; the trail being the only vehicle access. In theory it would be impossible to miss his arrival.

Cal lay alone in the dark bedroom, needing his own space for an hour or so to gather his thoughts and contemplate and organize his state of mind. He was changing. He could feel that he was becoming more than he had ever been. Each time that he entered someone else, he absorbed not only their thoughts and memories, but their entire knowledge; cultural background, religious conceptions and individual perception of the world around them. It was causing growth within him and adding new dimensions of experience to his own. He was, each time that he forged a mind-link, exposing himself to a vast array of emotions, creating a melting-pot; a fusion of love, hate, grief and joy, strength and weakness. He had perceived the full effects of other people's bereavements, illness and pain, with what seemed vivid actuality. It was difficult but possible to mentally deflect much of the misery and suffering; to not dwell on or allow the full force of each person's times of torment to be totally absorbed. Nothing could escape his observation, though. By ransacking unsuspecting brains of their contents, Cal had to endure everything from dark fantasies, hopeful dreams that rarely materialized, and real and –other than to him – undisclosed perversions. Each subject became an open book with no page left unturned. He knew facts that he had no wish to; that Belle masturbated regularly while Luke was away, which gave firsthand experience as no other man of a woman's orgasm, and so much more in relation to female sensations and feelings, both emotional and physical. And while in Rich Cole he had confronted the incidental fact that the agent was terrified of spiders. It was a fear that had been exacerbated to near phobia proportions when as a twelve-year-old Rich had been held down by supposed friends, who proceeded to empty a jar full of arachnids on his face, and laughed as he screamed. The nimble creatures had scuttled through his hair, under his shirt collar, and even into his open, wailing mouth. Rich had nearly passed out from the sheer undiluted horror that had assailed his brain. For just an instant, Cal had tapped into the ordeal, to fully appreciate the event, and to know the extent of the young Rich's fear. A second proved to be more than enough, as the sensation of darting, plump bodies and hundreds of scurrying, hair-clad legs crept over him.

Louise Gorman the reservation school principal came into his thoughts. He recalled how he had seen that the frosty and celibate spinster had secretly yearned for sex, dreaming on occasion of being fucked by one of her pupils, or by the science teacher, whom she had lusted after for years. It was clear to Cal that no one was what they appeared to be. Everyone seemed to be hiding their true personalities behind a façade, not allowing themselves to be seen for who they truly were; scared of appearing vulnerable or weak, and petrified of being condemned or ostracized for their deviant yearnings and aspirations. He pulled away, shutting off the barrage of other personalities, pushing them into a mental storeroom and locking it. He had constructed a metaphysical steel vault, capable of holding all the unwanted thoughts that he was unable to erase, to herd them behind an imaginary heavy door and swing it shut, to cut them off from his conscious mind; a sanity-saving facility.

So-called experts, who probe and study the convoluted lump of nervous tissue that is the brain, are honest enough to admit that the driving force that runs through it still mystifies them. It is a conundrum. Within its fragile matter lies the essence of sentient life; a neural network that empowering intellect. The organ is an enigma, and the potential within it, unfathomable. Intelligence is itself intangible, propagated and genetically handed down as race memory from generation to generation. The primitive within each individual is programmed with a wealth of set-piece reactions that may be bypassed, ill-used or denied, but still govern life. The brain is the universe within, that by some accident of nature, or by decree of some incomprehensible superior power, enables an instinctive awareness of being, but denies the ability to understand how or why we exist. Each of us is a part of, yet apart from all else, singular and self-contained, condemned to be born, exist, and then die alone within the confines of a weak and transitory host; to return to basic elements.

Cal had taken a step past his physical death. He now knew that the psyche could survive intact and be aware of continuation. In his new guise, he was the embodiment of what could be everlasting life. His capacity to govern his new-found powers and be able to keep all the thoughts and memories that he was amassing separately from his own was a mechanism that prevented him from overloading with more personalities than he would have been able to sustain. Had he not been able to create his 'storeroom', then he would have lost his singularity and been overwhelmed and assimilated into an amalgam of multiple characters, unable to function. He would have become insane. His unique ability allowed him to keep the information in what he thought of as files that he could access at will and then replace for future reference. He was scared that Rich was perhaps correct, and that he may not have the strength to stop using his powers. A small voice was already chipping away at his resolve. Why should he try to stifle a gift that however strange, was a reality? Was it necessarily right to not use his new faculties, just because other people did not possess them? Part of him wanted to explore the limitless possibilities that had been presented to him. He wanted to glide in the mind of an eagle and experience the rush of the wind over outstretched wings as he viewed the earth below. Or swim the ocean as a dolphin, sharing the thoughts of another intelligent mammal; perhaps being able to communicate and converse with it, as together they gamboled in the deep, expanding the frontiers of life on earth. But where would it stop? Would there not be more than a temptation to at all times enter the minds of others, to check their intentions and see if they were being truthful? If he did, who was to know to condemn him? It was a frightening concept. He already had the capability to enter, read and even manipulate others' minds, and felt that this was just the beginning; that his power was increasing.

It was feasible that he could right many wrongs, arrest the actions and rid the planet of tyrants, and by so doing, save countless lives. But no. He was no Paladin; no knight errant on a quest to right every wrong and save the world from itself. He had no right to take on the role of judge, jury and executioner in global matters. He would not set himself up as a modern day messiah. Let the world tread its own path through the minefield of life, death, continued evolution or extinction. He was a freak of nature to be back in the land of the living, with what was apparently a modified brain, rewired with many advanced, hidden extras. He was a top of the range test model; a one off, not for general release.

With the love and help of Sarah, Cal would aspire to contain his abilities and use them only for their personal growth, education and protection. If that was selfish, then so be it.

During the days that followed, while waiting for Luke to return, Cal decided to test drive his powers. He had not as yet determined over what distance he could 'jump'. Nor had he explored the full potential of his control over other people's will. And what else may he be capable of doing? He should know, for when they might have to put their lives on the line.

CHAPTER FORTY-FIVE

RICH was parked off the highway. He had reversed into deep foliage, invisible from the road, but with clear sight – through binoculars – of the trail entrance that led to the cabin. He was at ease, used to spending protracted periods of time spying on people and places. Surveillance was a major ingredient of his covert profession, although he was glad that he had decided on shifts of just four hours' duration. Long stints increased the risk of lapses in concentration. Boredom and mental fatigue caused by waning expectation lowered the odds of success, increasing the chance of missing a vital moment when it suddenly presented itself.

Mike drove by and stopped twenty yards ahead with the engine running.

Rich opened the window, looped the strap of the binoculars over a branch for the PI to retrieve, and then pulled out, accelerating away; a quick wave the only communication between the two men. Rich checked his rearview and saw Mike reverse into the shrubbery and vanish. Relaxing, he enjoyed the drive back down to the campground, with a tape of Sinatra in full swing, impeccably backed by the Count Basie Orchestra.

After a quick shower on board Ol' Betsy, Rich decided to go into town. He wanted to supplement their small arsenal with a high-powered rifle complete with scopes for day and night use, and maybe a 12 gauge pump-action. Better too much firepower than not enough.

Sarah filled a black plastic garbage bag with dirty clothing; mainly underwear, shirts and what seemed like a hundred assorted socks. There was a laundromat in town that she intended to patronize regularly while they were in the area.

Kissing Cal softly on the lips, Sarah joined Rich in the Explorer, waving and smiling back at Cal as they drove off.

Cal was in Rich's head, hitching a ride to test the effects of distance on the mind-link. It would be interesting to see if it could be sustained. He thought that maybe the signal, or whatever the hell it was, would weaken or become distorted. In all probability the invisible 'elastic band' would snap, jerking him back to be wholly by himself in the RV. He took no control, just sat back, so to speak, and enjoyed the trip.

Rich and Sarah made small-talk on the short drive into the center of Safford, and Cal was surprised that the agent did not quiz Sarah while having the chance to, at a time when he believed, wrongly, that Cal was not only out of sight but out of mind.

Rich parked-up opposite the laundromat, and both he and Sarah stepped out of the vehicle.

"See you back here in about half an hour, okay?" Rich said.

"I'll be having a coffee in the diner, Rich," Sarah replied, starting off across the street with the garbage bag slung over her shoulder.

Cal could not blame Rich for following Sarah with his eyes, admiring her tight, shapely butt, and having extremely lustful thoughts. Hell, he was getting aroused himself, just watching her through the agent's eyes.

The bell above the door jangled shrilly as Rich entered The Gun Loft and walked across to the counter. A mile away, Cal sat at the table, amazed that as he drank coffee in one location, he was within Rich in another. He could smell the gun-oil and leather, and feel the sun on Rich's face, as its rays slanted through the plate glass of the window. This was not just like being there, this *was* being there.

So, Cal thought, it was possible to travel at least a mile in someone else. Now for the next step, could he exert remote control as well at this range?

Rich lost his grip on the car keys that he held in his right hand, and they fell to the floor. Bending quickly, he retrieved them and thrust them in his pocket, completely unaware that Cal had orchestrated the small yet significant incident.

As Rich approached the counter, a gaunt looking man appeared from a door behind it, and Cal tried something new. As the salesman looked into the eyes of his prospective customer, Cal jumped and was instantly looking back at Rich from the business side of the littered, glass-topped showcase.

As Howie Whitmore talked rifles and scopes with the agent, Cal considered the implications of what he had achieved. He had traveled into town in one man and then transferred into a second person. It seemed safe to assume that he could move from one mind to another at will, without the necessity to return to home base.

Howie was anticipating a very worthwhile and profitable sale. The customer was a city slicker, but had surprised him with his knowledge of firearms, having chosen top-notch equipment. Rich had settled on a Weatherby .30/378 rifle that offered a deadly combination of long range accuracy and knockdown power, plus a dawn/dusk scope, a night sight, and a pair of night vision binoculars. His choice of 12 gauge was a Browning pump-action. Howie threw in five boxes of shells, free of charge, he said, and then added a hundred to the overall cost for his back pocket.

"That comes out at thirteen hundred even," Howie said, showing small, heavily-filled teeth with a quicksilver smile. "Now if you'd care to fill in these forms..."

Cal transferred back into Rich and decided to step in and stop the fed from being suckered by this hick country boy in food-stained and baggy calico coveralls.

"What's your name, son?" Rich said in a low and menacing whisper.

"Er, Howie. I'm Howie Whitmore. I—"

"Well, Howie," Rich came back fast, cutting off whatever further comment the young man was about to make. "I reckon that you're creaming about a hundred off the top of this deal. Or maybe you just made an honest to goodness mistake in your dumb-ass calculations. Which is it, huh?"

Cal was back with Howie, who listened in disbelief to himself as he commenced to make the worst deal of his life, breaking the law at the same time for good measure.

"You just caught me with my finger in the pie, sir," he said. "I was indeed tryin' to rip you off, and that's the shameful truth of the matter. But to avoid any hard feelin', I'm gonna let you have the whole motherfuckin' lot for three hundred bucks. And we can forget these piss-ass forms. Who needs 'em?"

Cal had Howie write out a receipt listing the goods and price, duly signed and dated. He then compelled the bewildered man to carry the packaged purchases out to the Explorer and place them on the rear seat. As Howie bid farewell to Rich with a parting, "Have a nice day and come back soon, friend," Cal directed the confused gun dealer to shut up shop and go fishing for the rest of the day. He then pulled back and was instantly within just himself, back on board Ol' Betsy.

Reviewing what he had accomplished and feeling pleased with himself and surprised that the jump back from town had been instantaneous with no sensation of travel, Cal felt ambitious, and optimistically thought that it would be possible to will himself back into Rich's mind, despite the distance between them. He came up blank and gave up after several concentrated attempts. It appeared that he had to be in sight of a subject to effect a melding of minds.

Movement caused Cal to look out of the window, to see a red transit van enter the campground and stop fifty yards away. A woman climbed out, huffing and puffing, a cigarette bobbing between her lips, and a large plastic container swinging from her right hand. She headed towards the water faucet that was bracketed to the side wall of the brick-built restroom and shower complex, which was strictly for the use of paying guests. She was junk-food fat, the rolls of flab swelling out and over her too-tight blue jeans, as she squatted to fill the container.

Cal slipped into her mind with ease. Transference was no problem. It was somehow connected to having the target in sight. If they were hidden from view, even when he knew their location, he couldn't jump. But, what the hell, even super-heroes have their limitations. Batman couldn't fly, and although Superman could, he was in the shit when Lex Luthor or any of his other arch enemies got their grubby little hands on a lump of Kryptonite, and they always did.

He had taken another step forward, though. He had, up until this moment, thought that he needed to make eye contact to transfer. If that had been the case in the beginning, then it wasn't now.

Cal withdrew from the woman's head almost immediately. He had absorbed more than enough of her sad life in a few fleeting seconds. He was not interested in her hopes and fears, or of what turned her on...or off. At thirty-six, Ethel Scheider was on the run. Not from the law, but from a marriage that for fifteen years had consisted of washing, ironing, cooking, being beaten regularly by her alcoholic, son-of-a-bitch husband, and an almost non-existent sex life, that at best had been a two minute wham-bang-thank-you-ma'am on a Saturday night. She had finally got angry enough to knock the prick unconscious with a skillet, pack a bag and leave. She was on her way to her widowed sister's place in San Antonio, having survived her own bloody Alamo and in dire need to start afresh.

Looking away from Ethel, Cal noticed a buzzard wheeling lazily on thermals in the steel-blue sky. It wasn't an eagle, but beggars can't be choosers, so he jumped.

He was inside the raptor's skull, within what was its brain. He gripped the edge of the table in the RV, giddy with the sudden sensation of also soaring high above the ground, needing a few seconds to adjust to the new experience of free flight.

Directing the buzzard's gaze to the woman far below, he marveled at the acute eyesight that focused so sharply and with such magnification that he could distinguish individual hairs in Ethel's tousled, golden mane. The periphery vision was soft, not blurred but hazy, cutting out any distraction from the main source of interest. As he thought to swoop down on the woman, it became reality. The wings were collapsed back and he was plummeting from the sky, only pulling up at the last possible instant, missing making contact with Ethel by less than six inches, before climbing steeply and gaining altitude. His stomach heaved threateningly with what seemed like G forces that would turn an F-16 pilot's guts inside out. The ride had pushed the best rollercoaster's efforts into a tame second place by a mile. He left the bird, and from the comfort of the bench seat, watched Ethel's reaction to the near miss she had just survived.

Ethel screamed out in surprise as the massive bird flashed into sight. The displacement of air from its down-beating wings as it pulled up blew her hair over her eyes and the cigarette from her mouth. She jumped backwards, falling on her well-padded ass, the half full container of water was discarded, and the open faucet soaked the ground, and Ethel.

"You motherfucker!" Ethel shouted at the departing buzzard, her anger mixed with an edge of fear, not knowing why the bird had attacked, and put in mind of the unforgettable avian Hitchcock movie.

Cal laughed loudly and heartily at the sight of the drenched woman, as she sat on her butt, water pooling around her, shaking her fist and badmouthing the receding raptor.

His laughter increased, and he held his aching sides, unable to compose himself as Ethel launched herself to her feet, slipped onto her face, and then scrabbled on her hands and knees, to pick up the container and hunch against the wall to fill it, keeping her eyes glued to the sky, expecting a further assault. Cal's eyes filled with tears as she then ran, zigzagging towards the van in a stinted short-stepped sprint, looking as though she had filled her pants. Within seconds of her climbing into the vehicle, it screeched away, leaving bare brown earth where there had been grass.

Strange, Cal thought as his laughter ebbed, how such a fatuous little episode could cause him to crack-up so completely. He had not laughed so much since...well, for many years in real time. He poured himself another coffee and watched the buzzard as it resumed its slow circular patrol far above him. Looking ahead, considering the showdown that would hopefully soon take place, he felt that with his array of powers there would be little problem in subduing the Indian, and Belle if necessary. He should be able to just throw a pair of handcuffs to Luke and compel him to put them on. He could then have him walk into a jail cell in Safford with all the meekness of a lamb to the slaughter; game over. But would, or could it really be that simple? Almost an anticlimax. Part of him hoped that it would be, but deep down, if he was honest with himself, an anger and hatred burned like an eternal flame, its fuel a blood lust, firing a need for a far more satisfying revenge.

Cal was still finding it hard to accept that the Indian had blown him away, and that he had committed the act with a smile on his face, undoubtedly finding perverse pleasure in ending life; the deed of no real significance to him, as commonplace as lighting a cigarette or taking a piss, but more fulfilling. He had caused so much pain and suffering that life was a gift he had no right to keep, even in the confines of a prison cell. Cal had to face the hard, undeniable truth that the reward he sought from this hunt was nothing less than bloody retribution. This was no noble crusade for justice to rid the world of a homicidal maniac, and in doing so make it a safer place. His motive was pure, unadulterated payback.

"I want the bastard to suffer for all that he has done," he said aloud to the empty motor home, needing to voice it, to hear himself state it, and in so doing acknowledge the pent up almost palpable dark force that was driving him.

Tears once more filled his eyes. But not the warm tears of laughter that he had shed just a few minutes previously. These were cold and bitter tears flowing from a well still deep with self pity; of a mourner at a funeral. And in these unique circumstances he was both mourner and deceased.

Ten minutes passed and Cal regained his composure, feeling better for allowing his emotions an outlet. Calmness replaced the brief storm within him. He was primed and ready for whatever destiny held in store.

BOOK FIVE

ON HIGHER GROUND

CHAPTER FORTY-SIX

LUKE had accepted a lift in a Freightliner from a Chicano who had made a delivery to Fat Al's. He couldn't be sure, but thought that Al was adding drug trafficking to his CV. The package that he saw change hands could have been a K of nose candy. He didn't want to know; it wasn't his scene, and the fat piece of shit knew it.

Ramon, the teamster, was headed west to San Diego, and so Luke hitched a ride and asked to be dropped off east of Bowie, the nearest point en route to the cabin.

"The Hacienda will do fine," Luke said as they approached a large truck-stop that sat back from the highway and was noted for serving up good helpings of cheap food.

Luke had just finished up a rare T-bone when he overheard a guy a couple of tables away ask a waitress for directions to Safford.

"Shucks, sorry, honey. I ain't got any idea," she said, shrugging her shoulders as she turned tail and headed for the kitchen with a stack of dirty dishes.

"It's about sixty miles from here," Luke said, smiling at the guy. "You need to keep west on I-10 till you see the turn for 666. That'll take you through the mountains and smack-dab into the center of Safford. I live on the way and could use a lift it that rests easy with you."

"Hell, I could use the company," boomed the guy. "If you're all finished up eating, let's haul ass."

As they walked across the lot to the light-blue Honda, Luke realized that the guy was a motor mouth. He was one of those jerks who had the need to prattle on incessantly, without seeming to have to come up for air.

"I'm Tom Patterson," the burly, balding, florid-faced guy said, sticking out a pudgy hand for Luke to shake as he introduced himself.

"Jim Santana," Luke said, his smile becoming more of a grimace as his hand was pumped vigorously by what felt like a sweating piece of raw liver.

Tom was a siding salesman, and as he drove at a little under the speed limit, he bored the shit out of Luke, relating his life story, and even showing him photos of his ugly fat wife and even uglier and fatter children, telling Luke that home to the Patterson family was a four bed, two bath tract house on the outskirts of Odessa in Texas.

He expounded the merits of his company's aluminum and pressed-steel products over those offered by their competitors, fishing in a pocket and handing Luke his business card as he promised him a one-off, extra special discount should he ever need 'the best in the west'. By the time Luke asked the guy to drop him off south of Turkey Lake, he had the beginnings of a headache. That Tom had met Willie Nelson backstage after a concert in Austin, and even carried a fucking photograph of himself with his arm draped around the old, IRS-dodging, marijuana smoking, guitar picker's shoulder, didn't impress him, but was a tad more interesting than siding. If he'd not been in his own backyard, he would have been sorely tempted to cut the boring bastard's throat, just to shut him the fuck up.

Luke climbed out of the Honda, thanked Tom and watched the salesman's car disappear round a curve, hoping that he would have a head-on collision with a Peterbilt. He then left the blacktop, slipping into the welcome peace of the forest, heading for the lake on a barely discernible deer trail. The scent of pine and the isolation quickly cleared his head. Tom Patterson was almost forgotten, and the prick's shitty embossed card had been ripped in half and trodden underfoot.

Reaching the edge of the lake, Luke sat with his back up against a tree trunk, fired up a cigarette and let the ambience of his surroundings percolate through him and wash away his tension. He gazed out at the expanse of shining water stretching before him, its mirrored reflection of pewter sky and trees disturbed only by the occasional fish breaking the otherwise placid surface. He was now eager to reach the cabin, and Belle. The winter months were a time for respite from his other self; a time to recharge his batteries. He ceased to burn with uncontrollable urges, his lust for blood reduced to a smoldering ash, the inferno capped as though the fall in temperature had also cooled his special needs. He was anticipating a time of calm, satisfied to be with his woman, to hunt and to be at one with the cleansing cold elements that would enshroud the mountain refuge.

Taking a last draw on the cigarette, he flicked the butt into the water and watched the spreading concentric circle of ripples race away. His time of killing was over until the melt brought him back out the following spring, sap rising within him and his compulsion to hunt and kill women renewed. He would then venture forth from a state of almost mental hibernation; a hungry and parlous predator in search of prey.

Skirting the north side of the lake, Luke cut back into the forest and approached the cabin with his usual stealth and caution. He knew that Belle would be eager to see him, and once he had stashed the large amount of money that he was carrying, and put the hair-covered souvenir from the Flat Top in solution, he would shower, have a few shots of tequila, bed Belle, and then catch up on some much needed sleep.

Cal was glad to see Rich arrive to start his shift. It had seemed a long four hours. The stakeout, even though shared, had begun to jag the nerves and become monotonous. The expectation of the Indian's return had, as the days passed, turned to disenchantment. What if he did not return? There were no guarantees that he would definitely show. And if he did, it may not be for another week, or even longer. While they had been trying to get a fix on him and were on the move, stopping, making enquiries and showing the drawings to people, there had been an almost electric charge powering and driving them on. Now, they were just stagnating in one location, playing a waiting game that had them all on edge.

Driving back to the RV, Cal had no way of knowing that Luke had just arrived at the cabin and that any advantage they had possessed was now gone. They had all assumed, unforgivably, that he would be driving, and would use the track that they were closely guarding. It was a serious error of judgment. They knew that he was highly dangerous, but had underestimated his wariness, and not appreciated that cunning and stealth were qualities that were second nature to him, built into his character and honed to almost an art form of self preservation. That he might always hitch rides, then use various routes on foot to reach the cabin had just not crossed their minds. They lived in the age of the car, were dependent on transport, and used to dealing with people who were of a like mind. The psychology of the Apache was outside their experience.

The truth was that if necessary Luke could live off the land, moving at night and staying in shade through the day. He could find water in cacti and tubers, and eat anything that walked, slithered, crawled or flew. In some ways he was as alien to his pursuers as a scorpion or sidewinder. They were judging him by standards that he did not conform to.

The tables had begun to turn, and their oversight would cost them dearly. The initiative was lost, and the hunt was now going to be conducted by the former quarry, on his ground and by his merciless terms of engagement. As a cornered rat, the Indian would attack with a tenacious will to survive, would never surrender, and would employ any and all means necessary to escape and remain free.

Belle met Luke at the door, and he returned her welcoming embrace before going to his room to secrete his ill-gotten gains in the secret compartment of the closet. He then stripped off his sweat and dust-grimed clothes and went through to the bathroom for a shower. Ten minutes later he rejoined Belle. He was now refreshed, and dressed only in a loose robe and soft kidskin moccasins.

Belle poured them both a drink, her hands trembling. She was afraid, but impatient to tell him of the strangers, who may or may not be looking for him, and were only a short distance away.

Luke took the glass from her, and noticed the tremor of her hand and the apprehension in her eyes.

"Talk. What's wrong?" he said, grasping her wrist firmly enough to hurt and promise bruising.

"St...Strangers, Luke. Whites. I think they're looking for you," Belle said, the words tumbling from her mouth in jerky, clipped sentences, staccato in delivery. "They were asking questions in the post office. They wanted to know where the cabin was, and Demi said that they were from the east, not local. They have a motor home parked at the campground outside town, and a rented 4x4. If it was me that they wanted to see, they would have just driven up and knocked at the door. So it must be you that they're waiting for."

Luke was silent for a few seconds, and a deep vertical crease of concentration furrowed his brow as he considered what Belle had said, and the implications.

"I'll check them out," he said, swallowing the tequila in one gulp and relinquishing his grip on Belle's wrist, leaving her hand numb and bloodless.

Back in his bedroom, with adrenaline stimulating his racing circulation and feeding his tense muscles, Luke felt a sense of immediate danger clutching at his stomach; icy fingers that kneaded his intestines as though they were a length of baker's dough. His urge to panic was held in check by a colder, stronger emotion; anger. He quickly dressed, donning olive drab camouflage clothing and rugged all-weather combat boots. He transferred his knife to a sheath that fitted snugly into a long pocket on the right leg of his trousers, and snapped the press-studded flap down with his thumb. Opening the back of his closet, he lifted a loaded Colt Python from the shelf, slipping it into a shoulder-rig under his jacket. He then took an extra clip for good measure and placed it in his left breast pocket. He was inflamed, his heart a drum-roll in his chest. He had to get away from the cabin, and fast. He imagined that whosoever was after him could be out there now among the trees, watching, moving in on him at that very second. Paranoia pierced his mind with the sprung force of a gin-trap's steel jaws. He visualized armed police surrounding the cabin, their weapons trained on the door and windows as they readied themselves to gun him down on sight. He had, to a lesser degree, felt this hysteria just once before, back in El Paso when the whore had started screaming her lungs up and he had been forced to run, and had briefly faced possible capture.

Sitting on the edge of the bed with his eyes closed and taking slow and deep even breaths, he told himself to relax and be rational. If the law was around, he would not have been allowed to enter the cabin. They would have shouted a warning, ordered him to stand still, to put his hands behind his head and to kneel or lay down in the dirt. They would then have rushed forward to frisk him for weapons and hook him up. Any untoward movement on his part would have resulted in them taking him out in a hail of bullets, filling him full of more holes than a colander if he so much as sneezed. No, he decided as his pulse slowed and his heart rate returned to the slow beat of a night-owl's wings. This was private, and that was fine by him. Whoever the whites were, they would be sorry-assed and painfully rewarded for crossing his path.

More composed, he got to his feet and went back through to Belle, his equanimity now almost intact.

"I'll leave through your bedroom window," Luke said, placing his hands on her shoulders. "Keep the lamps off, and if anyone comes to the door just aim the shotgun at it and stay quiet. If they break in, shoot them."

Belle nodded, and then followed him into her bedroom and watched as he eased the window open and crouched next to it, to feel the fresh breeze as it wafted the drapes and caressed his face.

He listened to the night and sniffed at the air, his senses acute and his awareness raised to an intense level as he absorbed his surroundings for any nuance of anything untoward. He was as alert as a nocturnal animal, satisfying himself by sight, sound and smells that no unbidden intruder was disrupting the harmony of the forest.

Silently slipping over the sill he vanished into the cloaking darkness. He searched the area, sweeping it in an outwardly spiraling circle, silently checking, even though confident that he was alone. Finding nothing to alarm him, he headed off through the trees, avoiding the trails and instinctively moving in the direction of the highway. With every step he took he became more certain that whoever sought him was ignorant of his return. He would find out what they wanted, and then if necessary, eliminate them.

Cal drove up the winding highway in Rich's car, the beams cutting a swathe of light through the gloom. He had the two-till-six shift, and no doubt Mike would be more than pleased to see him. The PI was doing Rich's stint, due to the agent suffering from a stomach bug which was forcing him to spend lengthy periods in the can.

Luke left the road as the glow of approaching lights lit the trees. He hid in the lush bracken, waited for the vehicle to pass, then once more moved out on to the blacktop to resume a steady jog downhill towards the campground. Ten minutes later he took cover again as an SUV sped by, heading in the direction of town. He had unknowingly been within just a few feet of Cal and then Mike as they had passed him like ships in the night.

Five-thirty a.m. Luke was ensconced in thick foliage bordering the site. There were only four RVs parked well apart, just dark shapes within the dimly lit perimeter. The largest vehicle had an interior light on, and a 4x4 was parked next to it. This was the one that Luke was interested in.

Inside the Cobra, Mike slept, as did Sarah. Rich was feeling weak, and although now in control of his wayward bowels, was taking plenty of toilet tissue with him, just in case of a relapse. His wristwatch alarm had jerked him from a fitful doze at five-twenty, giving him time to have coffee and fill a half-gallon flask with more, to see him through his six' till ten shift. Rich paused as he filled the thermos, a sudden prickling of the skin on his forearms putting him on instant guard. The sensation was brief, passing so quickly that he adjudged it to be from the low temperature, not an omen of impending doom.

At five-thirty-five Rich drove out onto 666 to make the now familiar journey up to the 'roost', as they had nicknamed the concealed off-road hideaway.

Luke moved fast and with no hesitation as the 4x4's rear lights vanished from view. He went straight to the side of the motor home and gained entry with the ease of a practiced locksmith, using the point of his knife to force the simple catch. He moved cautiously through the RV. The first door he came to opened onto a small, cramped bedroom where he found a man asleep. Leaving him, he went back to a much larger bedroom at the rear and studied the young woman who, as the man, was also sound asleep. He went back to the first bedroom, drew the Colt and aimed it at the head of the snoring man.

As Rich drove up the serpentine mountain road he assessed the current state of play. He was sure that when the perp returned it would be a simple matter to surprise him with ease. He doubted that they would even need to resort to employing Cal's supernatural powers of persuasion. The fuckwit Apache was at the end of his rope, his luck all run out like sand through an egg-timer, ignorant to the fact that they were poised, ready to move in and bring an abrupt end to his long reign of terror.

The local radio station's weather forecast broke his line of thought. Heavy snow was expected on high ground within the next twenty-four hours. Shit, thought Rich, it would seem that not *all* the Indian's luck had deserted him. Keeping watch on the trail would prove far more difficult, if not impossible, if the weather really closed in on them.

CHAPTER FORTY-SEVEN

MIKE'S sleep deepened considerably, changing to a different state of unconsciousness as the butt of the Colt impacted with his skull. He was unaware as his wrists, ankles and mouth were taped by the killer, who he and the others had been so anxious to catch up with.

Luke went through the bound man's pockets and found his ID, which caused him to feel relieved but very curious. The guy was a gumshoe from Washington D.C. This was a private job; an unofficial trace. But why? Who the fuck from the east could know, or want to know about him? It didn't make any sense, yet. This might just turn out to be something he could work out without having a blood-bath on his doorstep. He would much rather keep his low profile intact without killing people at the campground and attracting a whole mess of local lawmen and the State Police to the scene.

The bitch woke up real fast as he straddled her and clamped his hand over her mouth. He thought her eyes were going to pop out as she looked up at him with an expression of frightened recognition. He showed her the knife, which was a real attention-getter; the gleaming blue steel was a spellbinding sight that always had the same effect as a snake charmer's flute on a hooded cobra.

"Look at me," he said, withdrawing the knife from her line of sight and shaking her face, feeling her teeth through the flesh as he squeezed her cheeks hard to break the spell. "I really don't have the time to be fucked about, so concentrate. I want to know who you people are, why you are so interested in me, and how many of you are on my case? Now...before you answer, consider this. If I even think that you're lying to me I'll peel your face like a grape, and then cut your throat from ear to ear. The guy in the other bedroom is tied up and gagged, and when I get round to speaking to him, his answers better match yours, or you both die hard. Do you understand me?"

Sarah nodded rapidly, and he removed his hand from her mouth, touching his finger to his lips to remind her that silence is golden.

Sarah felt numb, paralyzed, as though she had been injected with a liter of Novocain and was at the mercy of a crazed and homicidal dentist. It was *him*, she thought. She was looking up into the living face of what up until this moment had just been a sketch on a piece of paper. Jesus Christ! This really was Luke Strayhorse. He was not just a mythical ghost, or as elusive as a shadow with no substance.

This was the psycho who'd murdered Cal all those years ago; the mutilator, rapist and killer of God knows how many young women. And now she was pinned beneath him, petrified and certain that she was going to suffer so much more than just a violent death.

"Speak," he ordered as she lay there slack-mouthed, watching him and taking in his sculpted Indian face, which was attractive in a cruel and hard way. But his eyes were evil, incarnate pools of raven-black, which showed no feeling; unreadable and as cold as pack ice, freezing her blood under their gaze.

"Th...There is f...four of us," she began, her voice a timid whisper. "A deputy sheriff by the name of Cal Morgan was murdered in Nevada, years ago, and...and his son believes that it was you that did it." How the hell could she tell him the truth; that a guy he had murdered over twenty-one years ago was now back from the grave, reincarnated and pissed, hunting for him after all this time. "The man in the other room is a PI, helping to look for you. And the other man is...is a friend, along for the ride."

"And what about you, sweetmeat? Which one of them are you fucking?" Luke said, running his thumb gently along first her top lip, then the bottom, tracing their shape as he smiled coldly at her.

"The one who thinks that you killed his father."

"Where are the other two?"

"Changing over, up near the trail that leads to the cabin. That's where they're watching; waiting for you to show up."

"And what did they intend to do when I did?"

"Take you in. Hand you over to the authorities."

Luke tilted his head back and laughed; a deep and mirthless chuckle that lacked any trace of real humor. It was the false laugh of a jackal or hyena, soulless and primitive.

"Okay, bitch," he said. "Here's what we're going to do..."

Cal stepped out of the car and saw an exploding starburst of orange. It reminded him of a corn marigold opening its petals to the sun of an autumn morning, or a firework blossoming in a bright expanding circle over the castle at Disneyland. In reality, he had been felled by a blow to the back of his head by the same bloodied gun butt that had rendered Mike unconscious. His stunned brain was vaguely aware of the Range Rover moving away, before insensibility wrapped him in a black embrace, and his face relaxed where it lay on a pillow of dew-sheathed grass.

Luke had taped Sarah's mouth, and had used more tape to bind her right wrist to his left. As the 4x4 stopped and a figure emerged, he pulled her from where he had waited outside at the rear of the RV, and rushed forward to club the driver down as he exited the vehicle. He recovered the car keys from where they dropped and pushed Sarah across the passenger seat, climbing in beside her and telling her to buckle her seat belt.

"Drive," he snapped, handing her the keys and then ripping the tape away from her mouth. "Head on up the mountain to the cabin."

Trembling and feeling sick with dread, Sarah somehow fumbled the ignition key into the slot, started the engine and drove away from the campground. She was consumed with fear. It was like a living entity writhing inside her, sapping her of all will and feeding on her terror as though it was sweet nectar. As she drove, she fought to regain some self-control, biting her lip until she tasted blood; using the pain to stimulate positive thought. She could not believe that this was happening. How could the Indian even know of their existence? He had just appeared from nowhere, a ghost in the night. All the planning they had done now counted for nothing. She was his captive, alone with him and vividly conscious of the atrocities he had committed, and the extent of the sick and depraved acts he was capable of perpetrating on his chosen prey. The tattoo on her right hip, although covered, felt like a flashing beacon that would draw him to it as surely as a porch light attracted moths. She knew his sickening modus operandi; that he cut tattoos from bodies, hopefully post mortem, but somehow she doubted that. He also raped, bit noses from his victims' faces, and cut their throats.

Driving on the winding road, with the bright headlights cutting through the dark pre-dawn, Sarah decided to be proactive; to attempt to make a difference and alter her fortune.

Rounding a curve, fully intending to crash the vehicle and take her chances, fate took over in the shape of a deer that was standing in the middle of the highway. Sarah braked hard and spun the steering wheel to the right.

Luke jerked his left wrist, pulling Sarah's right hand off the wheel, but he was too late to bring the vehicle back under control.

With tires screaming, leaving rubber on the black-top, the Range Rover slewed to the left and turned over, hitting the deer and killing it instantly as it was compressed and split open beneath the rolling vehicle.

After several bouncing revolutions, the 4x4 hit a steel guard rail, flipped over it and slid down a slope into bushes that brought it to a stop, resting on its side.

Cal pushed himself up onto his hands and knees, vomiting as nausea hit him like rolling thunder and forced the contents of his stomach out onto the ground in a steaming, stinking stream. He stayed on all fours as several more spasms racked his body. His mouth tasted of bitter bile, and strings of slimy mucus hung, swinging from his nose and chin as he slowly pulled himself up the side of the RV. He opened the unlocked door and clung to its edge, his head pulsating with pain, with dizziness threatening his already rubber-legged balance. Concentrating, fighting gravity, which seemed determined to pull him back down, he spat the foulness from his mouth and wiped at his face with the back of his hand. Somehow, driven by a sickening fear and the need to know what had happened, he stepped up into the vehicle and staggered to the rear, lurching from side to side as though he were a drunken passenger on a moving train, or a victim of mal de mer on the wave-lashed deck of a bucking, rolling schooner that was floundering at sea. He opened the bedroom door, praying that his worst fears were unfounded, and that his attacker had been nothing more sinister than an opportunist thief he had disturbed and who had struck him and stolen the Range Rover in a state of panic.

Sarah was gone. The bedding was in disarray, but there was no blood. On the pillow was a piece of paper; a note. Hands shaking, Cal picked it up. The bedside lamp illuminated the hand-written message that had been left for him. It read:

> You know who I am. I've got your bitch. Come
>
> to the cabin ALONE at noon. We need to talk.
>
> Fuck with me and the girl will make road kill

look attractive. Play it cool and we can all walk

away from this in one piece.

It wasn't signed. As if it needed to be. Strayhorse had taken Sarah from under their fucking noses.

Mike! What had he done to Mike? Cal went to the smaller bedroom, then hesitated, scared to open the door; a picture in his mind of what the Indian might have done to his friend. His hand seemed frozen to the handle, all strength gone, and the metal opener as immovable as a ten-ton truck. With his breath held, he forced it down, pushed the door back and saw the prone figure of the PI lying on the bed, bound and covered in blood. Mike groaned. He was alive. Cal scrabbled at the adhesive tape that secured Mike's hands behind his back, but was unable to remove it and so rushed out to the dinette and pulled a knife from the wooden block on the countertop. After slicing through the silver duct tape that was binding Mike's wrists, ankles and also wrapped around his head covering his mouth, Cal helped him to his feet and supported him as they both stumbled out of the bedroom to sit at the table.

"She's gone, Mike," Cal said in a ragged whisper as he handed Mike the note to read. "He's taken Sarah."

Cal poured them both large Scotches as Mike reached for his cell phone.

"He could easily have killed all three of us," Cal said. "But for some reason he didn't. I wonder why not?"

"Because he wants to deal," Mike said, stabbing Rich's number out on the keypad. "Sarah will be okay, and when you come facc to face with Strayhorse, you can do your stuff."

"Christ, I hope so. If anything happens to her—"

"She'll be fine. Just hold it together until noon."

Rich jumped; startled as in the darkness the silence and his train of thought were broken by the sudden urgent trill of his cell. He reached into his inside jacket pocket for it, having to pause to remove the bulky glove from his hand first.

"Yeah," he said, arms all at once alive with the prickling shiver of pimpled skin.

"Get back down here, Rich," Mike said in a distressed and agitated tone of voice. "The Indian's back and he's got Sarah. He took the Range Rover and may be headed towards you."

"I'm on my way," Rich said, breaking contact and throwing the phone onto the passenger seat as he started the engine, stalling as he tried to accelerate away too fast, and having to restart, using less haste for more speed. He pulled out and sped down the mountain, watching for the approach of the 4x4 as he broke the land speed record for that particular stretch of US 666.

Just the very rear of the Range Rover protruded from the dense bracken, but at an angle that concealed it from Rich's view, as his main beams swept by the site of the crash. He had passed within thirty feet of Sarah and the Apache on his pell-mell dash down the mountain.

CHAPTER FORTY-EIGHT

LUKE had been thrown around like a rag doll. He had not fastened his own safety belt. His left wrist – still taped to Sarah's right – had taken the initial brunt of the jarring forces that resulted from the Rover rolling. It was broken. And his head had slammed into the roof more than once, causing a deep wound on the crown that was flowing with blood. He was on the edge of blacking out, but the pain kept him conscious.

Sarah had fared far better. The belt had held her in the seat, and the driver's airbag had exploded from the center of the steering wheel, bouncing her off its billowing surface, winding her but preventing serious injuries. She was fully conscious. The only serious pain she felt was from her right leg, which had been twisted and also injured as the door caved in, and her bound wrist was badly sprained, but not fractured like Luke's.

It was obviously not the woman's fault that a fucking deer had been standing at the center of the highway, but Luke needed to vent his anger, and so punched her hard in the face, breaking her nose, and then hit her again, knocking her unconscious.

As Sarah's head drooped forward and the blood from her nose stained the airbag, Luke reached across and turned the ignition and lights off, to then sit back and evaluate the new and unexpected turn of events, before drawing his knife and cutting through the tape that held their wrists together. He then opened the passenger door, having to use his shoulder to release it, and gingerly climbed out of the vehicle. Gritting his teeth, he leaned back in, released the seat belt and pulled Sarah on to the passenger seat, to then fold her over his right shoulder. He stood upright with difficulty, took several deep breaths and set off in the direction of the cabin.

Rich looked from Cal to Mike. They were both ashen, with dark smudges under their eyes, and blood matting their hair and streaking their clothing.

"Christ, he got you both. Just cold-cocked you, one after the other," Rich said, due to it being obvious that there was no other explanation for what had happened.

“I was asleep, Goddamnit,” Mike mumbled, pressing a makeshift ice-pack of cubes wrapped in a dish towel to the back of his head. “I woke up bound and gagged.”

“I got out of the Rover and he slugged me from behind,” Cal said. “I heard him drive away, but I didn’t see a thing.” Cal handed the note to Rich, and as the agent read it he lowered his face into his blood-smeared hands, overcome by anguish and self indulgent with guilt at what had transpired. Mike had been right, he thought. He should have listened to him back in D.C. and not acceded to Sarah’s demands to join them. He should have been more stoic and just driven off without her. Not thinking it through properly at the time had been inexcusable. Several weeks ago, he had been too confident and had no real concept of just how dangerous this trip might turn out to be. Now, they were suddenly staring death in the face. He had caught up with his past, only for it to turn round and bite him like a rabid dog. This scenario should not have been a possibility. The combined police and FBI experience of the three of them, plus his paranormal abilities, had proved no match for one solitary Indian who had somehow outflanked, outsmarted and run rings around them with apparent ease.

“Cal, let me call the bureau, they have the resources,” Rich said, putting the note down on the tabletop. “We need help, and now. This situation has gotten away from us.”

“No, Rich,” Cal said, shaking his head and immediately regretting the action as the resulting pounding made him moan out loud. “I’m the only chance that Sarah has got, God help her. This guy isn’t going to give up or be talked down by some fucking hostage negotiator. He’ll live or die on his own terms, but he’ll never surrender. If he starts to believe that it’s the end of the line for him, he’ll kill Sarah and anyone else that he can, before probably offing himself rather than face the death penalty or the rest of his life in a prison cell. He could have easily taken us out. That he didn’t shows that he wants to bargain.”

Rich scratched at the stubble on his cheek, evaluating what Cal had said, knowing that although it went against all his training to go it alone, these unique and unusual circumstances might just warrant it.

“Let’s work out our next move, then,” Rich said, now decided, acquiescing to Cal’s logic without argument. “We need to know exactly what we’re going to do when we reach the cabin. Mike and I are going to be covering you every step of the way, and if either of us get a clear shot, then the bastard is history."

"I thought you wanted to take him alive, not whack him?" Cal said, surprised at the agent's sudden change of mind.

"Plan A was to take him alive. Now I've moved to plan B, which is to shoot the sonofabitch on sight."

Despite the pain from their head wounds, and the fear for Sarah's safety, both Cal and Mike grinned at Rich and his newly formed plan.

Sarah had prayed that Strayhorse was dead. He had been crashing into the roof and the console of the vehicle as it had turned over and over before leaving the highway. But he had survived. If Cal had not been wounded too badly by the blow to his skull, he and the others – if they were still alive – would somehow be able to save her. The Indian had left a note, so she reckoned that he must want to make some kind of deal, though she knew by just having looked into his malevolent eyes that he only dealt in death. Fortunately, Cal would be able to get inside his head and see his intentions and then outwit him, by manipulating him as though he was a marionette. All she had to do was somehow stay alive and wait.

"It's me, open up," Luke said, kicking at the door with his sound foot as he unceremoniously dumped Sarah on the ground.

Belle had been sat in near darkness, with only the glow from the fire lighting the walls with flickering, wavering shadows that danced and undulated to the music of the hissing and spitting logs. Her hands ached as she clenched the shotgun tightly to her breasts. When she heard the footfalls outside, she sprang up, pointing the weapon at the door and almost pulling the trigger, somehow stopping herself as Luke spoke. She put the 12 gauge down, unlocked the door, opened it and stood back. A mixture of shock and fear drained her face of color as she saw Luke's eyes, wide, wild and staring out from a mask of blood.

"Get her inside," Luke ordered, averting his gaze down to the moaning figure that lay in a heap at his feet, also covered in blood.

Limping into the cabin, Luke stopped at the center of the room to bend down and pull back the rug from the trapdoor that led to the cellar. Belle grasped one of the woman's ankles with both hands and hauled her inside the cabin, pausing for a second to let go of the leg, close the door and lock it.

Gripping the metal ring that was recessed into the trap's wood, Luke lifted it and let it fall back onto the floorboards where, with a heavy thud, it threw up a cloud of dust to coat his bloodied features in a gruesome patina that gave him the look of a zombie from a Romero movie. He stepped back towards where Belle had dragged Sarah, to grasp her wrist and swing her around to the opening, her momentum taking her over the edge to fall, bouncing down over the solid, inflexible steps, to come to rest spread-eagled on the hard-packed earth floor at the bottom.

"Go down and tie the bitch up real good," Luke said, pulling the reel of tape from a pocket of his combat jacket and throwing it to Belle, who fumbled and dropped it and had to chase it as it rolled across the floor.

"But what—?" Belle began.

"Shut up," Luke said. "Just fuckin' do it. Tape the cocksucker up."

He limped into the bathroom and leaned against the wall, light-headed and weak at the knees, closing his eyes, pausing until he felt able to undress, step into the shower and turn it on. He was more badly injured than he had at first thought. But he had survived and would mend.

Belle came through to find Luke now seated on a cabinet, struggling to pat himself dry. She toweled him, and with antiseptic poured over a wad of cotton batting she cleaned his head-wound and then bandaged his left wrist and forearm, immobilizing the limb, before fetching him painkillers from where she kept them in a drawer in the kitchen. After he had swallowed several of the Advil, Belle followed him through to his bedroom, and he was happy to let her help him dress in thick, warm outdoor clothes; clothes that he usually wore on his winter hunting trips.

"Get me a drink," he said as she finished tying the laces of his boots.

Belle left the room, pulling the door closed behind her, and Luke lifted his woolen sweater to fasten the sheathed knife to his belt by its leather, press-studded loop. Belle had already helped him back on with the shoulder rig that held his Colt. Taking a fleece-lined, thigh-length jacket from the closet, he went back through to the living room to drink tequila and wait. From what the girl had told him, the guy she had mentioned would continue to keep this matter private, between them, and would turn up at noon as instructed. Luke was not stupid, though. He knew that the other two men would be close by, ready to act if he gave them half a chance. But he would give them no chance at all. He wanted them up at the cabin, away from town, where he would, if possible, engineer it so that he could kill them all. He had no intention of making a deal.

CHAPTER FORTY-NINE

RICH parked off the highway, a good quarter mile from the turn off to Belle's cabin, and the three of them entered the trees, avoiding the trail, trying to fine-tune a simple plan as they drew ever nearer to the killer's lair.

"When we get close, I'll cut back on to the main trail and walk in," Cal said, checking the Glock as he moved, and then slipping it back under his belt at the small of his back and pulling his parka down over it.

"We'll come in from both sides and keep you in sight from the edge of the clearing," Rich said, patting the stock of the scoped Weatherby he carried as he spoke. "And remember, if I can get a clean head shot, I'm going to take it and finish this. He's too dangerous to fuck with."

As they walked, snow began to fall, light at first, then heavier. Within just a few minutes the ground was white.

Due to the forecast that Rich had heard on the car radio, all three of them were suitably dressed in appropriate winter clothing. And as Cal moved out on to the trail he pulled up the hood of his parka, tightening the draw strings and leaving just his eyes and nose exposed to the elements.

The clearing was completely whitewashed with virgin snow by the time that Cal stopped twenty feet from the front door of the cabin.

Reining in his jumping nerves, breathing deeply, not wanting to give away the mixture of fear and apprehension that he felt by betraying it with a wavering, cracking voice, Cal composed himself and forced a strong, confident and calm call from his lips. "Strayhorse," he shouted. "Luke Strayhorse."

"I see you, Morgan," was the immediate reply from inside. But there was no movement at the heavily draped windows, or visible sign of life. "Walk on in, hoss. Just step right up. There's no need to stand on ceremony," the disembodied voice continued. It was a voice that held both humor and menace, almost convivial, as though inviting a neighbor in to watch the big game and have a beer.

Cal obeyed. It was no real surprise to him that the Indian was too sharp to show himself. He would know that Rich and Mike would be nearby, watching. He probably thought that they would shoot him on sight, and if that were the case, then he thought right.

Cal walked across to the door. He could see spots and streaks of blood on the ground in front of it, now pink as snowflakes began to cover them, and prayed that Sarah was still alive. He opened the door and stepped inside, slowly.

"Close it," the voice ordered. "Then go over to the chair by the fireplace and sit with your hands clasped together behind your head, fingers interlocked."

Cal closed the door and walked across the room, unaware that Sarah lay injured and in pain, bound and more frightened than she had ever been in her life, just a few feet below him.

Luke appeared at the kitchen doorway, his gun aimed at Cal's chest, unwavering as he stepped into the room and pulled a straight-backed wooden chair away from a table with his foot. He then sat with his gun-hand resting on the tabletop, the weapon's barrel at no time drifting even a centimeter off target.

"So, now we talk, Morgan. And then I decide how this ends. Your bitch told me that you are the son of a deputy sheriff who you believe I offed a long time ago. I don't buy that. I want the truth, and if I think that what you tell me is a crock of shit, I'll just blow you away and take my chances with your buddies out there."

Cal had jumped the instant that he set eyes on the Indian, flinching involuntarily as the agony of Luke's injuries hit him. He partially blocked it out, mentally smothering the area of his brain that received the transmission of pain from the mass of damaged nerve endings. He was in a world of cold, calculating and destructive force. The Indian was unlike anyone else he had entered. He was what Cal imagined pure evil would be if distilled and bottled; a concoction of brimstone and liquefied malignity, more noxious than the fuel of hellfire. Strayhorse was psychologically unnatural, incapable of compassion or regard for anything other than his own warped desires. The neural pathways that should have allowed normal emotions to propagate and function were in some way shorted out, atrophied and redundant. His brain was a twisted and lethal organ, damaged but still capable of projecting a veneer of normality to shield his true nature from the attention of a world that was alien to him. He saw all other life about him as little more than a harvest to reap at will, or use to profit by. This was a predator that killed for the base pleasure that inducing fear, pain and death rewarded him with. It was the ultimate sport of hunting and culling; the domination and destruction of what he considered to be inferior beings that motivated him.

The part of Cal that was inside this human cesspool could hardly bear the images and sensations that were bombarding him. He saw all the killing and mutilation, and could smell the blood, sweat and body waste that the monster thrived upon. He was now infected with the abhorrent existence of the Apache, and would have to find a deep mental pit to bury it in, if he were to keep his sanity and survive the nightmare that was Luke Strayhorse.

Cal locked on to one event, muting and dampening all else. He witnessed the rape, brutal torture and slaying of the Henderson girl and saw himself through the eyes of the creature that had done, it after he had climbed out of his Jeep on that sauna-hot morning back in ninety-six. He stayed with it, right up to the moment when, from the Indian's viewpoint, he was looking into his own face. He could feel the surge of pleasure that followed the pulling of the trigger that ended – temporarily as it turned out – his life.

Being in possession of the other mind's contents was an instant occurrence. It was not a process that unfurled in sequence or piecemeal or even took time to assimilate. Once he had crossed over and gained access through whatever paranormal portal had opened up to him, Cal found it akin to looking at a painting on a gallery wall; seeing the whole picture and simultaneously picking out every nuance of the artist's brushstrokes, and absorbing the texture and richness of the pigmentation. He saw Luke as a baby being raised in a timber-framed house of cheap and poor construction. Outside the dwelling in the dust of the front yard stood a rusting old Pontiac that looked as if it had been placed there as some exotic garden ornamentation; a wheel less hulk; just one of many in the slum of the reservation. More importantly, he saw the Indian in recent hours, and zeroed in on the events following the car crash. He now knew that Sarah was beneath him in the cellar, injured, bound, but alive. Nothing that Luke knew could be withheld. Even memories that the Indian could not recall were crystal clear to Cal.

Cal 'saw' the compartment at the back of the bedroom closet, and was sickened and saddened at the sight of the grisly trophies of preserved flesh, adorned with artwork that the victims had once displayed with pride on vibrant living bodies. The multiple killings at the Flat Top Ranch had been his latest atrocity, and God willing, that poor family would be the last he would ever send so savagely to premature graves. Taking this ghoul alive was no longer even a consideration. He would kill him now, he decided, and not with the detachment of swatting a fly or stepping on a bug. He would kill Luke in cold blood, and relish the satisfaction that it would give him.

Allowing his will off the leash, Cal instructed Luke to put the barrel of the gun into his mouth and pull the trigger; no sermons, speeches or explanation. This was to be the swift slaughter of a wild beast; the destruction of a sick animal, not a human being.

Nothing! It didn't work. He had no control over this diseased mind. The corrupt mass that inhabited the brain-pan and governed the actions of the Apache did not respond to Cal's instructions, save for a slight and worthless tremor of the man's gun hand. All this had taken place in a matter of seconds, and looking at Luke from the fireside chair, Cal started to answer his questions, mindful now that he could not affect the situation with his powers, and would have to rely on his wits to stop the Indian, who on a whim could decide to shoot him. The only advantage he was left with was being able to monitor the killer's thoughts, mood and intentions as he tried to talk his way out of the hole that he was in.

Cal saw one small ray of light. He could see, literally, that Luke was curious and wanted to know why he was being hunted. He also wanted to get out of the situation alive, and with two armed men somewhere nearby, he knew that killing Cal or Sarah at that time was not the solution. Cal decided to hit him with the truth; all of it.

"My name is Cal Morgan," he said. "You and the two guys that you were traveling with – Johnny and Jerry – raped and killed a girl near the town of Benson's Creek in Nevada in July of ninety-six. When a deputy sheriff showed up, you capped him, too. Later, when Johnny died in the mine, you planted my gun on him. The important shit is, that I woke up in this body a few months ago. I'm a ghost from your past, Luke. I'm the cop that you murdered, and I can read your mind. There's nothing that you've ever done that I don't know. I'm what Swift Elk was warning you about when he called you Death Walking. And if you kill me again you'll just be plain dead."

Luke's expression remained impassive, but his brain raced, trying to comprehend how this young guy could know anything about Johnny, Jerry, Swift Elk, or long gone events.

“If you can read my mind, what am I thinking now?” he said, sure that there must be some other explanation for the stranger’s insight.

“You’re thinking several things, Luke. You plan on killing us all if you get the chance to. You also intend to tell me to hand over my gun, because you’re sure that I’m carrying. You’ve just thought that it might be better to shoot me now and keep the girl to bargain with. The truth is you don’t really know what to do. You aren’t used to being in the shit, only dealing it out. I think you should know what will happen if you do decide to kill me, though. I’m in your mind, and also in the mind of this young guy sat in front of you. I’m in two places at once, and if you shoot Danny...that’s this kid’s name, then I will only exist in one place, you. I would be living in you, part of you, and as time went by I would take you over, push you out into an eternal existence without a body, to drift in total isolation. On the other hand, I could transfer into someone else any time I chose to, and just cancel your ticket. Imagine it, Luke. You walk into Fat Al’s and I just jump into the slob, lift the sawn-off shotgun that he keeps under the counter and gut shoot you. Every minute of every day you would be wondering what I was going to do, and when I was going to do it.”

Belle Morita had listened to every word, and was frightened by the supernatural talk that she found hard to follow. Luke was – if the white was telling the truth – a killer, and although she did not want to believe any of it, she instinctively knew that it was probably true. She appeared at the kitchen doorway and stared at Cal as though he was a Martian or a three-headed dog. Luke sensed her standing behind him.

“Get me a drink, Belle,” he said, not taking his soulless, reptilian eyes from Cal.

As Belle turned, Cal moved into her from Luke, now seeing the kitchen through her eyes. She lifted a bottle of tequila from the oak counter next to the sink, and as she made to unscrew the cap, he took control of her. The bottle would do just fine. He compelled her to turn and stealthily re-enter the room, now holding the bottle by its neck like a club.

Belle knew exactly what she was doing – against her will – as she raised the half full bottle above her head. But she had no control over her actions and could not even voice a warning to Luke. Her lips felt sewn or stapled together, and she knew with a dreadful certainty that the stranger by the fire was working her like a glove puppet, using her as a living weapon. Tears of rage and trepidation dampened her cheeks as she brought her arm down in a full-blooded, sweeping arc, aiming the bottle at the top of Luke's already wounded head.

With a turn of speed to be admired, especially in a badly injured man, Luke not only half turned, but managed to move slightly to his left, which resulted in the bottle glancing off his already concussed skull, not striking him with the impact that Cal had intended.

Luke reacted instinctively, without thought as to why Belle would suddenly attack him. He swung his arm around and fired upwards twice from the kneeling position that he had assumed as he fell from the chair. Both bullets tore into Belle's stomach, a hairsbreadth separating the entry holes. The slugs erupted from high up in her back, taking a welter of blood and flesh with them, embedding into the ceiling timbers amid a crimson spray. She was thrown backwards, bouncing off the door jamb, spinning into the kitchen with her arms flailing, as if performing a macabre dance to music that only she could hear. And then she crumpled and came to rest in a sitting position against the wall with her legs splayed, hands curled up like dead spiders on the worn and brittle linoleum. Without a sound, Belle's head fell forward and was still. Her life had been extinguished in almost an instant.

Cal had left Belle as the bottle caught the side of Luke's head. And as the roar of the gunshots reverberated around the cabin, he drew the Glock and brought it up to aim at the Indian.

Luke kicked the wooden chair across the floor a fraction of a second before Cal pulled the trigger, causing him to flinch as the gun discharged, spoiling his aim, with the result that instead of seriously debilitating or killing him, he only managed to crease the shoulder of the Indian's already broken left arm.

Luke followed the chair, firing wildly as he moved, and Cal threw himself back over the armchair he had been rising from, to escape the bullets.

Stopping, Luke threw the rug back, and with the gun still in his hand, yanked open the trapdoor and leapt into the dark pit of the cellar, to land heavily at the bottom of the steps, just inches from Sarah.

As Cal looked round the side of the chair, Luke was vanishing from view, gone before he could get off another shot.

Luke holstered the colt and drew his knife, cutting the tape from Sarah's ankles before dragging her up on to her feet and urging her to move to the far end of the cellar, away from the weak shaft of yellow light that crept down the steps from the room above. Reaching up, he unlatched a small overhead door that was a purpose-built escape hatch from the underground bolt-hole. It took all of his strength to push it back with only one hand. The wood had both swollen and contracted through the passing of many seasons, and was reluctant to give. Finally it flew back, dislodging a thick matting of pine needles, twigs, leaves and earth that had built up over the years, concealing the exit from the outside. Placing a short wooden ladder against the rough, green-oak support timbers of the cellar wall, Luke slit the tape that still held Sarah's wrists together.

"Climb," he said, letting her feel the sharp tip of the knife in the small of her back as incentive for her to move.

Sarah dragged herself up the rungs, her right leg pounding with pain and her hands and feet throbbing with pins and needles as her circulation was once more allowed to pump blood through veins and arteries that had been starved by the tightness of the duct tape. At the top, she squeezed through the opening and rolled over the edge onto the fresh, cold snow, pulling her nightie down to cover the tattoo, sure that although badly hurt, the sight of it would incite the Indian to remove it at the earliest opportunity.

The shots brought Mike and Rich from cover in a dead run for the cabin. Mike took a flying leap at the door, kicking it solidly next to the handle; the wood splintering as the lock gave and the door flew back. He rolled and came up ready to shoot, searching for a target. Rich had dropped the rifle and was standing behind him, aiming his pistol two-handed into the room, also looking for the Indian.

The glimpse of Luke's head had been all that Cal needed. It had been enough to allow him to make the instantaneous leap and be in him again as he plunged into the cellar.

"He's outside in the Jeep," Cal bellowed at the other two, now on his feet and moving towards the door. "But don't shoot; he's got Sarah with him."

They heard the roar of the engine and ran out just in time to see the rear of the Jeep as it crossed the clearing, kicking up snow and veering out onto the trail that led to the highway. Rich *did* shoot, twice, aiming low for the tires, for one bullet to send up a puff of snow, the other hitting metal, not rubber.

"Fuck it!" Rich said, grimacing as the vehicle vanished, hidden from view by trees. "We've lost him."

"No we haven't," Cal said. "I'm with him, and he suspects that I am. He still needs Sarah as insurance, so she's safe for the time being. He knows what I can do, and that we can follow him."

"Stop," Luke said to Sarah as they reached the end of the trail. "Get that blanket from off the back seat and wrap it around yourself."

Sarah did as she was told, stopping the Jeep and pulling the thick Indian blanket – that Belle had woven the previous winter – to her, covering herself with it, glad of the rough wool on her shivering body.

"Okay, now turn right and follow the road until I tell you to make a left," Luke said in a soft, almost friendly tone of voice that seemed totally out of character to her, considering the situation. "It looks as if I'll be trading you for my freedom when lover boy catches up, so no more braking for deer or anything else. Both of us are banged up enough. Agreed?"

Sarah nodded, feeling for the first time since being abducted that she had a real chance of surviving the ordeal. She hoped that Cal was 'with' them, but couldn't fathom out why, if he was, that he didn't just control Luke and bring this nightmare to an end.

Back at the cabin, Rich went through to the kitchen to see if he could help Belle, but didn't even bother to check for a pulse when he saw her, knowing at a glance that the body sitting in the spreading pool of blood had severed all links with life. Happy or not, she was now in the hunting grounds that Indians reputedly believe in.

They closed the damaged cabin door behind them as best they could, to deter wild animals from obtaining easy pickings.

CHAPTER FIFTY

THEY jogged, their hot breath looking like streams of cigarette smoke as it hit the cold air and became vaporous. With no further need to be furtive, they moved side by side along the open trail, turning left at the highway and reaching the concealed Explorer soon after. Rich got behind the wheel, with Cal beside him as navigator – a psychic guide – and Mike in the rear, checking the weapons and settling his nerves a little with the help of a Marlboro.

"Three miles up and then hang a left," Cal said. "He's heading for a shack on higher ground that he sometimes uses for shelter when he goes hunting in winter."

"Let's hope we catch up with him before this weather closes in," Rich said, his eyes narrowed in concentration, wipers on fast, scudding across the windshield and whipping frantically backwards and forwards, fighting the wind-driven snow that threatened to obliterate his view of the road ahead.

The part of Cal that was in Luke, saw Sarah. She was driving the Jeep, a blanket wrapped around her shoulders, her hair and face wet and sticky with a mixture of melted snow and blood. Her nose and cheeks were swollen, eyes puffy, little more than bruised slits. He knew that she was safe, for the moment, but she was probably terrified and feeling abandoned and alone, with no hope of salvation. He transferred into her from Luke, screening out her past by imagining a wall; a force field to stop her whole life being absorbed. It worked. This was another escalation of his powers. He could choose to experience only her current thoughts, and felt only her present sensations. Christ! She was in such a world of hurt. Her knee was a bed of hot embers being raked with tines of liquid fire. And her whole face pounded with invisible rings of pain that radiated out from her fractured nose. She was scared, but hopeful, and was wondering if Cal was inside the Indian, tracking him. She was also perplexed. If he was in Luke, why hadn't he stopped him, immobilized him until they could catch up?

Telepathy was not a gift that Cal appeared to have in his repertoire. He tried to communicate with Sarah, but she was not aware of him. He stuck to what he knew he could do.

Sarah's right hand left the steering wheel without any conscious command from her mind, and reached forward to the windshield, which still had a three-inch wide band of condensation stretching along the upper inside surface. Her index finger moved against the filmed glass with inhuman speed, as a spirit writer, using a digit instead of a pen or pencil. The resulting message read: I'M WITH YOU, HOLD ON. Just five words, but five words that brought a flood of relief to Sarah, confirming what had only been a hope until that moment when Cal was with them. That he was invisibly present and watching over her like a guardian angel gave her renewed strength. The misty, dripping words bestowed upon her the resolve to endure her plight with courage.

Cal moved back into Luke and felt the rush of panic as the Indian stared in amazement at the writing that cut through the opaque veil with bone-chilling clarity. Luke knew that the girl had not been the author of it, only the instrument that had written it.

"Rub it off," he said to Sarah. "And stop playing fuckin' mind games with me, Morgan, or you'll be sorry," he continued, looking about him as though he might see Cal, although he knew that the other man's presence was purely ethereal. "I might have to keep this bitch alive for now, cop. But don't get too smart, or I'll start cutting," he shouted needlessly to the man within him. "You won't need any special powers to follow me; you'll be able to follow body parts."

Cal savored the undercurrent of fear that the Apache was trying to cloak with his verbal threats. He also knew that Luke's injuries were far more serious than he had first thought. The Indian's left arm felt as though it had been fed into a food processor; an agony that no amount of painkillers could alleviate. He was suffering, and his confidence was in shreds. Even more gratifying to Cal was the head injury. The concussion was now causing Strayhorse to almost pass out. He was fighting against the urge to just close his eyes and drift off into sleep for a while. Only pain stopped him from losing consciousness. He was in really bad shape, and that suited Cal just fine. At the moment, survival was the Indian's main priority, overriding his killer instinct.

"What's happening?" Rich said, redirecting Cal's attention back to the Explorer, although he still monitored Luke's every thought.

"He's badly injured and in severe pain. By all rights he should be out of it, but he has the willpower, determination and stubbornness of a mule. He knows that I'm with him, but still feels that he is in control of the situation, because he has Sarah. Having me in his head is a problem that he doesn't know what to do about. He's just hoping that he can deal his way out, or kill us all. One bonus, for me, is that he is reluctant to take me out. He doesn't know whether what I told him about living on inside him is true or not, and neither do I."

Rich opened the glove compartment and withdrew a fifth of Jack Daniel's. "I think we could all use a shot," he said, passing it to Cal to uncap.

The storm was early; a glitch in the normal weather pattern, even at this altitude. It had not been expected to be so severe, and was worsening by the minute, developing into a 'violent blow', as the locals would call it.

Bruce Norris was a veterinary surgeon. He was one of six that operated from a large group practice located just across the street from Centennial Peak Park in Tucson. At thirty-two he was in a relationship with a colleague, but still protective of his own space; not yet ready to commit to being part of a permanent double act.

Bruce had taken a week's break from cat-curin' and horse-healin' – as he referred to the vocation he loved – to pursue his other love, rambling in the great outdoors and enjoying the sights and sounds of its flora and fauna. These mountains were his favorite place.

He wore a large backpack containing a tent, sleeping bag, a sketch pad and pencils, and a little food and bottled water. Hanging from the pack was a coffeepot. He was an avid amateur artist, and made drawings that he would at a later date use as reference to paint large watercolors.

Bruce stopped for a while to catch his breath. The weather had turned. Earlier, the sun had been out, and after spending a night under canvas, Bruce had packed and continued on his way. But now there were storm clouds moving in at speed, and so he turned and headed back the way he had come. He could not outrun the storm, and was soon half blinded as he trudged wearily to lower ground. He was fearful, because this was perhaps the worst conditions he had ever been caught out in. And he had lost his bearings. He attempted to use his cell phone, but there was no signal, although he believed that if he called 911 he would get through to the emergency services. And then, as he considered making the call, he saw it.

The shack appeared before him through the howling squalls of driven snow, and with conditions worsening and his stamina almost depleted, he was relieved to have found a place to take shelter and sit it out. Tomorrow, he thought, he would be back down on route 666, and would spend a couple of days at his friend Todd's place – where he had left his SUV – before heading back to Tucson and the wonderful world of poorly poodles and other critters.

The shack was sturdy and windproof. Bruce was soon in his sleeping bag, warm and feeling safe.

He was almost asleep when the door burst open, startling him from his vagarious slumber. He looked up into the muzzle of a gun being brandished by an Indian whose head was bandaged and bloody, and who appeared unsteady, almost in a state of collapse.

"Get up," Luke said, taken aback to find someone in what he regarded as his shack. "Why are you here?"

"I got caught in the storm," Bruce said. "I…I'm a veterinary surgeon. I'm on vacation."

"Okay, Doc. There's an injured girl outside in a Jeep. Go and bring her in," Luke said, wondering if the guy might prove useful, or whether it would be simpler to just shoot him when he returned with the cop's whore. He mulled it over and decided that he might need the guy to drive. And he would serve as another hostage or human shield if need be.

Bruce carried the girl back inside and laid her down gently on his sleeping bag. She was conscious, staring at him with soulful eyes, but said nothing. He closed the door and then turned to face the Indian, who had sat down, back against the far wall.

Luke pointed the gun barrel at a coil of rope that hung on a rusted metal bracket behind Bruce and said, "Zip her up in the sleeping bag, and then tie it up nice and tight with some of that rope. Then you can set the stove going and get some heat in here."

Bruce removed the blanket from Sarah, not wanting to encase her in the wet material. The nightie that she wore was inadvertently pulled up her legs, and Luke caught sight of her sex, and an even more appealing image, to him...her tattoo.

"Stop." He said, and his eyes became more alert, glued to the garland that graced Sarah's right hip.

If his left arm had not been a bloated lump of hammering pain, and he had not felt so ill from the head wound's effect, then he would have probably raped and mutilated, but stopped short of killing Sarah. Even in his debilitated condition, Luke felt a stirring in his pants as he studied her nether regions and the intricate artwork. He told the guy to proceed, and watched the vet secure Sarah into the sleeping bag. He then drew his knife and handed it to Bruce, for him to cut the rope with.

"Now see to the stove," Luke said after Bruce slid the knife back across the floor to him. "My balls are turning blue. And once you get it lit you can take a look at my injuries. A vet in the hand is worth two doctors in the bush. Am I right?"

Sarah was warming up, and lying down and keeping still made the pain more manageable. Overcome by exhaustion, her mind drifted, her thoughts running wild as they courted sleep. She floated away from reality, soaring on gossamer wings of random thought. She was back in D.C. with her mom and dad, and then watching Danny slowly rising, face down through turquoise water, the billowing stain of blood from his head reaching every corner of what became a vast crimson lake, not the tiled pool in Alexandria. The scene melted, and she was arguing with Cal, demanding to accompany him on his journey west.

Sarah relived the emotions of falling in love with Cal; his being near to her; entering her; filling and fulfilling her in a union that seemed perfect on so many disparate levels. And then darkness as fear and pain enshrouded her and permeated throughout her being. She was suddenly transported and was curled up on a damp cellar floor. She could not move or see. The blackness was complete. Her wrists and ankles were bound tightly, and her right cheek lay on cold earth. She could smell her own stale sweat and the heavy, coppery scent of blood that was congealing around her head. A faint rasping, scrabbling, clicking sound alerted her. At first distant, and then slowly, almost imperceptibly moving nearer, the noises grew louder to become a frantic rushing of some alien horde that surrounded her, aware of her presence in their midst and creeping over the packed earth to devour her. As she tried to scream, her mouth was invaded and her cry stifled as they entered and bit into the soft flesh of her lips, tongue, gums and soft palate, causing her cheeks to bulge with their numbers. They were crawling, scuttling, squirming over and in her, forcing their way into her ears and nostrils. They pried open her eyelids with sharp claws and mouth parts, found their way into her anus and vagina, invading every orifice; eating her alive. She choked and swallowed, ingesting some of the thrashing mass, about to lose her reason as she shook in a frenzy of pain and revulsion. Above her, the trapdoor creaked open and a shaft of muted light split the tenebrous, crypt-like atmosphere. The cockroaches fled, climbing over each other in confused heaps as they withdrew from the glare and headed back to the cracks and crevices that they had emerged from to gorge on the fresh, warm, living food, as the Indian walked slowly down the wooden steps. He was naked, holding a massive, gleaming knife in his hand; the blade a silvery-blue with light dancing on the serrated edge. He knelt beside her, his groin just inches away from her face, and she could vaguely smell urine and semen. His penis began to thicken and rise, and then Sarah screamed as he cut the garland from her hip, as though slicing rare beef from a Sunday joint.

Sarah woke up feeling nauseous and very scared. The thought that all of the tomorrows she had envisaged could be taken away from her at any second was foremost in her mind.

CHAPTER FIFTY-ONE

THE shack came into view through the squall, appearing and then vanishing as the driving snow blew across the windshield. Rich stopped well back from the small wooden hut, but kept the engine running. They surveyed the surrounding white landscape. There were no other buildings. A craggy range of steep cliffs rose up behind the shack, protecting it from the full force of a now ferocious wind. Barely discernible to the south was a dense tree line.

"This is a stand-off," Rich said. "He could pick us off if we attempt to move in."

"Sleep," Cal said. "He needs to sleep. He's dog-tired, drained, and can't stay awake for much longer. He has another hostage in there now, a backpacker. He just made the guy tie Sarah up, and then light a fire in an old potbelly stove. Now he plans to smack the guy over the head and tie him up as well; which he knows won't be easy with one hand."

"Get over here and check out my injuries, Doc," Luke said.
"You're a certified horse doctor, so will be able to tell me what state I'm in."

Bruce went over to the Indian, and as he knelt down he was felled by a blow to the side of his head.

Cal had almost jumped from Luke to the other man, with the intention of using him to subdue the Indian, but stopped himself, scared that he could cost the stranger his life if he was unsuccessful. There was nothing that he could do to prevent the man from being knocked unconscious.

Luke set the pistol down next to him, crawled over to where the rope was curled up next to the sleeping bag, and then returned to use it to tie the vet's wrists together behind his back, which proved to be a difficult task with only one functioning hand. After rolling the unconscious vet over to the sleeping bag, he got to his feet and wedged the back of an old wooden chair under the door handle, and then limped back to the far corner and lay down on a thin, dust-laden mattress, with the gun next to his hand as he rested.

The heat from the stove in the confined space and his exhausted state combined to overwhelm him. His effort to stay awake was a battle that he lost, unaware as he slipped into sleep.

“He’s asleep,” Cal informed Rich and Mike. “It’s time to make our move.” He detailed the layout of the shack, the positions of its occupants, and the fact that the door had been wedged shut.

“Okay,” Rich said, drawing his gun. “I’ll go through the window, and you try the door, Mike. You stay behind us, Cal, and use all the juice you’ve got to try to hold him when he wakes up. And no holding back. We go straight in and shoot to kill.”

“You got it,” Mike said, checking the load in his revolver for the umpteenth time and snapping the cylinder shut.

They moved slowly, their approach covered by the blinding snow and howling gale force wind.

Standing against the front of the shack, all set to make his move, Rich held up his left hand, fisted, and mouthed, ‘on three’ to the other two. He then backed off a few feet, raised his index, then middle, and finally his ring finger, before running forward and hurling himself up and through the snow-encrusted glass of the window, arms covering his face as it fragmented. Twisting in mid-air, he landed hard, but came up on his knees, ready to open fire at the corner of the room where Cal had said the Indian was.

As Mike saw Rich’s third finger rise, he threw all his weight against the door, relieved as it flew back, disintegrating the brittle, timeworn chair, which fell apart.

Cal had stayed back, head in hands, eyes closed, concentrating completely on one act; keeping Strayhorse immobilized. The veins at his temples throbbed, and his face flushed a deep red with the effort as he filled the Indian’s brain with a repeated message: that he was paralyzed, set in cement, so weighted down with heavy chains that movement was impossible.

Luke came awake as both the window and door were breached, and saw the man hit the floor amid a shower of glass and come up in a kneeling position, facing him. He reached for the gun, but his hand, which should have snapped the pistol up instantly, betrayed him. His movement was sluggish, not responding fast enough. It was as though he was attempting to move in deep liquid as thick as molasses, and it took supreme effort and willpower to force his hand to slowly obey his command.

It was dark inside the shack. Rich did not immediately see the Indian lying on the mattress just a few feet from him. And a couple of precious seconds slipped by.

Mike entered through the wreckage of the door. He was ready to empty all six chambers of his Chief's Special into the body of Luke Strayhorse. His finger almost squeezed off the first shot, before he contained himself at the last possible instant. Rich was blocking his view. He had no shot and could only see his friend's back.

Rich saw movement in front of him and fired with hardly any hesitation as he saw the Indian raising a gun and pointing it at him.

With great difficulty, Luke managed to pull the trigger, even though a voice in his mind insisted that he could not. The bullet from his gun struck Rich in the side of his neck, driving him back and knocking him down. The back of Rich's head hit the floor hard and he fought to remain conscious.

Cal lost mental contact as the bullet from Rich's gun plowed into Luke's left side, to shatter a rib, ricochet and emerge from just above his pelvis and bury itself into the boards under the mattress he was sitting on. The shock of the slug's entry forced Cal to recoil from the Indian's brain, leaving him wholly outside the shack, the link lost.

Luke pushed himself up from the blood-spattered mattress. The fresh, searing pain galvanized him into action and he ran toward the open doorway, colliding hard with Mike, who was taking aim at him, to knock him back into Cal, causing both of them to lose their balance and fall in the snow outside the door of the shack.

Biting down, ignoring the pain that now encompassed his entire body, Luke ran into the blizzard, to quickly vanish from sight.

Mike and Cal got up and entered the shack to check on the wellbeing of Rich, Sarah and the other man.

Rich lay very still. Tried to talk, but couldn't. He could feel the blood leaving his neck in now waning spurts. There were a lot worse ways to go, he supposed. He was feeling lightheaded and knew that he would soon pass out, for what that long dead author Raymond Chandler would have called The Big Sleep.

Mike could do nothing. The bullet had disintegrated Rich's carotid artery, and he had already lost too much blood to survive. Mike just knelt next to him, gripped his shoulder and watched him die. He was distraught. The psychopath had killed his friend.

Cal had checked Sarah and the man lying next to her. They were both injured but not mortally, and so he went over to where Rich lay, and knew that the agent was dead by looking into his open, vacant eyes. There was nothing to say. Sometimes words are inadequate.

They had to continue, find Strayhorse and kill him. The Indian was in a bad way, and it was amazing that he was still able to function. But he would not get far in this foul weather.

Cal untied Sarah and Bruce, who both sat up, temporarily shocked into silence. Bruce's head was splitting as a result of the blow, and Sarah felt sick.

Bruce examined Sarah's injuries. There was nothing he could do. She needed hospital treatment.

"I want you to drive Sarah back down to Safford," Cal said to Bruce.

Bruce nodded, and winced as he did. He then picked up two of the broken chair's legs to fashion a splint for Sarah's fractured leg, to tie in place with some of the rope.

They carried Sarah out to the Explorer, where Cal helped Bruce settle her on the rear seat. As they did, Mike checked the Jeep and removed the key from the ignition.

It was time to follow Strayhorse and end this manhunt.

"I couldn't control him enough, and lost contact when Rich shot him," Cal shouted, to be heard over the wind that drove the snow almost horizontally at them. "But he took a bullet, so won't get far."

Mike looked about him, smiled and said, "Look," as he pointed to a trail of blood and footprints that were already barely visible in the deepening snow.

CHAPTER FIFTY-TWO

LUKE could not keep up a steady jog. After reaching the forest he slowed and limped along as best he could. He was in a world of pain, and covered in rapidly cooling blood that was seeping down into his left boot from the ragged exit wound on his hip.

As the trees became sparser he could make out the entrance to a cave high up on the rocky slope ahead, and so with renewed determination he made his way towards it. If he could make it up there he would have shelter from the storm and cover from his pursuers.

Although not steep, the climb almost finished Luke. By the time he had scrabbled up to the wide ledge in front of the cave he was totally exhausted. He paused at the threshold of the dark maw, gun held ready in case the cave was inhabited. Entering slowly and warily, he ducked a few inches to gain access through the low portal, which was maybe twelve feet wide and just over five feet high at the apex of the natural arch. The cave was empty, although a pungent animal smell hung in the air, and small bones littered the rock floor. Luke slumped to the bare rock. All he could do was wait and look out through a shroud of large snowflakes that were now falling almost vertically, due to an easing of the wind. He wanted his followers to appear; eager to kill them so that he could try to make it back to the Jeep and then somehow drive to the Buckeye and get Larry Loloma to arrange for a doctor, who would treat his wounds for a fee that would ensure his silence.

Cal strained to catch sight of the Indian through the snow and the firs. All he needed was the briefest glimpse of him to regain mental contact. He knew instinctively that the weaker Luke became, the easier it would be to control his actions.

As time passed, Luke became more than a little worried. The blood was still flowing freely and he was finding it hard to stay awake. The bitter cold and blood loss were threatening to overcome him. Perhaps he was finished. This could be where he would make his last stand. If so, then he wanted to perish as a warrior, not a reservation Indian, cowed and manipulated by the whites, or as his father had died, full of cheap rotgut whiskey and frozen to the ground in a dark alley.

"Up there," Mike said, pointing to the cave high above them, which they both immediately suspected that Strayhorse was in all probability sheltering in. They stopped at the fringe of the forest, and Mike lit a cigarette as they pondered over what to do next. If they attempted to approach and climb up to the cave, the Indian, if inside it, would pick them off like rats in a barrel. But waiting was not an option. The light was failing, and there was a possibility that he would be able to escape unseen in the darkness.

Keeping low behind large boulders, an unbelievable solution to their problem lumbered into view, cutting across the high ground above them, heading for the cave.

The present range of grizzlies outside of Alaska in the continental United States is primarily within the area of Yellowstone National Park, with perhaps a few in the northern reaches of Montana, Idaho and Washington. There had been no sightings of the species in Arizona since the nineteen-thirties. Mike and Cal were not to know that the huge adult male grizzly bear had escaped from the private zoo of an eccentric Mexican billionaire, and had somehow made its way over the border from Agua Pieta and headed north to its present location without being seen by a single person.

With a massive head that hung low between its muscular, rolling shoulders, the bear's ears lay flat, and its eyes were closed to slits against the snow and the chill air. Topped in white like a giant, iced plum pudding, it shambled towards its dry and sheltered den in the cliff face.

The shaggy fur rippled on the behemoth's flanks as it suddenly stopped and reared up with its snout twitching, testing the air. It could smell both blood and human spoor.

The bear was undecided, wary of the man scent, yet furious that an intruder had invaded both its territory and its refuge. It dropped back down on to all fours, swayed slowly from side to side and raked the snow with a huge front paw, as if unable to decide whether to attack or retreat.

"I'm going to hitch a ride," Cal said. "So whatever you do, don't shoot at 'Bruin', I'll be controlling him."

"You're going to go after Strayhorse inside that motherfucker?" Mike said, his eyes widening.

“Yeah,” Cal said. “And if he gets lucky and manages to deal with it, then we’ll be chasing Yogi’s ass in there to clean up. Think of it as a six hundred pound diversion.”

Cal looked up at the procrastinating bear, and then he reached out with his mind and entered its brain. He was immediately overawed by the size and power of the beast that he was now a part of. He could actually smell the Indian in the cave; a bitter blend of sweat, blood and traces of dried urine. The bear had an image of the trespasser; a blueprint to match the odor, which was filed in a catalogue of scents from the world around it. Like the coyote Cal had entered, this animal’s brain was a complex farrago of instincts, alien to him, and with no language or thought patterns that he could decipher, but with pure underlying emotions that were uncluttered and simple to evaluate. The grizzly made the decision to attack with no urging from him. It bounded forward as he took control, and was at once an automaton; a living tool following his instructions.

He entered the cave like a runaway express train, homing in on the Indian, looking out through eyes that were hot coals of anger as the bear drew its lips back to disclose lethal fangs.

Mike and Cal sprinted from cover and climbed as fast as the loose bed of time and weather eroded flakes of rock would allow, kicking up snow as they scrabbled upwards, knowing that the Indian had a more immediate and far bigger problem to deal with at the moment than the two of them.

Luke threw himself backwards, as with a thunderous roaring growl of unrestrained menace the bear rushed at him, appearing to almost fill the entrance, blocking out the light as it ducked down and slipped through the rock entrance with the raised hackles on its back brushing the limestone lintel.

Luke fired twice. The first bullet missed, ricocheting and whining around the cave in the manner of a berserk hornet. The second bullet ripped through the side of the animal’s head, taking fur and flesh, and forging a channel along the skull, but not compromising the brain. Cal was immediately dislodged by the sudden, searing pain. He was no longer in control, but had no need to be, as the enraged and wounded bear continued with independent and ferocious intent to rip the human to pieces.

Lashing out, the grizzly caught the gun, knocking it from Luke’s hand; the force taking his trigger finger – that was trapped in the guard

– with it. Standing upright, its bleeding head almost touching the vaulted ceiling of the cave's spacious interior, the giant ursine mammal paused, looking down at its helpless prey and readying itself for the kill.

Luke pulled the knife free from its sheath and waited, ready, knowing that if very lucky he might get one chance to use it. It flashed through his mind that the famous fur trapper, frontiersman and scout, Hugh Glass, had been attacked by a bear and dispatched it with a knife, surviving the terrible injuries that he suffered.

The bear dropped, lunging forward, swinging an enormous paw with three-inch long claws extended and scything the air with force capable of removing a face and destroying a skull as if it were no more robust than an eggshell.

At the last possible moment, and with split second timing, Luke ducked and thrust his arm out straight, elbow locked under the arc of the swiping paw, and like a spear – his arm the shaft, the knife its head – the ten-inch blade of razor sharp serrated steel entered the oncoming animal's throat, driven up by the creature's own weight and forward momentum to penetrate flesh, muscle and upper palate, before lodging deep into brain tissue.

The mighty grizzly was already dead as its claws made contact with Luke's head, to rake through his hair and scalp and gouge deep furrows in his skull. One of the keratin hooks removed his left eye, which burst like an overripe tomato and discharged its pale fluid onto his face, to mix with streams of blood. Luke screamed as the sweeping limb continued downwards, laciniating his cheek into segments and ripping his mouth open to the chin, taking away a large portion of gum and several teeth.

The twitching carcass fell forward, over him, and they lay as strange bed mates; the bear with one arm across Luke's chest, as if embracing him in sleep. He reached out, stretching with movement limited, and was able to retrieve the gun, pulling his amputated finger from the trigger, still not fully convinced that the grizzly was really dead.

Mike entered the mouth of the cave and approached the tangled heap of entwined bear and man; his gun aimed at the still body of the Indian, as Cal joined him and stood by his side.

"He's dead," Mike said. "Yogi did the job for us."

"In your dreams," Luke said; the word almost unintelligible through the ruins of his blood-filled mouth as he brought the Colt up and fired.

The shot spun Mike sideways and backwards, out of the cave's mouth and over the narrow ledge, to tumble down the incline that he had just climbed.

Cal jumped sideways and dropped to the ground, for the body of the bear to conceal him from the Indian's line of sight. He waited, and as the top of Luke's head slowly and cautiously appeared from behind the thick-furred back, he 'jumped' again, to once more enter the mind of his enemy.

Bruce pulled into an 'official only' parking slot outside the sheriff's office. *So ticket me*, he thought as he carried Sarah to the door, kicking it to attract attention.

The county sheriff, Joe Jansen, sent a deputy to fetch Doc Stewart, and then listened as Sarah quickly explained what had happened, and of the situation that they had left up the mountain. Her statement boiled down to the bare facts, that Luke Strayhorse – who Joe knew, but obviously not well enough – was injured and on the run. She explained that he was a wanted serial killer, and that he had shot and killed a federal agent less than an hour ago, as her companions had tried to apprehend him. Now, a PI and another guy were tracking him in high country.

Fuckin' ace, Joe thought. This was just what he needed. His shift had been almost over, and he had been all set to go home and enjoy a plate of meatloaf and mashed potato, and wash it down with a couple of beers'.

Bruce Norris – a vet for Christ's sake – told him the location of the shack, and the direction that Cal and Mike had set off in pursuit. He also said that the Indian was armed but badly injured, in no fit state to be able to travel any significant distance on foot.

The doctor arrived, examined Sarah and Bruce, and arranged for them to be transferred to the county hospital. Joe contacted the state police and the FBI and advised them of the situation, and then headed up to the shack with three deputies, using the only 4x4 that the department's funding stretched to. The Plymouth cruisers, even with chains attached, would have been hard-pressed to make it up the mountain track from the highway. He hoped that the State boys and the feebs moved their asses on this. He knew Strayhorse's reputation, and thought that this could get messy: The more firepower the better.

Mentally pushing the pain that Luke was suffering into the imaginary vault in his mind, Cal forced the door shut on it, separating himself from the Indian's intolerable physical torment. He fired the Glock twice as he advanced on the Apache, feeling the bullets strike their mark, but ready to shield himself from the sensation of being shot, all the while compelling the wounded man to throw down his weapon.

Luke took one bullet in the right kidney, the other in his bowels, as in disbelief he found that his middle finger proved not just awkward to pull the trigger with, but refused to. He then watched in horror as his hand betrayed him and threw the gun aside, out of sight and reach, into a pool of black shadow six feet from where he now lay with his legs pinned by the weight of the dead animal.

Standing over his nemesis, knowing that his mission was almost accomplished, Cal located and picked up the Indian's gun, and then turned and left the cave, hurrying, slipping and sliding and fearing the worst as he made his way to where Mike was sitting in front of a car-sized rock.

"Is he dead?" Mike said, a grimace on his blood covered face as he held his hand against the side of his head.

"Not yet," Cal replied as he pulled Mike's hand away to check out the wound. "He's working on it."

"How is it?" Mike said. "Will I live?"

"Yeah, you'll live, it's just a crease," Cal said as he simultaneously experienced Luke's thoughts and emotions, reluctant to let go and break the link. He took no real pleasure in the agony and misery that he knew the Indian was suffering. But neither could he feel a shred of compassion for the man who was nothing more than a deranged, cold-blooded serial killer, who had never himself felt any pity for his countless victims.

Luke was dying, and knew it. The pain from his many injuries was amalgamating, to envelop him entirely. He had not experienced much in the way of fear during his life, but was now terrified. He was about to expire in the gathering darkness on cold hard rock, and feared death and what might lurk beyond the veil in the spirit world. Shame at no longer being the warrior who had haughtily thought that this would be a good day to die also ate at his now almost nonexistent pride. But death could not be averted. He was hemorrhaging internally, filling up like the breached hull of a sinking ship, its bulkheads buckling and giving way. He was drowning in the liquid that had sustained his life, but was now gushing recklessly from his mortally wounded body.

Cal realized that the Indian was now aware of his presence within him. A somehow hitherto barrier had been removed and a telepathic link forged.

"This is it, Luke," he said, speaking in thought to the dying man. "You're on your way to a purgatory full of the people that you've tortured and killed. They're all waiting to welcome your rotten soul and make you suffer for eternity for your actions."

Luke watched in stark horror as the deputy sheriff – whom he had murdered so long ago – appeared, standing in front of him, smiling down at him with piercing blue eyes. And then more figures materialized, to gather behind the uniform-clad apparition of Cal Morgan, crowding into the murky cave, pushing forward; a staggering assembly of all his victims. They were as he had last seen them; the wounds that he had inflicted still raw and fresh; blood still dripping from slashed throats and the ragged holes where their noses had been. Like zombies, they reached out to him, moving spastically closer, even murmuring his name and demanding their tattoos; their noses; their lives back.

Now, at the very end, Luke was consumed with a petrifying dread, gibbering for mercy, and wailing at the terror of it all.

As they started to touch him and pull at him, he began to smell their corruption, and saw that they were now changing, rotting in front of him; flesh turning green, then almost black as it fell away from gleaming bones.

The figure of a girl straddled him, her eyes shriveling back into their sockets as her head sagged down – neck muscles withering – to within an inch of his face.

"Do you want a blowjob, honey?" she croaked through rotting vocal cords as a profusion of writhing maggots spilled from her putrid lips with the words. In that instant, Luke's brain seemed to fuse. A piercing scream erupted from the ruins of his mouth as his bullet-ripped bowels voided their contents of shit and blood. He crossed the border line between life to death as the corpse astride him put her mouth over his, forcing her pustule-laden tongue between his torn lips, capturing and inhaling his final breath.

Cal lingered in Luke's mind as the spirit of the Apache was ripped from his dead body by shadowy, darting, gargoyle-shaped demons, to be dragged shrieking into an infernal, flaming vortex that materialized in the cave like some holographic portal. The spine-tingling, inhuman cry of the Indian faded as the essence of what had been Luke Strayhorse faced an eternal damnation, and Cal was left alone in the cooling body.

The remains of those that had gathered in the cave became intact again, no longer decomposed, but returned to their once wholesome appearance. At peace now, they smiled at Cal's consciousness, and he could feel the overwhelming gratitude from what were fellow victims of the Indian. It was as if he had been their delegated emissary, given a second life to seek out and end the Apache's abominable existence. He now knew that his return had not been a freakish, supernatural accident. It had been a providential crusade, surely legislated by some higher authority.

The cave became awash in blinding light, and within its cleansing brightness, the audience to Strayhorse's demise faded and dispersed into the ether. Cal left the barren form of what had been a human devil and returned to the completeness of his own host body.

"He's gone now, Mike. He died hard," Cal said, turning away from the PI to vomit in the snow.

They set off back through the trees, and as they reached the snow-covered meadow they saw headlights appear next to the shack. Both of them smiled with relief.

EPILOGUE

IN the aftermath of the events that had resulted in the deaths of Special Agent Richard Cole, Belle Morita and Luke Strayhorse, Cal had to be very economical with the truth to keep his powers and true identity hidden from the authorities. The local sheriff's office and the State Police had no reason not to believe that Cal, Mike and Sarah had been caught up in Rich Cole's investigation, and had, for whatever reasons, been assisting him as good citizens. Cal's ability to read the minds of the three officials whom he was interviewed by separately, gave him the foresight to placate them by answering their numerous questions satisfactorily, with bullshit that he knew they would buy.

Mike was fine. It had just been a scalp wound. Cal had briefed him on what half truths and downright lies he had fed the 'suits' with, and gave Sarah the same script to use. The state boys and federal agents had taken all normal measures to prevent any collusion, but with Cal's new-found power of telepathy, they were playing against a marked deck.

Sarah had undergone surgery on her knee and nose. The nose-job had even straightened out a small kink that had annoyed her since kindergarten days. So now, with a straight patrician nose, she was like a kid with a new toy. Cold weather would always start her knee complaining and remind her of the nightmare that she had lived through, but with hindsight she knew that it had been a miracle that she had escaped with just a banged up leg and face.

Rich's supervisor proved to be no more than a minor problem. Paul Nicholl knew that Rich had been tailing them; knew that they had led him to the killer, but proving it was beyond him. Mike denied it and closed up like a clam; more tight-lipped than any priest being asked to divulge secrets of the confessional. And Sarah stuck to what Cal had told her to say, unshakably, word for word. That just left the fed with the young guy who he thought was Danny Clayton. For some reason, Clayton proved impossible to interview. When he tried to question him, he seemed to go blank and forget what he had been going to ask. Worse still, on one cringingly embarrassing occasion, every time he tried to discuss the affair, he found himself reciting 'Mary had a little lamb'. The episode was to haunt him for the rest of his career, and probably played a part in his failure to rise to the dizzy heights of assistant director; a position he had been given every reason to believe he would attain.

When the furor died down and time distanced him from what had taken place in the mountains of southeast Arizona, Cal felt empty and without purpose. It was as though he had only been reborn in order to hunt down the killer and exact a biblical act of retribution. Time, his love for Sarah and his father, and the bond of friendship that had developed between himself and Mike seeped into the void, reinvigorated his spirit and gave him a reason to live. He began to cherish life and savor each day for the gift that it was. He did not dismiss his past, but put it where it belonged, behind him, and moved forward, even changing his name legally from Danny Clayton to Cal Morgan.

Hank and Mildred had driven down from Benson's Creek to stay for a few days' at the lakeside bungalow near Meeks Bay, which was now home to Cal and Sarah Morgan.

Mike Cassidy was with them as they gathered around the large cedar top table out on the decking to enjoy the sunshine, the view of the lake, and the barbecue meal that Mike had cooked up single-handed. Ol' Betsy, the Cobra Phoenix, stood beneath tall ponderosa pines at the edge of the lake, almost eighty yards from the rear of the house. Mike had kept the promise he had made to himself, and now lived in it, happy to have free parking on Cal's and Sarah's property.

As for Danny Clayton: He was still missing, seemingly erased as though he had never been. His loss stayed with Sarah, but totally separate from the reality of her life with Cal. They had discussed Danny at length, and wondered where his consciousness might have gone. There was no way to know whether he still existed in some form, or had just ceased to be. His disappearance was as mystical as Cal's reincarnation; an anomaly that had no rational answer, defying all laws of physics, which was after all a science invented by man to try to define and explain everything relating to the properties and interactions of matter and energy, with more hypotheses than there are quills on a porcupine. It seemed fair to assume that Danny's fate would remain an unsolved mystery.

The grief of their loss had shattered Jim and Linda Clayton. Their despair made it difficult for them to even handle phone conversations with Cal. They naturally wanted their son back. As it stood, he was gone, as good as dead, but they had no body to bury and mourn over; Cal Morgan had it, which kept their loss an open, suppurating sore that would never heal. With a heavy heart, Cal made the decision to break all contact with them for the time being, if not forever.

Mike got restless after a few months' of fishing and sitting back watching the grass grow, and talked Cal round to going into business with him.

M & C Investigations was situated at a smart plaza in downtown Carson City, and specialized in tracing missing persons, though not serial killers. They were trying to keep it low key; just a sideline to give them a fuller appreciation of the time that they spent just hanging out. They were certainly not doing it for the money. Several times a year, Cal, Sarah and Mike enjoyed weekend trips together, hitting Reno and Vegas in turn. They would stay at the top hotels, catch a show, and then with Cal's unique abilities, clean up at the slots and tables. Call it morally wrong, but Cal could live with reading other card players' hands and benefiting by knowing when to fold and when to play. And gambling was the only area in which Cal used his powers. As a rule he kept out of people's heads, respecting their privacy. Maybe in time he would think of a beneficial way to employ the gifts bestowed on him. There was no hurry.

Sarah was writing a novel. It was fiction, but loosely based on a certain hunt for a psychopathic serial murderer, who just happened to be a Native American Indian. The book would be published the following year and prove successful enough to encourage her to try her hand at another. Therapeutically, the writing had helped flush the real life experience from her system; the blending of fact and fiction fragmenting and diluting the reality, thus dispersing the full horror of what she had been through.

Dawn broke over the turquoise lake on what had all the makings of being a baking hot late summer day. Hank and Cal Morgan had already been offshore in a small skiff for over an hour, fishing being the unneeded excuse to have time in just each other's company. A thin layer of mist hung in the still air over the glassy surface, until the sun rose, peering over the eastern mountains, and the gossamer blanket dissolved under its warming rays.

“Are you okay, son?” Hank said as he poured steaming coffee from a battered, blue thermos flask that had accompanied them on previous fishing trips, back in the early eighties when Cal had been a teenager.

“Yeah, Dad,” Cal said slowly and thoughtfully. “I do my best to believe that I got a second chance to put some wrongs to right. And I mean to make the most of being alive again. I still don’t really understand any of it, but I’ve stopped looking for answers. I’m just glad that it all seems to be working out. I won’t ever *really* know how or why I survived death. But when I resurfaced I needed to chase down the past and put it to bed for a lot of folks, including myself, and I did. Now I have Sarah, you, Mildred and Mike, and that’s a hell of a lot to live for.”

About The Author

I write the type of original, action-packed, violent crime thrillers that I know I would enjoy reading if they were written by such authors as: Lee Child, David Baldacci, Simon Kernick, Harlan Coben, Michael Billingham and their ilk.
Over twenty years in the Prison Service proved great research into the minds of criminals, and especially into the dark world that serial killers - of who I have met quite a few - frequent.

I live in a cottage a mile from the nearest main road in the Yorkshire Wolds, enjoy photography, the wildlife, and of course creating new characters to place in dilemmas that my mind dreams up.

What makes a good read? Believable protagonists that you care about, set in a story that stirs all of your emotions.

If you like your crime fiction fast-paced, then I believe that my books will keep you turning the pages.

Connect With Michael Kerr and discover other great titles.

Web

www.michaelkerr.org

Facebook

www.facebook.com/MichaelKerrAuthor

Raised To Kill
DI Matt Barnes 6

The initial crimes had been committed throughout the preceding decades, behind the walls of the now fire-gutted Gladstone House, which had originally been a Victorian lunatic asylum and then an orphanage, before being closed down following a headline-making exposé of gross sexual abuse by staff against many of the boys in their charge.

The current spate of murder victims were ex-employees of the orphanage, and it falls to DI Matt Barnes and his team to somehow identify and apprehend a killer that they believe has harboured a need to exact vengeance for many years. But all is not what it appears to be, and their prime suspect has cast-iron alibis that seemingly cannot be broken.

Also By Michael Kerr

DI Matt Barnes Series
A REASON TO KILL
LETHAL INTENT
A NEED TO KILL
CHOSEN TO KILL
A PASSION TO KILL
RAISED TO KILL

The Joe Logan Series
AFTERMATH
ATONEMENT
ABSOLUTION
ALLEGIANCE
ABDUCTION

The Laura Scott Series
A DEADLY COMPULSION
THE SIGN OF FEAR

Other Crime Thrillers
DEADLY REPRISAL
DEADLY REQUITAL
BLACK ROCK BAY
A HUNGER WITHIN
THE SNAKE PIT
A DEADLY STATE OF MIND
TAKEN BY FORCE
DARK NEEDS AND EVIL DEEDS
DEADLY OBSESSION
COFFEE CRIME CAFE

Science Fiction / Horror
WAITING
CLOSE ENCOUNTERS OF THE STRANGE KIND
RE-EMERGENCE

Children's Fiction
Adventures in Otherworld
PART ONE – THE CHALICE OF HOPE
PART TWO – THE FAIRY CROWN

24302352R00187

Printed in Great Britain
by Amazon